INFINITE BLUES

BLUES

A COLD WAR FEVER DREAM

GERALD BRENNAN

Other titles in the series:

Zero Phase: Apollo 13 on the Moon

Public Loneliness: Yuri Gagarin's Circumlunar Flight

Island of Clouds: The Great 1972 Venus Flyby

Alone on the Moon: The Soviet Lunar Landing (Forthcoming)

INFINITE BLUES

A COLD WAR FEVER DREAM

PART OF THE ALTERED SPACE SERIES

GERALD BRENNAN

TORTOISE BOOKS
CHICAGO, IL

FIRST EDITION, APRIL, 2021

Copyright © 2021 by Gerald D. Brennan III

All rights reserved under International and Pan-American Copyright Convention

Published in the United States by Tortoise Books

www.tortoisebooks.com

ISBN-13: 978-1-948954-18-1

This book is a work of fiction. All characters, scenes and situations are either products of the author's imagination or are used fictitiously. Any resemblance to actual events or locales or persons, living or dead, is coincidental.

Front Cover: Putorana Plateau image © ESA. Contains modified Copernicus Sentinel data (2016), processed by ESA, CC BY-SA 3.0 IGO. Used with permission.

Inner Image: Mohawk nuclear test, Eberiru (Ruby) Island, Enewetak Atoll, 3 July 1956. Image is in the public domain.

Tortoise Books Logo Copyright ©2021 by Tortoise Books. Original artwork by Rachele O'Hare.

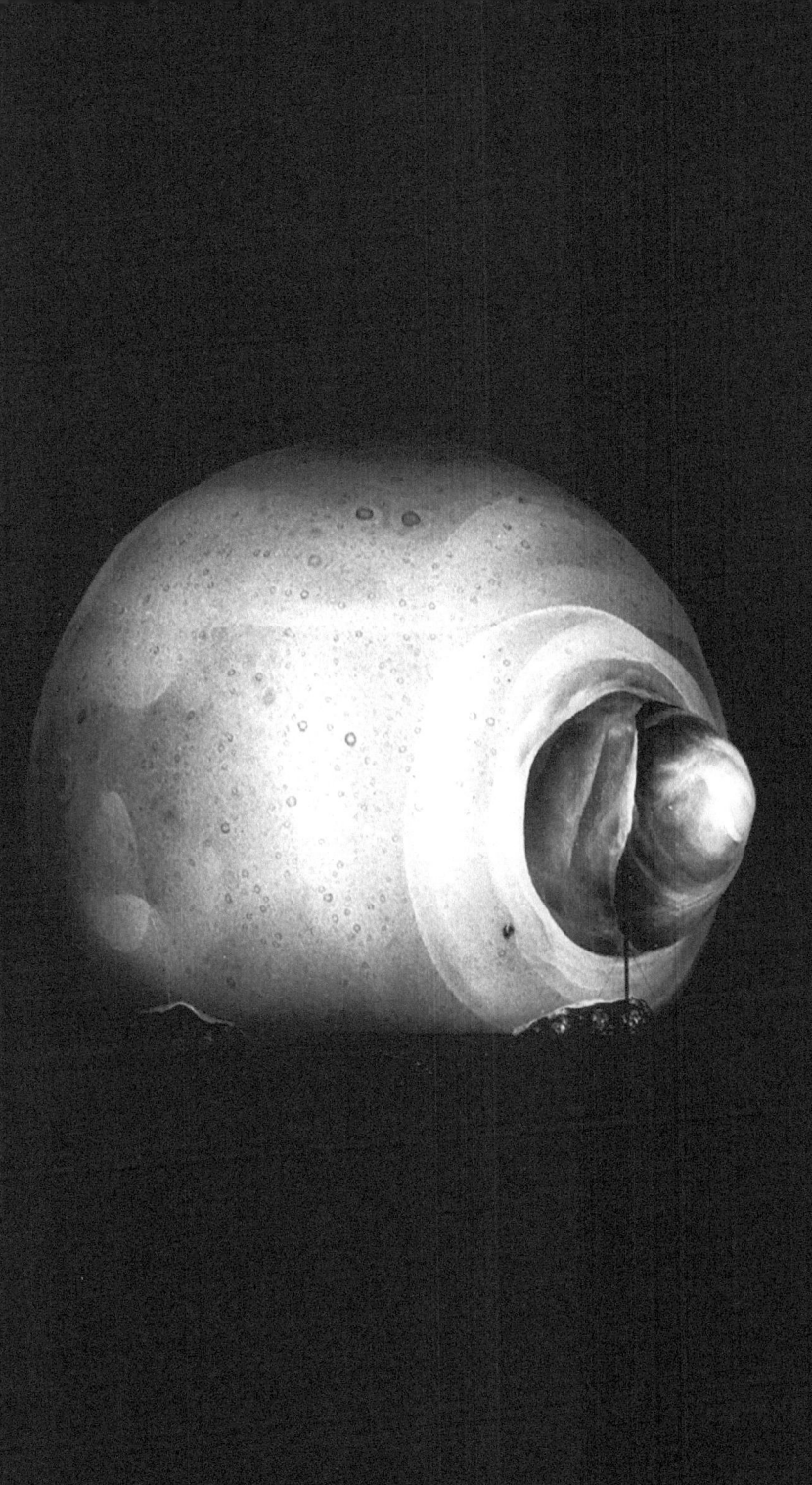

"It would not have been a better world if the unrealized possibility of these terrible weapons had been a secret shadow on our future."

> — J. Robert Oppenheimer, father of the atomic bomb, speaking in our universe.

"American Democracy was a form of self-murder, always. Or of murdering somebody else... The love, the democracy, the floundering into lust, is a sort of by-play. The essential American soul is hard, isolate, stoic, and a killer. It has never yet melted."

> — D. H. Lawrence

Reds

I first glimpse the space station as a blinking red dot, a distant light high above the curved dark horizon.

My X-20's in pursuit, crossing the Antarctic coast towards the Indian Ocean, sweeping soundlessly through starry space above the shadowed side of the planet. A God's-eye view: the earth without form, and darkness on the face of the deep. I'd been hoping to see the Southern Lights, but apparently the sun, too, has been silent. So: no color outside except that distant red beacon. Hank's there now: the only place to live up here in the heavens. My home for the next forty days, assuming the next forty minutes goes well.

Every instinct tells me to add power, climb in pursuit. Instead I key the mike: "Watchman, this is Falcon-2, I have visual, over."

Nothing. I scan the radio knobs. I know all's right on my end, but it never hurts to double-check.

"Watchman, Falcon-2. I have you on visual. Over."

Still nothing. Moderately concerning. I shift my weightless body. Touch every knob and switch on the comms panel, seeking reassurance through my pressure suit gloves. Touch each one again, just to be sure. Everything is set.

"Watchman, Falcon-2. Comm check. Over."

The red light climbs relative to me until it winks out, obscured by the top edge of the cockpit window. This part is as planned, but I thought we'd have comms by now.

"Falcon-2, Watchman." Hank Hartsfield's calm Alabama drawl gives me an excuse to breathe. "I read you five by five. Have visual as well."

Now I can dimly see the red light through the top hatch window. Nearly directly above, which is good: I have to get in phase before we raise my orbit. But that won't be until we're back in daylight on the other side of the planet.

I catch one last glimpse of the red light. Then it disappears again.

"Watchman, Falcon-2. Ascent was nominal. Spacecraft systems all nominal. Orbit is nominal."

"How'd you like the view?"

"Lotta ocean. Not much to see."

"There will be, Falcon-2."

This is a reconnaissance mission: sun-synchronous orbit, high inclination. The ground tracks for Mercury and Gemini were a low rolling wave with a peak at Cape Canaveral, bobbing up and down through tropical latitudes. Whereas we overfly polar regions, and every inhabited spot on the planet. Most importantly, the high arctic latitudes of the Soviet Union, all those ICBM fields being filled with new missiles designed to launch over the North Pole and shatter our country in a matter of minutes. All the sites we haven't photographed yet, the places we need to map, and target—assuming we can get the resolution on the cameras up to where it's supposed to be.

"Falcon-2, Watchman. Tananarive in five minutes."

"Roger, Watchman."

For now we're about to overfly the Malagasy Republic. Radio coverage. A chance to talk to fellow officers on duty at a lonely station, fighting sleep in some cramped radio shack, staying up late into the local night to speak to us during our workday. Then: Somalia, Ethiopia, Israel, Turkey, and a first nightward pass over the western end of our dark adversary.

"Falcon-2, Watchman. You can let go of the controls in the meantime."

I grimace; I am in fact gripping the controllers. It feels odd to just relax. Or try to: my bladder's edging towards discomfort. Outside my faceplate, the cockpit's bathed in cool electric light. My body says it's daytime, but this feels like night. Still nothing below. "Watchman, Falcon-2. It's not flying if you're not doing anything."

"Plenty of flying coming up, Falcon-2." Despite the futuristic setting, Hank's voice and demeanor are Old South. Not a boisterous good ol' boy, though...more the country gentleman, the quiet professional too relaxed to kick the accent.

A sickly little cluster of lights crawls across the horizon and starts inching towards us.

"All units, this is Tananarive. We have you on radar. Orbital tracks look good. No plane maneuvers needed. Stand by for phasing burn instructions. Over."

My launch from Vandenberg had been tightly timed to get me up here—a launch window measured in minutes. I suspected we'd gotten it right, but it's great to get confirmation.

"Tananarive, Falcon-2 standing by." We have, at most, about six minutes of communication with any given ground station. I watch the mission clock tick upwards. I'm eager to get this over with.

"Falcon-2, Tananarive, GO for phasing burn. GET of zero-zero plus four-eight plus three-zero. Burn duration three-zero seconds. Posigrade burn with the transtage. Zero degrees pitch."

I write the instructions on my knee pad. Read them back. Start flipping switches to prepare. Glance at the clock: time is short. Then: engine ignition. My weightless body settles into the seat and there's a smooth gentle pressure. All gauges look good.

"Falcon-2, Tananarive. Looks good here. GO for first-orbit rendezvous. Thule will have instructions. Over."

There's not much else to say, and not much time to say it. I bid them goodnight over the dark ocean. Still my bladder pressure builds; I'm wearing a condom and a urine bag, but I never entirely trust these things.

Northward we swoop, in sync now. Soon more lights are visible, little blotches of illuminated Africa, specks on a dark continent. Then: the Middle East. More light still. After that, a brief break to transit the Black Sea, and we're over Beria's Soviet Union, the evil madman's lair.

I'd pictured it as a dark hole on the face of the globe; it's a subconscious surprise to see that it, too, has cities with street lights, scraggly-looking patches coming into view beneath us. I spot Odessa and then, a minute later, Kiev.

Operationally we don't want to talk much right now. On an open channel, even bland conversations are bound to get picked up and analyzed. Hank transmits anyway: "Falcon-2, Watchman. If you've been looking for a rest stop, now's the time. Over."

"Watchman, Falcon-2. Not sure I copy. Are you suggesting bladder relief? Over."

"Roger, Falcon-2. Take a leak on those commie bastards." His tone's cool and professional, like it's just another mission task. "I think I'll shit on Minsk myself."

I smile. There's no chance of any friendlies listening right now, so Hartsfield knows he can let fly with the curses, among other things. I key my mike. "Watchman, Falcon-2. We shouldn't talk operational plans. If they're listening, we might...ahh...piss them off."

A ghost of laugh. "Too late, Falcon-2. I've reached the initial point. Target acquired. Three...two...one. Bombs away!"

"Don't say that on a hot mike, Watchman! Good Lord. You'll start World War III." We're just up here to take pictures. But there's been talk of attaching a weapons platform to the station. OB: Orbital Bombardment. Nukes from space. And for all the Soviets know, we've already done it.

Still, given the internal pressure readings, I can't resist letting loose myself. Sweet blessed relief. I wait for some sensation of wetness, slippage from the condom. But all is good.

"Falcon-2, Watchman. Did you follow me in? Little strafing run?"

He must be psychic. "Watchman, Falcon-2. That's affirmative."

"There you go, Falcon-2. Mark your territory."

Onward we fly. I cast a wary eye downward, as if I am indeed going to see ICBMs rising from silos, fiery plumes pointing them northwards to follow us over the frozen wastelands.

● ● ●

Soon there are color bands across the horizon, a glorious range of violets and blues and oranges fattening into a nuclear sunburst over a sunlit sliver of northern horizon. The cockpit floods with light; I blink away the bright.

Now in daylight I have a couple minutes to sight-see. The fjord-lined Norwegian coast glides past far below, infinitely detailed in the summer midnight sunlight. Then an expanse of ocean, and across it, a swath of white. Iceberg-flecked sea gives way to the edge of the polar cap: larger sections of thick ice interspersed by jagged leads of open water ranging inward. And finally: blinding whiteness, the top of the planet nearly featureless except for the thin pressure ridges that stretch across the ice. Only fifty-odd years ago, men saw this for the first time, and the only way to get up here was a hazardous journeys by dogsled; to conquer it so easily feels like cheating.

At last we are arcing along the northern edge of Greenland, and it's time for the real flying to start.

"Falcon-2, this is Thule. We have your rendezvous burn. Stand by to copy, over."

"Thule, Falcon-2, go ahead, over."

"GET of zero-one plus one-six plus two-zero. Burn duration zero-one plus zero-six. Posigrade burn with the transtage. Eight degrees pitch. Four-eight-point-four delta-v. Over."

I read it back and get started. The alien northland of ice and rock is still scrolling by, but I can't spend any more time on the scenery. Once the clock ticks down I fire the transtage. Rocket vibrations reach me through the spacecraft's frame as the ejection seat settles into my back. Soon I see the station at the top of my window, growing larger now.

It's still not much to look at, but it's more than it was: no longer a star but now a bright aluminum cylinder, like a metal relay race baton. I can't make out details, but I do see Falcon-1's triangular black shape perched at the docking spindle at the far end. Closer to me is the big eye, all the fancy optics: wide open, which is a problem. The biggest mission goal for my first week, the all-consuming priority, is to get the resolution up to where it needs to be. If I dock safely but there's thruster impingement on the main mirror, well, there's no point even being up here.

"Watchman, Falcon-2. Range five miles. Over." I push urgency into the words: I don't even want to know what kind of trouble we'll get into if we mess up the optics.

Nothing.

"Watchman, Falcon-2. Four miles. Over."

Still the station is stationary.

"Watchman, Falcon-2. Are you gonna turn that thing around, or what?"

"Falcon-2, Watchman. No need to get your tits in a flutter." Now at last I see my destination starting to rotate, and the optical cover closing. "You're clear to the hold spot. Drive safely."

"Roger, Watchman." I flip my switches. "Proceeding with checklist." It's in the clear knee pouch; I have it memorized but read it anyway. "Ejection seat: safe. Attitude mode: AUTO. Probe: deployed."

"Falcon-2, Watchman. Guy-ros disabled. Approach looks good. I'll let you know when it's stationkeeping time."

I keep my controller hand loose: physics and mathematics are still flying for me. The station's larger now but pointed straight towards me, the docking spindle's T-pipe end looming large, and Falcon-1 upside-down relative to me. Sleek black lines marred by the open cargo doors, and highlighted by the soft blue glow of Earth below.

About forty yards out, I can see Hank's face in the rendezvous window, motioning me. It takes a second to decipher his hand gestures: he's pointing up at the side with his space plane, shaking his head and swiping his hand as if to say no, don't park there. Then he points "down" at the open side. Gives a thumbs-up and an exaggerated smiling nod.

Wearily I key the mike. "Thanks, Watchman. Not sure I'd have figured that out on my own."

He chuckles, turns away. "All right, Falcon-2. Hold for station keeping."

I pulse the thrusters. Stop, then wait, for what seems like forever. "You gonna finish the job, Watchman?"

He turns back around, camera in hand. "Gotta snap some pictures. Air Force Academy needs new brochures."

I sigh. "You're serious?"

"Why, you forget your makeup?" He snaps away. "You'll like these, I swear."

Our Hawaiian ground station's coming up. We need to dock in daylight: only a few minutes left. Otherwise it's next orbit and Canton Island. Plus I'm eager to remove my urine contraption. I tend to final tasks: turning off the approach radar, opening the cargo doors. "All right. I'm ready for my close-up, Mr. DeMille."

Radio crackle: "All units, Hickam. Give us a status, over."

"Hickam, Falcon-2." Some weariness in my voice, I'm sure. "Waiting to dock. Over."

"Hickam, Watchman. Done with photography. Runway is clear and Falcon-2 is first in the pattern."

"Very good, gentlemen," Hickam says. "GO for docking."

My docking port is large and beautiful, but as I pulse the thrusters, I keep my eyes on the flimsy metal trapeze-looking contraption just beyond, making sure I'm lined up on the target portion. The world outside fades, all the vast spectacle; my universe is the task at hand.

I glide forward, smoothly closing the final feet, and my probe slides effortlessly into position.

"Excellent, Falcon-2," Hank says. "That felt good. I won't tell your wife, I promise."

It feels just like an aerial refueling. Always the same jokes, although here it's a fellow officer, not some anonymous airman. "Don't you have work to do, Watchman?"

I'm answered by a rippling metal groan that echoes through the spacecraft frame and through the seat to my body. Through my hatch window above, I can see the interior of the docking port, currently airless.

"We've got a hard dock," Hartsfield says. "Pressurizing."

My exterior hatch pressure needle starts to climb. We need it steady at 5 psi, to know there are no leaks. I can't shut down just yet.

"All units, Hickam. Sounds good up there. Over."

"Hickam, Falcon-2. So far, so good. Monitoring pressure. Preparing to disembark. Over."

"Roger, Falcon-2. Hickam signing off. Catch you on the night shift. Over and out."

I wait. The needle slowly reaches its goal. Stays there for a few seconds, then flickers. I peer closer, study it more intently. And: a startling knock on the top hatch. On the other side, Hank is floating upside-down and grinning, his wavy graying hair grown shaggy now.

I can't help smiling back. There's something impossible and amazing about getting up here to this empty place and seeing another human face. "Looks like it's safe to come out. Falcon-2 shutting down."

A flight safely concluded: always a relief after the thrilling dangerous freedom. Although I suppose I'm not really done for another six weeks. I flip switches and the cockpit goes dark. Memories flash: hundreds of landings in Super Sabres and Thunderchiefs, touching down at night and taxiing to some concrete apron in Germany or Arizona or Libya, then turning the airplane off before climbing out. Except we're still flying; I'm not at a runway, but a home in space.

The Earth pivots far below: a mass of blue and clouds moving soundlessly. Hank's off reorienting the station to normal attitude.

I look out the windows one last time and see: another fixed bright spot in the sky. Just above the horizon, too big to be a star or planet. Whatever it is, it's in orbit with us.

•••

Once the spacecraft's powered down, I slip free from my seat harness. Not much of a liberation in the cramped cockpit, but it's interesting to feel the physics of zero-g, the basic Newtonian actions and reactions that are making all this possible; with every twist, my body bumps against the cockpit confines. By the time I've stowed my helmet, I need to recheck all the switch positions. I glance at the pressure gauge one last unnecessary time before unlatching the hatch.

A whiff of unexpected odor—something of metal and combustion, like when you're at a gun range. I scrunch my nose. Hank's back floating above me in the narrow tunnel. "You go shooting or something?"

"How's that?"

Clumsily I push off and float upward. "I said, 'It smells like you went shooting!'"

He laughs as we shake hands. "That's the smell of space!"

It sounds like something you tell the new guy to pull his leg. "Space doesn't have a smell."

"It sure does! I noticed it when I docked, too."

I'm eager to get out of my pressure suit. Plus there are supplies to unstow. And it occurs to me that we need to figure out whatever it was that I saw out there, that other light in orbit. I awkwardly start to turn around in the narrow spindle.

"Leaving? You just got here."

"Gotta unpack." There's not much to see in the spindle anyway—bare metal walls, pressure gauges, a rendezvous window with a small control panel, hatches to each docking port, another hatch orthogonal to those for our EVA egress.

"Come on, let's take the grand tour first." Hartsfield pivots like a swimmer executing a kick turn in a pool; he pushes off with his feet and sails down the spindle into the main habitation area. I work my way around the T-bend, rattling off the walls like a BB in a tin can.

Past the spindle hatch: an octagon of angled storage lockers, flaring out to the sides. Everything familiar from training— food prep area, environmental control systems, comms panel. A curtain for the hygiene compartment. A round window, about a foot wide. And two sleeping bags stretched along the opposite wall like slender blue cocoons. Still I pause to take it all in: there's a freshness, seeing it for real.

Hank pauses for some quick aerobatics—another deft kick against a bare section of wall, propelling him into a fluttering somersault—then stabilizes himself. "I know, not much room, but it's quite a view. Rent's paid, too."

"Well that's a relief. Not sure I could swing this on a major's pay." It does look different than it did on the ground— different angles to everything. "Gotta say, I would have preferred a two-bedroom."

"Hey, at least it's not a studio."

"We're sleeping and eating in the same place. That's a studio. Even if the work's in another room."

He smiles. "Well, it's a short commute."

At the far end of the chamber, the octagonal walls narrow back down to another tunnel leading to the equipment section; he effortlessly pulls himself in.

I push clumsily off one of the storage lockers and ricochet into the center of the living chamber; for a second, I feel stuck, suspended. Anxious about grabbing the wrong thing, kicking some instrument: I survey the walls to find a handhold. At last I see a rail, pull myself up to the other tunnel. Look towards my feet and feel a flash of disorientation, all the internal gyroscopes off-kilter. The bottom wall of the chamber had been "floor," but now that I'm looking "down" past the end of my feet at nothing, I get a flood of angst, that fear you feel when you're about to fall. I look up, focus on my destination.

Hank's floating in there, waiting. "Disorienting, huh?"

Reluctantly I nod.

"I was the same three weeks ago. Mike was cracking up watching my clumsy ass. You'll get it."

Inside the equipment module I see more of what I've been training on: the Dorian viewfinder and light table, the comms panel, the attitude control console, a swath of binders. The narrow teletype printer—as innocuous as a roll of cash register paper at the grocery store. There's barely enough room for two people to work at once, although I can't help thinking it feels roomier than it did on the ground.

"And that's it," he says. "No TV room, no bowling alley…"

"No swimming pool," I add.

"That's outside." He grins. "We'll get you out there soon enough. EVA and recon. Until they send up the bombardment module, that's it."

"You think they're gonna?"

"LeMay wants it. The way things are going, Nixon's gonna let him have it."

LeMay. The name calls to mind strategy lessons at the academy, sterile classrooms brought to life with hellish visions of recent victories. Endless flights of B-29s showering fire on wooden cities, causing such infernos that the pilots in the later waves could smell the burnt flesh of civilians on the ground... "He sure has a thing for bombers, doesn't he? I mean, the fact that we're still doing the Chrome Dome flights..."

"Can't say I blame him. The man won the war with 'em. I mean, obviously MacArthur had to do some mopping up to do, come invasion time, but since we'd torched almost every city in Japan..."

It was a helluva thing to think about. You had to figure it'd saved lives in the end. Or saved American lives, at least. Still, it was a helluva thing to think about. "I didn't take you for a bomber nut."

"I'm still a fighter guy! But like LeMay says. 'Fighters are fun, bombers are important.'" He smiles. "I'm not nuts about recon either, but here we are."

"Recon always seems a little...passive. Fly in a straight line, get shot at, then KEEP flying in a straight line so the pictures don't come out blurry..."

"I hate to break it to you, but we can't really fly anything OTHER than a straight line up here."

"Which is good for bombing too, I guess." I think of newsreel footage, the early days of the MacArthur Administration: shots of a coral atoll, international observers walking around idly to see the "before," a B-36 circling at the ready, and then, from a distance: the impossible fireball. Observers watching, mouths agape, through the windows of the C-54 as they fly back over the island, a mile-wide blue void now carved into its side. The unspoken, unspeakable message to the communist aggressors: imagine what this weapon would do to a city. Imagine if we dropped it on Moscow. "Not that I want to actually do it..."

"Well, that's the military...you might spend your whole career training. Never actually doing your job, in a sense. And that's probably for the best. But you can't help wondering..." He doesn't need to finish the sentence; like anyone that's worn a uniform in peacetime, I know what he's talking about.

"The scary thing is, the unimaginable does tend to happen, eventually..."

"Well, there's that theory. That eventually we forget about the last big war, and have another one. And there's only been...what? Fifty years without war, in all human history? But..." He shrugs. "Questions beyond our pay grade. If they wanna bolt a couple nukes on this thing, that's their business." He floats for a moment. "I will say this. If the shit does hit the fan and it's a question of actually DOING something, or just snapping pictures of the rubble afterwards...I mean, unless they figure out a way to put a cannon on the X-20..."

I laugh. "That'd be the day, huh? Space-to-space combat...I'd take that over a bombardment module any day." There's something noble about fighters: you'll never end up killing anyone who isn't trying to kill you. At least, not in normal circumstances.

"Whatever happens, I just hope Nixon has the balls to stand up to Beria..."

A skeptical look. "He did in Berlin."

"Are you kidding me? They still put a wall around our half of the city." A frown. "He tries to talk tough, but everybody knows he's no MacArthur."

"Is anybody?" I glance at my watch. "That reminds me...we popped the hatch...what, ten minutes ago?"

"I guess so, why?"

"Fullerton and I had a bet. How soon you'd start talking politics. The over-under was fifteen minutes. Looks like I lost."

He chuckles. I push back towards the living room so I can get my pressure suit off. A thought flashes, a warning indicator at the corner of my brain. "Oh, by the way. I saw something out there."

"Out there?"

"In orbit with us. Like another satellite or something. Behind us. When you reoriented, I saw it."

"You don't think it was something from you, do you?"

"From me?"

"Debris. A piece of the transtage or something? What else could it be?"

The alternatives aren't great: either something came off my ship in orbit, in which case I may be in trouble when I try to come home, or...what? "Satellite, maybe?"

"We didn't hear about any launches. Ground woulda mentioned it, if they'd seen something on radar."

"You'd think...but, I mean...this thing. It was out there. It's something."

"I wish I'd seen it."

"Would it be too big a deal to reorient now?"

"That's...probably doable, actually." He checks his watch. "We'll be running out of daylight soon, though."

"Maybe we can catch see it coming out of darkness. When the light hits, after we cross the terminator."

"Sounds like a plan," he says. "You get settled in. I'll handle the flying."

For the next forty-five minutes, I attend to normal tasks—changing from the bulky pressure suit into the light flight coveralls, then dipping back to the X-20 to get my gear. The interior storage area—above and behind the ejection seat—is only accessible when the hatch is open. Even then it's an awkward job, dangling upside-down and rooting around to get everything: replacement lithium hydroxide canisters, tubes of food, small bag of personal items. By the time I am finishing up, I'm feeling a little unwell.

Back in the station, Hank's finishing the maneuver, and although the nausea has moved my focus somewhat indoors, I take up my position by the window.

We flash into daylight high above the North Sea, equidistant between Norway and Scotland. The hazy terminator recedes beneath us on the surface of the water, and I peer into the darkness and count to ten. If there's something following us, we should catch it as it, too, catches the light. But: nothing.

"We have another comms window with Thule on this pass. We'll call it in." Hank suggests. "See if they see anything on the scope."

I am feeling too awful to do much more than nod. I am not a happy camper.

●●●

"Thule, this is Watchman." Hank's left me to my own devices; between waves of discomfort I am putting away gear and listening in on my headset.

"Watchman, Thule, we read you five by five. Give us a status. Over."

"Thule, Watchman. We had a bit of a…UFO sighting. Over."

"Uhhh…say again, Watchman." In the capcom's hesitation I read his thoughts: wondering if we're about to start raving about silvery saucers.

Hank chuckles. "Sorry, Thule, bad choice of words."

Radio crackles: "Say again, Watchman."

"Thule, that was a bad choice of words! Falcon-2 saw an object behind us in orbit. Somewhere from ten to fifty miles back. We reoriented for another visual but couldn't see it. Figured we'd have you check your radar. Over."

"Watchman, it's...uhhh...funny you mention it. We thought we saw something on the scope last orbit. Over."

"Were you planning on telling us?" A long incredulous pause. "Over."

"Watchman, we were focused on rendezvous. And we wanted to get another look this pass. But looking at the scope now...we do not see anything following you in orbit, over."

"Roger, Thule." He gives me a look and a shoulder shrug. "Keep your eyes out, will you?"

"Will do, Watchman."

This is not good news. It may well have been something smaller and closer I saw, something loosened by launch that came off during the rendezvous burn. I start mentally inventorying the tail end of the transtage, imagining the handholds I'll need to grab to get down there during EVA. Thinking about what might have come off, and whether or not I'll need it to get back home.

"Thule, ahhh...how'd you get stuck there, over?"

"Watchman, Thule...not sure I copy, over."

"How did you get posted to northern Greenland? We had Hawaii on the last pass. Those guys can get off work, go to the beach, find some maidens in grass skirts. You've got...what, seals and Eskimos?"

A radio laugh. "Don't forget the B-70s, Watchman. Valkyries in Valhalla."

"A beautiful airplane doesn't make up for an ugly base. Especially when you're not flying it. Who'd you piss off to end up there?"

"Long story, Watchman. I try to look on the bright side. Like this time of year. Daylight 24/7. You need good shades to sleep, but it does wonders for your mood."

"So it sounds like you're…on top of the world," Hank adds; I grin despite my misery.

"Until six months from now," I chip in.

"We won't think about that," Thule says bitterly.

"You just gotta prepare, is all," Hank says. "Find a warm Eskimo woman and a cozy igloo."

A chuckle. "Roger, Watchman. Will do."

"Keep an eye on the scope in the meantime, Thule. Watchman out."

"Will do, Watchman. Thule out."

"Well," Hank says to me. "I guess the aliens have an invisibility shield, huh?"

"If it's from the transtage, I'm in trouble. That'll screw up the flight manifest, if they have to send up a Gemini to bring me down."

"One thing at a time. Get settled in. EVA tomorrow. We'll figure it out."

• • •

I don't have much else to do, which is just as well, because I'm not. My head is puffy and my stomach's empty. Evening rest period comes as a blessing.

We pull the window cover closed for a break from the relentless cycle, forty-five minutes of daylit Earth scrolling by every orbit. The white "daytime" interior lights go off, and the red "night" ones come on. But once I float feet-first into the sleeping bag and close my eyes, I feel no different than I had before. There is something about surrendering to gravity at the end of the day, the natural progression from walking, to sitting, to laying down. Without that, and with a head full of new sights and memories, it's impossible to wind down.

I float there, eyes closed; I realize my body's tense and tell myself to relax, but still it's all so strange. I consider taking a Seconal, but don't want to risk the secondary effects. It's all I can do to keep from waking Hank; I spend as much time as possible motionless. Worrying about the EVA. Fantasizing about Greenland in winter, dark and quiet hibernation. Eventually there seem to be gaps in time, some semblance of sleep.

By breakfast time, the white lights are on. But when I pull the shade, it's night outside: somewhat off-putting. Weary and groggy, I drift over to the food locker to retrieve our breakfasts.

"Good morning, sunshine." Hank floats out of the hygiene area, bright-eyed and upbeat.

"Uhhh…night…" I nod towards the darkened planet, shake my groggy head.

"Tough one, huh? Happened to me, too. Believe it or not, you'll get used to sleeping up here." Seeing the food packets in my hands, he adds: "Here, I got those." He sets the water gun to HOT, puts the Canadian bacon on the nozzle, and starts injecting. "You're good for EVA still?"

"Yeah." The other meal pouches contain Tang, and cubes of cinnamon toast. "I'll be fine once I get moving."

An appreciative nod. "That's the spirit."

"Indeed." The Air Force seems to like sleep more than the other services, given the safety issues of going without. But nobody gets far in the military by coming up with reasons not to do what needs to be done that day. The logic for having EVA today is pretty impeccable—we want daylight coverage by U.S. ground stations, and we won't have that once we've shifted the station schedule to Soviet time. But as usual in the military, impeccable logic wreaks havoc on the human body.

Hank places the bacon pouch in a vacant bit of airspace between us, then starts adding cold water to Tang. I open my toast cubes and get to eating. They're coated in gelatin to keep crumbs from floating everywhere. But food is food. "Your UFO comment made me chuckle. Talking to Thule."

Hank smiles. "He didn't know what to say, huh?"

"Seems like that's the only acronym the Air Force discourages."

"I don't blame 'em. Can't have the boys in blue talking about little green men. We'd cause a panic. Some *War of the Worlds* type of a thing."

"Yeah, probably."

"We wouldn't even have to say 'little green men,' either. The way the press...blows things out of proportion. Mention a spot of light in orbit, next thing you know, somebody in the media says you saw a flying saucer."

"Lord knows there's enough other things to worry about down there." A nod earthward: Berlin surrounded, ICBMs fielded, Asia under the communist thumb except for Japan and Taiwan and Singapore, Africa dotted with Cold War hot spots. A red stain spreading across the globe, barely contained.

"Lot to keep an eye on." Hank places a gelatin cube in front of him, floating suspended, and eats it out of the air. Free of care.

•••

"...airlock pressure coming down. 3 psi...2.5...2." I'm back in the docking spindle, encased in my space suit now. Visor inches from my eyes, and the sickly gray-green metal of the hatch just beyond that. Yesterday it felt narrow; now it's a metal tomb.

"Everything looks good." Hank is smooth and reassuring.

"OK. Coming down still. 1...0.7..." The needle's descent slows. I move my helmet closer to the illuminated gauge. "...0.4...0.3...not quite getting the last of the air out here."

"That happened with me, too," Hank says. "Give it a minute. Under 0.1 should be fine to unlatch."

"OK." At my feet I feel the umbilical floating loosely. Bend my hips forward to catch a glimpse of it. My lifeline coiled and undulating, a writhing white snake. Clipped to my chest, the film canister, twenty pounds of pictures waiting to go home, everything Hank and Mike took before the latter's departure and my arrival: food for the Mushroom Factory, even if the resolution's still bad.

"Watchman, sounds good up there," Thule says.

"So far, so good. Unlatching now." I pull the lever.

The silent planet scrolls by far below. Bizarre to just spring the hatch and step outside—like opening the door of an airliner mid-flight. A quick instinctive handrail grasp. In front of me: jagged glaciers of Greenland and northern Canada, all strangely clear of clouds. Our normal orientation is different from when I docked; the hatch is "down" and subconsciously I think I'm expecting to fall out, but of course nothing of the sort happens. And the quiet's reassuring. I relax my grip on the inner handrails and pull myself out into space.

An expansive limitless view: ice and water and rock, daylit under skies of black. It's dazzling, disorienting, amazing: far more than a panorama, well beyond what you'd have time to take in through the bubble canopy on a Super Sabre, even. The serene icy scene moves smoothly and steadily, scrolling on implacably, all those whites and blues and flecks of brown.

"All right out there?" Hank can't see me easily on this side of the station.

"Quite a view."

"It is something, huh?"

"Yep." I turn my back on the beautiful view, pull down my tinted visor. "All right, proceeding with the rail inspection." We do, after all, have work to do.

I find the handrail that leads to the other side of the docking spindle. Glance up at the nose of my X-20, sleek and beautiful, gleaming softly in the earthlight. I've practiced this in the water tank, but I take extra care as I pull myself around. For the benefit of the others, I narrate: "Carrier rail is free and clear. Carrier is locked in position at the end of the spindle."

"Sounds good," Hank says.

"Moving to the payload bay." On the other side of the docking tunnel, another handrail leads me to the small cargo bay, and my workstation. My grip isn't great and I almost slip off; we've trained on the Vomit Comet and in the water tank, but here it's easier for your body's inertia to get the better of you. Finally I get a good grip in the payload bay. Guide my feet into the restraints.

"Anything missing in there?" Hank asks.

"Missing?" I'm not sure I understand.

"Our little UFO from yesterday. Didn't come from there, did it?"

"Oh. Good thinking." Mentally I inventory the cargo bay. "Everything's in place. Proceeding to extraction."

The first reentry canister is in front of me: a blunt black mass two-and-a-half feet wide. As big of an object as you can comfortably manhandle during a spacewalk. I know I must work very methodically to get it where it needs to be.

"Working on the first latch." With a twist and a pull, I release the metal arm from the top of the canister. Fold it out of the way, then move on to the next one.

"Two latches removed. Proceeding to film insertion." Before I pull the reentry bucket from its cradle, I have to get the film canister in; I release the chest clips carefully. (Bad pictures or no, I still don't want to lose them.) The canister slides snugly into position deep in the reentry bucket; I fold the inner and outer covers into place, double-checking every latch and lock. "Film deposited. Removing the final cargo bay latch."

"You got the lanyard attached, right?" Hank asks.

"Uhhh, roger. Will do." If the canister drifts out of the bay, we may not be able to retrieve it. Hence the lanyard. It's tough work in the pressure gloves to hook it in. But finally I release the last latch, and the bucket rises towards me.

"All right, getting my hands set." The vessel's massive enough that it could easily damage, say, the hinges to the cargo bay doors; I make sure I have a firm grip before I move it up to chest level. Weightless but it still has mass. The muscles in my forearms strain to keep it under control.

The next part's, by all accounts, the hardest; despite all the training, I'm not entirely confident. I bring the film bucket over towards the carrier, guiding the snap towards the attachment point. I can't quite see it; I try to bring everything together blindly, but when I feel the bucket bump the carrier, I know the snap hasn't engaged.

"No dice."

"Took me three tries," Hank says. "You've got this."

"All right. Take two." Again I guide the canister towards the snap, slowly and deliberately. Now, a brief tremor, transmitted through the metal and gloves into my hands. "There we go."

"Nice job. One-upped me."

My breathing: heavier than expected. Condensation creeps in on the edges of my faceplate. "Getting some visor fog."

"Take a breather."

"I want to get this up there while it's still daylight."

"You will. Plenty of time. Take a breather."

Despite the commander's benediction, I feel I don't deserve it. Plus, a quick glance at the Earth shows that Arctic landscapes have given way to summer greens and browns. Quebec or New Brunswick, or maybe even Maine already. "Wait, are we talking to Loring?"

"Watchman, this is Loring," the headset says. "The world is passing you by. Over."

"Taking longer than I thought. OK, moving back to the spindle."

"You've got the lanyard, right?" Hank gently reminds me.

"Uhh, roger. Getting the lanyard and moving back to the spindle."

I move patiently, looking around as much as possible to keep my bearings. We talk to Loring, we talk to Cape Canaveral, we talk to ourselves in the empty space of the Southeastern Pacific. Now I have only the vaguest sense of the spectacle rolling by beneath me: a distraction from the work. As Antarctic darkness approaches, I guide the reentry bucket onto the spring launch platform.

"Well done," Hank says as the blackness swallows us. "Relax and enjoy the view."

It sounds like a joke. Still I settle in to the footrests, acutely aware of the ache in my hands and arms from muscling my body around on the rails. It seems like I should be lying down if I'm going to watch the stars. Instead I slide up my visor and ride the back of the station into darkness standing up, like a cowboy atop a speeding train.

Above me now: the universe in full, a glorious spectacle. The most complete night sky I have ever seen: indescribable. The mottled cloudy Milky Way sharply defined, subtly colorful, full of stars in mind-blowing abundance. And beyond: infinity. Distant galaxies everywhere. How many stars? Planets? God knows.

Distraction: a streak far below. My spine shivers: I'm looking *down* on a meteor. Heading northward over the Indian Ocean, the moon casts a soft hint of silver on the waters far below. Then come the dim shapes of cloud formations, illuminated from beneath by flashes of lightning: silent and distant, awe-inspiring. Mine eyes have seen the glory of the coming of the Lord...

I realize at last how long I've been silent. "I didn't think you were serious. About the view." This pass is light on radio coverage; we're west of Carnarvon and east of Tananarive, so there's no need for radio identifiers.

"Oh, you're still out there," Hank chuckles. "Thought you'd drifted off. I was gonna radio down. See if I needed to recover you."

"Very funny. Seriously, though. It's incredible, isn't it?" Now we're past the clouds. A strange coast approaches, clusters of lights arranged along the shoreline. Memory tells me it's India; we're passing west of Calcutta.

"Join the Air Force, see the world. Can't wait to get back out there."

A glance back heavenward. My childhood was spent under city skies, stars washed out by the streetlight backscatter; the first time I camped out upstate, it was a revelation. And now it's all far beyond anything I've seen down there, even on dark country nights. A subtle and overwhelming beauty, the whole universe at night. What is humanity, even next to our own galaxy? From a distance we, too, must be lost in this.

Now in the darkness I see jagged lines and patches of snow catching the moonlight: the Himalayas. Then a dark swath of western China that I know will shortly give way to the Soviet Union. We'll be observing it in detail and in daylight, soon enough.

Again I look up. You watch the *War of the Worlds* a few times and come up here, and you can't help wondering. Could there be anyone out there? Could there *not* be, in that infinity? Are they keeping an eye on us? Listening to our radio stations? Watching our television signals as we stumble skyward? Or are those transmissions still headed their way— for another hundred, or thousand, or ten thousand years? Will it all just be gibberish to them? Will they be curious enough to decipher them? Will they want to meet us? Perhaps we'll meet them halfway. Perhaps we'll kill ourselves off, and they'll journey here only to find the ruins of ancient cities.

Flash back into daylight near the northern end of the Urals, high above the mouth of the Ob river. Sightseeing's over, nose back to the grindstone. I move back into position to retrieve the second bucket. (This one will stay empty until Hank's second EVA.) Again I undo the latches and attach the lanyard, working hard as we pass over the Arctic. Hands tired enough now that I am truly worried about losing it. Despite the practice, it takes me five tries to get it snapped on to the carrier. We pass back down our side of the planet and chat with a string of SAC bases, Thule and Grand Forks and Cheyenne Mountain; I'm sure the pictures in our buckets will be in their briefing rooms soon enough. Especially once the resolution's better.

Eventually the carrier and the second bucket are in position for Hank. Then I am connecting the hoses to feed in nitrogen and replenish the cold gas thrusters from the resupply tank in the transtage. But it's hard to focus, thinking of the object I saw yesterday. I drag myself back to my X-20. There's a rail behind the cargo bay that leads to another on top of the transtage; I pull myself along it to the end of the spacecraft. Once there I spend a long couple minutes looking over the silent rocket nozzles. Everything looks normal.

Wearily I pull myself back towards the airlock. We are crossing the empty southern Pacific in daylight as I head inside; there's not much to see, and I'm tired enough that I don't care to look anyway.

It takes a bit of effort to get the hose inside and get the hatch closed. I am thoroughly spent.

"Not bad for a day's work," Hank says as the pressure gauge rises.

I sigh, exhausted. "Two days," I remind him. The clock says it's just been a morning. But it does feel like two days.

●●●

Inside and de-spacesuited now. Hank's warmed up lunch: Salisbury steak and mashed potatoes. Flash back into daylight outside, and the day's work's far from done; we need to eject the loaded film bucket soon so it can reenter in time for the recovery aircraft to pluck it out of the air over the Pacific. We eat in ravenous silence, high above the Barents Sea.

Soon the radio crackles alive. "Watchman, this is Thule. Awful quiet up there. Over."

"Thule, Watchman. More like awful hungry." Hank scarfs down another spoonful in lieu of radio courtesy.

"Thule, you're awful chatty today," I fill in. "Over."

"Not much else to do here but talk. Over."

"I bet." Hank pauses, next spoonful halfway to his mouth. "I'm picturing you as a lonely man in an igloo. Talking to strangers on the radio 'cause there's nothing else to do."

Static and a chuckle. "Not true, Watchman! It's a Quonset hut. Over."

"I don't mean to be rude, but we do have the film drop coming up," Hank says, by way of explanation. "Over."

"Understood, Watchman. Just make sure you talk to Cheyenne after that. Over."

"Shorter acquisition this pass." Down at that latitude, our ground track will be a good thousand miles west of where it'd been on the last orbit. Near the limit of their useful coverage. "Anything you can't tell us? Over."

"They want a little extra privacy," he says. "Over."

"Got it," Hank says. I envision the Soviet "fishing trawler" that's doubtless plying the icy waters of northern Baffin Bay—far better equipped to catch signals from the air than fish from the sea. Usually we don't entirely care, and for ease of comms we often talk on clear channels. But this situation calls for double protection: encryption, and a discussion over the continental United States, far from foreign boats and ears.

"Everything's on track for the drop?" I ask.

"It's not about the drop, Watchman. That's all I can say. Over."

"Understood. Watchman out." Hank kills the radio. And to me: "Little cloak and dagger stuff, huh?"

I chuckle. "There you go. It's not…boring old recon. We're spies!"

"Move over, James Bond."

I scrape the last of the mashed potatoes into my mouth, put spoon and pouch in the trash, and check my watch. "Four minutes. Plenty of time. I'll get started on the sequence."

Before I can move, Hank floats over there. "I got this one. You've had your fun for the day."

"You sure? I figured since I set it up…"

"All right. Fine." Under Hank's smooth surface: traces of annoyance and amusement. "You wanna flip for it?"

"Like, flip a coin?"

"Sure, why not? Can't exactly wait for it to hit the ground, but…here." Hank produces a MacArthur silver dollar. "Heads I win."

He sends the coin spinning; it tumbles end over end and drifts slowly towards the side of the station I think of as "ceiling." He plucks it out of the air, slaps it against his forearm, and moves his fingers to reveal the verdict: heads.

"All right, here we go." He floats to the console. "Platform is enabled, latches are released. Timer is activated and counting down…and…enable." He presses the button telling the computer it's OK to release. The timer hits 11:50 and there is a slight bobble. I drift over to the window.

"Clean separation. Retrograde direction."

"OK. Retro armed." Hank flips the last switch. "And we're done. Hope they like it." The capsule's now set on its fiery path, its deathless plunge through the upper atmosphere. If every latch holds, if the rocket fires properly, if the plunge goes smoothly and the altimeters function properly, it will soon be hanging under a parachute, waiting to be hooked by the recovery aircraft.

"Resolution's still bad, huh?"

"Last test strip I shot, it was maybe a foot and a half. That first calibration, we missed half the targets. The Mushroom Factory really pushed hard to schedule another one."

"You think we'll get down to four inches?" The hallowed, secret number. Our whole reason for being.

"We'll do our damndest."

Below now: the Rockies. Ragged mountains: a light dusting of snow lingering on one side, and mottled plains of tan and green stretching eastward. "We don't need to talk to Grand Forks, do we?"

"I don't think so."

"OK." I check my watch. "Couple minutes until Cheyenne."

"Better set the scrambler." Hank pulls the comms binder from a sleeve next to the radio and places it in the air in front of him.

"Might get a look at LA this pass, huh?"

"Yeah, should be. Noontime pass." Hank scans his finger along the day's code page. "Let's see...radio mode is SECURE. And we've got...E-O-P." He dials it in. "I prefer the night ones, to be honest. I told my girls to keep an eye out. I like to think we're seeing each other."

"We saw you the other night. I took my kids out in the backyard. It was kinda neat. I mean, obviously I told them the bare minimum, 'Daddy's gonna be in space for forty days' and all that. 'Daddy's gonna send you telegrams.' But I told them they could see us. And we caught you. It was neat."

"Cool."

A glance at the watch: another minute until Acquisition of Signal. "I used to fly over the house back in New Mexico, at Cannon. I always told my wife to keep her eyes out. I'd get as low as I could. Waggle the wings a bit, so she'd know I'd be home in a half hour and she could put on the roast or whatever. I don't know if it ever actually worked out that smoothly, though. I mean, it wasn't like she was in the kitchen staring out the window all day long. But it was fun."

Hank speaks, mock-serious: "I'm gonna officially recommend that we *don't* try that on this pass."

"Haha, yeah." I imagine the station reentering, melting, spinning apart: a bright daylight meteor. "Might be a little dangerous."

"Your wife would notice, though."

I chuckle. "Yeah, probably."

Radio crackle. "Watchman, this is Cheyenne. Come in, over." Our ground man's serious, humorless. A soft accent not unlike Hank's.

"Cheyenne, Watchman. Bucket is released and we are getting ready for maintenance tasks. How can we help you? Over."

"Watchman, we have info on the object you witnessed after Falcon-2's arrival. We believe it's a Red satellite. Over."

"Say again, Cheyenne?" Hank sounds like he heard just fine but doesn't want to believe.

"Watchman, Cheyenne. The object Falcon-2 observed. We believe it's a Soviet satellite in your plane. Over."

"In our plane? How the hell did that happen, Cheyenne?" Calm exasperation. "We missed a launch from Baikonur? Over."

"Watchman, we asked the Mushroom Factory. Apparently Plesetsk has been busy all spring. They wanted to put it on the target list last week, but we told them to wait, because of the resolution issues. Over."

An angry Hank head-shake. "Cheyenne, we'll take care of the resolution. We need you to keep an eye on the radar scope. Where they are now? Over."

"Watchman, they're out of phase. Higher orbit. We are going to try and get some ground-based imagery. But we do think..." The conversation dies in a crackle of static.

"Well that's just great." My watch confirms what the radio already told me: we're out of range now. "A Soviet satellite. In our plane. What do you think they're doing?"

He purses his lips. "Watching us. What else?"

"Why?"

"Why not? See who's coming and going. See if we're putting any modules on that they might not like. Hard to know for sure until we get a look at their platform, but..."

"Now we need a satellite to watch their satellite."

Hank chuckles. Through the window I see blue, and I groan. I float closer and position myself at the edge of the window and look across the water; I can just barely see the edge of Santa Monica receding behind us, bright in the high noonday sun. Our neighborhood's already out of sight.

• • •

Relentlessly we orbit: another pass over the dark Antarctic, then up across Horn of Africa and the deserts of Arabia. Another look at the midnight forests of the Soviet Union, before once more the blinding north. The night part of the pass had conspired with my tiredness into making me think my day was done; the sun's blast reminds me I need to be up and active after all. I float into the bathroom, wipe my face with a washcloth, and get ready for Round 2.

"All right, let's go," Hank says when I float out. "Ocean observation. You wanna spot, or target?"

I need to practice both tasks up here; I feel like trying the easier one first. "Spot."

"Me too." Hank could pull rank—he's in charge until he leaves—but he pulls out his silver dollar. "You wanna flip for it?"

"Sure. Can I be heads?"

He smiles. "I'm always heads." Still he flips the coin. Sure enough: heads. He puts the coin away before I can get a good look at it.

We pull ourselves into the observation section and man the Dorian console. Because we're re-calibrating tomorrow, we need to spend today practicing the scope work. I slip into my workstation footrests and press my face into the rubber console mask of the viewfinder. A blurry circle, just under a mile wide: pure deep North Pacific blue.

"All right," Hank says. "I am dialed out."

"Dialed in. Track mode on." The spotter scopes start their cycle, looking "ahead" and then panning backwards for ten seconds as we pass above; this gives us a little more time to figure out what we're looking at. Still, ten seconds isn't much.

"I have a wake at two o'clock, midway out. Try and get the ship."

The goal is to pick up the target and focus before the scopes recycle; I scroll up and to the right but don't see anything. For tomorrow, we'll have to consistently get the targets in the center of the camera field in the middle of the cycle. So I'm anxious to get it right today. But my scope is a bland blotch of blue.

"Wake direction northwest," Hank prods. "Getting up on the scope."

I breathe heavily. Scroll upwards. See: a smudge of white foamy seawater, which disappears almost instantly as the system recycles.

"Just barely caught the wake. Gone now." Unsaid, all the implications. If we can't pick up targets, we can't recalibrate. And if we can't do that, we're useless.

"All right, we'll find another." Hank dials the knobs. "Here we go. North-south wake. Bottom of the scope. Five o'clock."

"All right. Scrolling down." I'm anxious to prove my worth. But: nothing. An empty mile-wide circle of ocean.

"Drifting up. Three o'clock now."

"OK. Scrolling up a bit." Relentless pressure: time and work, and orbital mechanics working against me. "Nothing yet."

"Moving up."

"Retargeting." Then: a white smudge on the water. But I scroll the wrong way and it peters out. By the time I realize my mistake, the ship has passed from view. "Missed it."

"All right." Is Hank angry? Does he get angry? I can't tell.

Still, I'm mad at me. The American taxpayer has spent millions to put me here. If I can't do my primary task, it'll be an absurd waste of money. "It's such a narrow field of view. Like looking through a soda straw."

He lifts his face from the scope. "And I have to look through a toilet paper tube to tell you where to point the soda straw."

His tone is soft, but the message is clear: no use complaining. "It's tough, but it's doable. You'll get it."

I am racking my brain for lessons from training, but the memories are a hazy blur. "I feel like I'm missing something. Any pointers?"

"For me it's about minding the search pattern. Scrolling perpendicular to what the spotter calls out. A north-south wake, if you rush down to catch it, you're liable to miss it and have to backtrack. Scroll east-west as you drift downwards. The sooner you make that initial acquisition, the more time you have to hone in."

"Thanks, yeah. Perpendicular search. Don't know why I blanked on that."

"Probably because you trained weeks ago and you've done a million other things since then."

"Well, yeah, I guess that's true."

"Remember, it's all still practice."

His mellow tone's disarming. It's like going to confession with a laundry list of sins and only getting one Our Father as penance. "Well, practice makes perfect."

When Hank calls out the next one it is heading northeast-southwest; I swivel in smooth diagonals and catch the wake, then follow it as it narrows and whitens, twisting the focus as well to sharpen my view. "All right, I got a ship."

"There you go."

My resolution's about ten feet, just enough to make out a series of large white blobs just about as wide as the ship; I can see the angle changing as we pass overhead. "We'll call it commercial. Bulk carrier." When the cameras are on, they will do the rest, taking sharper pictures, imprinting date and time and telescope azimuth—everything necessary for a photographic interpreter to locate the target and have some actionable intelligence.

After the pass, a bathroom break over the Indian Ocean, then a long night pass over Africa (I imagine mighty jungles, sleeping lions, although surely there must be cars, cities, buildings) and the Med and Central Europe. Then another arc over the Arctic, brief pleasantries with Thule and Eielson. Finally: more oceanic target acquisition, northwest of Hawaii now, slicing down across the ocean again.

"Got a few wakes here," Hank says. "West by northwest, seven o'clock."

"Got it. Scrolling in." I catch the largest one, follow it easily. The controls feel smoother now, natural, like that day in flight training when it all clicks and you stay ahead of the airplane and it starts to feel like a part of you, something you can control as easily as your own limbs. At the head of the wake is a distinctive ship shape, squarish and asymmetrical. I scroll over, catch a destroyer and a cruiser before the recycle. "I'll be damned. That's a carrier battle group."

"There you go," Hank says, and leans back from the scope. "That's a good win to end the day."

"Jesus, if we had the cameras on they would have probably picked up the deck numbers."

"Pretty neat, huh?"

"It's amazing. Like playing Battleship and seeing the other board."

"Battleship?"

I chuckle. "You ever play that notepad game when you were a kid? They got this new version. Boards and pegs and little plastic ships. Got it for my son last Christmas."

Hank smiles. "That's what I get for having girls. It's all…Barbie dolls and tea parties."

"Missing out." I nod back at the scope. "Although it's more fun playing it live. Aircraft carrier, cruiser, destroyer, that's three fifths of the ships…"

"Except here it's real…I mean, carrier battle group, near Hawaii. We know it's ours, but imagine if it wasn't? Imagine if we had this ability in 1941…"

It's a sobering thought; it's easy now to imagine the Japanese fleet plowing through the seas below, sinister gray carriers moving into position for the fateful blow.

Hank goes on. "We had reconnaissance planes, we could have *maybe* caught the strike force once it was close enough to strike already, *if* we'd been lucky. But can you imagine if we'd had this?"

I've heard the Pearl Harbor analogies before, of course. They're on everyone's mind; they're why we're here. To stop something that already happened. Or to stop the atomic version, at least. So many Red surprises: the atomic bomb, Sputnik, Vostok…who knows what else they're willing to spring on us? "Just to be devil's advocate. We still might've missed them, scanning the seas at random. Couple days of bad weather..."

"We could have watched their bases, all the time! We could have seen that harbor in the Kuriles all full of carriers. We could have seen it empty out. We could have caught them leaving the Home Islands, rather than waiting for the first bomb to fall..."

"Except it still would've taken a while. They'd still have to alert the fleet, decide what to do. Maybe alert the president. I mean, we couldn't have just...attacked them without provocation on the open ocean."

"Maybe once they launched planes..."

"Still, you'd need some kind of executive decision. Those things take time..."

"Well, yeah. You need a fast enough decision cycle."

"Do you think it *can* happen fast enough?" We've talked about these things before, of course; we've known since selection what we're doing up here, and why. But something about seeing it for real, seeing the world laid out before you, all the kingdoms of the world... "If we get attacked now, we won't have a week to prepare while they're steaming towards us. The older ICBMs...a day. Now, half an hour, tops."

"That's why I think we'll get the OB. If we can strike while they're still drawing their sword...cut off the head before it can issue the final command..." Hank looks straight through me. "We could save the country from catastrophe, you know."

I nod. We are bobbing freely in front of the console, light and loose, but alive to the seriousness of why we're here. The need for four-inch resolution, the need to get good pictures in front of decision-makers as fast as humanly possible...

The radio intrudes. "Watchman, Hickam. How are you this fine afternoon, over?"

"Hickam, Watchman. We're doing well." I smile. "Keeping you safe from Admiral Nagumo's task force. Over."

"Watchman, Hickam. I...uhhh...do not copy. Over."

"Hickam, Watchman." Hank gives me a look, more disappointed now than when I was messing up on the scope. "Never mind. Bad joke. Over."

•••

We work until dinner and then eat in silence. After that: close the window cover and put on the evening lights. In the soft red glow everything feels calm. I float into the hygiene area and treat myself to a bowel evacuation and a sponge bath, which eats up a good half an orbit. After that comes a few minutes of mindless reading, Dashiell Hammett's *Red Harvest*, something to remind me that it is, in fact, time to wind down.

And yet on this last pass before our sleep period we'll be passing back over the continental United States. An ascending node now, south to north over the Great Plains on a short summer night. We are close to Texas when the radio crackles to life.

I float over to listen better. "Watchman, Cheyenne Mountain, come in, over." They're on a clear channel, which surprises me.

"Cheyenne, this is Watchman." Hank sounds moderately annoyed. "We didn't get a secure comms request. Over."

"Error on our part, Watchman." A soft drawl, not unlike Hank's. "End-of-the-day decision. We should be able to say what we need to. Over."

"Go on, Cheyenne."

"First off, package delivery was successful. I repeat: package delivery was successful."

Hank rolls his eyes, mutes the mike, looks at me. "Well that's a helluva secret code."

I smirk. "Good thing they got it, huh?" Always that worry, that the Soviets will grab a bucket before we can get to it. If the recovery aircraft had missed, the capsule would have splashed down in the Pacific. They're designed to sink after a few days, but there's always the chance the Reds will snag one first. Especially if they know we missed it.

Cheyenne is droning on. "...object you mentioned, we obtained imagery from a ground-based asset. Unfortunately we couldn't see much. It looked like a blob. Over."

"Cheyenne, Watchman. You said a blob, over?"

"That's affirmative, Watchman. Normal-sized. Probably the standard model. Over."

Hank mutes the mike. "Zenit 2?"

"Sounds reasonable." It occurs to me that we can look outside without messing up our internal clocks; I slide the window cover up and watch lights scroll by: streetlight maps of cities and towns, more vibrant than on the Soviet side of the globe, a crooked bright spiderweb on the black earth.

Ground is still talking. "...ish we had more information, Watchman. We do appreciate the pictures. Even with the resolution issues. Over."

Hank transmits: "Somebody's gotta keep an eye on the bad guys."

"Well you picked a good call sign, Watchman."

"Wasn't my decision," Hank drawls. "I wanted it to be 'War Eagle.' But some Yankee higher-up thought that sounded...belligerent. Figured the Russians wouldn't catch the Auburn reference."

"War Eagle." Cheyenne repeats it like it's a dirty phrase.

"We're on track for tomorrow, right?"

"Uhhh...that's affirmative, Watchman. Circularization looks good and you are steady at eighty-five nautical miles. Vandenberg is a GO. No change orders."

"Good," Hank says. "Might be a short mission for my friend here otherwise."

"Actually...stand by, Watchman. Someone just handed me a high-priority message."

My pulse quickens with his tone. I check my watch: we're coming up on the end of the comms window.

"You want I should put on the scramblers?"

"No time, Watchman." Urgency's crept in to his voice. "I'll read it phonetically. Stand by to copy."

"OK." Hank plucks pencil and paper from the sleeve by the radio. In the soft crimson glow I see concern on his face.

"Romeo-Oscar. Lima-Lima. Tango-India. Delta-Echo."

Suddenly it clicks. I watch Hank's pen on the dim red-lit paper; he makes it through R-O-L-L and T-I-D before he figures it out.

"You sonofabitch," Hank shakes his head. "All right, good night."

There's laughter from the Alabama stranger. "Cheyenne out."

"'Bama grad. That's as bad as a communist," I joke.

"Crimson tide bullshit," Hank grumbles, and looks around at the submarine night-lighting, as if that too is part of the joke. "I'll tell you what, red is *not* my favorite color."

His quiet gripes somehow sound endearing, not annoying. "Good team," I point out. "Bear Bryant."

Hank shakes his head. "Bear. That's a Russian animal. On top of the whole red thing. Now, I'm not saying they're communists, but it does seem a little unpatriotic. Especially compared to an eagle. Don't you think?"

"Sympathizers, maybe."

"You know that sonofabitch was in the navy?" Hank says. "And I'll tell you what. He was navy, he'll find out: the tide is receding. They are not gonna win another championship this year."

"You say so." I can't help but smile.

"Roll tide." Hank chuckles. "Man, I can't believe I fell for that."

There's a Thule comms window coming up, but neither of us cares to relieve their boredom. We maneuver floating bodies into sleeping bags, and I figure a way to pull my arms in and tighten the drawstring from inside, to give my body the illusion of gravity's pressure. I'd brought a small family picture and taped it on a spot of bare metal next to me; I look at them, remind myself to send a message tomorrow. I say an Our Father. A couple blank minutes later, sleep overtakes me.

•••

I wake an hour early, and we're still lit red. It's early enough to go back to bed, but nature calls, so I float over to the bathroom. On the way back I notice Hank isn't in his sleeping bag. And he's not in the working module, either.

My mind can't quite process this. Not many places for him to go. At last I notice a flicker of motion through the little hatch window to the docking spindle.

Now I'm curious. The hatch is closed but not locked; I push it open, catch the faint sound of music. Dvořák, *From the New World*, dramatic and urgent. Hank's feet are in front of me; I touch them and he startles.

"Up early?" I ask.

"Couldn't sleep. Wanted to think." He floats feet-first back out of the tunnel and pushes a small Philips tape deck towards me. "Figured I'd take a sightseeing break. Wanted a little musical accompaniment, but I didn't want to wake you up. You'll have to try it. Get up close to the rendezvous window and tilt your head back, you kinda feel like Superman."

I chuckle. Through the docking window I see deep daylit blue. A descending pass over the center of the Atlantic.

Hank closes the hatch. Now again all is red. "That satellite. The Zenit. It's odd to me that they'd launch in our plane."

"They probably want to keep an eye on us."

"They can't change orbits, right? The Zenit. If I remember correctly, they have no on-orbit maneuvering capability. They can't raise or lower it at all." His face is red and quiet and serious: a crimson king.

"That's right, as far as I remember."

"So it's odd to launch in our plane. I mean, what, they get one guaranteed look at us, and then...what?"

"They'll get others. Different conjunction opportunities."

"That seems like an awfully big effort. Launching a satellite just to look at us occasionally."

"Well, they get normal recon passes. The high-inclination orbit works for them, too. They can observe our missile fields at the same time every day. Same length shadows. They can see if missiles are being trucked in or trucked out, or maintained, or whatever. As for watching us, it's like any military decision. You've got a limited resource, if you have a chance to do a couple things with it, you do. Two birds with one stone, and all that."

"But what if that's not it? What if it is just us?"

"Well, like ground said. They're out of phase now. Higher orbit. And if they can't maneuver..."

"Maybe they can, now," Hank says. "Maybe it's not an ordinary Zenit. Either way, I wanna get a look at them."

●●●

By breakfast, we have made another lap. The lights are day-duty white. Outside: the Caribbean, waters of all depths, every shade of it I've ever seen: dazzling azure to sparkling turquoise, and everything in between. An infinite variety of blues.

I pause between bites of reconstituted eggs. "Man. Wish I'd gotten a better look at that yesterday."

"That's the tough thing about being up here on the taxpayer's dime. Not much time to sightsee." Hank gazes at the window, wistful. "It's worth losing a little sleep to get some extra window time..."

The radio interrupts. "Watchman, Antigua. Come in, over."

"Antigua, Watchman. We are finishing breakfast and getting ready for the workday. Over."

"Roger, Watchman. We are going to push your burn instructions and target list summary up through the teletype. Over."

"Thanks, Antigua. We'll keep our eyes out. Over."

"All right. It's on the way. Antigua out."

Hank turns off our mike. "Aaand they're all done for the day."

"Good beach day there, I bet." Behind us in the work module, the teletype starts clattering.

"It could be for us, too." Hank smiles.

"Ha! Yeah, I suppose so." Our X-20s were designed to be maneuverable after reentry: gliders, true, but starting from a great enough height that we can steer a good thousand-plus miles crossrange. Given that, plus our orbital inclination, we could literally set down anywhere on the globe on any given day. "Do a retro burn over the Arctic next orbit. We'd end up...what, over the Bahamas? Or steer back this way a bit. Pick out an island after reentry. Find a flat stretch of road..."

"Hell, just eject once you're low enough."

Losing the spacecraft...obviously not ideal. "Well, if you're gonna get in trouble anyway...I mean, I'm sure Uncle Sam would come looking for us soon."

"Yeah. Caribbean might not work so well. Probably only get a couple hours on the beach before they hauled you off to the brig. You'd have to get a little further away…South Pacific, maybe…"

I laugh. "You've been watching too much *South Pacific*. 'Some enchanted evening…you will meet a stranger…'"

"Can you imagine, though? Dropping out of the sky onto some…Polynesian island where they're all…members of a cargo cult…"

"What the hell is a cargo cult?"

"You never read about those? They sprang up during the war, on some of those islands. The Solomons. Or the New Hebrides. I mean, it kinda makes sense. Like, imagine how mind-blowing that was, if you were living down there. Maybe some of them had been colonized already, but others…I mean, there are places down there where there had been no contact with the outside world until this century. Places now where there's still no contact. Like the Sentinel islands. So imagine. You're going on about your day, the way your people have for…thousands of years. Cut off from the outside world. The most advanced technology at your disposal is the…axe you use to make your outrigger canoe. Then next thing you know, there are…massive steel ships in the waters off your island. Men flying airplanes from the ships, and you've never even seen an airplane, let alone one that could fly off a ship. Then maybe people are putting an airstrip on your island. And you see them talking into a radio, and you don't even know what a radio is, but all this stuff starts…magically appearing. Quonset huts! Food in cans, flown in from the sky! Can you imagine how that would look to you?"

The teletype continues its soft clatter. "We must've been like aliens to them."

"Aliens or gods, yeah." Hank smiles. "Anyway, a cargo cult...some of these islanders, they'd imagine the person on the other end of the radio. They'd give them one name, because they would think it was one person. A mystery god, responsible for all of it. John Frum. Tom Navy."

"Tom Navy."

"Yep. They'd imagine the person responsible, and they'd worship them. Because why not? I mean, if some...mysterious distant entity is making things happen that you can't comprehend..." Hank smiles. "So yeah, that's what you gotta do. Drop out of the sky on...Espiritu Santo or something. Meet all the island maidens. Tell them you're John Frum."

I laugh. "I wouldn't have much in the way of supplies."

Hank muses. "You could just...just tell 'em it's on the way."

"I wouldn't have a radio."

Hank's eyes brighten. "Ham radio."

I laugh. "Ham radio?"

"Sure, why not? We can access those frequencies. Single Sideband mode. Get your X-20 down in one piece, rig up a power source, start talking. Find some rich civilian in...Australia or New Zealand maybe...some lonely guy with a boat...talk him into buying supplies. You'd be set!"

"Wait, how am I the one doing this?"

Hank laughs. "Well I'm not gonna do it! I've got a solid Air Force career. Wife and kids to go home to…"

I chuckle, shake my head. Imagine the freedom. Behind us, the teletype printer has gone silent. Hank secures all the breakfast trash and snags a few wayward crumbs from the air. I float back to the working module to pick up our orders for the day.

•••

"Loring, Watchman. Ready for target acquisition. Over."

One orbit later, another descending node: the green forests of southern Quebec flashing by below. We're back at the Dorian console, seeing, at best, a six-mile slice at a time. Our orders are all transcribed, our plans for the day now deciphered into plain English, the relevant maps pulled from their binders and placed in their transparencies, with a grease pencil line on each one to indicate our ground track. The weather forecast is excellent: thunderstorms in the southeast, clear everywhere else; even God is cooperating. But peeking through the scope with the tracking off, and seeing the terrain with its myriad details whizzing by at 4.6 miles a second, it becomes all the more apparent how little time we'll have for the task.

"Watchman, Loring. Trucks are in position." Our controller's curt, direct: no time for pleasantries. "You should have the maps ready. Details as follows. Target one is at a service station on U.S. Route 5, just south of St. Johnsbury. It's a double-cloverleaf interchange, just north-by-northwest of the I-91 to I-93 interchange. Over."

I scan the map, locate the spot, make a tick mark on our orbital track. "Loring, we copy. Next target, over."

"Target two: ten miles west of Springfield, Mass, on a pulloff on the south side of I-90. Just west of where the interstate passes over U.S. Route 20 and the Westfield River. Over."

Again I scan the map, find the spot, make the mark. "We copy, Loring. Over."

"Target three is in a parking lot at…" (Garbled.) "…west of Bridgeport, Connecticut. Over."

Anxious. No way to place that. "Loring, Watchman, say again all after 'parking lot.' Over."

"Watchman, parking lot at Fairfield University, north of I-95 and west of Bridgeport. Over."

"Loring, we copy 3 targets. South of St. Johnsbury, west of Springfield, west of Bridgeport, over."

Hank is hunched over the spotting scope. "Track mode on. Crossing the St. Lawrence." He flips a switch. "Cameras on."

"Watchman, Loring, it'll be forty seconds between one and two, twenty seconds between two and three. Happy hunting. Out."

Not much time at all: very little real estate to play with before we cross the Connecticut coast. I've turned the maps upside-down, and Hank looks up from the scope to study the landmarks that will precede each target; I mark off a quick initial point for each one: the spot where I-91 and Route 5 come together like tree branches north of St. Johnsbury, the state highways north of I-90, a bend in I-84 before it crosses a river near Newtown. Then I put my head back down.

With tracking on, the motion's smoothed out; now I can pick up blotches of dark green and light, patches of forest and field. "Loring, initial points are set and we are on scope. Watchman out."

"First IP," Hank says, and hits the button to reset the scopes. "Recycling."

"Aaand here we go..." I pick up the thin twin strand of I-91 as it arcs around the tiny town; a quick scroll and focus, and I see it feed into a two-leaf asphalt clover. "Two interchanges, there we go." The counters tick and the cameras click: red numbers just outside the telescope field climbing steadily upward.

"Great. Next settings."

I glance at our notecards and tweak the focal length and exposure to the settings for Target 2. Then, head back down. More forests, crooked roads, ragged granite lakes.

"Second IP. Recycling."

With a quick north-south scan I pick up I-90 and focus in. "Wow. Got it. There we go."

Again everything clicks; I adjust the settings again, but now things are happening faster and Hank calls "Third IP" before my head's back down.

"All right, scanning..." Now I'm seeing a thicket of confusing suburbia; I catch the landmarks too late, and then everything cycles and it's gone and I'm looking at the blue of Long Island Sound. "Damn! Not sure we caught that one."

"We'll check the film," Hank says. "Never know 'til it's developed."

"They should have done Long Island for that truck."

"It's already a long drive from Loring to Connecticut. Add New York traffic, then getting back east…"

"Yeah." I'm hit by a quick blast of childhood nostalgia. Day trips downtown: the long Manhattan avenues stretching out to the horizon, the low morning sunlight turning limestone to gold, the city panorama from the Triborough Bridge with its infinity of buildings.

"We'll try those settings out west. I think we have a couple pick-up targets."

Preparations for the next pass: cleaning the transparencies, inserting new maps for the targets from Grand Forks and Cheyenne. There's a lot more land to play with out there, and the trucks will be more evenly spaced, spread across Minnesota and Iowa and Kansas and Oklahoma, with probably a solid minute of acquisition time between each one. And there's a third pass coming. Targets in Idaho and Oregon, Nevada and California—much more to prepare for. But for the moment, we're over open ocean and I'm thinking back to those snippets of image: imagining what it's like to be down there on the target trucks, waiting. Maybe taking a morning nap in the cab after the long redeye drive across New England, waking hot and sweaty, checking your watch to see if it's time to fold up the target panels and get back on the road. Or: wandering off to some roadside diner for coffee and cigarettes and bacon and eggs, milking the airman's uniform for whatever it's worth, flirting with the waitress, dropping coy hints about a secret mission...

"What do you think they're doing?" I ask Hank.

"Who?"

"The guys driving the trucks."

He chuckles. "No idea. Nice lazy duty day now, I bet. Take their time getting back on the road, easy summer drive back to Maine..."

"Yeah." I'm not sure what I'm feeling; I don't think it's jealousy. Maybe just an awareness of how many pieces there are in this whole operation, or in the government itself: tax dollars paying not just for our orbiting home and the space planes that flew us here, but the mundane stuff, too, all the odds and ends, the customized semis with their large metal target panels, the airmen and their uniforms, the money they're spending at the diner and the gas pump, the salaries of the accountants who will tally it all up at the end...

"I'll tell you what...those guys down there...we get the resolution where it's supposed to be, we'll be able to see 'em for ourselves."

●●●

The day's last target is the only one that's not a semi, the only one I've seen from the ground: a large concrete pad baking in the California sun at Vandenberg, painted black and white, no doubt destined to be repainted every few months by some airman on a work detail with no real clue what he's doing. We're over the hill-cradled farmland of the Central Valley now, almost there. I'm eager to catch the last target, eager to atone for my many failings.

Head down, I watch the scope recycle. Flashes of familiar shapes: mountains, railroad tracks, perimeter fence. "...aaand there we go." Then a quick scroll southward: a familiar structure. "Oh! Launch pad!" Over the radio: "...3...2...1...and liftoff! Your Centaur is on the way..." and see before my scope recycles: a bloom of smoke and fire, a rocket rising up to meet us.

The scope resets: blue Pacific again. I float away, more than thrilled to be done for the day.

"Vandenberg, Watchman, we caught a visual," Hank says. "Thanks for sending that."

"Anytime, Watchman. Hate to see all that hard work go to waste. Over."

"I hope it wasn't a waste, Vandenberg." Picking out targets on the Great Plains was harder than expected: the long straight country highways and patchwork farmland looked far more samey-same than the glacier-hewn granite terrain of New England. The westernmost pass was better: blue mountain lakes and winding roads, rivers snaking through arid valleys. Still, I don't know if I was good enough.

A crackle from the radio. "Tough day on the scope, Watchman?"

"Roger, Vandenberg. We'll see what the pictures say."

"I think he did great," Hank says. "Very productive duty day. You might even call it…" (A pause for a punchline.) "…the high point of his Air Force career. Over."

"Watchman, that's the kind of joke my dad would make. Awful."

"I thought you'd like it! You seem like a good guy. Very…down-to-Earth."

"Watchman, keep that up and we'll bring *you* down to Earth."

"Come on, Vandenberg, there's no need for…pun-ishment."

A light chuckle from the radio. "All right, Watchman. For the sake of your crewmember, we'll get you some more high points."

What goes up must come down, at least if it's in low-Earth orbit. The fringes of the upper atmosphere will eventually drag the station from orbit and turn it into a molten metal meteor. The rocket now ascending will push us into an elliptical orbit that won't decay as quickly, one with only one low-point—over the targets we'll be photographing in the Soviet Union.

"Telemetry is looking good," they continue. "First stage sep will be after LOS. Tananarive will have more for you. Vandenberg out."

On go the red lights: our work module's now a darkroom. I wind up the target film, unload the canister, attach it to the developer mechanism. The small tail of film sticking out gets threaded onto the sprockets, and the mechanism winds the film through the developer chamber.

"Busy day," Hank says. "I didn't get to ask Cheyenne about our stranger."

"Stranger?"

"The Zenit. If it is a Zenit. I want to get a look at it."

"With the station? That'll take some work." I press the buttons: send fluid into the chamber, start the centrifuge, start the timer.

"Not the station. Me."

"The X-20?"

"Sure, why not?"

"On your departure day?"

"Tomorrow."

"Transtage fuel budget might be tight. When it *is* departure day, you don't want to shove off and then not have fuel for a burn." The timer climbs.

"It's low-Earth orbit," Hank smiles. "I'd come down eventually."

"It'd take a couple weeks. Might get hungry in the meantime." The timer runs out. Stop the centrifuge, set it to drain, give it a few quick manual spins, then feed the film into the stop bath drum.

"You can't tell me you're not a little curious."

"Well, yeah. I mean, they talked about this as a possibility. I didn't think the Soviets would actually launch something in our plane, though. You think they're that eager to keep an eye on us?"

"It could be more than keeping an eye on us. I mean, we're assuming a Zenit, but..."

"What else could it be?"

"Some kind of hunter-killer."

The words stop me. "You think?"

"Sure, why not? I mean, it's in a higher orbit than us now, right? Why would they put a recon bird in a higher orbit? Higher orbit than us, but same plane. We know how hard it is to get something in the same plane, with no wedge angle..."

I finish the stop bath. Move on to the fixing stage. Thirteen minutes in the centrifuge. Hank floats back to the main room to talk to Tananarive and prepare for the rendezvous. I am not at all certain that it's going to work out well. So many things must go right, and if they don't, it will be at least two weeks before they can send up another booster. But there are bigger things to think about now.

My hands and eyes keep working as if on autopilot, but my mind keeps wandering off to that bright spot following us in the night sky, and those words: hunter-killer.

•••

"Watchman, Thule. Approach complete. Verify camera closure. Over."

"Cameras are buttoned up," Again that fear: our lenses and mirrors getting schmutzed up from the thrusters.

"Thule, Watchman. Good telemetry here. Going to TV now." With the flip of a switch, a grainy black-and-white image appears next to Hank: our station from an unfamiliar angle, opposite our docking spindle, down on the mirror end, off-center on the screen, still a bit distant. "We have a clear picture, Thule. Over."

"Turning over control, Watchman."

"Roger. Testing thrusters." Hank's hands move ever so slightly, and the picture rotates; a small black cross now visible against the Arctic below. "We have control. Over."

I watch, amazed. For all my knowledge of our systems and capabilities, there is something miraculous about seeing it all work as designed.

"Watchman, you are GO for final rendezvous. Over."

"Thule, we copy GO for rendezvous. Bringing it in now. Over." Hank works confidently; another pulse on the controller and our station's image grows larger as smoothly as a ship stuck in a *Star Trek* tractor beam.

"Coming up on LOS. You should have Eielson shortly. Over."

Hank's busy, so I take it upon myself to reply. "Thank you for your help, Thule. Excellent job. Watchman out."

Within seconds, the radio comes back on. "Watchman, Eielson. We have AOS. Over."

"Eielson, Watchman. We are on final approach. Over."

"Roger, Watchman. Let us know if you need anything."

Back to the screen: the black target cross lined up with the reticle on the far end of the station, and everything looking so perfect I can't believe it. Surely this is where it will all go wrong: collision, decompression. But then at last comes a very slight bump, the groan of the docking latches. I finally allow myself to believe that it's all going to be OK.

"Looks like we managed all right, Eielson," I say, then to Hank: "Nice job." I pat him on the back; it feels as awkward as the rendezvous was smooth.

From Hank: nothing. No sigh of relief, no sense that anything could have gone any way other than how it did. He scans the indicators and flips the switches, all the electrical connectors now complete, and we are all joined now, one spacecraft, for the time being.

We swoop southwards, above Arctic islands speckling the ice pack, then giving way to the Yukon, empty lakes and snow-capped peaks.

•••

Another orbit later and we're crossing the north coast of Alaska: smooth pack ice followed by a slice of dark water, then the fast ice of the coast giving way to green summer tundra. Soon we'll be at roughly the same latitude as the bulk of our Soviet target areas. In other words, it's time for the burn.

"I'll flip you for it," I offer Hank.

"For the burn?" he smiles.

"Sure, why not? You did the rendezvous."

"All right."

Again the same coin; he sends it end over end, but I snatch it from the air before he has time to react. I inspect both sides. Sure enough: two MacArthurs. "Are you freaking kidding me?"

He laughs. "It's become a bit of a station tradition. You'll get it at the change of command."

"A double-headed dollar."

"We prefer to call it a non-binary command authority augmentator."

"Has anybody ever refused any commands up here? I mean…" The rest goes unsaid: we—the pool of Air Force astronauts—are not exactly the rebellious type.

"You know how these things are. I mean, hell, you were in the first class at the academy, right? You had to make up some traditions, I'm sure…"

Flashes of memory: ATOs yelling in our face outside the old wooden barracks at Lowry Field, heated debates with classmates about whether we wanted to be falcons or tigers. "Well, yeah, but…"

"That's all this is. Half the fun is just seeing how long it takes the next guy to figure it out. You were faster than me, I'll give you that." A glance at the clock, then: "All right, let's go."

Outside, the peaks of the Brooks Range. Stark and white in the summer sun, scraping away the sky.

Hank scans the instruments. "Attitude and orientation are correct. Ready for command entry."

I read the teletype: "Burn commences at Two-two-five-one Hours Greenwich Mean Time. One-two-niner seconds."

Hank types it in. "Commands entered. Timer set."

"All right, then." Below now, Alaska's ending: the Aleutians stretch off into the distance, the North Pacific deep and dark blue in the late afternoon.

"Engine enable." Hank presses the button and smiles, his free hand on a railing. "Might want to hold on."

When the engine kicks in it is not dramatic, but I do find my floating body drifting rearward a little more quickly than expected. I grab for a handrail and miss, then catch another further back. The acceleration isn't great, maybe a tenth of a g, and there's no damage to anything other than my ego.

Hank looks back and smiles. "Half the fun is seeing how long it takes the new guy to figure it out."

•••

This will be our last night on American time, but it's early morning in the central Soviet Union, so we're going to pretend dinner is breakfast, pretend we're fine working another workday at the tail end of this workday. For now we're pretending we woke up early to get a few things done. So: on go the red lights again.

The fixing stage is finished and the film is no longer light-sensitive. Time to cut up the negatives and find our enlargement targets. We've pulled the porthole cover over, to help our internal clocks reset. Blind to the outside world: we might as well be in a submarine. But we know where we are.

"Coming up on Siberia soon," Hank observes.

"Be nice to get the time shift over with." We've been drying the film for the last couple orbits. On Earth it would be a simple step, hanging it on a line, but here even simple things are complicated, so the target film's loosely coiled in a drying chamber, with a fan to stir the stagnant air.

"It's different. Different rhythm to the days."

"How so?" I feed the first foot of film out, find a line between frames, cut it, and hand it to Hank.

"More alone time. More time looking at them in daylight." Meaning the Reds. Beria's ruthless police state. "If they do try anything, that's where it'll happen. Over their territory. Out of our radar coverage."

If they do try anything. Those words again: hunter-killer. "You think they would?"

"I wouldn't put it past them. I don't know if we can afford to wait and see." He slides the film onto the light table and gives it a quick scan. "Still north of the first target here."

"Maybe they're just preparing. Making sure they have the capability." Feed and cut again. "I mean, if they did try something, they'd have a lot of political consequences to deal with."

"If they admitted to it." Hank feeds the new slice of film onto the light table but ignores it for now. "It's not like there'd be much evidence. Pieces of orbital debris, which would reenter soon. Nothing anybody'd ever see. They could just say, 'We're sorry for the tragic loss of these brave Americans. We don't know what happened to them. Space is a dangerous place.' Or if we *did* have evidence they'd shot us down, they could claim it was a violation of sovereignty. Say they have a right to defend their airspace, even up *into* space. I mean, we know it's bullshit, we know this is different than, say, shooting down a U-2. We know everybody's satellites cross everybody else's territory all the time. But in the court of world public opinion...these people in the Third World aren't going to make that distinction. If the Soviets said we were flying over them and they were defending themselves, some people would buy it."

"Maybe."

"Or, hell, maybe they don't care. Maybe that'll be their *causus belli* for a larger war. Us being up here."

"You think they want a larger war?"

"Not sure if they want it, or if it's just...inevitable. Man's never built a weapon that we haven't used in anger at some point. And the missiles they're building..." Finally he scans the new negative, consults the map. "Still not there yet."

"All right." Feed and cut.

"Either way, I'm sure they'll try and hit us in the first phase."

I breathe and float. Imagining the first shots of World War III, aimed at us.

"I mean, it's only logical," he goes on. "Even if they know we don't have a bombardment module. Any kind of military action, that's the first thing you do when the shooting starts. Take out the sentries, blind your enemy. And they are up to something."

"Just because they launched a satellite in our plane doesn't mean…"

"It's not just the satellite. Our taskings lately…we haven't just been counting up ICBM fields. We've been stretching out the duty day to get pictures of Eastern Europe, too. It sounds like they're massing forces. I think that's why the Mushroom Factory is so eager to get the resolution up to where it's supposed to be. They want to be able to tell cars apart from tanks. Figure out what kind of forces we're facing. If they changed their minds and decided to take out West Berlin. Or attack West Germany." He scans the third strip. "Still nothing. Getting close."

Feed and cut once more. "Do you think they know our capabilities?"

"They've know we can provide some kind of early warning. And even if they don't know the full capabilities…imagination can be worse than knowledge. They're not gonna wanna take chances." Once more he scans the images on the light table: miniature black-and-white shots, with fields and forests reduced to blotches of dark and light gray, and roads like silver ribbons. "Almost there."

"We've got other assets. Unmanned. There's usually at least another Corona up here at all times. Sometimes two. They wouldn't be able to take out everything at once."

"The Corona doesn't have the resolution we are supposed to have. It can't be retasked as quickly as we can. Half the time it's taking pictures of cloud tops, because it doesn't know any better."

I have to concede the point. But then again… "If they wanted to take us out, they would have launched in the opposite inclination as us. Not the same. Then coming towards us, they'd just explode the satellite a couple dozen miles out. Big debris field, like a shotgun. Go for the kinetic kill. At those closing velocities, it wouldn't take much…" The possibilities are vague but terrifying: the station vaporized in an instant, or peppered by smaller strikes that would drain our air or destroy our X-20s. "Whereas this way, they'd have to close in slowly. They'd run the risk of us maneuvering out of the way. We have ground coverage, we'd get a call at some point…"

"That's why I think it'd happen over the Soviet Union. They could start a maneuver after we cross the U.S. on a descending node. Some of those orbits, we don't have coverage again until Thule. Plenty of time for them to close in…"

"They'd have to get pretty close."

Hank purses his lips. "For all we know, they've got a nuke on that thing."

For the next hour we are feeding and cutting film, studying it under the magnifier when necessary, circling the frames with the target trucks, placing those strips into paper sleeves so we can enlarge them later. Before long we've found every target, save that third one in Connecticut. I take a bathroom break and then sneak away to the docking spindle.

Below is Siberia again, the Magadan Oblast. Low brown mountains cut by jagged green rivers. Empty of friendly eyes: the perfect place for a crime. As our next orbits take us further west, we'll be even more isolated. The coast approaches, the Sea of Okhotsk.

Then, over that foreign horizon: a quick twinkle. An object just visible through the bend of the atmosphere, then rising above it as it follows us in orbit. A pang of angst: the enemy star, bright and menacing.

"It's back," I tell Hank. "The satellite."

"Sonofabitch."

"Did we get a warning call?" A question, but I already know the answer.

"No. Where's it at? Higher orbit still, or lower?" Meaning: is it closing in, or did we pass it without realizing?

"It's...ahhh. Tough to say."

He floats into the spindle, jostles up next to me so he can see. "We need to talk to Loring. Set up a secure chat with Cheyenne."

On the flip side of these orbits, another set of comms windows is opening: ascending passes over the U.S. at night. "You're right. Maybe we should have you fly up there. We need eyes on that thing."

●●●

The day stretches on, the endless double day, an edgy blend of work and paranoia. With no gravity, our bodies don't get tired. And our minds have more than enough to keep us occupied. We take turns warily eyeing the spindle window, making sure our fellow traveler isn't closing in.

But after our second breakfast, it's time again to hunker down and work. The enlargement phase: red lights. We float head-to-head around the machine; I feed the first negative strip into the film carrier.

"Gotta admit, I'm curious how this'll turn out." I scroll to the target frame, focus the image on the baseboard.

"You've always seemed like the kind of guy that's never sure you've done a good enough job."

"Growing up Catholic. That's what it does to you." The image resolves, blurry to clear, or close to it, at least; I see the trucks at last, top panels unfolded so they look like crosses, but I can't quite make out the resolution marks. "Be perfect as your heavenly Father is perfect, my mom used to say."

"High standards, huh?"

I smile. "The highest."

He surveys the blown-up projection. "Looks good."

"You think?" I fiddle with the focus a little more, hoping against hope that we got it right on the first try.

"As good as this one's gonna get. Print it."

"Might be better on one of the later ones."

"I'm sure it will be. Let's practice before we get there." He floats gently, observing. "We'll be all right. We caught a lot of targets, compared to last time. All but one."

I expose the print paper. On goes the white light; I watch the timer carefully.

"When you say, 'all but one,' I hear, 'missed one.'"

"Like I said, on the initial calibration, we missed five," Hank says. "All on one end of the scale. And the scale was probably off."

"Yeah." Off goes the light, and the print paper comes out. "Still, there's a big difference. Comparing yourself to others versus...just trying to get it right. In high school, everyone else was hoping the teacher would grade on a curve. I was always trying to ace the test."

"Blow up the curve for everyone else, huh?" Hank says. "I can respect that."

The print paper goes into the centrifuge: a couple minutes of spinning so the developer gets everywhere it needs to, then more spinning with the drain plugs open, then more spinning with the stop bath, and then we drain that, and then fix the image.

When it's done, the print isn't quite perfect. We see it all, the parking lot and the cross of the truck panels, the highway ramps and roads, but it's still out of focus; the larger resolution marks on the truck are visible, but down the scale they muddle quickly into a blob of gray.

The reference binder floats next to us; Hank grabs it from the air and flips over to the panel diagram. "What is that, maybe twelve-inch resolution? How 'bout that. You can see my johnson from space."

"Yeah, right." I snort, shake my head. "You wanna print this one again?"

"Come on, that was funny."

"I'm an astronaut, not a...pornographer. If I see anybody's twelve-inch johnson..." I shake my head, look back at the picture. "We might have to burn it."

"No need to get jealous," Hank says. "We've got an enlarger if you need one!"

Despite myself, I laugh. "I don't think it works that way." Then a nod at the print. "No, seriously, though. Burn it a bit?"

"It's as good as it's gonna get. Let's move on."

Again we work through the process. The second truck is a little sharper; we're picking up the ten-inch symbols now. We'd tweaked the exposure and focal length settings over each target, and the third and fourth prints each come out a little clearer.

"What's that, six inches?" I finally survey my handiwork with something other than disappointment. "You can see *my* johnson from space."

Hank chuckles. "There you go. Practice makes perfect. I got a good feeling about this next one."

But the next print's off. A parking lot in Kansas: we can see puddles of standing water in the wheat field next to it, and a couple cars on the road, but the resolution squares still peter out at the six-inch row.

"Well...crap." I shake my head. "I thought this one for sure..."

"It still might be. Here, look at this." Hank points at the cars. "Dark car looks a little more well-defined than the light one, right?"

"Yeah, I guess."

"Might be a bit blown out. This one we can print again. Dodge it. You want detail in the black *and* detail in the white."

And when we print it again, sure enough, the final squares are visible. I allow myself to feel satisfaction, at last.

"That's four-inch resolution right there," Hank says.

"*Now* we can see your johnson from space."

He gives me a dirty look.

"Come on, that was funny."

"Don't quit your day job." But he smiles. We're both in too good of a mood to take anything personally. The bucket of film we sent home was taken using the old settings: bad pictures, no better than what they're getting from the Coronas at far lower cost. But finally we're accomplishing something.

Still, I can't relax and enjoy it. I pull myself back to the spindle, anxiously scan for the Soviet star. Again it is gone.

●●●

"Cheyenne, Watchman. Do you copy, over?" The scramblers are on and we're bobbing wearily: Hank speaking, myself mute.

"Watchman, Cheyenne. We read you five by five." Again, the Alabama drawl of our crimson antagonist. "Little late for a secure chat. Over."

"Cheyenne, we're well aware of the time." Greenwich time stares up at us from the digital display: just after 6:00 a.m. on June 24th. But our listeners are under a mountain in Colorado, burrowed behind massive blast doors in the electric futuristic 24-hour command center; for their bodies, it's just past midnight yesterday. "We've had some urgent developments up here. Over."

"Watchman, if this is about the Zenit..."

I step on their response. "Cheyenne, we had a conjunction we were not expecting. No warning call from the ground, and we saw them. Over enemy territory. And we're still not sure it *is* a Zenit. Over."

"Watchman, we're monitoring the situation. There's a global network of ground sites. We'll get word to you if it starts getting too close. Over."

"Cheyenne, that's far too...reactive," Hank says. "We'd like to get some visual information about their capabilities as soon as possible. Over."

"Watchman, how are you proposing to do that, over?"

"Well, Cheyenne, we do have two spaceplanes up here. I can fly one of them up there tomorrow. Take some pictures with the Hasselblad, develop them up here. Get ahead of the power curve. Over."

"Watchman, uhhh...this has already been discussed at the highest levels. It's not something we're ready to do at this time. Over."

"Cheyenne, what *are* you ready to do?" An edge in Hank's tone. "Because we're not comfortable waiting for them to make a move. Over."

I make the mistake of opening the window shade, looking at our dark continent below; our pseudo-daylight interior clashes with the obvious night, further discombobulating me.

"Well, Watchman, you are riding the biggest and most expensive camera ever constructed. I'm pretty sure we can take pictures with that. Wait for a conjunction, roll the station on its back, point that big mirror up at the sky, and snap away."

Hank bobs, shakes his head. "We've always discussed an X-20 rendezvous as an option, if we had an opportunity like this. Not sure why we wouldn't go ahead and do it. I guarantee we'll get better pics that way. Over."

"Watchman, this has already been discussed at the highest levels," Cheyenne drawls. "Schreiver and LeMay levels. We think it's safer to go with the conservative approach. Get pictures in this next bucket and get them analyzed before we authorize a rendezvous. They launched into an orbit they knew we could reach. They had to know we'd be thinking about this. Schreiver says maybe that's what they want." There's a pause, but I can tell there's more: we float and wait. "For all we know, the satellite's booby trapped."

"Well I wouldn't put it past 'em," Hank says.

After LOS we eat. Gelatinized bread and bologna. Depressing.

"So if we don't do anything, it could hunt us down and blow us up." I chew, ruminate. "But if you go look at it, it could blow you up."

"Or it could just be an ordinary recon bird."

"Or it could be just an ordinary recon bird." I shake my head.

"But I doubt it. Schreiver's right, I bet it *is* a trap. They surprised us with the launch, but they put it where we could get to it. They had to know how tempting that'd be."

"How would they trigger it? Ground signal?"

"Maybe as a backup. But that couldn't be the only way. They don't have *that* much radar coverage."

"Yeah, you're right."

"Would they have an active radar on the satellite itself?"

"Maybe. Or IR sensors. But if it's a trap, maybe not. Maybe they want it to look like a normal Zenit, so we'll feel safe going ahead with a rendezvous."

"They'd still have to trigger it."

"Yeah."

"They've gotta have some sort of...optical alignment sensors, right? Even on the normal Zenit. Cameras or sensors on the sides. Make sure the bright globe is down and the dark sky is up."

"Yeah, they'd have to. I mean, that's pretty much a bare bones requirement for a recon system. Make sure your camera's not just...pointed off into space."

"I bet that's how they'd do it." He takes a deep breath. "Have a device connected to the alignment sensors. Arm it. And if any kind of object appears, point yourself at it. Blow it up."

"You think if we *do* get pictures we'll be able to tell, one way or another?"

"I don't know. But we do need to get some kind of look. They've surprised us so many times. A-bomb, H-bomb, Sputnik, Gagarin...who knows what they're planning here?"

The afternoon drags. There's not much on the schedule, other than staying awake. A few routine tasks, but they eat far too little of the clock. I treat myself to a long bathroom break, get back to *Red Harvest*. My mind's so tired I have to read every page twice. But I do make some sense of it. A plot as knotty as the darkest corners of the ugliest heart. Bloodshed, betrayal, lies. Not exactly comforting.

●●●

In the morning, the mystery satellite has receded from my mind. We prepare breakfast with the white lights on, a simple day of reconnaissance ahead of us. Outside, the dark Atlantic sweeps past as we head north towards Thule and our instructions.

"Good night's sleep?" Hank asks as we float and eat.

"Best I've had up here." The breakfast is one of my least favorite options, reconstituted eggs, but I don't even mind, I feel so good.

"Amazing what a difference it makes."

"Yeah. I was worried. Still am, a little. But it does make sense to do it like they said."

"Yeah. It only costs us a few frames of film. I can still fly up there if everything checks out."

"You think we'll get good pictures from the console?"

"Should be doable. Especially with them in our plane." Hank pauses, thinks. "Even doing this, we have it easy, compared to the folks at the Mushroom Factory. All we have to do is take pictures. They have to see the future."

"How do you figure?"

"Well, that's what they're there for. To be fortune tellers. Using the world as their crystal ball to figure out what the Soviets will do. Whether it's Berlin or Africa or the Middle East or wherever. Or with the missiles. Counting up ICBM sites last month and the month before that. Determining how long they take to build one, then...stacking up computer punch cards in some basement, crunching numbers and plotting graphs and drawing trend lines. Trying to figure out how many ICBMs they'll have next month, and next year, and the year after that. Because we do need to know! How many ICBMs do *we* need this year, and next year, and the year after that? 100? 1,000? 10,000? How many ABM sites will we need to shoot down their missiles? Is it even *possible* to build enough sites to do that? Or can they just keep building more missiles, putting more warheads on each one, putting decoys next to the warheads? How much is it going to cost us to keep up a credible deterrence? How many tax dollars will we have to collect and spend to keep the American people safe? Tens of billions? Hundreds of billions? When they draw up the pie charts for each branch of the service, how much does each branch get? If the Air Force gets a fatter slice, who gets to eat it? LeMay and his bomber bozos? The fighter mafia? Schreiver and the steely-eyed missilemen sitting in their silos in North Dakota? These are tough questions. They have to find answers in those buckets."

We clean up, place trash into the airlock, set the scramblers so we're ready for Thule. Below, night gives way to light, sunrise flashing by in a matter of moments: daylight on the deep. Blue waters followed by Greenland's ragged southeast coast: pale, but living up to its name.

"Watchman, this is Thule. We have a list of today's targets and we're pushing it up through the teletype. Over."

In the observation chamber, the machine clatters out a series of abbreviations and coordinates. I float over and give it a cursory look while Hank keys the mike. "Thule, Watchman, we are receiving. Over."

"Watchman, FYI it is low on priority targets this pass. Weather reports are a little iffy. That telemetry station near Petropavlovsk is Priority 3. Otherwise it's general hunting. Next pass gets you near a Priority 1, the ICBM site at Svobodny. You did some spotting work for it last week. Mushroom Factory says keep your eyes out for those access roads. They can find the silos themselves..."

For a minute it goes on like this, professional chatter. From the briefings I recall that access roads for remote ICBM silos tend to follow a common pattern: long straight roads with very gradual turns and no right-angle corners. Unpaved forest roads that any vodka-drunk Soviet private can navigate while driving a semi-trailer with a nuclear missile on it.

"...and that's it for today, Watchman. Also, Cheyenne talked to you about photographing a certain unidentified object. They are drawing up an operational plan. Should be on the schedule for tomorrow. Over."

"Thule, thanks for the brief. Very solid job. Over."

"My pleasure, Watchman. Hoping to get up there myself someday. I put in my packet yesterday. Over."

"Now why would you want to leave the frozen glory of northern Greenland?"

"You talk like you've seen it, Watchman."

"Thule, we see everything." The teletype clatters to a stop; I scan it to make sure we have the END TRANSMISSION line. "We're like Santa Claus. Flying around the world, seeing who's naughty..."

"Naughty? I wouldn't mind being naughty. It's a little light on female companionship down here. They told us on the way up that there was a woman behind every tree. And when we got off the airplane...totally barren! Over."

I shake my head. Back at the academy, we'd taken a class trip to Japan; there was a fueling stop in the Aleutians, and they'd said the same thing. The whole Air Force inventory contains just five jokes, reissued endlessly.

Hank smiles. "Thule, you still haven't found any lovely Eskimo ladies, over?"

"Watchman, only females I've seen are caribou and polar bears. Over."

"Well I'm sure you're lonely, but don't give in to temptation, Thule."

From the airwaves, a stifled chuckle.

"Thule," I interject. "That's still more females than we've got up here. Over."

Hank gives me a look like: What, are you jealous they have caribou?

"All right, then," Thule says. "Coming up on LOS."

"Thule, congrats on the packet," I interject.

"Yes, congrats," Hank says. "We'll put in a good word for you. Over."

There is no response; we've passed out of range, not knowing if he heard. But I don't feel too bad for too long: out the window I can see swaths of Arctic pack ice, the open polar cap scrolling by as we swoop towards the Soviet coast. Clear air, visibility unlimited: the world is our crystal ball.

We take up station at the Dorian console. But over that small stretch of open ocean just north of the shoreline, I see the first wisps of clouds whipping past the scope. Soon they thicken. We set the cameras to standby and scan for a break, but for the entire first pass, every sweep of the scope ends with the exact same thing: an opaque circle of greyish white.

•••

At the end of the day there is not much new for the bucket. Nothing from the first or the second passes. Only scattered breaks in the clouds for the third and afterward, and none above our main targets. We take advantage of a comms window on the dark side of the globe to ask Cheyenne about the satellite photo session. Hank's Alabama adversary reiterates what Thule said: we'll have an opportunity tomorrow. I'm eager for it: clouds can't stop that, at least.

Back on the bright side of the globe, the bad weather returns. Even Berlin is socked in.

"Does this happen often?" I ask as we're shutting down.

"It happens." Hank shrugs. "Think of it this way. The Coronas would have burned up yards of film on those passes, for buckets full of nothing. Pictures of cloud tops. Sometimes our value's knowing when *not* to take pictures."

"Shoot. I could have stayed home and not taken pictures. Saved the Air Force some money."

"We'll get some. Don't worry. We'll have more frames for the satellite now."

We read through the checklists. Power down the console. Exit the module. Prepare dinner. A segue from professional tasks to personal ones.

My first pouch: meatloaf. Inconsistently warm, far drier than it should be. "That'll make you miss your wife's cooking, huh?"

"Judy's is miles above this, that's for sure. Much as I love being up here, I do miss that."

"When my wife found out I was going up here, she was happy for me. When I told her how long, and that it'd be the height of summer...not so much. Kids out of school...I'm sure she has her hands full."

"Prime reconnaissance season. Best lighting of the year. Can't expect a wife to understand that, when they don't even know what we're doing up here."

"Yeah. The lack of communication, too. I mean, I know it's necessary, but..."

"You mean, not talking to them while we're up here?" Hank gives a look I can't quite interpret.

"Well, just the secrecy in general. She's a great Air Force wife, she's been as supportive as I have any right to hope for, but when I told we wouldn't be able to talk, and gave her the telegram protocols..."

Another look from Hank, like he's thinking about saying something. At last: "So what else did you tell her?"

"I mean, I told her what I could, but obviously..." Everything about our mission is classified, except the fact that we're up here. An unidentified spacecraft launched on an undisclosed mission for an indefinite period of time. So I could only talk to my wife in the vaguest terms. Still, she seemed to understand, and I'm sure the same's true for Hank's wife. The only secrets in our marriage are the professional ones.

"The Reds probably know more than our wives, at this point."

"Probably." I chew another reluctant spoonful. "Might have to type up a telegram. I really do miss the little buggers."

"I miss family dinners. Reading to the kids. Hell, having them come in to the bedroom in the middle of the night when they're afraid."

"My son used to do that! I'd wake up and hear his door open, hear him just…scampering down the dark hall, like he was running a gauntlet."

Hank smiles. "A voyage through the unknown."

"Man, it used to bug the crap out of me!"

"Yeah. The girls did the same stuff. Especially during thunderstorms. Although sometimes, if I was on TDY and came back, or even if I got home really late, they'd come in then, too. They want that reassurance, that you're keeping an eye on them."

"Yeah. Man, it used to bug me! But now…"

"Yeah. You come to miss it. Everything you thought was annoying." Hank finishes his pouch, crumples it up. "I'm sure we'll miss all this when we're back down there, though."

"Yeah." I can imagine: eating reconstituted eggs, seeing Greenland's pale green coast. The Caribbean and its multitude of blues.

"Obviously for now you know you'll have more chances to see everything. But there'll come a time when you'll see these things for the last time."

"I am hoping to get back up here."

"Me too."

"Pulling for winter. I know it's not as good for reconnaissance, but..."

"Yeah. I know what you mean. I've seen the whole world, but I haven't seen Antarctica."

"It'll be nice to get home in the meantime. Tell the kids about everything we've seen up here."

Again he gives a look I can't quite place. "All the declassified stuff, at least."

"I'm sure they're curious what we're doing."

Hank shrugs. "Keeping them safe. All you can say."

I think of the wasted day, the empty film bucket, everything under the clouds that we could not see. Keeping them safe: I do hope it's true.

●●●

In the morning over the blinding white Arctic we read through the day's targets with Thule: assorted airfields, the port of Vladivostok, more ICBM sites, the TALL KING radar installation north of Moscow. It's such a full list, I don't notice what's missing.

Hank at least is paying attention. "Thule, what about our UFO?"

"Say again, Watchman."

"The satellite photography? That thing in orbit with us that might be able to kill us? We were supposed to get a look at it today. Over."

"Change of plans, Watchman. Weather looks good. The ICBM site at Uzhur is your top priority. Over."

"Thule, I photographed Uzhur last week! Even with the resolution issues, it should have told them something. We need to look at that satellite. Over."

"Watchman, I'm just the messenger. Take it up with Cheyenne. Over."

Hank looks at his watch and shakes his head. There are fewer comms windows for Cheyenne, so we can't talk to them until lunchtime.

In the meantime, we have our marching orders. After LOS, we start prepping for our first pass. Studying target landmarks, making notes, and planning. The weather is mostly clear over the Kamchatka peninsula, and we get pictures of the airfield at Klyuchi. Then more prep work; on the second pass, we catch Vladivostok under crystalline skies: no easy feat, Hank says. The third finds us photographing the Drovyanaya ICBM site, east of Lake Baikal: some clouds nearby, but not too bad.

Then, lunch: we start heating up the packets over the scattered green islands of Indonesia, and soon we're eating and staring down at the Indian Ocean, hungry and empty and blue. Antarctica brightens my mood: above the darkened continent we catch a dazzling dancing *aurora australis*, pink and purple and blue and green and orange and gold. But then comes a long dark pass over the far eastern end of the South Pacific.

We cut across the Mexican coast in the middle of the North American night. Through the hatch window on the docking spindle I can see our Soviet star on the far horizon; I imagine we'll be overtaking it soon, probably near Uzhur.

Hank floats over to the radio as we swoop north. Keys in the secure code.

"Cheyenne, Watchman. We have visual on the Red satellite. Looks like there will be a conjunction. Any reason we're passing on taking pictures, over?" Under Hank's lazy drawl there is some simmering resentment.

"Good evening, War Eagle..." Hank's Alabama antagonist says the words slowly, just inside the edge of professionalism. "...excuse me. Watchman. Uzhur came as a high priority request from the Mushroom Factory. They made it clear it overrode all other considerations. Weather forecast is good, it's time to do it. Over."

"Cheyenne, I'm not sure what's a higher priority than determining whether that satellite is a threat to this station. Bad resolution or no, we already imaged that site. Over."

"Watchman, it's because of those pictures they wanted another look. Even with bad pictures, they could tell something's missing. Over."

"Cheyenne, we don't have time for twenty questions. What is it?"

"Fueling facilities. We think they're deploying the SS-13." Cheyenne pauses to let this sink in.

Hank purses his lips, displeased.

Cheyenne continues. "You can see how that would make it a priority target, given current tensions." And indeed we can: it could mean a lot of retargeting on SAC's part. Changes to the SIOP. New decisions for our political leadership. "We're all playing for the same team here. And the same coach. Right, War Eagle?"

Hank still stews, but the burner's off. "Cheyenne, I read you loud and clear."

"Watchman, we appreciate your understanding." Cheyenne sounds conciliatory now. "Rest assured we are eager to keep you safe. We should have plenty of conjunction opportunities. And of course weather won't be a factor. It's all coming down in next week's bucket anyway. Over."

"All right, Cheyenne. We'll do our damndest."

"Coming up on LOS. Happy hunting. Cheyenne out."

"SS-13," I observe. "That's their first solid-fuel bird, right?"

"Yes it is."

"So they're finally catching up with Minuteman. I guess that is a big deal."

"It's a huge deal," Hank says. "The Berlin Crisis, that's why they had to settle for building a wall. I had a long talk with

Schreiver about it once. He said for all that public panic about Soviet missiles, they had maybe ten in all. All LOX/kerosene, so it would have taken them a full day to get them ready for launch. They didn't even have any hypergolic birds. Whereas we'd just deployed the first Minuteman squadron; between those and the Titans, we could have destroyed them before they could get a shot off, at no cost to ourselves. Followed up with LeMay's alert bombers…we could have clobbered them. All their missiles, all their airfields. But now…two-three minutes for them to launch, too. Depending on the gyroscopes."

"Gyroscopes?"

"That was another thing Schreiver said. It isn't just solid fuel. That first generation of gyros, they couldn't leave them on all the time. Too much wear and tear. Then you've gotta take the bird down for maintenance all the time. But you couldn't just leave 'em powered down…they took a good twenty-thirty minutes to spool up. We realized with Minuteman we'd need something better. So they designed these air-bearing gyros. Always spinning, always ready. Solid-fuel bird with good gyros, all you need to do is confirm the launch command, turn the keys. Two-three minutes, tops."

"And the Soviets might have them, too."

"The way they steal stuff, yeah. Which means next crisis, they might not back down."

Daylight bursts through our window over far northern Canada. We prepare for the fourth pass, studying sketches and target maps. Then, the console. I keep waiting and wondering if we'll pick up clouds, but the coast is clear. We turn our camera on; we feel the tremble of the motor as the head swivels back and forth, sweeping across swaths of Soviet territory, committing it all to film; our heads are down on the scopes, observing the ground too, obedient.

Then at last: Uzhur, nestled in brownish-green farmland amidst blotches of forested hills. I catch a few shots containing what I think are silo access roads. It doesn't look much different from the sites we've already photographed. But knowing it is makes it so.

• • •

In the middle of the night I half-wake. Float to the bathroom, groggy and confused. Heading back to bed it occurs to my sleep-addled brain that I don't see Hank. He's not in the spindle, either.

The curtain is drawn for the observation module.

I float over, pull it aside: Hank is at the console, head down on the scope. Which I don't understand, because we're over the eastern United States.

"What's going on?"

"Oh, you're up!" He gives the sheepish look of a man caught doing something he doesn't want to explain. "Didn't want to disturb you for this."

"Are you taking pictures?"

"Just a little something for Cheyenne," he says cryptically. "A target of opportunity. Figured after the bad weather yesterday we could spare a few frames."

I float back to bed, baffled.

• • •

In the morning we are dragging. Breakfast passes in near silence. Hank's late night photography session feels like a dimly remembered dream, one it'd be embarrassing to talk about. Thule reads the day's targets and we listlessly jot notes as the teletype clatters. But at last we are aiming for the satellite.

Before the second pass we make our move. We're sacrificing the chance to photograph the gold mines of Kolyma, the worst of Stalin's gulags, still full under Beria: not a crucial strategic target, but an essential moral one, a reminder of who we're fighting, and why.

Hank keys in the commands and the cold gas thrusters fire; the high Arctic rotates out from under us. We see the thin haze of atmosphere hugging the curved horizon, and the endless black infinity above. A quick survey of stars: the Big Dipper and then Polaris, steady and reliable. And our target.

"I have visual on the satellite." It is thrilling to be doing this. The other day it felt like Cheyenne was making us jump through hoops; today we are determined to be the best hoop jumpers possible.

"Attitude adjustment complete," Hank announces. "Heading to the console."

"Holding at one-five-zero degrees of rotation." I check the teletype printout and glance at the radar. "Target angle should be roughly four-zero degrees. Range about ten miles."

"Camera on manual. Target scope is dialed out. Aaaand...target acquired. Steady in the crosshairs."

"OK. Heading over." This is all going far more smoothly than I'd imagined. I pull myself into the observation chamber, position myself at the Dorian station, slide my feet into the restraints, press my face into the hood. "Zooming in."

The blurry star becomes something else: distinct bright edges of collected metal shapes, foreign and solid and crude. My breath quickens: I feel alive seeing this dangerous stranger, this faceless enemy. I nudge the controller a notch too fast; the satellite disappears.

"Lost it. Might be off-center. Zooming back out."

"Let me know when you pick it up again. I'll give you control."

"OK." Now I am dialed back out and the satellite is in my lower right quadrant. "Got it now." It's more work for me now; I have to aim and focus at the same time. The blurry satellite bobbles around on the scope. But I'm getting used to the task. Soon the image is centered and zoomed. We're in a lower and faster orbit, though, so it does not stay in either condition very long.

"We're going to overtake it soon," Hank says.

"All right. Five exposures." A quick succession of button presses and then I stop. The satellite is high on the scope and blurry again. I re-focus. Re-center.

"How's it look from your end?" Hank asks.

"Like a Zenit. Just like in the briefing books. Although..." I snap five more frames. There are puffs of what must be thrusters firing, and our target rotates slowly. It does have a large spherical module, and a ring of spherical tanks between that and the service module. But near the service module I notice something I don't remember from any briefing.

"What is it?"

"I don't know. Some kind of...extra module maybe?"

"Well that's interesting."

"Yeah." The target is sliding and our range is changing; I try to focus in a little better, but then I notice the bright numbers projected below the scope image. Alarm. "We're gonna run out of scope travel here!"

"Crap. Let me rotate. Another sixty degrees, maybe." I hear Hank leave his post, head back to the controls. From the main room: "You're gonna need to zoom back out to reacquire!"

"Will do." Reluctantly I dial my scope back. "GO to maneuver."

Hank rotates the station and I sweep back up, looking for our target. It flashes across the scope, a bright white firefly. With some effort, I trap it in the crosshairs and start zooming again. It grows once more, this alien thing; in a flash I imagine its past, being manufactured in some grubby assembly room in Krasnoyarsk by uneducated factory workers in denim coveralls, each with a hammer in one hand and a bottle of vodka in the other, although no, all of that must be wrong. The details are blurry; I twist the focus knob a little more...

"We're gonna lose it again. Get what you got."

"All right. Five more." I snap away again; the angle isn't great to see the extra module, and even as I try, our metal stranger slides out of view.

"Did you get it?"

"Christ, I hope so." I look up from the scope. "Are we gonna reacquire?"

Hank scans the printout of instructions, which I'd left floating between us. "Not sure if we can."

I think about the extra module we've now seen. Equipment of uncertain purpose. We need to know more.

•••

At the end of the day I am winding down when I catch a glimpse of the small photo I stuck to the wall by my sleeping bag. Sometimes when an object's always in the same place, you stop seeing it after a few days, stop noticing it. But tonight, my family's bright eyes summon love and guilt; there's a task I've been neglecting. Over the past few months, I've been busy with training, promising things will be different after the mission—we'll go putt-putt golfing, we'll go to the beach, we'll take a family vacation, go camping together in the mountains. And yet I haven't even bothered to do this.

I check the mission clock, do the simple math made arduous by the mental fatigue of a long duty day after a sleep-disturbed night: night for us, afternoon GMT, morning in Loring. It is time, after all.

I float over to the teletype and compose laboriously:

BEGIN TRANSMISSION

BEGIN PERSONAL MESSAGE FALCON 2 FAMILY

ARRIVED SAFELY AT MY HOME ON HIGH STOP

SAW THE CITY FROM UP HERE AND I HOPE YOU SAW ME TOO STOP

ALREADY MISS HOME COOKED FOOD AND FAMILY DINNER AND ALL OF YOUR FACES STOP

LOOKING FORWARD TO PUTT PUTT AND THE BEACH AND A FAMILY CAMPING TRIP STOP

The way my training schedule ramped up pre-flight, it's been months since we've had a real vacation; we've had a few Sunday afternoons by the pool out back, or at the beach, but I promised the kids a camping trip, and every time I look at their picture on the bulkhead, I know they're going to hold me to it.

I LOOK AT YOUR PICTURE EVERY NIGHT BEFORE BED BUT IT IS NOT THE SAME STOP

I pause, think. What else can I say that will make them understand? They should know I'm busy. Keeping an eye on the bad guys? No: too much information. I opt for the simple:

BUSY KEEPING YOU SAFE STOP

LOVE DAD

END PERSONAL MESSAGE

END TRANSMISSION

Once it's sent, I use the bathroom one last time. While I'm in there, I swear I hear the teletype. I wipe in haste, float out and over to the printer: somehow something's there already. I push myself closer.

BEGIN TRANSMISSION

BEGIN OPERATIONS ORDER FALCON 1 EYES ONLY...

Hank's hot on my heels. "Uhh, can I help you?"

"I...uhhh...thought that was..."

Hank yanks the paper, tears it free in haste. Eyes me uneasily. "You thought you were gonna get an answer that quick?"

"I guess not." I know, intellectually, everything that has to happen first: our duty officer needs to read it and make sure there's no security issues. Then he needs to put it in at Western Union. Then: transmission across the country, and the Western Union messenger biking to our house through the relentless summer heat, and THEN my wife reading it, showing it to the kids while they're getting cleaned up for dinner, maybe writing a response together afterwards, adding a task to her to-do list. THEN, if I'm lucky, making it to the Western Union office tomorrow and sending it off to Vandenberg. And of course, the duty officer deciding where on the globe they can push the message up through the teletype... "You'd think there'd be an easier way to keep in touch..."

"You'd think so, huh?" Hank smiles, and in it there's something unsaid.

•••

"What do you say I take the target scope this pass?" Hank asks on Friday afternoon.

We're over the Arctic yet again, coming up on Novaya Zemlya. More ice and rock scrolling by. It is not boring—with the infinite varieties of cloud cover and ice movement, it's never boring—but it takes some effort to see it fresh.

"So me on the spotter?"

"Yeah. I wanna get a little practice in."

"Sure thing."

We've been doing this just long enough that I'm starting to have favorite regions to photograph. Mornings take us over vast stretches of Siberia and Red China; targets are fewer and farther between, and generally lower in priority. And the earth itself is more interesting: vast swaths of trackless forest carved up by meandering rivers, followed by the cold deserts of Mongolia, and the sharp mountains of the high Himalayas. Whereas here we'll be east of Moscow and west of the Urals, near Nizhniy Novgorod and Saratov: flatter terrain, more farmland, and targets piled up on top of one another, which only seems to get worse the further west we go. So I don't entirely mind swapping.

I settle in on the unfamiliar console, scan our maps in their transparencies, the grease pencil markings of our orbital track. I'd meant to take a bathroom break before we started this round, so there's some discomfort there, but once I get started the work itself feels as easy as a pair of weekend slippers: the wider spotting scope sweeping smoothly across the northern islands, and no need to retarget.

"Cameras on auto," Hank says.

"Getting a good swath of terrain here." Pictures of the frozen north: nothing too exciting just yet, but then we cross ice and open sea and make landfall on the Soviet coast. "Coming up on Oskolvo-2."

An icy airfield. "Got it."

The pass passes. Hank seems smooth and assured, picking up targets like a pro, which I guess we both are at this point. My bladder pressure's still building, though, so I'm eager for the end of it.

"All right, last target." I call it out, eager for relief. "Kapustin Yar." My feet slip from the restraints and I turn toward the bathroom.

"Can you stay on for a minute?"

"Was gonna get a break here."

"Just let me know when we're about to cross the coast." He's got another map next to him, one that doesn't correspond to any target Thule gave us; he turns a dial, cranks the assembly to an orientation well east of our ground track. "I need to get some oblique shots."

Reluctantly I put my face back down. "OK. On scope."

Beneath us the land scrolls by, rolling countryside. No military targets that I can see; not much of anything, really. Then: resort towns and beaches, the far eastern end of the Black Sea. "Crossing the coast."

"OK." The cameras click away. "Thank you much."

A floating dash to the bathroom: quick activation of the suction hose, and then blessed relief. Another image flashes back through my mind: another bathroom trip, possibly last night or the night before, but NOT the night I saw him on the scope, because this time he wasn't there, wasn't anywhere. Was it a memory or a dream?

• • •

The end of the workday: a long sweep over the Norwegian Sea. We have a secure comms window with the ground station in England, our last bit of business before dinner.

"Watchman, Lakenheath. Come in. Over." The voice is a new one, professional but with a touch of angst.

"Lakenheath, Watchman. We read you five by five," Hank says. "You're...a...not the guy we've been talking to. Over."

The Soviets no doubt know what frequencies we use; it has occurred to all of us that they could easily mount an impersonation operation. Put a fishing trawler in the ocean near one of our sites, have a man behind the microphone, and an antenna pointed at the sky. Maybe figure a way to jam the normal ground site. But our scramblers are on. All the settings look normal.

"Your duty officer took ill," the radio voice tells us. "Had to fill in last-minute. Ready for your report. Over."

"Ahh, well. Pretty normal workday," Hank says. "We got everything they sent us. Ready for the end of the duty day. Over."

"Watchman, any weekend plans? Over."

"As if we'd get a free weekend up here! Couple hours Sunday morning, maybe. We get a target list Saturday, same as any other day." Hank chuckles. "How about you? Off to the pub?"

"Watchman, I haven't been leaving the base much. Always protestors at the gate these days. Total Nuclear Disarmament types. Last time I went to the pub, I got an earful about Nixon and the Berlin Crisis."

Hank: "Not exactly grateful for the protection, are they?"

"They did live through the Blitz," Lakenheath points out. "And V-2s. You meet someone the right age, chances are they grew up going to the bomb shelter every day. Chances are they lost family."

I cut in. "So they don't like risking nuclear war for the sake of people who used to bomb them?"

"Well, beyond the German angle," Lakenheath says. "They've seen their cities bombed and ruined. Missiles falling from the sky. They're not eager to repeat that on a larger scale. Still, it's no fun to get a...diatribe when you're trying to get a pint and some dinner. I like fish and chips, but not that much..."

While they finish chatting, I get started on the dinner pouches. But I am thinking back to what Hank said. It wasn't a normal workday, after all. Not with that odd pass.

At last Hank joins me. We dig in to reheated chicken, and the day's events. "That was nice. Getting to spot for a bit."

"Yeah. I think we got some good shots of Kapustin Yar."

"That was their first launch site, right?"

"The first one we knew about," he says. "Before Baikonur. Odd place. One of the few that's always a priority target, even when we're taking oblique photos. Always always always."

"What's the appeal?"

"I guess they've gotten...strange human intelligence out of there. Stuff they can't make heads or tails of. Reports of lights in the sky that don't correspond to normal launches or airplane flights."

"Lights in the sky."

"Yeah. Just...lights. Dancing around, zipping off in different directions. Real mysterious stuff."

Now I'm really confused. "So what, like Soviet UFOs?"

Hank laughs. "Yeah. I'm sure it's nothing. These human intelligence reports, they're...unreliable. Which is why we're up here. Spies lie. Or their stories get...twisted up. Listen to enough of them, you start to think the Soviets are ten feet tall. In cahoots with aliens."

"Why bother listening, then?"

"You know how it is. Everybody's got their own budgetary axe to grind. Sometimes a story suits their purposes. Then next thing you know, the press is reporting that the Russians have some...mystery weapon that we need to counter with a weapon of our own. The good thing about what we're doing..." (A nod toward the cameras.) "...is it lets our leaders see through the bullshit. The pictures in this bucket, I guarantee you they'll be on Nixon's desk in a couple days."

I chuckle. "So, if they do develop the film and see Soviet runways full of flying saucers..."

Hank laughs. "I will say, if there are little green men, maybe they *should* talk to the Reds. I mean, they are the backwards ones..."

Silent eating. A few chews of bland, dry chicken. A question grows in me. "You think there is anyone out there?" A nod at the impossible universe.

"Hard to imagine there isn't *someone*, somewhere in all that."

"Yeah."

"But of course, nobody's come here yet. Nobody's signaled us, even."

"As far as we know. Maybe they're watching us. Keeping an eye on things." I nod towards the observation module. "Trying to see if *we're* dangerous."

"Unless they're this close, there probably isn't much to see."

"Well...we are sending out transmissions all the time. TV signals. Radio waves. They could have an...electronic intelligence unit."

"If they have means to decipher TV signals, they'd have to be within thirty light-years or so to have seen anything yet. Maybe forty-five light years for radio. But still. That's a very very small piece of the galaxy, let alone the universe. If there is anybody out there, they probably don't know we exist yet."

"Unless they're here in the Solar System." I chuckle. "You never know, they could have an observation post on the moon."

"We'd see them."

"Or…I don't know. Venus or something."

"Venus?" Hank smiles. "Kinda hot and nasty, isn't it?"

"It'd be perfect, if they didn't want us to see them. Someplace we'd never think to look. Someplace we'd never want to go. Just a little observation post. Telescopes and antennas floating above the clouds. Home base down below. Maybe some sort of…subspace transmitter, sending signals back to the home planet, faster than light."

"Now you just sound paranoid." Hank shakes his head. "I'll tell you what, though. People get really nuts about that stuff."

"They do."

"And it doesn't help that you've got the media whipping them into a frenzy."

"No, I guess not."

"I mean, look at *War of the Worlds*. The radio thing. People really panicked!"

"*War of the Worlds*." A warm burst of nostalgia. "They had the movie on TV on Sunday. Last day home before my flight. Spaceships and heat rays and all that. My son was so scared! He kept putting his hands over his eyes. But he kept peeking out. Then that night, we tried to keep him in his room. And he kept running out. I kept telling him, 'It's just a movie.' But, man, he was scared. It turns out he thought they were going to attack me when I got up here."

Hank chuckles.

I continue: "That's the funny thing about being scared. People kinda like it. They don't admit it, but they like it. Making up stories about whatever's...out there hiding in the dark. When you look at *War of the Worlds*, the radio one...there wasn't any atomic bomb back then. There wasn't any fear of nuclear war. People didn't have...memories of the Blitz, or whatever. They tuned in anyway. They let themselves get whipped into a frenzy. You can't entirely blame the media...nobody made 'em watch."

We finish eating, tend to trash and chores; I imagine Soviet UFOs, Russian parents talking to their children. Kapustin Yar. A priority target.

And yet Hank stayed on the scope afterwards, taking more pictures. It wasn't his priority.

•••

I end my workweek working on maintenance chores. Trying not to get worked up about everything else. Given the mysterious module on the Red satellite, we're pretty sure they won't let Hank fly in for a closer look.

Hank hasn't received any family telegrams. But he seems strangely unperturbed. My own anxious wait finally ends on Saturday night; we pick up a signal from Loring, and the machine starts printing.

BEGIN TRANSMISSION

BEGIN PERSONAL MESSAGE FALCON 2

SO GLAD TO HEAR FROM YOU DAD STOP

WE ATE CHINESE FOOD LAST NIGHT AND EVERYONE USED THE CHOMPSTICKS STOP

Chompsticks. One of those family words that crop up: my daughter started calling them that, and it was too cute to correct her, so we all started saying it. It warms my heart.

THEN WE WENT OUT LATE AND SAW YOU FLYING HIGH AND BRIGHT STOP

UNDERSTAND THE NEED FOR SO FEW WORDS BUT WE LOOK FORWARD TO PUTT PUTT AND CAMPING AND TALKING MORE ABOUT ALL YOU HAVE SEEN AND DONE STOP

WE DO FEEL SAFER WITH YOU WATCHING OVER US AND HOPE YOU FEEL LOVED KNOWING HOW MUCH WE LOOK UP TO YOU STOP

SENDING ALL THE LOVE A FAMILY CAN GIVE STOP

END PERSONAL MESSAGE

END TRANSMISSION

I read it and re-read it, wishing for more.

•••

I wake to knocking in the night.

It is just a simple knock, like someone on a door. Chilling. *Knock. Knock.*

It is outside.

"You hear that?" I ask Hank.

He's not in his hammock. He comes floating back from the spindle, perplexed. Again comes the sound. *Knock. Knock.*

Again: "You hear that, right?"

"Yeah, I hear it."

"It's..." I feel crazy, saying this. "It's outside, right?"

Reluctantly he nods. "It does sound like it's outside."

"You don't know what it is, do you?"

He smiles thinly. "I dunno if it's a *what* or a *who.*"

This is real. This is not a dream. Again it comes: *Knock. Knock.*

I am more awake now. A quick stab of panic at that word: who. I picture: a green alien. Bare arm? No, they'd need a spacesuit, too.

Or maybe: a cosmonaut.

"It does sound like someone's trying to get in, doesn't it?" Hank muses. The noise seems to be on the wrong side of the spacecraft for us to see its source out of the window. He floats back towards the spindle, all the windows and hatches.

"Well, don't open the door."

He chuckles. I'm still anxious. Again the noise. *Knock. Knock.*

"Oh!" He glances at the comms console as he floats past. "Left the antenna in track mode. Must be in a gimbal flip region. Like it's cycling between two stations."

The knocking stops.

He smiles, reassuring. "I guess your son's not the only one that gets scared about things going *bump* in the night."

• • •

"...and the hatch is open. Preparing for egress."

"Roger, Falcon-1." Through the docking spindle hatch I can see the clean spiral coils of Hank's umbilical cord, an orderly snake, important: Don't Tread on Me. "Coming up on the terminator."

Daylight hits. Over eastern Siberia, north of the sea of Okhotsk, on an ascending node: ostensibly a nightward pass, but these latitudes don't see much darkness in July. Outside: empty forests in the low sun. Vast spaces, places I will never see up close.

"All right. Out I go." The snake uncoils, following Hank out the hatch. "Man, what a wonderful view!"

"Nothing you haven't seen before," I remind him.

"Well, I'll tell you what, it never gets old."

"Nobody else out there, right?"

He chuckles. "No, nobody else out here."

We are talking to ourselves. Everything's been planned so we can work without our orbiting neighbor observing. So for the next few minutes there's no ground coverage, although we will catch Lakenheath and Ascension on the descending node. I'm scheduled for a second spacewalk during my command shift, when Bob Lawrence is here and I'm near the end of my forty days. Still, I can't help being a little jealous.

"All right. Coming up on the bucket."

"How's everything look?"

"You did good. Carrier is locked in position. Bucket looks good. Everything in its right place."

"Fantastic. Good to hear."

"Lanyard is attached. Unlocking the carrier. Moving it towards the platform…"

I listen along as he repositions the reentry bucket and unsnaps the bulky film canister from his chest. Always the calm Southern drawl. Undoubtedly for him there's the excitement of a difficult task in an exciting setting. But for me it's smooth to the point of boredom. Which is good, I guess. Better than troubleshooting noises in the night.

We arc over the high Arctic. Today even that's bland: clouds blotting out ice and sea. I stifle a yawn. My eyelids get heavy. I shake my head, then glance over at the slender teletype printout of my family telegram. Somewhat stale now: I've squeezed all the feeling I can get from it. Now I want something to…well, not go wrong. But happen, at least.

Further south, leaving the North Sea for Scotland, I get my wish.

I'm taking a quick bathroom break when I hear a garbled transmission. Float to the radio: more garbage. Then: "Watchman, Lakenheath." Something's not quite routine in his tone. "Please go secure. Over."

A flare of panic: Oh, Christ, I forgot to set the scramblers. "Lakenheath, Watchman. Wait one. Over." I set the code book in the airspace in front of me, flip hastily through it, scan for the day's code and frequency: every second I take is one less we have to talk. Then, the dials, anxious. At last it is set.

"...man, Lakenheath. Are you receiving secure? Over."

"Lakenheath, Watchman, we read you five by five." A floating sigh of relief. England scrolling by far below. "EVA is proceeding smoothly. Over."

"Watchman, we're tracking your orbiting follower on radar. Separation is much lower than expected. Range: eight miles. Over."

Eight miles! Again, angst. "Lakenheath, we were told we were out of phase. And no conjunction this pass. Over."

"Watchman, they must have lowered their orbit. Range now five miles. Over."

My pulse pulses. Hank's anxious musings: a hunter-killer satellite closing in on us from below. I can see nothing but blotchy clouds, and snippets of the Bay of Biscay: the intruder is on my blind side. "Lakenheath, I can turn on the station radar."

"Might not want to do that while I'm out here," Hank pipes in, still cool and collected. "I see him. Jesus, he's close."

Still my head says: DO SOMETHING. "Lakenheath, do we need to take evasive action?"

"Range: four miles," ground says. "Coming up on L…"

Their transmission ends in a static crackle. Loss Of Signal. We are alone to deal with this.

I take a deep breath: memories of the academy. Junior officers yelling: FUNCTION. I scan the controls, the cold gas thrusters. They're good for changing attitude. Moving our orbit might deplete them too much. Still, if the station is in danger… "Hank, do we need to maneuver?"

"Hold one."

"How close is he?"

"Closer than we've seen him. He's…you might wanna get the Hasselblad."

"How close?"

"Hard to see from here. I think he's…"

The pause is maddening. I am blind and angry.

Then at last: "He's directly beneath us now. Still a couple miles away. Look out the window, maybe you can spot him."

And now at last I *can* see him down there, staring up at us as we cross the Spanish coast. I shake my head. Maybe this was the whole point of them launching in our plane: to get pictures of our operations.

"Can you get him on the Hasselblad?"

"I can try." I unstow the camera, snap a couple pictures, although with the bright planet beneath I wonder if I'm getting the exposure right. A quick glance at the console: I could power it up quickly, get some better shots. But no: we haven't loaded this week's canister yet. Just minutes ago I wanted something more. Careful what you wish for.

"Kinda wish I could moon him," Hank says calmly.

At last I relax. "Might be dangerous."

"Next EVA. You'll have to write the checklist. Removal of Spacesuit Posterior in Vacuum Environment..."

• • •

After another dark side orbital pass and some final work over the central Atlantic, Hank is back in the airlock; the top of his helmet's on the other side of the glass, and I can just barely see two large food containers near his feet. Cargo from the Centaur.

When the pressure is equalized I crack the airlock; he unlocks and raises his visor.

I smile. "Thanks for getting groceries."

"My pleasure." He unlocks his helmet and places it in the air near me; I stow it in the locker. Then he floats in to the living area so he can doff his suit.

"They really pulled one over on us. With that maneuver." I un-Velcro the end of the torso zipper and pull it down his back.

"They sure did."

"I'm a little worried now. Maybe they've cracked the scramblers."

"They certainly picked the right time to photograph us." Grunting and contorting, twisting a little as he floats, Hank works his head down through the neck ring and out the opening in the back. "Maybe it's a good thing, though."

"How do you figure?"

"That extra module...the old Zenit couldn't maneuver in orbit. But this one can. So maybe that's it. Not some booby trap. Just a little extra capability." The suit comes off and he's down to the liquid-cooled undergarment now.

"You think?"

"I'd bet money on it. They'll have to let me fly in closer now."

As Hank finishes changing, I report in to Pine Gap. Central Australia: just about the only spot outside the continental U.S. where we can talk without any possibility of interception. Our duty officer confirms the ejection time for the film bucket.

Coming up over the Arctic, it is time to launch it. Atlantic drop for this one. Hank allows me to do the honors, although there really isn't much to it. I read carefully from the checklist. Everything happens when it's supposed to happen, and when the reentry bucket separates I catch a glimpse of it glinting in the sunlight as it sails cleanly away. Everything looks absolutely normal.

•••

Drifting off to sleep that night, cocooned in my sleeping bag in the soft red lights, my weightless mind flies forward into the fantastic future. Visions of President Nixon walking into the Oval Office for his morning intelligence briefing and seeing massive pictures on easels, all the important targets: solid-fuel ICBMs being loaded into silos, Soviet tanks massing around West Berlin, and the mysterious maneuvering satellite. The president marvels at the sharpness and clarity of every photo; he picks up a red telephone and barks at Chairman Beria. Then he asks to know who's responsible for this great work, so he can convey his great gratitude, and the nation's appreciation...

There's only one problem: we haven't received acknowledgment that they've picked up the bucket.

● ● ●

Tuesday is a normal workday: daylight passes over the Soviet Union, somehow now routine. Except the ground stations still aren't sending up any updates on the film recovery.

We are taking our lunch break on the dark side of the globe when we get the bad news.

"Watchman, Cheyenne. We...uhh...hate to break it to you, but we've lost the bucket. Over."

A pang: all that work, lost. Possibly incinerated. I key the mike. "Cheyenne, Watchman. What happened? Over."

"Watchman, according to Antigua it reentered long. Our aircraft were in position, but the radar track was high. They realized they'd never be able to make it. We held off on telling you because we didn't want the Soviets to pick up on the extra chatter. There was a chance it splashed down north of the Brazilian coast, so we dispatched a destroyer that was on standby. They haven't found it. Now we're wondering if it's on land. Over."

Land. That means recoverable. My heart sinks. It's bad enough to lose it, but if the Soviets grab it before us, our hard work will be doubly counterproductive: they will know our capabilities.

"Well that's a shame, Cheyenne," Hank says. "We got some good shots in there. I even stayed up late and picked out a special target, just for you. Over."

I look over at him, curious, remembering the mysterious late-night telescope session.

Ground's puzzled, too. "Watchman, Cheyenne, we do not copy. Over."

"Cheyenne, we were fat on film. Because of the weather. And since we're up here to photograph places we want to destroy, I figured I'd stay up late and take target practice on Tuscaloosa. Swear I caught Denny Stadium in there..."

A radio laugh. "Too smart for your own good, War Eagle."

I shake my head. The humor takes the sting out of the loss, but only so much.

"Atlantic drop..." Hank shakes his head after we sign off. "Shoulda stuck with what we did last time. The Pacific is a much bigger target."

We haven't budgeted any time for self-pity, though. There's a full target list for the next pass. And our third canister won't be coming down in a bucket; Hank will be flying it home in the X-20. So whatever went wrong this time won't go wrong the next time. There's motivation in that, at least.

• • •

In the night I awaken alone.

Hank isn't in his sleeping bag, isn't back on the console, isn't using the bathroom. Through the window of the docking spindle I see emptiness: bare metal and the end window, a slice of black sky with clouds beneath, daylit in the summer sun.

I'm at a loss. Sleep-fogged, but curiosity's burning through that. Although it makes no sense, I open the lockers for the EVA suits. Mine and Hank's are both stowed normally.

There's only one place he could be. Well, two.

The docking spindle's unlatched; I float into the airlock, down to the hatches leading to our X-20s. I peer around the corner and yes, he's in there; easily visible in the hot glow of daylit Earth filtering in through the cockpit windows. He's more or less sitting: not strapped in, still in his underwear, but in position. The main cockpit lights are off but he's powered up the console; I'm looking down at the top of his head and can only see slivers of face, but I can tell he's talking to someone. Talking on the radio.

It occurs to me I'm seeing something I'm not supposed to see; I keep waiting for him to sense my presence, to feel he's being observed, to look up. But: nothing. I float, mesmerized.

Then: a stab of panic. Whoever it is on the ground, they'll be coming up on LOS soon. Which means Hank turning off the radio and coming back to bed.

I push myself back into the module, heart pounding. Pressure in my bladder now, too. Should I use the bathroom? No: I don't want him to know that I know he was awake. I cocoon myself in the sleeping bag, pretend I'm using it for its intended function, even as my anxious heart, busy brain, and almost-bursting bladder conspire to prevent that possibility. We're peers, but I feel like a kid trying to pull one over on my father. Maybe there's something childish in this: he has secrets, and I want some, too.

When I hear him coming I close my eyes and wait, and wait, and wait there in the darkness.

•••

In the morning I'm confused, like a computer trying to read a stack of disordered punchcards. The programs are not running to completion, not without some extra effort to put things back in place and restart the processes.

We prepare breakfast. Coffee summons thought, somewhat. I should talk, should sound normal, even if it takes work. "Looking forward to flying home?"

"I am." In the shortness I hear his tiredness. "Should be a hell of a reentry. You can simulate these things all you want, but…"

But: I do know his thoughts—training never compares to the real thing. Especially this. Slamming into the atmosphere at Mach 25, watching through the windows as the thin air turns into a fiery furnace, swooping in for a landing at Edwards, knowing you have only one chance to get it right...

He gives me a look. Does he know I know he was up? I should say: what? "Crazy yesterday, huh?"

"Yeah. After that little stunt they pulled, I feel the need to one-up them." He opens his pouch: pancakes in gelatin. "I'm sure we can get closer, if they let us."

"I guess that's an advantage for us." I nibble cubes of bacon. "Having a person at the controls. Rather than just steering from the ground."

"That's the advantage of a free system that encourages independent action." He smiles. "Like the old joke goes: teach their fighter pilots initiative, next thing you know they're flying to West Germany."

I chuckle. "We had one of those when I was over there. A defector. He must've flown at fifty feet all the way to the base, to keep under the radar. Straight-in approach, didn't even make sure the runway was clear. Touched down, rolled to a stop, popped the canopy on the MIG, came out with his hands up. Next day the CIA was shipping it back to the States in crates."

"Never happens the other way around."

"No. No it does not." A reminder that our systems are not equal, no matter what the egghead intellectuals say: this is a struggle of freedom versus tyranny. "That satellite. How close do you think you can get?"

"Close as they let me. Closer, even. Obviously I don't want to lose my ticket for the next ride. But you know how these things go. As long as it goes well…"

"Yeah."

"Sixty feet, I bet."

"You think?"

"Closer than that I don't think would be useful. I don't think it's booby trapped, but who knows? And no sense risking a collision. Sixty feet, though. Should get some nice pictures."

"They'll let us do that."

"I'm sure they will."

"It does bug me that they didn't want to give us a choice in the matter…"

"There is a choice," he says. "It's just that it already happened. You choose to make a commitment. The Air Force, it's like marriage, it's another marriage. You contemplate your options before you get into it, but then you choose. And those other options fall away. Which is just as well, because they would have fallen away one way or the other. Then your only choice is whether or not to stay on the path. Keep doing what you're supposed to do, or go fly airliners. You can fly an X-20 up here, and put up with all the rules and restrictions, or you can go do laps between Chicago to Denver in a 707. That's your choice."

I eat for a bit, contemplate this. "You can still choose where to go. It's not like the plane's on rails."

"You can only choose so much. And every choice limits you. Take...reentry. I mean, sure, you can do a burn that'll put you down anywhere on the globe. But after that...you've gotta fly the profile that keeps you alive."

"The tyranny of physics."

He chuckles. "Something like that."

I think about our earlier talk: Polynesian fantasies, landing on some remote island and convincing the natives you're John Frum. "And we're not the type of people who are gonna set down anywhere on the globe."

A wistful look. "Well it's fun to think about, at least."

We go through the motions of preparing for the day's operations; breakfast has made things better, but there's still that sleep-deprived mechanical strangeness to it all. And the angst. Knowing he's got secrets.

•••

It isn't easy up here to do things without the other person knowing. But there are ways. I time Hank's bathroom breaks throughout the day, guesstimating when I'll have a longer window.

Then in the afternoon he announces it. A nod towards the toilet: "I'm gonna be in there for a minute."

I pretend it's no big deal. But once he closes the curtain, I am floating off towards the spindle.

Feet-first, I pull myself through the hatch into Hank's X-20. Look around and see: nothing.

What did I expect? I don't know. Everything looks normal, all the gauges and switches just like mine, despite that vague feeling of unease, the unsettling symmetry of things that are identical but not the same.

I strain my ears, trying to hear in the thin air. Usually for a long bathroom break we strip naked: it's easier to clean feces from skin than from cloth. So I should have time. But if I'm caught, I won't have excuses.

I look and think, think and look. When I put my hand on the side of the ejection seat, I feel his kneeboard with his checklists. Clipped to it: an index card.

On it, four codes. Three have times. So:

K7TRV

W6EZV 16:55

K7UGA 19:58

K8KOR 19:59

Suddenly: that feeling of being observed. I look up with a start, sure I'll see him watching me. But still: nothing. Carefully I copy the card down. Then I return everything to its right place, and glance around one last time. My eyes settle on the radio panel. The mode selector knob is on the last setting: SSB. I write down the frequency.

But who's he talking to, and why? Based on our workday clock, those times, especially the first, would put us over Eastern Europe. A thought flashes: ridiculous, perhaps, but there nonetheless: he's a Soviet spy. If the whole gung-ho Cold Warrior act is a front...

Enough. Time to get back. I look one extra extra time to make sure everything's exactly the way it was. Then I pull myself back up and out, and through the spindle to the main room, expecting Hank's accusing eyes.

He's still in the bathroom.

I close the spindle hatch just in time. He pulls the curtain aside and floats out.

"Good break?" I ask, trying to sound nonchalant.

"Not bad."

I take a breath. Try to relax. "Good."

He looks me straight in the eyes, and I swear he sees right through me.

•••

The workday passes. Still no word about our bucket. In my tiredness, my thoughts wander into paranoia and absurdity: I imagine Hank purposefully plugging wrong numbers into the computer and deliberately sending the bucket off course. Then: teams of Soviet agents hacking through the Brazilian jungle with machetes, snatching it up before us so they can glean its secrets, learn our capabilities, take appropriate countermeasures.

But when I really think about the times on the notecard, I realize the error of my ways: if they were workday times, I'd have still been awake. They're Greenwich Mean Time. So we were over the Eastern seaboard on a daylight pass, during our sleep period. Which does make sense.

Still I don't know what to say. There's nothing in the station SOP that covers this sort of thing.

At dinner Hank gives me a knowing look. "You know, I was thinking today about our little chat at breakfast."

Instantly I'm edgy, defensive. "What about it?"

"Well, there is another freedom, once you've made a commitment. The freedom to do a little extra. To go above and beyond. You can coast by and just check off all the boxes, or you can help write the checklists. You can punch in and out on a schedule, or you can go to work early and stay late. Do something extra for the bosses."

I nod, contemplating this. But I still don't know what to say. Not yet.

•••

We settle in again for the night. Again I pull the sleeping bag tight around my weightless body. Stare at the metal panels and think. And when the time is right I am still awake, and it feels like the natural inevitable thing to float into the spindle myself and take up position in my X-20.

Our ships are connected via umbilical power to the station. Power requirements while docked are very low—a couple pumps for the coolant lines, to make sure nothing on the dark side of the spacecraft freezes up. I only have to push one circuit breaker to turn on the radio. I set it to Single Sideband mode.

I'm not sure if this is the craftiest thing I've ever done, or the stupidest. "Whiskey-Six-Echo-Zulu-Victor, this is Kilo-Seven-Tango-Romeo-Victor. Come in. Over."

Nothing.

Again: "Whiskey-Six-Echo-Zulu-Victor, this is Kilo-Seven-Tango-Romeo-Victor. Come in. Over."

A call into the void. Is there anybody out there? Anxious and alone, I transmit again. "Whiskey-Six-Echo-Zulu-Victor, this is Kilo-Seven-Tango-Romeo-Victor. Come in. Over."

At last, a reply: "Kilo-Seven-Tango-Romeo-Victor, this is Whiskey-Six-Echo-Zulu-Victor." The voice is familiar. I gasp with realization. He continues. "Didn't expect to hear you tonight. I take it you've had the talk. Over."

"Whiskey-Six-Echo-Zulu-Victor..." Everything is upended. "This is not the usual operator at this station, sir. Over."

"Kilo-Seven-Tango, no need for formalities. I know who you are. Do you recognize my voice? Over."

I do, of course. It's my commander's commander's commander's commander's commander. The man who firebombed Japan. The Chairman of the Joint Chiefs of Staff. General Curtis LeMay.

Again: "Kilo-Seven-Tango, do you recognize my voice? Over."

I sputter. "Whiskey-Six-Echo...that's affirmative." (Every fiber of my being wants to add a 'sir.') "This is all...very unusual. Over."

"Kilo-Seven-Tango, obviously this is a departure from normal procedures. The other operator at your station will fill you in. Get some sleep. Over and out."

"Whiskey-Six-Echo. Copy your last. Over and out."

I shut everything down, pull myself out of the darkened cockpit. Surely now Hank will be awake and waiting. But he's still in his sleeping bag, oblivious.

•••

In the morning I have slept soundly, despite the abbreviated schedule. Everything seems all right again: the punchcards stacked neatly in the metal bin, feeding smoothly into the machine. We go through the normal meal prep routine and I don't say anything, not yet.

Then, after sucking my first sip of coffee from the pouch, I take a deep breath and spit it out: "I...uhhh...know about the radio sessions."

Hank doesn't flinch. "I know."

"You know?"

"You left the spindle hatch open the other night. When you peeked in while I was out there. And you're bad at pretending to be asleep. Worse than my girls." He smiles serenely.

"Sonofabitch." I chuckle, shake my head. Then: "I talked to him last night."

"Which one?"

The one was surprising enough that I'd forgotten about the others. "LeMay. It was...a surprise. To say the least."

"Yeah, he's really into amateur radio. Has been, for decades. Which is odd, because he's not very talkative in person. But, yeah, really big on the…"

"No, just…talking to him! From here!" My disbelief pours forth at last, all the strangeness of this. "I mean, after all the lectures they gave us! Schreiver on down, lecture after lecture! Operational security! Using the scramblers, avoiding the media! EYES ONLY transmissions! And then to just…talk to him. Him! Him, of all people, on a civilian frequency…"

"It's not *just* a civilian frequency. There's the MARS network for civil defense…hell, every bomber in SAC has a Single Sideband option…"

"But why, though?"

A shrug. "I think he likes the performance of the shortwave frequencies."

"No…" I sigh, exasperated. "Why are you doing this?"

"We'll get to that!" He smiles. "I will say, it is a useful set of frequencies. Down there, hell…bounce a signal off the ionosphere, you can talk around the globe. Set up some code words, you can recall the bombers at the last minute, which you *can't* do with an ICBM. He wanted that option. And if you want to chat with a hobbyist on a ham set, there's that option, too." Hank bobs in front of me calmly, as if this were just a normal conversation. "How did he react, anyway? Getting a call from you out of the blue?"

"He…" (I shake my head.) "…didn't seem fazed at all."

An appreciative nod. "Yeah, that's how he is. Takes it all in stride. Back during the war, his crews used to call him 'Iron Ass.' The man is completely unflappable."

"That's one way of putting it."

"We were going to have to fill you in anyway. Today or tomorrow. That's actually what we were talking about the other night."

"Fill me in on what? Who are the other call signs?"

Hank smiles. "I can't tell you. Not yet."

"Can't tell me?"

"Well, this wasn't the original plan. This was all supposed to be over and done by the end of my shift. What I *can* tell you is we're talking to a friend of ours in civilian leadership..."

"Not the president."

"No, but...up there. Someone with the leverage to ask for something like this. Our friend had some...bold targeting ideas. Very sensitive ideas that he didn't want to send through the normal bureaucracy. He approached LeMay, and they looked through the crew lists and picked me."

"Sounds pretty hush-hush."

"Yep."

"Then...well, pardon my French, but why the fuck are you talking to them on an open frequency that any two-bit idiot with a ham set can listen in on?"

Hank laughs. "We're not saying much! Hell, all the really secret stuff is coming through the teletype, scrambled, EYES ONLY for me. The voice comms were just an afterthought. They briefed me orally on all of this. In person, locked room in the Pentagon, just the two of them. Made me memorize two targets. Made arrangements to send me teletype messages if they needed to get me something securely. But they're both ham enthusiasts, and...well, do you know how it is when someone gets an idea, and they're so excited it's possible that they don't stop and think whether it's a good idea?"

"Yeah."

"That's kinda how this was. They started briefing me, and they told me the targets and the contingency plans, so I'd know how important this was, how many lives were at stake. And the briefing was done, it was all done! And this...civilian leader...said, 'Can we talk to him directly while he's up there? Like an actual voice conversation on the radio?' And LeMay, he kinda rolled his eyes, but he said, 'Well, they do have Single Sideband...' And our friend, he's a ham enthusiast, too, and he looked like a kid with a new walkie-talkie. I swear, he just wouldn't let it go. All excited about...code words and secret messages..."

I shake my head. "So everything we talked about in our briefings...Soviet fishing trawlers...we can't even talk to our families, for Christ's sake!"

An indecipherable look. "This friend of ours...it's not someone you can just say no to."

"Not even if you're LeMay?"

"Not even him."

"But it's not the president."

"He's…one of the men who holds the purse strings, let's just say. And we tried! We talked about operational security, we talked about all of this. And he kept saying he thought it'd come in handy. To have a direct line of communications. He was very persuasive. I mean, hell, sometimes it is a good idea to talk on an open channel…" (Hank sounds like he's trying to convince himself.) "I mean, nothing too detailed, nothing that actually allows them to interfere. But it's useful sometimes to let the enemy know you're up to something. Rattle the cage a bit, psyche them out, make them think you're a little nuts. Get them thinking big scary thoughts. Like during the Berlin Crisis, General Power sent the DEFCON-2 order out on an open frequency. We wanted them to know we were doing something big and they had no way to stop it. And here they don't even know what it is we're up to."

"I don't even know what it is we're up to!"

"We'll get to that! This is all…need to know stuff. And…well, up until now, you didn't have a need to know."

I shake my head.

He goes on: "Like I said, it was supposed to be wrapped up already. They briefed me on two targets. I was supposed to get all the pictures during the last few buckets. And they had taken care of the other end, down at the Mushroom Factory; they had a person who was going to make sure those pictures got to them. And then things were going to go back to normal. But given the resolution problems, and the fact that we lost this last bucket, LeMay figured I'd have to brief you on what we're doing. Which is helping them draw up a contingency plan."

"A contingency plan?"

"A plan to win the Cold War."

I float in stunned silence. Everything about the current situation with the Soviet Union seems etched in stone; an end hardly seems possible. "How?"

"Well, first...ask yourself this. If you could go back in time and kill Hitler, would you do it?"

"I guess it depends on when. I mean, back when he was a kid, or an art student, or whatever..."

"No. After the Rhineland. During the Sudetenland Crisis, maybe, before Munich. Or after Munich, in the lead-up to Poland, before the war started. Or maybe...maybe right after the invasion of Poland. Once people knew he was a serious threat, but before the bulk of the death and destruction."

"Well, yeah, of course. I mean, it's only logical. You'd save the world a helluva lot of trouble..."

"Well that's what we're figuring out how to do."

"A...decapitation strike?"

"Yep."

"Beria?"

Hank nods solemnly. "He's...he's an evil man. About as evil as they get. A murderer and a rapist, running a country..."

"A rapist?"

"That's what they say. He has his minions...abduct women off the street. MVD agents...picking up young girls. They take them back to Beria's place so he can have his way with them. If they refuse, if they resist...they disappear. As a father to two girls, when I heard that, it's..." He shakes his head. "But obviously it's...I mean, it's not just that, it's everything else. All the deaths in all the camps. He's worse than Hitler, in a lot of ways. Hitler never held the nuclear sword over the world's head..."

"Beria." Again I say it: the name that has haunted our lives for these past fifteen years, and longer. The sinister name. Beria, orchestrator of purges, responsible for who knows how many deaths—numbers with commas. Beria, the spymaster whose agents stole our atomic secrets. Beria, the ruthless administrator who drove the Soviets relentlessly to build their own atomic bomb—the man responsible for all of this, in a sense. Beria, the Machiavellian leader who outmaneuvered his rivals after Stalin's death, executing and exiling so many men: Malenkov, Molotov, Khrushchev. "How?"

"Well, that's the fun part. A leader at that level, you know in a general sense where they are, but only *if* they're doing public events. Speaking at a party congress, or what have you. On the average ordinary workday, you might not know for sure if they're...in the Kremlin or whatever. And even if you did know, and you wanted to...target them in a bombing raid or something, in the olden days the bombs just weren't big enough. They could take cover once bombers were spotted. Get down to a shelter, what have you. The bombs are bigger now, though. Big enough to make sure. Of course, you still have the problem of collateral damage. And that's the good thing here with Beria. It is known, in a general sense, where he goes on vacation. There's a dacha in Kuntsevo, just outside Moscow, there's a resort home at Gagra..."

A flash: the daylight session where Hank had taken the controls. "...on the Black Sea coast."

"Exactly. That's the preferred target, I believe. That would be the cleanest option."

"We...can't carry out a strike, though. There's no bombardment module up here."

"We can spot a line of cars. A Soviet prime minister and his entourage. If we photograph a spot we know they go, at a time he might be there...if we can spot three or four black limousines, all lined up in a row, in a country where hardly anybody has a car..."

"Still, if we launched an ICBM...I mean, they'd pick it up on their northern radar fence, they could still launch everything..."

He purses his lips. "The Chrome Dome flights. The alert bombers. The ones everyone thinks are a...useless anachronism."

"The ones out of Thule?"

"There are routes out of Thule, yes. But there are other routes around Europe. Over the North Sea, I believe, and over the Adriatic. And recently, rather than ending the flights, they've started more over the Eastern Med. If someone gives the order, at any moment they could turn and head for their target. Penetration mission..."

"If they survive the SAMs."

"Well, yes there's a lot of dispute about survivability in a general war. Even for a Mach 3 bomber. That's the genius of this particular plan, though. We've established a pattern of regular behavior. A pattern that probably seems mildly stupid to the enemy. The old bomber general, maybe a little nuts, so devoted to his favorite weapon that he's kept it alive even though we've developed and fielded ICBMs in such numbers that even the most advanced manned bomber is obsolescent...it seems slightly dumb to keep flying them, right? To keep...fantasizing about the day you'll win another war with bombers. But when an enemy thinks you're doing something routine and slightly dumb, they stop paying attention. And that's the idea here."

I find myself nodding a little.

Hank goes on. "Beria...like Stalin, he's from Soviet Georgia. The intelligence says he goes back to Gagra fairly often. But when he leaves the Kremlin, we don't always find out where he went until after the fact. Anyway, the next time he starts pressuring us, the next time he does something like...Berlin, then we'll have that option. We'll wait for him to leave the Kremlin for a weekend, and we'll take some pictures to confirm where he went. And then a B-70 over the Eastern Med is going to have engine trouble. That's what they'll announce, anyway. They'll call an in-flight emergency. Mayday on all open channels. They'll get permission to head to the nearest airbase in Turkey for an emergency landing. They'll keep descending, keep making calls, 'Not sure we can make it back to base,' and all that. They'll drop into the mountains. Off radar. And then...a dash north, as low and as fast as they can go. Out of the mountains, over the Black Sea, under Soviet radar, timed to avoid any fighter patrols, that big beautiful white bomber skimming fifty feet over the waves. Then at the last-minute, too late to stop, they pull up and release their payload. Medium-yield nuclear weapon. That kind of launch profile, it'll head up in a ballistic arc...Circular Error Probable of a few hundred yards, but a big enough bomb that it won't matter...meanwhile our bomber turns tail and heads out of the way. And boom! Goodbye Soviet leadership."

Gently I float, taking all this in. The catastrophic perfection of a well-honed plan. "So is this...is this definitely going to happen?"

"Oh, no, it's not definite. I mean, I don't think it's definite. Nobody *wants* it to happen. I don't think."

"You don't think."

"Anyway, that's a question beyond my pay grade." Hank shrugs. "I think it's just a contingency plan. Something they want to have in their back pocket so we don't get pushed around. A couple pages in the SIOP for when they break out the nuclear football."

"So one nuke, and that's it."

"Well...that's a good question. Taking him out, would the whole regime just...collapse? Quite possibly. Personally, I think we'd need more, just to be on the safe side. I'm pretty sure our friends have discussed that. A small salvo of missiles. Take out their command and control, and their ICBMs, in case they did want to retaliate. Even if we only get...ninety-five percent of the ICBMs, the Sentinel system could shoot down anything that does launch. Still, the contingency plan...it would buy us some time. Give us an actual chance to win things."

"That's..." I nod appreciatively. "That's a helluva plan, actually."

"Isn't it?" Hank smiles. "I thought you'd like it."

•••

Knowing the plan brings an edgy new energy to my days.

The time flows, smooth and routine, the last of Hank's week here. Daylight pass after daylight pass, cold bright ice pack leading to empty green of treeless summer tundra, followed by deserts or grassy steppes. Our faces glued to the rubber masks on the targeting scopes, a little extra antsy any time there's cloud cover, a little more excited when skies are clear. We photograph all the ICBM sites we can, intent on finding every one; we take pictures in the knowledge that, should the balloon go up, we might actually have the chance to smash them all before they can get a bird off. Counterforce strikes, no need to target cities or civilians: a way to kill the nuclear swordsman holding the world hostage. The only humane way to fight a nuclear war.

Provided, of course, the first part of the plan happens. Which, we still need to prove it's possible.

Then on the weekend, it all comes together. Beautiful pictures late on Friday afternoon of the western Moscow district where the party bigwigs have their dachas, and then Gagra on Saturday. We don't know for sure that Beria is at either one this weekend, and Hank says I'll need to keep photographing both locations until we've confirmed we've caught him at each site; still, I imagine he is there. I imagine it perfectly, imagine it already happening: the leader of the Soviet Union plotting the invasion of Western Europe, then changing into a bathing suit and walking down to the beach to get some sun on his fat corrupt body before he forces it on more innocent nubile young Muscovites. I picture him all alone, slapping his belly and staring off at the water, but then again there must be a couple of guards, too, MVD agents, hard scarred men who tortured people in the Siberian gulags, men wearing their full uniforms and low quarters, even at the beach—bodyguards with pistols on their hips, pathetically inadequate to stop what's coming. Maybe they're looking across the water, too, as the beautiful white Valkyrie pulls up at the end of its desperate ride, maybe they can catch a dim glimpse of the bomb in the distance and open their mouths in wonder as it starts arcing towards them. Then: a flash. And now they are all gone, only the guilty men, a stretch of beach now turned to glass. A sucker punch, a quick stunner to the face, a bolt out of the blue before the body blows rain down on the missile silos. But all is fair in love and nuclear war.

When the last pass is done, we wind the film into the bulky canister. No reentry bucket for this one, no need to worry about C-119s plucking it from the sky, or Soviet agents hacking their way through the jungle to find it on land. No, this one is going down with Hank: a hand delivery of our most important imagery. He floats down the docking spindle to stow it in his cockpit; I watch, as anxious as a first-time father.

•••

There is one target from the bucket we haven't re-shot—the satellite.

It has been stalking us lazily all the while, staying in its low elliptical orbit, visible occasionally through the end of the spindle, on Hank's mind more than mine. Given the fact that it hasn't maneuvered since his EVA, the speculation is that they're conserving maneuvering fuel, trying to stretch out the end of their mission, with budgets at their limit and conservation on their mind. Given how low our orbit is, it's amazing theirs hasn't decayed yet. But we want to take advantage of that. So Cheyenne's finally relented; they've given him permission to work up a plan, to reschedule his departure and fly up close and get some great pictures. While their explanations and speculations and calculations sound plausible, I suspect there's something simpler underneath it all: we want to get better pictures of them than they could possibly ever get of us.

•••

Then at last it is Sunday. For Hank: Departure Day. We spend the morning doing inventory, taking stock of what's lost and broken, seeing what needs to be crammed into Bob Lawrence's cramped cockpit storage area before he flies up on Tuesday.

"Excited about the change of command?" Hank asks.

"Oh, of course. Finally get to relax a bit up here! Jesus." I chuckle because none of it's true.

"Eager for my reign of terror to come to an end, huh?"

"If anything, I just want my part to go this smoothly."

"It didn't go that smoothly," he says. "We lost a bucket, we had them up here taking pictures of us…"

"It felt smooth. It felt like we were taking care of everything. Both the EVAs went fine. Camera resolution's where it needs to be. You made it look easy! In fact, if you have any pointers…"

"Well, like they say, work like a duck," he says. "Keep the surface calm, paddle like hell underwater. You'll do fine with the work. You're not the type of guy to take anything for granted. Just…take a breath when you need to, too. Don't punish yourself too hard."

This sounds fair. But then again… "You have to punish yourself a little, though. Make sure you're not taking privileges your subordinates don't have. The commanders I admire, that's what they do. Like…well, hell, like LeMay." Memories again from the academy: firstie year, a bright clean classroom at last, mountains in the distance, case studies in air leadership.

"He is something." Hank pauses.

"They say back in England, he ordered his crews to stop taking evasive action during bombing runs. To fly straight and level through the flak. He'd done the math; he knew it was the smart decision. Very little extra risk in exchange for much more accurate bombing. Because why risk lives, if you're not going to accomplish the mission? But he didn't just order it from the safety of a desk: he gave the order and then flew lead plane on every mission."

"Indeed. Helluva guy. Great combat leader."

I almost get back to work, but another thought comes: "You know, in a way, I think that's what we're up against. They're doing the opposite of that."

"Who?"

"The Soviets. These...targets we're observing. Beria and the others, driving around in motorcades. Limousines going to vacation places in a country where the average worker doesn't even get a car. When...Ivan Q. Public is stuck...standing in line for their ration of toilet paper, or whatever. When leaders take privileges their subordinates don't know about...that's tyranny."

Hank nods, contemplating. "Yeah. Tyranny."

I flip through the binders with the paper maps, looking for places where we've misfiled them in our haste; soon we've put each one back in its proper place. Some of the cover transparencies are nearing the end of their useful lives, though. I pull those aside, and Hank adds them to the equipment list.

Then, out of the blue: "You've heard of MARS, right?"

"Well...yeah..."

"Not the planet. Military Affiliate Radio System."

"That's a Civil Defense thing, right?"

"Yeah. Civilian ham radio operators. They go through a course and get certified to participate. Basically if there's a war, and bases get knocked out, they can go on the air and act as an a resource. Listen for news and bulletins from the government. Act as a liaison with local authorities. Anyway, there's a station on the MARS network I may have you call down to. Maybe next week. There may be someone you want to talk to on the other end."

Thoughts: Is he talking about what I think he's talking about? Do I even want to know? "Is that...authorized?"

A crooked look. "Do I look like the type of person who would do something like that without authorization?"

"Well..."

"Just to assuage your Catholic guilt, this...uhhh...policy modification has been cleared at the highest levels. Anyway, I wanted to let you know. Call down to the MARS station. Here's the call sign." He etches it neatly on a notecard: K8KOR.

"When?"

"Good question." He ponders this. "We'll have to figure that out after I get down." Then: "I'll tell you what. You and I are scheduled to talk in a few days. I'll let you know then. Should be during a normal daytime Los Angeles pass."

"All right." I look at it in disbelief. It feels like a *Wizard of Oz* type of a situation, a click-your-heels-and-go-home ending, something absurdly complicated somehow becoming absurdly simple.

On goes the inventory. A bit of mental lint from the academy sticks in my mind, an A.T.O. talking about the three functions of every inspection: accountability, serviceability, cleanliness. Make sure something's there, verify that it works, see if it's clean. Accountability's surprisingly tough here—small things drift off, big things get placed in the wrong storage locker. But whenever you clean, you find things, and so it goes here. We verify serviceability as we go, making sure everything works and we don't need spare parts. And cleanliness: after some scrubbing, the place is inspection-worthy.

Finally I'm filling out the requisition form. We've radioed everything down so they can start preparing; still there are the formalities: a carbon copy for some clerk somewhere, numbers for the accountants to balance the books. I read it over, sign it, hand the yellow copy to Hank. "All right, here goes."

He scans it over. "Looks good."

"That's it?"

"What, did you want a change-of-command ceremony?"

Memories again: baking at attention on various air base aprons, sweat stinging eyes and no way to wipe—or worse, inside a hangar, with commanders using the covered venue as an excuse to pontificate a little longer. "Never did enjoy those."

"Nobody does, except the commanders."

"Can't exactly stand in formation up here, either."

"No. Although…there is one thing." He reaches in his pocket. Produces the double-headed silver dollar. "Command Authority Augmentator, Non-binary, One Each. Sometimes two heads are better than one, but it helps if both are of the same mind about the big decisions. And if minds need to be changed, here's a piece of change that's sure to do the trick." He presses the coin into my hand. It's warmer than I expect.

"Bob's a good guy. I don't imagine we'll have any issues." Our next crewmember, soon to be the first Negro in space. Given Hank's background, and the changes of the past few years, I'm curious about his thoughts on the matter, any private things he didn't say in training.

"No," he says. "Probably not." He floats off to the X-20 with the Hasselblad, getting ready for departure.

●●●

"Spacecraft hatch is sealed," Hank calls out in my headphones.

I'm floating in the spindle, looking through the hatch window as he settles in to the cockpit. The Hasselblad's stowed in front of his ejection seat, and my mind's on the risky task he faces: a covert rendezvous with a hostile foreign spacecraft. Conversations flood back, speculations about automated self-defense mechanisms: it's entirely possible all this is a trap. With my bare hand, I touch the black metal of the spacecraft skin. "Looks good. Happy hunting." I'll see him on the ground in three weeks, or never.

"Still wish we had a cannon on this thing."

"That'll be the day, huh?" I fold the spindle hatch into position, lock the locks into place. "Spindle hatch is sealed."

Through its window I still see him, helmet and lap distorted a little by the extra glass, reading the checklist on his kneeboard. "Ready for interhatch depress. Cabin pressure's good."

"Dumping the interhatch." I flip the switch and the valve opens; I eye the pressure gauge as it drops. "Pressure coming down."

"Steady in the cabin," Hank calls. "Looks like we're in good shape."

My other gauge is steady. "Good here, too."

"Attitude control on standby. Ready to undock."

I look everything over one extra extra extra time before taking the step that cannot be undone. Then: the latch switch. A creaky forlorn metal noise as the station gives up its commander. "And…spacecraft is released. Godspeed."

"Thank you, Watchman."

The picture in front of me had looked permanent, inner hatch and outer in a fixed arrangement, but now there's a bobble, and the window to Hank gets slightly smaller. He pulses the thrusters and slides backwards out of view; I see the nose of his spacecraft, black and moonlit, sharklike against the night ocean.

Over to the spindle window. Through patchy clouds I catch the Indian coast. Soon we'll be over the Soviet Union. Gradually the separation builds.

"Watchman, Falcon-1. Preparing for deorbit burn," Hank says, even though he is not. "Over."

"Copy that, Falcon-1. Looks like you'll be on the ground in forty minutes." Also not true. Flashes of the Honor Code, then Winston Churchill's words: In war, the truth is so valuable it must be surrounded by a bodyguard of lies. "Have a safe trip down. Over."

"Watchman, I think we're going to lose comms in a minute. Over."

"Copy, Falcon-1. Over." This is my signal. I pull myself back to the comms panel, flip the switches. "Falcon-1, this is Watchman on secure channel. How do you read, over?"

"Watchman, Falcon-1. Read you loud and clear. We'll try and give you a play-by-play. Over."

Now: back to the spindle window. Beyond the undocked X-20, I can see the Red satellite, a star newly risen over the horizon. Soon it will be known to us.

"Translating," Hank says.

"Looks good by my clock."

I peer through the glass. Hank's far enough back now that it's tough to make out the contours of his spacecraft; I strain to see the thrusters, trying to see: what? Flame? Nothing.

"Looks like he's catching up with us."

We'll have acquisition from Thule in a few minutes, but for now we're still alone: active participant and passive observer.

I feel the need to fill the silence. "Roger, Falcon-1. Good to hear. Over."

"All right. Radar is on. Set is warming up. There we go. Range: 50 miles."

Into daylight we fly, high above the Soviet Arctic coast, the terminator now noticeably north of where it was when I arrived three weeks ago. Very few clouds today: I see water, Novaya Zemlya, and then a long cold emptiness stretching all the way to the North Pole. Can I tell the kids I was almost above it? Probably not, even though the Soviets obviously know our inclination...

My headset comes on: finally a friendly voice. "Falcon-1, this is Thule on secure channel. We have you on radar. Waiting for updates. Over."

"Thule, Falcon-1. Radar is on and we're hunting for bear. Over."

"Falcon-1, Thule, we see your target as well. Working out the calcs for the approach burn. Over."

"Roger, Thule. Standing by to copy."

A brief wait that feels interminable. "Uhhh...Falcon-1, can you give us a range? Over."

"Thule, I have him at...crap. 52 miles. Over."

"Falcon-1, it...uhh...looks like we're seeing some planar separation. Over."

"Thule, did you say planar separation, over?"

"Roger, Falcon-1."

My mood flattens. Mouth goes dead. Heart…well, "sinks" isn't the right word up here. But: a flood of disappointment.

The silence of contemplation, minds stretching plans to cover changing circumstances, the yawning separation. Then: "Thule, Falcon-1. Can we still attempt a rendezvous? Over."

I feel every second tick by, pulling us further from the plan. "Falcon-1…that's Cheyenne's call now. We'll phone it in, tell them what we're seeing. But I don't think a burn would be productive. Over."

They're probably right. No point dropping Hank into the lower orbit now; the Zenit will be miles off to the side by the time he gets there. And there's no time or fuel to make planar maneuvers. If we keep trying, it will probably take an extra rev to bring him down; by then our orbital track will be far out in the Pacific, a thousand-plus miles west of Edwards, too far to steer him safely back to shore.

"Roger, Thule." It's not often I can hear disappointment in Hank's voice. "Not sure how this happened. Over."

"All units, Watchman." I chip in even though I'm stepping on their response. "Maybe they were waiting for this."

"Watchman, not sure I follow. Over."

"Falcon-1, they track our departures. It's a full rev before normal. They had to know we'd be thinking rendezvous. Then, chatting secure…predictable move on our part. Over."

"Copy, Watchman." Dull, resigned. Then: "Coming up on LOS. Over."

We are down over Hudson Bay now. We—no, I. I have grown used to thinking in plural, the two-headed crew doing everything as one. For now, at least, it's no longer the case.

Hank is far back now, a distant star. High above I see Polaris, fixed and true, looking down in gentle accusation on our evasions. We have nothing to show for our petty lies.

•••

Soon Cheyenne confirms what we know in our heart: no rendezvous. I'd imagined myself breathlessly following the action as Hank closed in, listening for the thrill in his voice that would tell me what he was seeing. Instead he listlessly copies down times for his final de-orbit burn while I stare down at the empty heartland. There is a flatness to it all.

My day's almost done. I picture Hank fighting off sleep in his cramped cockpit during the long blank period before his burn. Meanwhile I catch up on personal tasks—some cleaning, a bathroom break, a long sponge bath—and in between I catch glimpses of the world. America ends. Mexican mountains slide by in silence. We swoop down across the western South Pacific; a geographic fact floats into my mind, how all of South America is east of Jacksonville, Florida. Then it's into orbital night; there are no comms windows again until Thule, and it's past the end of my normal workday anyway, but I force myself to stay awake. It occurs to me, not for the first time, that I may be the one who ends up rendezvousing with the Zenit. Did I want this to happen?

And now we are coming out of night near the White Sea. I put the headphones back on.

"Falcon-1, Watchman. Still awake in there, over?"

An emptiness. Then: "Watchman, Falcon-1. Up and at 'em. Ready to go home. Over."

"Falcon-1, how's your orientation, over?"

"Watchman, I am upside-down and backwards. Watching the world fade away behind me. Over."

Another academy memory: a history lecture about how the Greeks viewed time. Walking backwards, blind to the future, watching the past recede before your eyes. A lonely voice, teaching classics in that Space Age setting. A poem from class: I am Ozymandias, king of kings...

"Still there, Watchman?"

"Uhh, yeah. All right, Falcon-1. Coming up on the burn."

"Copy, Watchman. Counting down. And...ignition. Everything looks good. Over."

Back I float to the spindle window. There is nothing to do now but watch, and not much to watch, not yet. Hank's still a speck in the far distance. I know his engines are pointed at me now; still there are no dramatic fire plumes, no exciting visuals to the rocketry. Everywhere else I look, the whole vast space spectacle is boring old reruns: the same old show, no way to change the channel. Again we are near the northern limits of our orbital track. It's somewhat clear; I see patchy clouds and endless bright ice below.

"Watchman, burn is complete. Too bad it's not Christmas Eve. Over."

"Falcon-1, Watchman, not sure I follow. Over."

"Watchman, flying home to LA from the Arctic…a roll of film to see who's been naughty…I feel like Santa Claus. NORAD could use my position updates for their tracker. Over."

I think back on another academy bit, some engineering professor calculating the aerodynamic heating on any object attempting to cover all the distances that would have to be flown on Christmas Eve at the speeds required for prompt delivery. The result: temperatures far hotter than any alloy could handle. Let alone reindeer. "Not sure Rudolph can handle Mach 25, over."

A chuckle from Hank: warmth across the airwaves as the Arctic slides beneath. "Maybe that's why his nose is red. From the heat."

A glance towards the North Pole. If I told the kids I was this close, I'd still have to lie about what I saw—they're both young enough to believe in Santa. What would I see if all that were true? Icebreakers laden with containers of raw materials plowing their way northwards, tearing long dark streaks in the sea ice: a neverending logistics train. Barracks full of elves hot-bunking so the factories can cram in three shifts a day, a manufacturing cruelty abetted by the midnight sun and the months of endless daylight—no need for anyone to work against their Circadian rhythm, like I'm doing now.

Now I can see Hank; now I see the fiery plume arcing down over the islands of the Northwest Territories, a human meteor, a blowtorch so blindingly incandescent it looks electric. The hot white flame pulses brighter and my heart quickens; it flickers and flashes, spewing a steady stream to the rear, a dragon's flaming breath. It goes on for an impossibly long time; it goes on and on and on, falling away, falling behind; I stay stuck to the glass, mesmerized. Comms blacked out now so there's no way to verify. But it's hard to believe my friend is alive in the middle of all of that.

I wish upon the shooting star, say a prayer for his safe return.

After an eternity of minutes, it goes out, far behind me now. What's left? A glider or a cinder, I can't tell.

On comes the radio, ground calling for him: "Falcon-1, Edwards, do you read? Over."

And nothing.

"Falcon-1, Edwards, do you read?"

Nothing.

"Falcon-1, Edwards, do you read?"

These anxious moments feel like hours. Long enough to imagine all the scenes, not just the minister making the reluctant walk up to Judy's front door, but also the service (closed casket, picture on top), the missing man formation, the grieving brunch afterwards at some sad dark restaurant, everyone picking at their food and making awkward conversation with me, the last man to see him alive.

But then: "Edwards, Falcon-1. We're down through it. Over." Cool and flat and professional. Not even an exclamation, just a status update.

"Falcon-1, Edwards. Chase planes orbiting at Angels 10. Over."

"Falcon-1, Watchman. Santa Claus is real! Great to hear your voice. Over."

"Roger, Watchman." A clipped acknowledgment, the best I can hope for: he's busy now. "All units, Falcon-1 descending through Angels 100. Over."

I look to the empty hatch on Hank's side of the spindle, then at my own X-20, listening all the while to the radio chatter, everything executed to perfection. But I'm faster, far ahead now, coming up on LOS; their voices cut out right before Hank links up with the chase planes. I don't have another comms window until Tananarive, and I don't plan on being awake for that…

I look up at the hatch and my empty cockpit, and stare, and think.

● ● ●

Monday is a lazy lonely day.

I wake to the news that Hank landed safely. Everything went according to plan, apparently: the T-38s timing their orbits perfectly and picking him up at 10,000 feet and following him down towards the dry lake bed, the landing skids deploying cleanly, the small black spacecraft touching down and shuddering to a halt, the three-letter-agency men picking up the film canister and whisking it away on a plane to Washington. No catastrophe, no discrepancy at all between planning paper and reality. I have no idea why I imagined otherwise.

There won't be more film until Bob flies up tomorrow, so there are no photography passes. Ground has given me a list of maintenance tasks to fill my workday. Still I spend time on the scope, scanning and scanning. The contingency plan is still on my mind and I want to recognize everything, want to know it and study it in case I need to take some photographs. Our—my—ground track's far enough off from Gagra that I can only see obliquely. But I do get a good glimpse of Moscow.

After dinner I have time to read. *Guns of August* now: bloodbaths on a massive scale, war plans grinding up people in numbers never before seen in human history. They had forgotten the destructiveness of a general war; they couldn't imagine how easily the new technology would facilitate a slaughter. I stay up late, reading and imagining. I'm not sabotaging tomorrow: every launch in the program is a daylight launch on a descending node, so I'll need to be active on California time for at least one more day.

At the appointed hour, I slip into my cockpit, turn the radio on without fear of observation or need for explanation. The only station I don't know. "Kilo-Seven-Uniform-Golf-Alpha, this is Kilo-Seven-Tango-Romeo-Victor. Come in, over."

There is no response.

"Kilo-Seven-Uniform-Golf-Alpha, this is Kilo-Seven-Tango-Romeo-Victor. Do you copy, over?"

Over and over. No response.

• • •

"...and liftoff. Beautiful launch, beautiful day, Falcon-2 is on the way!"

I'm watching on the scope again, just like when they sent the Centaur. A unique perspective: a strange quick glimpse of sunlit metal shapes exploding into action. Still I can't help wishing I was down there. This feels like another rerun. I've seen launches from the ground before, of course, but there's more to enjoy: beautiful California weather, then a leisurely drive home down the P.C.H. It'd be a rerun of a favorite episode, at least.

"Vandenberg, Watchman, looking good from up here. Over."

"All units, Falcon-2." (With the change in shifts there's been a change in call-signs.) "Roll program complete. All systems nominal. Over."

I swoop down once more with the telescope, trying to catch Bob in the boost phase; I dial the zoom back out and catch the plume, but when I try to follow it to its source I run out of scope travel. No matter.

There isn't much I need to do. I fly around the station anyway: arranging objects on Velcro, straightening binders in sleeves, scanning for stray stains and spots. First impressions set the tone, and I want the place to look immaculate. Memories come back, countless inspections at the academy, time spent standing and waiting for A.T.O.s. I am in charge now, of course, but for me that always means more pressure, not less. It's hard to command when you know there's some flaw visible to your subordinates; I want them to look up and see perfection.

The station passes into southern darkness. Distracting visuals: *aurora australis* below, a tantalizing ghostly glow. I catch a glimpse but force myself to keep working.

At last comes the call: "Watchman, Falcon-2. I have visual. Radar range 30 miles."

"Falcon-2, Watchman. Read you five by five. Over." I'm on the other side of the looking glass now, reliving my rendezvous from the opposite perspective—boring now, drained of mystery.

"Watchman, Falcon-2. Ascent was nominal. Spacecraft systems all nominal. Orbit is nominal."

"How'd you like the view?"

"Lotta ocean. Not much to see."

"There will be, Falcon-2." I feel like we are rereading transcripts of old dialogue: a shuffling of roles in endless succession, the understudy taking place of the actor, who was himself once an understudy. Infinite repetition. "There will be."

●●●

"...very good, gentlemen," Hickam says. "GO for docking."

The rendezvous burns are done and the approach is nearly complete; I'm at the end of the spindle watching the spectacle, the black daylight sky and the endless blue Pacific. The X-20 had been stationary, floating in formation, but now it's closing in, a silent shark on a string. My excitement's shot through with angst; my eyes dart back and forth as yards turn into feet turn into inches. In the final moments, I crane my neck and move sideways on the glass for a better angle. I imagine some wayward flick of Bob Lawrence's wrist sending the spacecraft lurching towards me: crunching metal, decompression, cataclysm.

But no. The indicator light comes on and I barely feel a bobble. "And we have contact. Well done. Excellent job." I resist the obvious sex jokes.

Bob does, too. "You...ahhh...have something to do, Watchman?"

"Oh." My face flushes with embarrassment as I flip the switch. Metal against metal: the latches engage. "Hard dock." Through the hatch I see the inner rubber lip smooth and flush against the black metal: an airless kiss. I flip the other switch: "Pressurizing the interhatch."

"There we go," Bob says.

"Sorry about that. I was expecting some dumb sex joke."

"Me too. Surprised it's not on the rendezvous checklist."

"Right? Lame joke about probe penetration? Aaaand...check." I chuckle, but it feels forced. "Clearly you've spent too much time in the Air Force."

I second-guess this as soon as I say it: Does he think I think he *shouldn't* be in the Air Force? For all the training Bob and I have done together, I feel strangely conscious of the differences. The first Negro in space.

If this rubbed him the wrong way, his voice offers no indicators. "All right, finishing my checklist." Even and professional.

"And we're equalized. Opening the spindle." The first hatch folds towards me neatly and I see him more clearly, flipping switches and working methodically. "Hold one." I fly back through the station for a quick bathroom break, and one last look to make sure everything's in order.

By the time I return, he's popped his hatch and floated up into the spindle. "Anybody home?" He smiles as he sees me coming back, the simple joyful smile I surely had: seeing a familiar face in space.

"Sorry about that. Welcome! Congratulations." We shake hands vigorously. Although it's hardly the first time, I catch myself noticing my hand in his, the contrast of pigments, the odd way their hands get pale in the palms. A stab of awkwardness: does he notice me noticing? Does he care?

"Thanks. Glad I could make it."

"You smell that?" I wrinkle my nose.

"Smell what?" His eyes narrow warily.

"That...like, metal smell." This all feels uncomfortable, compared with Hank's easy welcome.

"Oh. Yeah, what is that?"

"That's the smell of space."

"Space doesn't smell."

"I didn't believe it either." I nod back towards the main living area. "Come on, I'll show you around."

We float back into the open main station; I turn to see his eyes wide with wonder, a grin like a kid in a candy store...no, happier than that, like a kid who's been given the keys to the store. A long way from the South Side of Chicago. "Place looks good!"

"Move-in ready. We cleaned the hell out of it."

"More than I can say for some of my landlords."

"I bet." I look to gauge his reaction. "So you like it, huh?"

He grins. "I love it! Man, this is something."

"Good, we'll let you stay." I say this without thinking but I think I see the grin turned down a notch, a furrow on his brow. Another sudden stab of self-consciousness: Did I say the wrong thing? Equal Housing Opportunities. "I mean...well, what'd you think of the flight up, anyhow?"

"Oh. Well, like I said, wasn't much to see on the ascent. But man, what a kick in the pants!"

The thrill of memory. Something we share now. "That was something, wasn't it?"

"They're trying to get it where it's some regular routine thing...operational, rather than experimental. There is nothing routine about it, though."

"No, no there isn't." I smile. "I don't think we want it to be, either. Not in our heart of hearts. I mean, that's half the fun of this job, doing something dangerous. Walking past ordinary people on the street and knowing you're different. I think that's why they never redesignated the plane after the solo flights, why it's still an X-20, and not..."

"What else could you call it?" he asks. "No cannon, no missiles...can't be an F-20."

"Much to Hank's chagrin," I chip in.

"B-20, if they want to put a warhead in the payload bay. Although I think they'll probably just do a bombardment module instead."

"You think they're gonna?"

"Pretty sure it's built," he says.

It does feel strange, hearing something this...definitive. "Could be just a rumor. You know how this program is. Everything's so secret we all spend our free time playing fortune teller. And for every accurate prediction there's twenty others that don't come true."

"It's built. They're just waiting for the right moment politically."

"After the election?"

"Depending on the election."

Politics. Kennedy versus Nixon, assuming the latter can hold off Goldwater. "Lotta things...up in the air, huh?"

"Very funny." No laughter.

"Still..." Stumbling through words now. "Could be just a rumor."

"Well, let's put it this way. Just last week, final training for me, two of the others got pulled into some super-secret briefing. Macleay and Neubeck."

"Are they on the flight manifest?"

"They just got assigned. November and December. And I saw them come out of the meeting. They looked like they had the weight of the world on their shoulders."

I think to Hank and the contingency plan, everything he knew that I didn't, everything I know now that Bob doesn't. "I guess that's how it works, huh? Need-to-know." That's the flip side of the rumor mill. Everybody knows at least one thing you don't. And only the speculators get to talk. "Still...that's heavy stuff."

"Yeah. I'd prefer just taking pictures. Boring as it probably is after a while." A nod back towards the space plane. "As much as I hate to say it, R-20's probably most accurate."

I laugh. "None of us wants to admit we're reconnaissance pilots! And it doesn't actually have the cameras, it just hauls the film."

"C-20, then."

"Cargo, that's even less sexy than reconnaissance!" At last I feel at ease, feel like we're clicking. "I mean, not that I'm the arbiter of sexy, but still. U-20, maybe. I'm not gonna push for it, though."

"Me neither," he smiles, and I feel a connection, floating there in the living area of our orbiting home. The two of us, experimental pilots, the only two humans in space, until the next Red adventure.

On to the observation module. "I will admit, it does get kinda boring. The flight up is exhilarating. The flight down, at least from what I saw, probably more so. But you'll spend most of your time chained in here, slaving away..."

He flinches, just a little, and I look again at his skin and realize what I've said.

"Lemme...uhh..." He looks back towards the spindle. "Lemme get my stuff. Thanks for the tour."

I can't think of anything to say besides: "Yeah, sure."

• • •

Soon we're preparing dinner in silence, injecting hot water into irradiated meal packets. I look for evidence of nausea, extra bathroom breaks, any indicators he isn't at home in space. But: nothing. For me: a pang of jealousy, memories of my misery. We are different people. Separate. And if equal means the same, then the equation is out of balance.

The frozen Arctic Ocean slides by far below beneath intermittent clouds. We are in need of an icebreaker. "Any news?"

"News?"

"Yeah. World events, what-not?"

"There was this...East German who got shot by the border guards, trying to escape. Wounded really bad, gut-shot. He fell in some...no-man's-land area, this dead zone not quite in the West. People from our side were throwing him bandages. Encouraging him. But they couldn't cross the line to help him. He spent an hour in agony, moaning in pain with their guards just standing there, watching him die. And when he was dead they just came and got him. By that time, there were television cameras watching from our side. So it was all over the news."

"Bastards."

"Yeah. It's an embarrassment for them. People trying to leave their...socialist paradise."

"Funny how it never happens going the other way." I am relieved. He was as eager to talk as I was.

"No, I guess not." He inspects his package, looks back to the timer. "The first thing on my briefing was actually Czechoslovakia," he adds.

"Czechoslovakia?"

"Apparently that new leader, Dubček..." (He pronounces as perfectly as an Eastern European émigré: DUB-chek. This surprises me, although perhaps it shouldn't.) "...made a major speech last week announcing a new round of reforms. They're loosening some restrictions on speech. Travel. There's talk of them moving towards a free market. Opening their borders."

"Well that's a good thing." Talk of foreign politics: it feels like a refuge. We're all Americans here.

"It could be," he says. "A chink in the Iron Curtain. But they briefed me because they don't know how the Soviets are going to take it. If they're going to go along, or put it down like they did in Hungary and East Germany. Rumor has it Beria's called some leadership conference for this weekend."

Instant angst. "No shit." Thoughts of the contingency plan. Will we be dropping bombs or taking pictures? Do they need more pictures? I don't even know.

Bob goes on, oblivious to my secret worry. "So if we get taskings for random places in Eastern Europe, that's why. Potential staging areas. They want to see if the Soviets are massing troops."

The timer dings and we open our pouches. It's been a long day for both of us. Back to the cameras tomorrow. Slaving away: what a stupid thing to say.

"Look, Bob, I...uhh..." I'm in charge but I feel weak, speechless. "I feel like I said something dumb, earlier. I was thinking of...I dunno. Roman galleys, slaves behind the oars. Spartacus or something."

"Spartacus." He throws it back out there flatly.

"I mean, I didn't mean it as any kind of..."

"I will say, it's not the worst I've heard. Not by a long shot."

Something in his tone makes me feel something less than relief. "It was a dumb thing to say."

"Well I know the difference between 'dumb' and 'malicious.' The career I've had, you learn to tell the difference."

For all the time we've spent together—simulating spacewalks, or practicing on the photography console, or enduring survival training in Panama or Alaska—this is the first I've heard him acknowledge things have been different for him. "I haven't heard you talk about that stuff."

"I don't want that to be all people see, when they think of me." A long pause. "I mean, don't get me wrong. I'm proud of who I am, I'm proud of where I've come from. But I want people to see the rank and the uniform." He scoops a spoonful of food, stops again to talk. "I mean, that's the point of the uniform, right? To make everybody the same. With rank as the only distinction. And we pretend it's really true, we pretend everyone at a given rank is really interchangeable, even though that's the first thing you realize when you get in the service, what a fiction that is." He brings the spoonful up to his mouth, but there's more in there. "Maybe that's asking a lot. Trying to be the same. I mean, you see someone from a distance, that's the first thing you notice. Skin color. Before you notice anything else, whether they're a man or a woman, old or young, that's the first thing you see. I don't want it to be all people see, though."

"Have people treated you differently?"

He gives me a look like I really am clueless. "I can't think of too many people that *haven't*. And that's not to say everyone's calling me 'nigger' to my face. Some are at least...trying to prove they're giving me a chance. 'We're all wearing blue in here,' or words to that effect. And a chance, that's all I need. But you do feel like the standard's higher. Full afterburner, 105% of rated power, all the time. You know some people have that preconception that you're a little bit lazier, a little more stupid, prone to...drink or drugs or running around on your woman. So you feel like you have to work a little harder than the next guy, be a little sharper, just to prove you're not there on accident, just to prove you're not some Yankee politician's integration selection, some choice foisted on them by Old Man MacArthur to make sure all his kids are playing nice with each other. Stone cold sober with a perfect family life, just to be treated the same as somebody else. Because people do pay attention, they do notice..."

I nod, taking it in.

He goes on: "They do notice. Eventually. It depends on the area of accomplishment, but they do notice. You kick their ass on the basketball court, it's no big deal. To be expected. You join ROTC, out-soldier everybody else, join the Air Force and outfly them, it's more like, 'Huh.' You turn in a dissertation on *The Mechanism Of The Tritium Beta Ray Induced Exchange Reaction Of Deuterium With Methane and Ethane in the Gas Phase* and get your Ph.D. in Physical Chemistry, and finally they're impressed. Then you get a different vibe from some people. Like you're the exception that proves the rule. 'Why can't they all be like him?' As if every white person was...earning PhDs. As if there weren't white beggars, white hoodlums, white...idiots."

I nod and ponder.

"Anyway, enough of that." He turns back to his food, and we finish in silence. I can't tell if the ice is re-forming.

•••

My scope sweeps the blue Atlantic; we're south of Iceland, getting close to the sea lanes between the U.S. and Great Britain. "And...there we go. I've got a wake, west to east, maybe five o'clock."

"Got it," Bob calls coolly. "There we go. Looks like…freighter, maybe."

"Sounds good." More sweeps, more targets, and no indication from Bob that any of this is remotely challenging. I remember my angst on the scope, the torment of thinking I'd be a failure at this. If Bob feels that, I haven't seen it.

Soon the targets are thinning out. I feel the need to fill the void. "It was a different vibe, doing this over the Pacific. We caught a carrier battle group."

"Really."

"Yeah, near Hawaii." I scan and reset, scan and reset, across miles of empty blue, remembering warmer conversations. "It was amazing. Really easy to think about what we could've accomplished by being up here in the last war."

"Not so much over the Atlantic, though."

"Well…we could have spotted convoys, but those were ours. Obviously the main threat then was under the sea. U-boat wolfpacks. Which I guess we could have seen when they were surfaced."

"But not when it mattered."

"We could've helped at some point. Kept the Titanic from hitting the iceberg, maybe. But yeah, over the Pacific, it really brought it home why we're up here. Trying to prevent a nuclear Pearl Harbor."

"Prevent one, or plan one?"

I lift my head from the scope, and he's already off his. Looking straight through me. Does he know about the contingency plan? Am I authorized to tell him? "H...how do you mean?"

"Well, assuming they do put the bombardment module up here, it seems like that'll be the operational use, right? Have it on hand for some...decapitation strike."

"I...don't know. Haven't given it that much thought."

"Well it's been on my mind. Ever since I saw Macleay and Neubeck come out of that briefing room. The look in their eyes..." He shakes his head.

"Yeah, I bet." Glance at the scope: a flash of green, the eastern nose of Brazil. No need to get back to it yet.

"I know it's one of those 'decisions beyond your pay grade' things we all grow accustomed to. Except there'd have to be a decision up here. I mean, they wouldn't put it up here and control it from the ground..."

"Probably not. Although you could."

"You think?"

"Sure. I mean, if you wanted to get really clever, you could automate it entirely. Do a dead man's switch." My mind expands into all the dark corners of possibility. "No manned platform at all. Just a satellite with nukes on it, and a transmitter in Washington that's on the air 24/7. Just a steady encrypted signal. And program a computer on the orbiting platform so that if it ever passes over the Eastern seaboard and that transmitter's off the air, it'd assume they'd attacked us. And it'd nuke Moscow."

"Well that's a little...morbid."

I shrug. "Ehhh...It'd be sort of like...an insurance policy."

"Death insurance." A skeptical smirk. "I can think of a couple ways that could go wrong."

"I'm not saying it's a great idea." I smile a little. Dark humor, although I don't want to use that phrase.

"I guarantee you some RAND think-tank type is lying on the beach in Santa Monica right now, getting paid a lot more than us to come up with ideas like that." Bob smiles a little, the first time I've seen his teeth since my stupid remark. "With that kind of mind, you could be a professional paranoid."

"Why stay amateur, right?" I chuckle, breathe a bit. Nuclear war: just what we needed to break the ice. "I'll tell you, up here alone with Hank, we had lots of time to imagine worst-case scenarios. Especially when we spotted that satellite. And still...I mean, we have no idea about the Reds. What their intentions are. But you do have to assume the worst."

"I disagree." His tone grows cold again: "When you assume the worst of anyone, it gets very very easy to do the worst to them."

I see his face again, the color of his skin, stories of lynchings down south; I think on the MacArthur years: 12 years of incremental integration and desegregation, trying to keep the rabble rousers at bay, all those Negro preachers and famous figures, Martin Luther King Jr. and Paul Robeson and such. The public communists, and the possible sympathizers. "The Soviets are not the good guys, Bob."

"If I thought they were, I wouldn't be wearing this uniform. I just want to make sure I can stay proud of it. If we did fire the opening shots in a nuclear war, the number of civilians..." A weightless shudder. "We'd put the SS to shame."

"Well, I trust our leadership to be...responsible. Plan for the worst, hope for the best, expect the realistic. I'm assuming they'd do a missile silo arrangement up here. Two keys at opposite ends of the module that you'd have to turn simultaneously." I reach into my pocket, feel the two-headed dollar. Regret: I'd meant to flip it before we got on the scope, meant to pass along the tradition. "So it wouldn't be on you."

"I disagree. It'd be completely on you. If you alone could stop it, by not turning your key..."

"Are you saying you'd refuse?"

"I'm just saying if you transmit every order, you're not really making a decision."

"Are you saying you'd refuse, though?"

"I'm saying I don't know what I'd do. And you don't either. It is a conundrum, though. If you do everything that's asked, they may as well replace you with an automated platform. But if you don't transmit every order, you're an unreliable part. There's no decision there, either, because you'll get replaced by someone more...uniform."

"My understanding of the silo arrangement is you both look at whatever comes over the teletype. Compare the codes to what's in your binder. You have sixty seconds to decide whether it's a legitimate launch order. Then you both go to your opposite corners and turn your keys. Or not. So that's the only decision: Is it a valid order? So, verifying, and providing a safety layer."

"A safety layer." He scrunches his face. "Have you ever heard the phrase 'foleyadoo'?"

"Foley a what who?"

"Folie á deux." My ears now resolve the words properly, as French; he pronounces them with the casual aplomb and perfect accent of a native Parisian. Which, again, shouldn't surprise me. "*Folie á deux*, the madness of two. When two people, possibly in isolation of some sort, get caught up in a shared psychotic delusion. Or any other mutual craziness. Like…what was that movie last year? *Bonnie and Clyde*. I mean, a two-key system's better than a dead man's switch. But still…"

"Folie á deux." I think on Hank, our late-night red-light conversations, spinning through scenarios, thoughts rattling off one another, echoing off the metal walls with nothing to stop them. Would that count? "Well there's a madness to all of this, right? I mean, obviously, Mutual Assured Destruction…"

Bob gives me a look like: no shit. "There's a sanity, too. I mean, the best insurance policy is if both sides know they can't start anything, because it'd be bad enough for both that it wouldn't be worth doing."

"Well, if they do put a bombardment module up here, it'll just be that. Another insurance policy." I think again of the contingency plan, wonder if I'm telling the truth.

"You know…" He nods back towards the scope. "The main threat today is under the sea, too."

"How do you mean?"

"It's easy to think about your counterparts on the Red team who are in the same branch of service, more or less. All the people in the silos. Strategic Rocket Forces, or whatever. It's easy to think of them and say, 'OK, all we need to do is find every ICBM field.' Which we can do from up here. And those guys are easy to kill. But the hard targets are the ballistic missile submarines. Hidden in the depths, every one with a dozen missiles trained on cities, ready to kill millions of Americans with the turn of two keys." He looks up at me and, again, through me. "If you don't get all of them, every one of those subs, you might as well not try. And we can't spot them from up here."

• • •

End of the day, arcing down towards LA, watching western mountains roll by, lonely and dry.

On comes the radio. "Watchman, this is Vandenberg. We have a friend that wants to talk to you. Over."

I press my bookmark deep in *The Guns of August* so it won't float out; I push myself over to the radio and press TRANSMIT. "Vandenberg, Watchman." My voice brightens. "I hope it's who I think it is. Over."

"Watchman, Vandenberg." A familiar Southern drawl replaces the other voice. "Can't believe I'm using this stupid call sign now. Over."

I grin. "It'll be my turn soon enough. How was the ride down? Over."

"The ride was fine. The tough thing's trying to walk afterwards. Tell you what, when you pilot a space plane down to a landing in the high desert, you feel cooler than Yeager. But when you stand up and feel so woozy you have to sit back down…not so much. Over."

"Well it looked impressive from up here." And it was a success, after all, from a medical standpoint: we've proven that a man can be weightless for over a month and still fly himself home. We can stick to the expanded schedule. "How's life on planet Earth? Over."

"Busy, Watchman. Lots of debriefings. But I talked to the…uhh…local chain of command. And we did schedule a time for our local MARS Network affiliate to be on the air this Saturday. Over."

My mind shifts gears. "Uhh, roger, Vandenberg."

"We may even invite some people you know to observe. Over."

I catch his drift. Then a guilty feeling as I look up at the bathroom and see Bob emerging: no mention of his family. Still, I can't pretend I'm not looking forward to this. "That sounds good, Vandenberg. That sounds real good. Over."

"Watchman, that's it for now. I am turning the mike over to the duty officer. Over."

"Vandenberg, thank you much. Over."

Behind me I hear the soft clatter of the teletype.

"Watchman, we also received an encrypted message for you. We are pushing it up through the printer right now. That should be it for this pass. Vandenberg out."

"Thank you, Vandenberg. Watchman out."

I float over to the teletype, buoyed by a sense of pleasant anticipation. But the message deflates me.

BEGIN TRANSMISSION

BEGIN OPERATIONS ORDER FALCON 1 EYES ONLY

NEED VISUAL RECON THIS WEEKEND OF CONTINGENCY TARGETS IN MOSCOW AND GAGRA STOP

TRANSMIT CONFIRMATION OF TARGET PRESENCE VIA TELETYPE FRIDAY EVENING STOP

END OPERATIONS ORDER

END TRANSMISSION

I read the slender printout over and over again.

My mind won't settle. I drift to the window, gaze down at the empty blue Pacific. Encrypted…so possibly neither Hank nor the duty officer knew the contents of the message. Bob glances over, but I can't talk about this, not yet.

Who can I talk to? One name comes to mind.

I turn back to my book. The Battle of Tannenberg: unfamiliar to me. Wireless was so new back then that the Russians were transmitting orders in the clear as they marched westward into Germany. And the Germans were intercepting everything, translating everything; they used this knowledge of the enemy's movements to rapidly move their own forces by rail, and encircle and smash the Russian Second Army. A massive military defeat, based entirely on signals intelligence: not exactly comforting, given the conversation I want to have tomorrow.

•••

Our workday begins impossibly early, slicing down across the eastern Soviet Union. Time to fill another canister.

We work together well, Bob and I; cloud cover is bad for a bit, but we capture a silo site and a couple airfields, and anyway I do enjoy the spotter role even more, the wider field of view, the bigger picture.

"How long before you think they're doing this to us?" Bob asks after the second pass.

"Who?"

"The Reds."

"They already are, with the Zenits." I remember our orbiting stranger: easy to forget about, now that he's out-of-plane and so much else is going on.

"With a manned platform, I mean."

"Tough to say. It's a costly program. And they don't need as big of a reconnaissance budget as we do."

"You don't think?"

"We're an open society. They can just…buy a few newspapers. Tune in to Walter Cronkite."

"They can't read about *us*." Meaning the platform. Our names are known, but little else: when our launches hit the papers, there are a couple brief paragraphs, barely any information.

"Well obviously we have some secrets. But not like them. I mean, for some intellectuals I think it's fun to think of them as just a mirror image of us. A reversed copy on the other side of the globe. It's night and day, though. I mean, hell, that's why we're here. They have launch facilities, nuclear sites, that aren't even on the map..."

"The Manhattan Project sites weren't on the map. Oak Ridge, Hanford, Los Alamos..."

"Lot of good it did us." I'm feeling cranky, Hank-y: all the revelations from the trials of the Truman years, all that bad press that swept MacArthur and Nixon into power in '52. And the executions: the Rosenbergs, Greenglass, Fuchs, Oppenheimer. Democrats: the party of treason. "Bad enough that we poured all that money into a bomb that wasn't ready in time for the end of the war. But the fact that all that research went right out the door...I mean, Beria stole it all! They had a bomb of their own in no time, because of the man who's in the Kremlin now! Just like what they did with the Tu-4."

"That was their B-29 equivalent, right?"

"More than equivalent! They completely reverse-engineered the aircraft!" My agitation surprises me. "The Soviets had three production B-29s in custody by the end of the war. From aircrews that had made emergency landings in...Vladivostok or whatever. And they'd had no real luck developing anything comparable. So they held on to those planes! All the help we were giving them, ostensibly our allies, and they held on to those planes. And the next thing you know, they're...flying B-29 clones over Red Square during the May Day parade. And we're scrambling. Trying to figure out what to do if they send a fleet of them on a one-way mission to destroy Los Angeles, Seattle, Chicago..."

"Maybe they were scared. They saw what we did to Tokyo, all those other cities. Maybe that was their way of saying 'What you did to them, we can do to you.'"

"They're not the same as us. We have an economic system that works. It made us rich enough to rebuild the world..."

"The world we helped destroy."

"We didn't start that war! And still, we were generous when it finished. We could rebuild Europe. All the Soviets could do was steal from it. The two systems are totally different. Night and day. Dark and light."

A moment's delay. Then: "I don't think you're going to convince me darkness is a bad thing."

Again I look at his skin. Think about where his sympathies lie. But he's up here with me, for a few more weeks at least. I force a chuckle. "No, I guess not."

•••

I float through the quiet module, seeing vague shapes in the dim red light.

In the spindle I fumble towards my ship. Pull my weightless body into the cockpit, power up the radio.

"Whiskey-Six-Echo-Zulu-Victor, this is Kilo-Seven-Tango-Romeo-Victor. Over."

Nothing. Will he be listening? I crouch in darkness, looking up to the tunnel, waiting to see the shadow shape of Bob watching me. During training, we were out at night and some instructor said: crack a smile so we can see you. Which is offensive, apparently.

"Whiskey-Six-Echo-Zulu-Victor, this is Kilo-Seven-Tango-Romeo-Victor. Over."

"Kilo-Seven-Tango-Romeo-Victor, this is Whiskey-Six-Echo-Zulu-Victor. Read you loud and clear." The voice: clipped and precise, unmistakable. "We sent instructions. Did you have questions? Over."

"Uhh, Whiskey-Six-Echo-Zulu-Victor. We can get new pictures. But we can't drop them off until Tuesday. Over."

"Kilo-Seven-Tango, we need to know on Friday. Over."

A stab of fear: the contingency plan. They're actually going to do it. "We'll have to...reschedule the delivery then. Over."

"No time for that, Kilo-Seven-Tango. You can develop the film yourself. All we need is a yes or no. Over."

"Whiskey-Six-Echo..." What would he say if I just dropped the transmission? Claimed some technical fault? "With all due respect, sir, this is...somewhat irregular. Over."

"Kilo-Seven-Tango!" A sharp disciplined burst of anger. "I need you to take pictures. And tell me what you see. So we can have options. That might save lives. Please confirm. Over."

A tight breath. "Whiskey-Six-Echo, that's affirmative. Over."

"Kilo-Seven-Tango, I'll expect a full report via teletype on Friday. Over and out."

After everything's shut down, I drift back to the main room. But I can't shut down everything. All this news burns within me, a coal mine fire trying to reach the surface, unstoppable. I think about waking Bob up; this is a lot to bear alone.

Possibilities spin: my mind's consumed. Friday night in Washington, early Saturday morning on the Black Sea. Will everything else be in place? A B-70 flying its racetrack pattern over the eastern Med, weapons in its belly, waiting for that fateful transmission so it can go winging through the darkness towards that foreign shore. A sneak attack on the unsuspecting Reds, a nuclear Pearl Harbor…

But like Hank said, man's never invented a weapon we haven't eventually used in anger. So maybe war is inevitable at some point. If so, is it right to wait for it? Or is this a once-in-a-lifetime opportunity to stop it before it starts? The range of outcomes is unfathomable. Millions of dead. Or: a quick bright end to our problems.

•••

"You ever spend any time on the radio up here?" Bob asks the next day.

We've finished a Soviet pass and I'm strangely wakeful, wired still despite a near-complete lack of sleep. Skimming over the Yellow Sea, aware enough to be wary of the question. "On the radio?"

"Yeah. I mean...apart from the normal check-ins?"

I can't tell him. As much as I want to, I can't. "Why do you ask?"

"Well, I mean, it just occurred to me we could probably pick up some stations here and there."

"Stations?"

"Yeah. Just normal radio. AM, FM, whatever."

My weary mind recalculates, recombinates. "We wouldn't have much time to listen. I mean, the longest possible acquisition time is...what? Nine minutes?"

"Nine minutes isn't bad. Catch a song or two. News. Who knows? Kind of a radio roulette. Feel a little connection to this world we're observing."

"Right now?" Below us: the innumerable islands of the Philippines, rough emeralds set haphazardly in the silvery sea. "We have to check in with Pine Gap in a couple minutes."

"It doesn't take that long to change frequencies."

"All right, what the hell."

We turn the radio on, wander through the static, stumble upon a low measured voice speaking: Tagalog? I know there are other languages down there, too many to learn, too many for us to identify, even.

"Huh." Bob looks intrigued.

"I can't even tell what they're talking about." In my pocket I feel the silver dollar, the non-binary decision augmentator. I should have brought that out when he asked about the radio. Kept the tradition alive, pretended he had a choice in the matter.

"News? Sounds like news."

Somehow looking at the world feels different now: seeing and hearing. "It's funny. Hank and I talked about how we can basically...come down anywhere on the globe. He spun these...fun easy fantasies about landing on some Pacific island. Maidens in grass skirts and all that. But the language barrier alone...I mean, who's to say anyone would welcome you?"

"It is interesting." Bob's eyes are lost in a dreamy gaze out the window. "We did all that survival training. Coming down in the jungle, coming down in the desert, coming down on the polar ice cap. But nothing about coming down in some...random village on an island you've never heard of."

"Chances are you'd end up like that Rockefeller kid. The governor's son. Eaten by cannibals somewhere."

"Lack of technology doesn't make you a savage," Bob says. "Given the tools we've developed...you could argue the opposite."

I turn the radio back to our operational frequency. But routine is boring. We endure the usual: a perfunctory check-in with Australia, and the long comms blackout over the empty dark void of Antarctica.

And then we are on an ascending node, coming up on South America in the dead of night: Buenos Aires spreading away from the coast, a massive electric stain, brightest where it meets the black ocean. Or, no: half a leaf, with veins of light. Intriguing. "You know what? Let's try the radio again."

"Sounds like a plan." Bob's already next to the knobs; in seconds he's scanning the FM spectrum, and soon we hear a stadium roar, an excited announcer jabbering in Spanish.

"Soccer game." I look at my watch, do the math. "Late night."

"*Futbol,*" he says.

I follow his gaze back out the window, down at the city a hundred miles below; somewhere in that patchwork of streetlights is a stadium. What would it be like, being down there? Anonymous in the thrilling crowd, the green field spread out under the klieg lights. Another scene I'll never see, but there's some connection in listening, and knowing it's in sight. We stay tuned until LOS.

"You didn't bring any tapes with you?" I ask at last.

"Tapes?"

"Music. You wanted to hear the radio, I figured you forgot to bring your own."

"Oh. No, I brought my five."

"Blues?"

He laughs. "Just because a black man's from Chicago, doesn't mean he loves the blues."

"Well, I didn't think..." Was that a racial thing, what I said? I didn't think it was a racial thing.

"I mean, I like it, but...I'll take jazz over blues any day."

"Really?"

"Yeah. Monk. Coltrane. Ahmed Jamal. I'll listen to the blues here and there. But jazz feels like a more...original form. Something new. America's greatest musical contribution to the world. I mean, I love classical, too...I brought Beethoven's *Moonlight Sonata* as one of my five. And when I listen to Coltrane, it feels like we've done something every bit as good as that. We have something that'll stick around for a few hundred years."

It occurs to me that "we" could mean Negroes, or Americans. But I don't ask.

"As for blues...there's a Chuck Berry line I always think about. 'How many times have you heard this song: If I had what he had, my blues would be gone.' And that always sums it up for me. There's a lotta great blues, but sometimes it all feels like...worry and sadness and heartache. People whining about what they don't have."

"You don't ever feel that way?"

"Oh, I definitely get is. When I was in flight training, I was at Malden. Back in the Delta, practically, not too far from where my father had left to find a better life. You risk your life training to protect everyone, and then you take off your uniform and go off base and you can't even buy a cup of coffee...for sure, I had the blues. Then later on, they decided to make me a flight instructor. And I was a great instructor, but I think they didn't want a black man telling Southerners what to do, so they sent me to Germany, training pilots for the *Luftwaffe*. And those guys were great, but...you realize their dads probably spent the war...invading Poland, or rounding up Jews, or something. I had the blues then, too."

"I bet."

"But...I grew out of the blues, in some ways. I think it was something I listened to mostly to spite my folks..."

"You don't strike me as the rebellious type."

He chuckles. "That was about the limit of it. My mom's pretty religious, and blues is the devil's music, to her. She'd always quote Mahalia Jackson: 'When you sing the blues and you're done, you've still got the blues. Blues songs are songs of despair. Gospel songs are songs of hope.'"

Flashes of Catholic school: marble statues in plaster alcoves. The Stations of the Cross. Jesus whipped, weakened, falling, broken. "I never thought of crucifixion as a hopeful message."

Bob smiles a little. "Me neither. To me it's jazz that's hopeful. Out on the town on a Friday night, going to see a hot quintet in some hole-in-the-wall club, and outside it's just rained, and you see the city neon reflected in the puddles..." His gaze goes distant, nostalgic. "I used to play piano, you know."

I had not, in fact, known that. "Piano?"

"Yeah. Parents had a piano. They spent good money for it, so they made me practice, so the money wasn't wasted. And I actually started to really like it. I got good, as a teenager. Thought about pursuing it, as a career. But my parents...good Lord. They didn't want me growing up to play music in some club. My dad's a teacher. 'Make something of yourself,' that's what he always said. The way my parents figured it, every musician ends up an...alcoholic reefer addict. Anyway, I went away to college and...next thing you know, I hadn't played in months. And, I mean...I made it up here, so I guess I can't complain. Still..." He gazes longingly out the window at the darkened planet.

We turn on the radio, call down to the Cape as liberated Cuba rolls by. Bay of Pigs, invaded: the closest thing we've had to a war since Tokyo was smoldering. A pacified hemisphere at least, thanks to MacArthur—except for the riots in our own cities.

Northward we fly, parallel to sleepy Florida, crossing the coast over the Carolinas. Westward the darkened Republic stretches, dreaming about deposing more tyrants. Downward Bob gazes at the blotchy patches of streetlights, imagining, perhaps, the city scenes, his face strangely serene, mind empty of the heavy things I know.

•••

It occurs to me, of course, that everything could go horribly wrong.

I remember Bob's words about Soviet submarines, nukes trained at cities; I imagine rockets of light stabbing upward from the sea, arcing through the dark while my family sleeps. (We still haven't made the move to Vandenberg, although that's coming soon. Would they be safer now if we'd moved already? Impossible to know.) The western Anti-Ballistic Missile sites are just becoming operational, so perhaps: more rockets angling off into the high stratosphere. Nuclear flashes in the distance, ours obliterating theirs. Still...would any sane person want to depend on something like that? No. It only takes one to get through. So: better to get everyone out the city. But how? If I wait to talk to them on Saturday, it may be too late.

After several minutes of mental debate, I type up a message, push it down through the teletype over Grand Forks:

BEGIN TRANSMISSION

BEGIN PERSONAL MESSAGE FALCON 1 HOUSEHOLD

WE TALKED ABOUT A FAMILY VACATION STOP

YOU GUYS SHOULDNT WAIT FOR ME STOP

YOU SHOULD GO CAMPING WITH UNCLE HANK THIS WEEKEND STOP

TELL HIM IT IS A CONTINGENCY TO PLAN ON STOP

END PERSONAL MESSAGE

END TRANSMISSION

●●●

The planet rolls merrily by beneath us, oblivious. Every orbit brings our ground track a thousand miles west. Closer to Moscow. Closer to Gagra.

When I plot out the ground track I realize we can't get good pictures of both on the same pass. If we catch Moscow from above, we'll be well west of Gagra. We can slew the cameras, of course, and take oblique pictures, which is what Hank had done when he'd had his turn on the console. But it makes for lower resolution in the photographs.

The more I think about it, the more it bothers me. We can do better. And it does feel vitally important. Especially if they are at Gagra.

We need to adjust our orbit. Nudge it upwards, just slightly, and we'll be able to get Gagra on the previous rev. I've done some back-of-the-envelope calcs, and the orbital mechanics should work. The human factor, on the other hand…

"We need to do a little stationkeeping with the cold gas thrusters," I tell Bob, high above the Indian Ocean, two orbits before our target.

"Stationkeeping?"

"Yeah. You know, nudge the orbit up a bit, keep from burning up."

"That's…" He rolls the sentence around in his head; I can tell it doesn't sit right. "We didn't get any instructions."

"They were going to have us do it tomorrow. I'm just moving it forward a day."

He gives me a look I don't like. "Thule already gave us our target list. Isn't that going to throw us off?"

He's right. But I can't tell him that. Why won't he just listen? "Commander's discretion."

Dutifully he takes up station next to me and reads off the checklist while I prepare.

Then, at last: the command. Our thrusters pulse gently. Not as substantial as a Centaur burn, just a little nudge upwards: what goes up must not come down, not quite yet. Based on my Kentucky windage calculations, the slight boost should bring our primary target within a couple dozen miles of the ground track. Which will make for much better pictures. Assuming that's what we want.

We arc back around through the darkness, the black void of Antarctica at night with no Southern Lights, the emptiness of the dark Pacific. Mexico, then America, south to north.

"Watchman, Cheyenne," the radio comes on. "Comm check. Over."

"Cheyenne, Watchman. Read you five by five. Over."

"Watchman, our AOS was a little late. Over."

"Cheyenne, we went ahead and moved up our stationkeeping. Over."

"That's...highly irregular, Watchman."

"There were a couple maintenance tasks I wanted to get to tomorrow. The motor on the scrubbers sounded odd. Over."

"Well that's...news to us. Anything else we should know about, Watchman?"

"Not at this time, Cheyenne. Over and out."

"The scrubbers sound...pretty normal," Bob says. "Don't they? Am I missing something?"

"It was last night. You were asleep. It might be nothing. I just want to be extra careful." A guilty memory of something Mom told me: You can never tell just one lie. Because you have to say another to cover for it. And another. And another.

Then it is the last ascending node before the fateful pass, and we are heading northward through Pacific night, arcing towards the southern coast of Alaska. "I'm going to run some test shots on this pass," I tell Bob.

"Test shots?"

"We need to do a darkroom refresher. In case you need to recalibrate the cameras after my departure."

"Shouldn't we do that over the U.S.? Western Europe, maybe?"

"It's something we have to do. Might as well do it now."

I can tell he can tell I'm being less than honest. He doesn't say anything. How did Hank do it to me? Did he lie? Or just withhold the truth? Try as I might, I can't quite recall.

Bob's first film canister is still half-done, all that long perfect celluloid wound beautifully through the intricate machine. Taking test shots requires us to go to darkroom mode, swivel the camera head into neutral position, pressurize the mechanism, open it, release the rollers, and wind enough film into the canister that we can swap it out for a test cartridge. It's quite a bit of work, and I realize in the middle of it that we may not get it done in time. We're racing against the clock, slashing down across the Soviet Union, passing multiple regular targets so I can have a crack at the one from my secret instructions.

The rollers take longer than expected. My pulse pounds as I release the last one, wind the film, and ease the large container out of the way. To Bob I almost shout: "You got the test cartridge?"

"We've got all of Africa this rev," Bob points out, as if to say: What's the rush?

"Commander's discretion!" I snap. "Let's get it done already."

We are scrambling now, rushing to thread the film and swivel the delicate metal rollers back into place, all that expensive and finely machined equipment; I feel like I'm manhandling it, but at last everything's in and the inner cover is closed and locked and I don't even take time to close the cabinet, just pivot upwards to the console, to press my face to the scope and see if we've missed Gagra, and...

Clouds.

Miles and miles of clouds.

There is an odd feeling, conflicting waves of emotions crashing at odd angles, surges and lulls. Maybe it's a good thing. Maybe this is God's way of keeping it from happening.

I remember the telegram I sent my family. Did they understand? Are they packing the car? What will they think if nothing happens? Better to plan for the worst and have nothing happen, than to not plan at all.

"This...uhhh...should be breaking up soon," Bob says. "Like I said, we've got all of Africa, if you want to get test shots..." And it's true: we'll be sweeping down from the corner of Egypt down over Sudan and Zaire and Rhodesia and South Africa: the whole continent, from the Red Sea to the Cape of Good Hope.

"Nothing worth seeing there." It comes out cold but I don't care.

He glares.

The silver dollar's in my pocket; I could have played this with far more finesse. "Commander's discretion."

Bob turns to the film bay, as if to swap the film back out. There are, after all, priority targets in Eastern Europe.

I remember Moscow, the Kuntsevo dacha. We need pictures of that, too. "Leave it. We'll swap it back out tomorrow."

•••

We do get some bad oblique pictures of the Moscow target area. Develop them: nothing definitive. Dutifully I push the report down via the teletype. Still there is still the damnable curiosity: how will they take it? How will he react? So: back to the X-20. Friday, night for us, end of the workday for Washington.

"Whiskey-Six-Echo-Zulu-Victor, this is Kilo-Seven-Tango-Romeo-Victor. Over." I'm afraid of what he's going to say.

"Kilo-Seven-Tango-Romeo-Victor, this is Whiskey-Six-Echo-Zulu-Victor. We received your report. I suspected you'd call again. What seems to be the issue? Over."

"Whiskey-Six-Echo, we had weather visibility issues. Over."

"Kilo-Seven-Tango. Understood. You'll have another chance tomorrow, correct?"

A heavy exhale. "Uhh, roger, Whiskey-Six-Echo."

"Report back then. Via radio. Over and out."

• • •

In the morning we get up in slow motion, tend to breakfast and morning ablutions, make our standard check-ins with our ground stations.

Except they're not standard. I had known somewhere deep down that it was not quite over. The test cartridge is still in the machine, so we can't go back to our normal routine. Which of course means more lies.

"Thule, Watchman. We needed to do some maintenance work on the console. We will…a…not be able to make any progress on the target list today. Over."

"Watchman, Thule…ahh…did you discuss this with Cheyenne? Over."

"We'll fill them in later, Thule. Over and out."

But without the normal workday routine it is even more painfully obvious that all is not well, that some level of trust has been broken. There is no way to avoid the silence.

At last it's too much. "Look, Bob…"

He turns towards me, eyes heavy, looking like he knows we have to have a Talk.

"I didn't handle that as well as I should have, yesterday."

He waits a few moments. "It would help," he says with an excess of deliberateness, "if I knew what you're trying to handle."

"We have to do the darkroom refresher. I probably didn't pick the best time to do it, but…"

"You're not a very good liar, you know." Again he waits. Uncomfortable seconds that drag and drag. "But I can tell you don't like to do it. And knowing what I know about you and following orders, I can only assume you know something I don't know."

I almost talk.

He goes on: "If this is some…commander's-eyes-only need-to-know basis thing, it's your right to tell me as much or as little as you want. Or nothing. I am not up here to cause trouble. I know how to read a chain-of-command chart, I know how to read a flight roster. And I want to keep flying as much as the next guy." His eyes are relentless. "But whatever it is that needs to get done, it'll probably get done a lot easier if I'm not getting in the way. So it's probably wise to let me know…something. Just…tell me what needs to happen."

I take a deep breath. "We need pictures of a resort town called Gagra on the Black Sea coast. We need them on the test roll so we can develop and interpret them up here."

"All right." He smiles, a smile I feel I don't deserve. "That wasn't so hard, was it?"

•••

I float about, mind still distant. We wind our way around the globe, south to north and north to south. It turns beneath us, pulling us towards our dark assignment.

In the meantime we have a workday to kill.

"Any plans for the day?" Bob asks "Since we can't work on the normal target list?"

"Do you want to get a look at the scrubbers?"

Beneath the mask of professionalism: a very slight glimpse of bemused skepticism. "Is there actually a problem with them?"

"Well...this way when we check back in, we can honestly say we took a look and didn't see anything wrong."

"You really don't like to lie, do you?" We float over to the scrubber and he starts unlatching the cover panel. "I mean, I'm not complaining, but..."

"My parents raised me to be honest. Catholic school. 'I am the way, the truth and the light' and all that. The surest way to get them mad was to get caught in a lie."

"'...the way, the truth and the life.'" Bob eases the cover panel up and into the empty airspace above our heads; it floats gently. "Not 'light.'"

"Well...you get the idea. And four years at the academy after that. When you were supposed to sign in at 12:00, and the clock said 12:01, you had to put 12:01 in the log book, even if it was gonna get you in trouble. I mean, I was the type of guy who was always back by 10:00, but still..." A glimpse at the humming machinery, the pumps which give the breath of life. "We should have powered it down. Let me get the checklist."

"Is it worth taking it offline for this?" Meaning, I suspect, a task that isn't strictly necessary right now.

"Should be fine." I float past the window, see Siberia far below; I prefer to pretend this is a normal workday. Blue binder: station stuff. Environmental Control System Maintenance Checklist. Circuit breakers to be pulled, which I do, in proper sequence. "I guess what I'm saying is: you internalize it there. How important it is to have high standards. Ideals. Something to measure yourself against."

"Lord knows, I know all about high standards." Bob shakes his head. "When you live with perfection as the standard, though, the thing you realize is...everybody falls short, sooner or later. People are flawed."

The machinery goes silent. "Not everybody cares, though."

"True. But still. People are flawed. The world is flawed."

"We had a lot of traditions to establish, back at school." I study the equipment, ease the latches off the filter. "First year, first class. When it was time to name our yearbook, we chose 'Polaris.' The sun and the moon, they go up and down. Every star arcs across the sky. Only one is fixed in place. Steady and reliable. Yes, the world is flawed. But if you aim at something that isn't..."

"It is good to have an ideal," Bob concedes. "Even if you can't ever reach it."

We vacuum out the filters, reassemble the machine. There are a few hiccups when we power it back up, and each one makes me question my judgment, my unnecessary decision to turn it off. Soon, though, it is back to normal.

Then: lunch. Over Brazil we play radio roulette and hear music, thick fat horns, all mood and no words. We talk about other things, and all the while Gagra draws closer. We running out of ways to avoid doing the terrible thing that must be done.

Before the final pass I retrieve the proper map from the binder. A map: a representation. Projecting a round world onto a flat piece of paper gets distortion. Still, we are working to get everything on the map. Studying the world from outside the world. Before all this started, there were targets in the Soviet Union we couldn't place within 30 miles. And by the time it's done, we'll have it all down to six decimal points of latitude and longitude. We want the maps to be reliable, perfect for targeting; we want ourselves to be reliable.

I review the approach with Bob, show him where the ground track will cross the coast. I do this with plenty of time to spare.

Down below everything scrolls by in its usual sequence: Arctic ice, summer tundra, the Urals. Flecks of clouds. As we go south they get fewer and farther between before disappearing entirely. I have the terrible knowledge that this is actually going to happen.

And on the approach: perfection. Smooth easy sweeps of the spotting scope over the approach terrain: the vast empty steppes the Nazis crossed on their way to Stalingrad, the ragged summer Caucasus still flecked with glacier ice, the lush green mountainside sloping down to the fatal shore. Clicks of the shutter. I know before we even develop the film that we'll see the line of cars.

I think of the plan. I remember classes at the academy, learning about the H-bomb. Aerial shots of coral atolls with miles-wide nuclear craters blasted out of them: Will this coastline look like that tomorrow?

I think, too, of my family, hoping they understood the message.

•••

A blur of activity: developer centrifuges and stop baths, strips of film on the slender light table. Then, the magnifier. Confirmation. The image looks familiar somehow, like a memory, like something I've always seen.

Bob and I talk a bit at dinner, but my mind is elsewhere. I can't help thinking that the less he knows, the better. Can he tell as he gets ready for sleep that I'm incapable of it?

I pretend to be Hank and park myself in the spindle; I spend hours gliding over the world like Superman flying backwards, watching the past recede before my eyes.

At last I am on the radio. "Whiskey-Six-Echo-Zulu-Victor, this is Kilo-Seven-Tango-Romeo-Victor. Over." Will he respond?

Of course he will. "Kilo-Seven-Tango-Romeo-Victor, this is Whiskey-Six-Echo-Zulu-Victor. Go ahead. Over."

A heavy breath: this cannot be undone. "We have positive visual confirmation at the southern target. I repeat, we have positive visual confirmation at the southern target. Over."

"Kilo-Seven-Tango, I copy positive visual confirmation. Thank you for your service. Over and out."

A study in economy: the bare minimum of information, words that would mean little to anyone listening. And yet, and yet, and yet...

I rustle up the tape recorder, listen to Dvořák as the world rolls by, oblivious to my observations, for now. Two full revs between DC and LA, two full trips around the world, the daylit United States and the nighttime Soviet Union, the enemy we're trying to catch asleep. Will I see it from up here? Will we be in the right place at the right time to see any of it? Underneath the fear lies a dark anticipation, a damnable curiosity.

I have done my duty. Have I done the right thing? I don't know what else I could have done, what anyone else would have done. Should I have told Bob? Probably. Is it too late? Possibly.

I am waiting to call down to LA. Hoping I talk to them, hoping I get no answer, hoping contradictory and impossible things. The message I sent: Was it enough to get them to leave town? Possibly not. They might be waiting to talk to me, see what it's all about.

In fact, I can see it now, the scene down at Hank's: the kids' distorted reflections in the convex TV, Judy pulling a glistening roast from the oven, Hank checking his watch and then turning on a radio console, and the sudden burst of static annoying everyone. Maybe they will listen if I tell them, in no uncertain terms, what's going on—an actual emergency, time to evacuate, this is not a drill, etc. But who else monitors the MARS Network? And what will they do— what can they do, besides alert local authorities? And what will that cost—if I call down, a prophet of disaster; if I cause some *War of the Worlds*-type local panic, and nothing happens—what will it cost? Will it cost me my career? Maybe they are listening. Maybe it will be worth it.

Coming south over the daylit Rockies, it is time. "Kilo-Eight-Kilo-Oscar-Romeo, this is Kilo-Seven-Tango-Romeo-Victor, over."

I wait. I cannot stand the wait.

Again: "Kilo-Eight-Kilo-Oscar-Romeo, this is Kilo-Seven-Tango-Romeo-Victor. Come in. Over."

Static and silence. Maybe my telegram was enough. If it worked, I will not know. I imagine them at a campsite, glistening in the desert heat. Still, I would like to know.

"Kilo-Eight-Kilo-Oscar-Romeo, this is Kilo-Seven-Tango-Romeo-Victor. Come in. Over."

Nothing. Is that a good thing? There's a hollow spot in front of my heart.

"Kilo-Eight-Kilo-Oscar-Romeo, this is Kilo-Seven-Tango-Romeo-Victor. Come in. Over."

Again I imagine a campsite, a fire in the high desert, the kids complaining about sunburns, my wife cursing my name, Hank reassuring her without giving specifics. Maybe they will soon see flashes on the horizon, below the ragged line of mountains: a sudden and horrible understanding.

But: nothing.

I keep calling until LOS. And after, for an extra minute, just to be sure. Then I leave the spindle, float back to the main chamber. I know sleep will be impossible, but I should try anyway.

One last glance into the work module. There is a short stub of paper drifting up from the teletype.

BEGIN TRANSMISSION

BEGIN PERSONAL MESSAGE FALCON 2

KIDS ARE SICK STOP DINNER PLANS CANCELLED STOP RESCHEDULED FOR NEXT SATURDAY STOP

END PERSONAL MESSAGE

END TRANSMISSION

They haven't left town. None of my visions have come true.

The hollow spot grows larger, big enough to swallow me. On the other side of the globe will be the Horn of Africa, the Eastern Med, Turkey, the Black Sea: all now trying to sleep through the night. Will I be close enough to see a flash of light? From training I recall the two sets of extra dark goggles we have stowed away: emergency eye protection. I wonder if I will need mine.

I float back to the spindle as the station plunges south over the face of the waters, heading for darkness.

●●●

In the morning I am not sure if anything has happened. Surely they would have woken us up for war, right?

Not that I needed a wake-up call—what sleep I got was beyond fitful. No tossing and turning up here, of course, just a constant effort to be still, to will the mind into submission. Scattered fragments of oblivion. Nothing more.

Now at last I have surrendered to consciousness. I drag myself into and out of the bathroom, float wearily over to the window, pull open the cover, stare blankly down at the world below. Everything looks normal: pristine ocean scenery, no sign of anything amiss.

On comes the radio, the first check-in after the long Sunday sleep window. "Watchman, this is Kadena. Come in, over."

Bob is heating up pouches of bacon but floats over to take the call. "Kadena, Watchman. How are you this fine morning? Over."

"Beautiful, Watchman. Peaceful Sunday on Okinawa. Hope all's well up there. Over."

"Roger, Kadena. Late start to breakfast. All systems running normally. Looking forward to a relaxing day. Over."

"Watchman, we...ahhh...heard you had a relaxing day yesterday, too. Over." Something snide in his tone.

"Kadena, we...uhh...did have some unscheduled activities that required our attention. But things should be back to normal this week. Over." Bob looks to me, as if for confirmation.

"Sounds good, Watchman. Over and out."

Bob hands me my bacon pouch. "I know I'm not the one making decisions here. But things are back to normal, right?"

"Believe it or not, I'm not the one making decisions, either."
All the craziness, the bizarre late-night comms sessions, the
photograph I thought would be fateful: it all feels like a fever
dream. "But...normal. Yes, it does appear to be that way."

I dig into my pouch. Take a tired forkful of bacon cubes. Eat
in silence.

We relax into our day of rest. But soon: a crackle from the
radio. A summons from our earthly masters. "Watchman,
Thule. Come in, over."

"Thule, Watchman. Go ahead. Over."

"Watchman, be advised Cheyenne is requesting secure
comms on your next pass. Over."

Odd for a Sunday. "Thule, copy secure comms with
Cheyenne. Over."

Again around the globe, and at last the oddness of a
lunchtime pass over sleeping America: darkness at noon.
"Watchman, Cheyenne, calling secure, over."

"Cheyenne, Watchman. Go ahead, over."

"Watchman, be advised, there will be an above-ground
nuclear test at Eniwetok Atoll this week. Over."

"Cheyenne, Watchman. You said nuclear test? Over."

"Watchman, that's affirmative. They've been thinking about
it for a while. Given current events it was decided to go ahead
this Tuesday. We would like to have you observe it. Over."

Bob and I trade perplexed looks. "Cheyenne, Watchman. That's...interesting news. We...uhh, have an EVA scheduled, too. Over."

"This will be first thing in the day, Watchman. Might have to set your alarm clocks. We'll have details later. Over."

"All right, Cheyenne. Keep us posted. Over."

"Will do, Watchman. We'll let you get back to your Sunday. Cheyenne out."

Glances of concern from Bob. "That's...the first above-ground test since MacArthur."

"Yes, I suppose it is." A nuclear test: a gentle reminder to our enemies. We can destroy you.

•••

On Monday we are back on the cameras. The world spread out before us, all the kingdoms of the world. Jesus and the devil viewing all of it from on high: all this can be yours. Surely that's the first step in making people do what you want: observing.

But there is no peace in it. Not when your life and security depend on it. So: less "observation" and more "anxious vigilance." The news about the nuke test, the density of the Monday morning list, the sheer number of new priority targets in Eastern Europe...whatever brief relief I felt on Sunday morning, it is clear that things are building again. Gagra was a spike, a peak. Or: not a peak, a high ridge. A looming wall of stone reaching up into low clouds—high enough we didn't know if we could clear it, and we couldn't see beyond it. Rough rock reaching up towards the bare metal belly of the aircraft. And now, having juuuuust baaaaaarely avoided that fate, the weather on the other side is at least clear. But we don't see the hoped-for fruited plain, only more jagged high terrain.

Still, as uncomfortable as it is, sharp-eyed anxious vigilance still beats the sheer terror of blindness, or the dull worry of dim vision. For the past month, the Mushroom Factory has been telling stories based on the vague outlines of things we could barely see. Rumors of war: troop movements in Eastern Europe.

Long story short, they believe action is imminent. They're eager for clear pictures.

So we work briskly, filling up the bucket, making up for the lost days pursuing the contingency targets. I'm eager to atone; on one of the comms passes, I float the idea of rescheduling Bob's spacewalk, giving us an extra day to work, to fill a perfect bucket. But Cheyenne says no. They want pictures for Nixon NOW. We are, after all, still just an eye in the sky, steered by the whims of our earthbound rulers.

•••

And Tuesday. The big day.

We wake up early, retrieve the blast goggles from the storage locker, watch our watches as the station streaks southward over the morning Pacific.

"Quite an event," Bob says. "First test in years."

"First atmospheric test," I point out. "They've been doing underground shots in Nevada this whole time."

"You think Nixon's trying to send a message?"

"That would seem to be the case." A glance at my watch.

"Surprised they're not worried about EMP. Having us within line-of-sight…"

"I'm sure they did their homework." Either way, we're keeping the optics covered up. Another time check. "All right. Five minutes. Goggles in hand?"

"Goggles in hand."

We wait. Touch everything we need, one last time: goggles, camera, notepad.

"Two minutes," Bob says.

"All right. Goggles on."

We wait, blind for now. And then: bright sunburst circle, colored green by our eyewear.

"…three…four…five…six…" (It grows and fades.) "…seven…eight… nine…and goggles off."

Below now, a billowing roiling cloud. It is not huge from our altitude—just an odd strange formation, like a puff of smoke jetting up from the blue ocean, a man-made multicolored volcano, interesting and harmless. A small deformity, cause for concern but not alarm, like a skin tab behind your ear. Bob casually snaps pictures with the Hasselblad.

Only when I move my head from the window do I realize the station lights are out, and everything is going silent. Pump sounds gone, gyroscopes whirring down.

"Did that..." I start.

"Wow, that did take us down, didn't it? Good old EMP."

We float over to the panel to figure out how we're going to get it all running again. Everything dimly lit by the blue backscatter of the ocean below.

Working in the semi-darkness, it takes a couple minutes to locate the appropriate systems binder, bring it over by the window, and leaf through the pages to the ones that discuss the fuel cell system. There are restart procedures, but they assume that we are running the cells in standby mode while the station is on battery power. No one ever envisioned starting the fuel cell system cold.

Push in three breakers. Can it restart?

Blessed relief as the systems come back online. An experiment with unintended results: we take copious notes.

●●●

"Oh, wow, what a tremendous view! Man, I feel like...Superman out here." Bob's excited voice in the headset summons a strange mix of emotions: jealousy because he's out there now and I'm not, nostalgia for my own first trip into the void, anticipation of the next one.

But above all that: tiredness. It's been a long day. Within a rev of the blast, everything was back to normal. Another day taking pictures of the Soviet Union, of Eastern Europe—

whatever it is we're trying to deter, whatever future catastrophe the Reds have cooking. And now, unlike Bob, I don't have the adrenalin to keep me excited.

"Neat, huh?" Through the window I glance at the fog-shrouded Arctic. "Imagine it on a clear day."

"I bet. All right, time to get down to business." After that first burst of excitement, he's every bit as professional as any of the rest of us. Did I expect otherwise? I've trained alongside him long enough to know better.

"Sounds good." I follow along as he works his way to the bay of his X-20, retrieves the first bucket, transfers it to the carrier rail. Amidst all that, a routine check-in with Thule. All things I've done before.

Outside, the world slides by: Arctic clouds give way to Hudson Bay. A Gospel verse pops into my head: in my Father's house there are many dwelling places. Meaning: different places to live on Earth? Different planets in the universe? We roll on down towards America.

Again the radio interrupts. "Watchman, Cheyenne, calling secure. We'll take an EVA status. Over."

"Cheyenne, Watchman. First bucket in position. No major issues. Over." Bob sounds like he's done it all before.

A memory from Hank's walk, the Red satellite encounter. "Cheyenne, any sight of our orbiting companion? Over."

"Watchman, sounds like you miss the guy. Over."

"Cheyenne, I know he's out of plane...just like to know where. Over."

"Watchman, funny you should mention that. Looks like he'll get within fifty miles this rev. Over."

"Cheyenne, I heard the tapes from last time," Bob says. "They made it sound like Hank almost bumped his head on the thing. Over."

"It wasn't that bad!" I interrupt. Next to the radio I can see the new Hasselblad, the one Bob brought up. "Cheyenne, did you ever crunch the numbers for a rendezvous on my departure date? Over."

"Watchman-1, Cheyenne. We tried to make it work. But we can't do a plane maneuver and bring you down safely. Every scenario puts us way over budget on the transtage fuel. Over."

"Roger, Cheyenne." I try to reply as mater-of-factly as possible. Still it's a disappointment. I think of the nuclear test, the target list. It feels like we are in passive mode, that we are allowing things to happen to us. Depressing.

On we go: green America fading into Mexican brown, swept away in turn by Pacific blue. Bob works efficiently, hits all the timeline checkpoints. I find myself nodding off here and there. And at last we are settling in for the night pass. "Should be quite a show," I tell him, hoping it's true. I've seen it all before.

"Wow. That sunset's something, at least," Bob says.

"Yeah, quite a sight." Darkness hits like a hood thrown over our heads. Then below: ribbons and sheets of lights, yellow and purple and green.

"That aurora. Wow."

I drift down to the window. "That's…one of the better ones I've seen, actually." I look at the Hasselblad again, resist the urge to pull it out. Nobody who's not here will ever see it as well as we can, no matter how many pictures we take. Best not to ruin the experience.

"Nobody ever told me there were this many stars!"

"That's what we get for being city kids."

"Geez, that is quite a sight."

"Yep."

Soon that blip of excitement, which is really just the dim reflection of Bob's, fades again; we are off into the boring night part of orbital flight. Time for a bathroom break…

I'm just getting down to business when Bob calls it out. "I am…uhh…seeing a bright object. Something off to starboard."

"Whaddaya got?"

"I do believe that's a reentry."

"No shit." I throw my underwear back on: no shit. Back in the living room I press my cheek against the glass, look over as far as I can: no luck.

He continues: "Looks like two major objects…one falling behind a bit, burning brighter. Pretty fiery for both, just these long fire trails with bright white spots at the front. Man, that is something."

"That's gotta be the Zenit." I don't know why this hadn't occurred to me: their mission was always going to be over before mine. No buckets for them: the working assumption is it's all in there, cameras and film and everything all coming down at once. A crude design, inefficient and inelegant, like everything they do. But apparently it works. "Reentry module and equipment module. Same as the Vostok and the Voshkod."

"Yeah, that's what they briefed us on." A gentle reminder: we've been in all the same rooms. "Surprised they're bringing it down at night."

"Might still be daytime, up around Plesetsk."

"Yeah, maybe...wow, that is really something!"

I remember a similar image burned into my retinas, fading now: Hank's flaming descent. I can only imagine how much better it is to see one in darkness. So: another pang of jealousy...

But another thought: maybe they'll launch a new one.

•••

Breakfast Wednesday. Pancake cubes in gelatin. Floating and talking. After yesterday's long workday, the plan is for an abbreviated schedule at last, a temporary respite from the late-day Eastern Europe targets.

"Man, that EVA was something." Bob's eyes are distant: the waking dreams of memory.

"It's neat. Being out there."

"Is it just me," Bob smiles, "or did you fall asleep on me?"

"I may have conked out once or twice."

"I was worried I was gonna have to knock on the hatch," he chuckles. "Wake you up to let me back in."

"It was a long day."

"I'm not accusing you!"

"It is always a downer. When you've lived something like that yourself, and then you're…observing from the other side of the looking glass." A sip of coffee. "Same thing goes for the rendezvous. When you're inside and passive, it isn't quite the same."

"I'd imagine not."

"It's funny, when I was a kid, I'd lie in bed at night. I'd see my dad sticking his head through the door to check up on me. Then it stopped happening, and I forgot about it. For decades. Then I *had* kids, and one night I was sticking *my* head in the bedroom door, and I got a little flashback, like, 'I'm on the other side of the looking glass now.' But it felt…flatter, somehow."

"It's flatter because you know more," Bob says. "You've seen the other side."

"You think?

"Sure. When you're a kid, it's all a…big scary mystery. Everything outside your room. I mean, you've seen it all by day. The hallway, your parents' room. But you know there's other things going on at night, and you don't know what they are. Bumps and noises. Maybe you've walked in on your folks...rolling around in bed or whatever..."

"That happened to me once." A stab of embarrassment. "My dad just yelled: 'GET OUT!'"

"Exactly. You saw something, but you didn't know what it was. Then maybe later, you find out the facts of life, but it's all still hearsay. Then you grow up, and it happens, and it's exciting! Hopefully. Eventually it's no longer a mystery, it's just your normal life. And next thing you know, *you* have kids, and it's *you* looking in from the hallway. Observing. Or keeping secrets...in the bedroom with your wife, trying to remember to lock the door so the kids don't barge in."

I shake my head, shudder at the unpleasant memories of close calls. "I guess that's what it means to be in your thirties. You've been in all the rooms."

"Well, I'd hope so." A chuckle.

"I mean, beyond all the...mommy and daddy stuff. Like, look at us. Top-secret program, highly classified briefings, and now we're up here. We've experienced...about all it's possible for a human being to experience. And you know what? It gets...boring, after a while."

"Maybe. We've made it from the kids' room to the master bedroom, at least. But there's still rooms we haven't been to yet."

"Such as?"

"Old age. Death. The surface of the Moon. Everything else out there, all those places we've never been to." He nods towards the spindle window, the vastness of space. "Or just the other side of the globe, even."

After some quick housekeeping, we float over to the cameras. I'm looking forward to something like a normal workday, by space standards: just the usual routine, daytime photography of Soviet ICBM sites. Another thing we've done already. Nothing's left that's new, other than the trip home.

Then, on the dark side of the planet: "Watchman, Cheyenne. Come in, over."

"Cheyenne, Watchman. Pretty normal workday up here. Decent weather on the other side of the globe. Making steady progress on the target list. Over."

"Watchman, hate to break it to you, but it's not a normal workday. The Red Army is rolling into Czechoslovakia. Over."

"Cheyenne, you said…Czechoslovakia? Over."

"Watchman, that's affirmative. Some kind of crackdown. Tanks in the streets. Over."

"Cheyenne, that's…" I shake my head. *Disappointing* seems too mild. "For what it's worth, we should have good imagery in yesterday's bucket. Over." I feel so impotent, saying this. The tyrants of the world are clamping down, and we're snapping pictures.

"Watchman, I'm sure they're interpreting it now. In the meantime we'd like some more today. Over."

A reluctant sigh: anxious heart, tired eyes. But I know better than to protest. "Understood, Cheyenne."

"We're pushing up an amended target list now. Over and out."

I drift over to the printer to retrieve our new orders. Look on our new work with despair.

"I guess we shouldn't be surprised," Bob observes behind me. "They can't afford to keep the clamps on Berlin and let the Czechs open up to the West. That'd be a pretty long chink in the Iron Curtain."

"You say that like it's understandable, what they're doing." My blood rises as I float. "I've got family in some of those countries." I am imagining distant relatives trying to leave and failing, making the journey to the Czech frontier too late, being turned away by Red soldiers with machine guns, or maybe slipping into the forest to search for a secluded spot along the frontier, a place to breach the barbed wire— making their bid to escape, and getting cut down in a hail of bullets. Or, worse: thrown into prison camps, new gulags, the only way tyrants can hold power in the end. "Every time something like this happens…East Germany, Hungary…it always ends in a bloodbath. And we never do anything about it."

"We're in a better position to observe than we've ever been. If it does get violent, we'll get some great pictures."

"If they're willing to declassify them." Therein lies the rub: if we had perfect visual proof of the Soviets cleaning up after some…massacre in central Prague, would we publish the pictures? Let the world know? No. Four-inch resolution: the hallowed secret, never to be revealed. What good is it seeing everything if you can't tell anyone what you saw? If you can't stop anyone from getting hurt? An eye in the sky: useless.

A thought back to the contingency plan: whatever Beria's up to, we could have stopped it.

•••

Night finds me on the radio, alone in the darkened X-20. "Whiskey-Six-Echo-Zulu-Victor, this is Kilo-Seven-Tango-Romeo-Victor. Come in. Over."

Nothing. I want to do something.

"Whiskey-Six-Echo-Zulu-Victor, this is Kilo-Seven-Tango-Romeo-Victor. Come in. Over."

Nothing.

"Whiskey-Six-Echo-Zulu-Victor, this is Kilo-Seven-Tango-Romeo-Victor. Come in. Over."

I want to do something. But: nothing.

•••

The next morning: more nothing.

"Thule, this is Watchman. Ready to start the day. Over."

(In garbled static, I hear something like our call signs, and a word that sounds like "incident.")

"Thule, Watchman. You are loud but not clear. Repeat your last. Over."

(The static improves.) "Watchman, Thule. We…" (Something something.) "…incident. Over."

"Thule, Watchman. Transmission still not clear. We copy an...incident of some sort. Over."

"Watchman, how do you read now? Over."

"Thule, we read you loud and clear. We copy an incident of some sort. What can you tell us? Over."

"Watchman, ahh..." (Hesitation in his voice, that worry about whether to trust the scramblers.) "...we had a Valkyrie crash twenty miles from base. In the interior. Chrome Dome flight. Possible Broken Arrow. Over."

Broken Arrow: lost nuclear weapons. Bob and I trade uneasy glances. "Thule, we copy possible Broken Arrow," Bob says. "Over."

I step on their response. "Thule, do we have a target list? Over."

"Watchman, no list this pass. This just happened thirty minutes ago. Comms with Cheyenne are tied up. Obviously a lot to sort out down here. Over."

"Thule, any word on the crew? Over." Bob's question makes me feel like an ass for not asking it myself.

"Watchman, we received a return-to-base call a few minutes after takeoff. Engine fire. They could see them losing altitude. Got a couple Maydays and they dropped off the scope. That's all we know. Over."

A Chrome Dome flight. One of the airplanes on the northern route—not part of the contingency plan, I don't think...although if they had one standing by for the Moscow option...

A flash, a stab of panic...could this be that? Maybe it's happening after all. Be careful what you wish for.

I cut in: "Thule, Watchman...any other...uhhh...instructions for us at this time? Over."

"Watchman, Thule. Take whatever pictures you can and stand by. Over and out."

Soon comes LOS. Over the cloudy Arctic we prepare for our first pass; we prepare blind, unsure what we're looking for. I miss having a target list. Routine feels mundane until it's no longer possible. Then the ordinary things become as refreshing as...well, breathing. And of course, there's that nagging worry: things are happening thousands of miles away, big heavy things we'll only find out about after the fact. What if they had a war and nobody told you?

We settle in on the scopes, scan and scan. Endless circles of grey: no breaks in the clouds. Without the Thule update we're a little fuzzy on how long this pass should last, but there comes a time when we know, logically, that it must be over. We push away from the scopes.

"I guess we didn't need the target list," Bob says.

"No, I guess not." I try to sound at ease with it all, but I don't relax, really, until the next check-ins, Kwajalein and then under the globe to Ascension, repeated confirmation that there is, in fact, nothing going on.

•••

An empty circle of rock and ice. Scan and search. Scan and search.

We are on the scope again over barren southern Greenland, coming up on Thule: an ascending node, more or less, although at this latitude there isn't much higher to go.

"Thule, Watchman." Headsets on as we scan. "We have eyes on scope. Over."

"Watchman, Thule. Say again, over."

"Thule, we're on the scope. Let us know if you need pictures of the crash site. Over."

"Watchman, Thule. Uhhh, we do have a helicopter on-site. One crewmember deceased, one missing. Unsure if weapons have been recovered. Sun doesn't set until August, so we can search 24/7." The unspoken message: we may not need any help. "But a few pictures can't hurt. Over."

More ice and rock. More ice and rock. Brown and grey lowlands, and glaciers flowing slowly from the snowy peaks. Our scopes tracing the contours of the desolate earth. Without roads it is difficult to get bearings, hard to make sense of the terrain. Geography pushes the coast under our flight path as we near Thule, but even with the jagged inlets we don't entirely know where we are looking.

"Thule, Watchman. That's a…godforsaken part of the planet you've got there. Over."

"Watchman, Thule. Quite aware of that. Over."

"Thule, I mean it's hard to find landmarks. Over."

"Roger, Watchman. They took off on Runway Zero-Eight, so find us and look east. Over."

"Copy that, Th…"

I catch a glimpse of the base: its big American concrete runway and long clear taxiways, a marvel of engineering, by far the biggest man-made object this far north. A quick scan east. Possibly I see something, a black smudge on the barren earth, but it all happens too quickly to know for sure.

I let the cameras go for a minute, then shut them off.

"Who are they?" Bob steps on me this time.

"Watchman, Thule. Say again. Over."

"Thule, the crew. Do you have their names? Over."

"Oh…uhh, roger, Watchman. Deceased is D'Mario, Major Alfred D'Mario. Missing is Svitenko, Captain Leonard Svitenko. Over."

Svitenko. A flash of memory: nametag and face, back at the academy. "Thule, Watchman. Did you say Svitenko? Over."

"Uhhh, roger, Watchman. Captain Leonard G. Svitenko. Over."

"Copy, Thule. We may have gotten some shots. Over and out."

●●●

Over lunch, Bob asks: "Did you know that guy?"

"Yeah. Svitenko. He was a doolie when I was a firstie." Summoned memories: a face and a nametag. "Different squadron, but the academy was pretty small then. You couldn't help seeing everyone."

We eat in silence for a minute. Hot dog bites, warmed over cubes of potato that are meant to approximate French Fries. My thoughts scan the contours of the frozen earth. I imagine Svitenko hiking back to base, head full of hard-imparted lessons: Survival, Evasion, Resistance, Escape, with only the "S" being necessary here. Or: nursing injuries, trying to drag himself across barren Greenland to the crash site and rescue. Or: unconscious, still strapped into his escape capsule, fallen in to some shadowed crevasse, unseen from the air. Or...

"Class of '62, then?"

"Yeah. They were the first normal class. The first to go through with a full set of upperclassmen. The first that spent all four years on the actual campus." Memory cycles back: eager tours of beautiful new Space Age buildings, the best Skidmore, Owings & Merrill had to offer, quite a step up from the drafty wooden barracks at Lowry Field. "We hazed the hell out of them for it. 'You haven't earned the right to look around yet, doolie! You don't deserve all this! You never had to put up with the shit we did. You think you know what it's like to suffer?' Honestly I think we were jealous. They got all the new stuff right off the bat. We had to wait three years for it."

"Musta been quite an experience. The academy."

"It was. Especially for us, being the first. I mean, one week you're a normal high school graduate. Walking to the movie theater with your buddies so you can...drool over Marilyn Monroe in *The Seven Year Itch*. Going home to eat leftover pot roast. Next thing you're out in Colorado, and the eyes of the country are on you. Everything was different, it was like a second birthday. Walter Cronkite was there, he broadcast our dedication ceremony, and I remember thinking: That is actually Walter Cronkite. Cecil B. DeMille, he designed our drill uniforms. Little Hollywood connection. MacArthur himself spoke at our graduation. He wished us well—in all things but football. All these...mythical figures who'd been up on Mount Olympus, all of the sudden they're real people making decisions that impact your life. You see that they really exist; you've been...boosted up to that same level."

"You get very...nostalgic talking about it."

"We bitched about it all the time." I smile. "All. The. Time. It was tough. A third of my class didn't graduate." I think of summer training. Marches and calisthenics in the thin high Colorado air. Cadences: *Standing tall and looking good! Oughta be in Hollywood.* Drill and ceremony: how you have to learn basic obedience long before you can hold a weapon or fly an airplane. "But one of our instructors said, 'You want it to be tough. In your heart of hearts, you want it to be tough. So it means something. So you'll have stories to tell your kids.' It was hard for us. And we made it hard for them." I nod back in a retrograde direction, towards the past: Svitenko and the crash site, the reel of photos that may eventually help the accident board determine the cause, or that may just show a bunch of rock and ice. "We made it hard. Hopefully hard enough to survive this sort of thing..."

"You do want it to be tough."

"Well...yeah. But you also want all the suffering to mean something." I polish off the last of the hot dog bites, leave the potato abomination unfinished. A glance at the window:

sparse night lights, northern Canada, still not quite at the terminator. A little time. "I remember one of my instructors telling us about the B-17, the first B-17 that flew. I mean, now, obviously, it seems…archaic, something for the history books. But everything the B-70 is now, the B-17 was then. Absolute state-of-the-art bomber, nothing like it in the world. Just an incredible technological accomplishment. It was the plane that was going to save Boeing. And it crashed on one of the first test flights. Killed the pilot and copilot, injured everyone else. Nothing was wrong with it, though! It crashed because someone forgot to flip a switch. So after that, they started making checklists. And it became standard aviation practice. Ticking off all the boxes. Trying to be as methodical as possible. It was like everyone just decided: OK, this crash, all this suffering, it *has* to mean something."

"You feel bad for the people that had to die for that lesson to stick."

"Of course you do! But you hope in the end it saves lives. Maybe down the line some airliner full of people *didn't* crash, because someone used a checklist. That's how it goes, though. You always remember the painful lessons."

Bob smiles, an uneasy grimace. "It's weird, though. This profession. You also know the crashes are going to keep happening. Every funeral you attend, you push those thoughts away. You hope to God the guy in there just…messed up. Because otherwise it's all about numbers catching up to you. And that's the dark heart, the silent center of those thoughts. That fear: that could have been me. That could *be* me, next time. You push those thoughts away, because otherwise you couldn't function. But the suffering means something because it could happen to *you*."

"Sounds kind of...narcissistic, when you put it that way."

"It is. In a way. And Lord knows I'm not immune. I see pictures of a young Negro kid...beaten to death for whistling at a white woman, I see his...mutilated body staring out of an open casket, I'm going to think about it more than you. I see pictures of some guy...lynched in Oklahoma, and his body lit on fire, with a crowd of people all around, I'm going to know it could have been me. And you..." (A bitter chuckle.) "...well I won't insult you by saying you'd have been in the crowd. But you wouldn't have been hanging from the noose."

"No, I guess not." I shake my head, affirmation through negation.

"Same goes for war. We remember Pearl Harbor. But the Russians lived through a much worse sneak attack. And I guarantee you it's on their mind, every time they look up us." Bob plucks the empty floating food containers from the air and nods towards the front, posigrade, the next pass over the Soviet Union, the pictures we'll take that the analysts will use to provide target lists for the triad, the unholy trinity: Minuteman silos and Polaris submarines and B-70s, the fleet of beautiful white aircraft, numbers now diminished by one.

•••

We find out the next day that Svitenko's gone, too. Ejection malfunction, some failure of the escape capsule parachute. And the weapons from the bomber: still unrecovered. There's a feeble attempt on Thule's part to steer the conversation elsewhere, to cheer us up with petty complaints about the shortness of their summer, and how the absence of cruelty gets mistaken for kindness, and how a fifty-degree-day in Greenland gets everyone breaking out the Bermuda shorts.

Still I keep thinking of the search party finding Svitenko. A morbid scene on the lifeless landscape. If I close my eyes I can remember his face. Sobering stuff: it puts me in a funk for the rest of the day.

But we go on about our business: documenting the Soviet clampdown in Eastern Europe, one pass at a time. Cheyenne sends up news stories to go with the pictures: official communiques from members of the Communist Party of Czechoslovakia requesting "fraternal assistance" from the Soviet Union, armored spearheads rolling towards Prague, protests in the streets, deaths. (I find myself remembering the news from Berlin, at the end of the crisis: when they built a concrete wall and called it an "anti-fascist protective barrier" and started shooting at anyone trying to leave.) We are powerless to stop all of this suffering.

My mood only picks up late in the day, when the teletype starts clattering:

BEGIN TRANSMISSION

BEGIN PERSONAL MESSAGE FALCON 2

WE MISS YOU DAD STOP

HAVENT HEARD FROM YOU ALL WEEK STOP

LOOKING FORWARD TO A MESSAGE STOP

LOVE YOUR FAMILY STOP

PS GOING TO SEE UNCLE HANK FOR DINNER TOMORROW STOP

HE SAID TO TELL YOU WE ARE GOING TO LEARN ABOUT THE MARS NETWORK STOP

END PERSONAL MESSAGE

END TRANSMISSION

A pang of guilt: I've been minding the other side of the planet and ignoring my family. And they don't seem to mind. They just want to hear from me.

My heart warms a little. But then, more guilt: A chat with my family? Whatever Hank said, I can't believe anyone in our chain of command is OK with that.

•••

"Kilo-Eight-Kilo-Oscar-Romeo, this is Kilo-Seven-Tango-Romeo-Victor. Come in. Over."

A pleasant scene from the X-20 cockpit: western mountains scrolling by, not a cloud in the sky, only the smallest patches of snow visible on the northern side of the highest peaks. The warmth of anticipation.

Again: "Kilo-Eight-Kilo-Oscar-Romeo, this is Kilo-Seven-Tango-Romeo-Victor. Come in. Over." I know they're going to respond.

And they do. Each phonetic letter comes through twice, a soft adult prod followed by a loud kid repetition, like a backwards echo. "Kilo...KILO...Seven...SEVEN...Tango...

TANGO...Romeo...ROMEO...Victor...VICTOR." My son's hesitant voice, with Hank feeding him lines. "We hear you loud and clear," followed by "WE HEAR YOU LOUD AND CLEAR." And another muffled cue: "We are a MARS Network station standing by for your updates," followed by the same sentence again.

My smile feels like it's going to split my face. "Kilo-Eight-Kilo, I am...glad you're participating in our civil defense initiatives. Over."

"THANK YOU," my son says. And Hank, now: "Kilo-Seven-Tango, the...uhhh...other operators at this station want to know how you're feeling about them, too. Over."

"Kilo-Eight-Kilo, I miss them! Over."

A muttered drawled "See, I told you he missed you!" to my daughter. It breaks my heart. Then Hank again: "Kilo-Seven-Tango, that's more like it. Over."

"All right, Kilo-Eight-Kilo...ahh...is my wife there? Over."

"Kilo-Seven-Tango, I respect your priorities. Here you go..." Followed by a familiar feminine "Wow, I didn't think this was actually going to happen. It is really good to hear your voice, honey. You're not going to get in trouble for this?" Hank's muffled "Over," followed by her "Over."

I'm not happy that she mentioned trouble; if anyone happens to wander across this conversation, they might figure out it's not two normal earthbound stations. "Kilo-Eight-Kilo, there's been...uhhh...support for this at high levels. Over." It occurs to me yet again that I'm taking Hank's word for it, that this is OK.

"Kilo-Seven-Tango, we were…uhhh…confused about your message last week. About the camping trip." Another Hank-prompted "Over."

"Kilo-Eight-Kilo, did you…ahh…talk to Hank about it?" A piercing angst: I used his name on the air. Surely we're going to get in trouble for that. Embarrassment, shame: I want to bang my face on the console. At last I remember: "Over."

"Kilo-Seven-Tango, I did not." (Even with the radio distance, I hear sternness in her voice.) "Even if the kids…" (Crackle.) "…sick, I was not in a big hurry to take them camping in Southern California in late July! So I made a command decision not to…" (Static.) "…up. You know how hot it is down here? It's fire season! Over."

Visions of atomic fireballs. What can I tell her? "Kilo-Eight-Kilo, I need you to trust me. There were good reasons for those instructions. Over."

"Well, like we discussed, we'll take them camping when you get back down. Over."

Back down. An exasperated head shake: I am alone in my frustration. "Can you put Ha…can you put him back on? Over."

"Is that all you've got to say to me? Over."

"We've only got a few minutes, honey. Over."

"Very well. I'm glad we got to talk." Then, Hank: "Kilo-Seven-Tango, how may I help you? Over."

"Kilo-Eight-Kilo...uhhh...our friend wanted some...uhhh...weekend work last week. On a contingency basis. Over."

"Rrrroger, Kilo-Seven-Tango." Slow drawn thoughts: a smeared response. "Is there a question? Over."

"Kilo-Eight-Kilo, I...uhh...tried to get word down to the MARS Network..." (Another stab of panic: now I said 'down.') "...in case you wanted to...uhh...take precautions. Over."

"Roger, Kilo-Seven-Tango. It...uhhh...certainly sounds worth ...uhh...trying to get word out about something like that. Over."

"Kilo-Eight-Kilo...is that it? Over."

"Kilo-Seven-Tango...uhh...not sure what else to say on this channel. We'll talk at a later date. Let me...uhh...put the little ones back on. Over."

"Roger Kilo-Eight-Kilo."

"Kilo-Seven-Tango." Singsong now: my son and my daughter. "It's good to hear you, Daddy." Hank's "Over" and then "Over."

"Uhhh...Kilo-Eight-Kilo, are you being good for mommy? Over." Now the Pacific below: Los Angeles crawling backwards as we fly towards LOS.

"Kilo-Seven-Tango..." The voices track together, barely, for the call sign, then fall apart into "Yes, Daddy!" and "We are!" and another prompted "Over."

"Kilo-Eight-Kilo, we are keeping an eye on you. Every night."
A white lie. "Keeping you guys safe." Another one, maybe,
when you think about the contingency plan. "Looking
forward to telling you all about it." Still another, kind of.
"And...uhhh...looking forward to going home." At last, the
truth. "Over."

But instead of a proper response I get garbled static, the
angst of not knowing. LOS. I repeat my benign lies one more
pointless time. Troubled thoughts: Am I keeping them safe?
We're certainly not stopping the Soviets from doing
anything, being up here.

I float for a minute, bobbing up and down in the silent
cockpit; I turn off the lights; I scan the empty ocean as if I'll
find an answer.

•••

"Aaand...coming up on the terminator." It's my second EVA
day at last; outside, I ride the station's bright metal hide into
the dark of the Antarctic night.

"Excellent. Great work out there." Bob's voice in my ears:
calming and reassuring. His belief makes me believe. "Enjoy
the view."

Below I'm getting my own Southern Light show, but there's a
melancholy air to it: this is the last exciting thing until
departure day. And then: What? Fear I will not get back up
here, fear that this will be the biggest thing I ever experience
in life. A few minutes of quasi-covert communications with
my family: it casts a long shadow in my mind. Whatever Hank
said, I can't quite believe our chain of command would be OK

with what seems to me like a massive breach of operational security. I haven't told Bob it's even a possibility; I wonder if I'm doing him a favor.

I try to enjoy the show. Who knows if I'll see it again?

"Actually, let me add to your enjoyment." Bob's voice in the headset. And then: music, the *Moonlight Sonata*. An amazing experience, a great gift, twinkling piano accompanying dancing lights, an experience no human has ever had. I feel guilty now: it never occurred to me to do this for him; he must have wanted it during his rest period.

Then the lights fall behind. Miles and miles of empty night ocean. Nowhere near as dazzling, but compelling in its vastness. As we fly north I catch patches of silvered clouds gathering together. Soon, lightning flashes: bursts of light on the waters and within the clouds, and some above, bright and blinding. Then the clouds are separating again and we are passing the Horn of Africa, coming up on the Arabian Peninsula. A few glimmers could be lights of ships— freighters and tankers funneling in to the Gulf of Aden. Then: mountains of Yemen. And empty moonlit desert.

"Good to be back out there, huh?" Bob says.

"It is. Thanks for the music."

"My pleasure."

Now I look skyward, into orbital night brightness. An amazing crowd of stars and galaxies. By day on Earth the sky is boring, reduced to manageable elements: sun and sometimes pale moon, our entire sphere of existence seemingly knowable, and known. Only in darkness can we see the universe as it truly is: mysterious, infinite.

I look north, and in that vastness I find the one true thing, Polaris fixed in its place. Have I been that reliable? To whom? God, country, family, the Air Force Academy, my crewmembers, LeMay, Schriever. The idea of reliability itself. My own hopes and dreams. To thine own self be true, the saying goes, which to me always sounded a bit...well, selfish.

Below now, an empty swath of water. I think I see a single light, a ship in the night. Black planet, black freighter, Black Sea. All of it at peace. No thanks to me?

And now, up across the Soviet Union. Sad little clusters of lights creeping by, far less vibrant than anything on our side of the globe. Those walking in darkness have not yet seen a great light. Godless communism. God loves his children, but can a father love a child who ignores him? A child who tortures his fellow children? I get angry thinking about it: Berlin separated, Prague subjugated, Paris and London perpetually threatened by this...stain on the globe. I could not love the world entire. Not yet. Not until everything is the way it's supposed to be.

The source of all the darkness creeps down toward us. Moscow, ring roads surrounding it, a crudely drawn target. How much more smoothly would everything go if it were gone? If we could reach down and smite the men responsible—just the men responsible, just a dozen or so men, for the sake of the billions around the globe? Or would it need to be more, to be safe—every missile silo crew, every sailor on a missile submarine, every bomber pilot at every

Soviet airfield? Still: a few thousand. Ten thousand, perhaps, for the safety of billions. Surely that would be an acceptable ratio, no?

We are creeping up now towards the terminator: God's shadow on the world. The second reentry bucket from Bob's X-20 is on the rail. Soon we'll send it earthward, full of photographs, documentary evidence of Red tyranny. Surely with enough information our leaders can rule wisely and peacefully.

I look north now and catch a flash of light: a temporary star ahead of us, coming out of the night. Not twinkling, but bright. My pulse quickens as I realize what it must be: a new Zenit. When did they launch it? Just now, from Plesetsk, before we had a chance to photograph the launch pad?

I force my mind back to the final EVA tasks; I put myself to work as we pass into daylight over summer Scandinavia and the rugged fjords of the North Cape. We are flying out over the Norwegian Sea, getting ready to skim across Greenland and come down south again. And even before Thule comes on, I know what they are going to say: We are tracking a new object in orbit with you.

I can feel it in my bones: we will get a look at this one. I will get a look.

•••

And now it is departure day. Another week in the can. Pictures of Prague and Berlin, clear shots of everything hidden the Reds have hidden behind the Iron Curtain.

Floating with my head and arms through the hatch and my body in the spindle, I slide the bulky canister into position above the wide head of the ejection seat. In my mind I am reentering hours from now, and as we slam into the atmosphere it flies forward, and either hits me on the head, cracks one of the windows, or smashes up the instrument panel. So I double-check the latches, then triple-check. Then: a little tug as I attempt to jiggle it loose, just to make sure.

We are a day ahead of our original schedule—we moved it up to surprise the Soviets. Monday, 29 July. Did I know all along this would be the real day? Something about the 30th seemed off. So many bland calendar dates acquire meaning as you get older: 11 July, once nothing, then becomes the day you started at the academy, a second birthday of sorts. So, too, 21 June, not just the summer solstice any more, but now also my first day in space. 29 July: my last? The day of your death circles past you once a year as an empty calendar square: you stare at it unknowing, until the end.

I push myself back up into the spindle and float back into the living room. Eyes trying to see it all new, to drink it all in. Telling myself: this was so familiar you took it for granted, and now: God knows when.

"Hasselblad is loaded." Bob waits until we make eye contact and then pushes it gently through the air towards me. "You want a couple more rolls?"

"Gimme all you got."

Bob smiles. "What's that? Seven?"

"I'm gonna go full Japanese tourist on this thing. Besides, I'm taking the only camera."

"For now."

"I'll make sure you get another one!"

"Fullerton's gonna be pissed. He's gonna have film in every pocket of his flight suit."

This calls to mind the change of command ceremony, the two-headed dollar in my pocket. I never used it with Bob, never had cause to pretend I needed to pull rank on him, so it does feel odd passing on the tradition. But I should. I should.

"We need to...ahhh..." (A quick last-minute test of internal pressures. The needles on my mental gauges are uncomfortably high, given the hours I am about to spend in the tiny X-20 cockpit. I could just using the fecal containment garment later. Still, the thought of piloting the world's most advanced spaceplane through a covert rendezvous with a Red satellite, down into a fiery reentry, and finally swooping over the desert mountains and Joshua trees like a victorious falcon to make a perfect touchdown on the dry lake bed, all with a diaperful of shit: that thought does not appeal to me.) "I'm gonna hit the bathroom quick."

It's never quick, though, what with the near-total nakedness required to minimize post-defecation cleanup. Once the flight suit is off I pull myself into the toilet area and get down to business, which takes longer than expected. I catch myself anticipating another simple pleasure of home: parking myself on the throne with the Sunday paper, lord of all I survey. So many little things to look forward to: ordering Chinese takeout and cracking open fortune cookies with the kids; spending a Sunday splashing in the surf in Santa Monica, then walking along the pier at sunset and going on the Ferris Wheel at night; tooling around LA on Saturday with the radio on, enjoying the relative lack of traffic (although, to be honest, part of me even misses the traffic); all of these things are…

"I think we're getting close on time." From the other side of the curtain, Bob's voice brings me…well, not back to earth, but you get the idea.

"Right, right. Couple more minutes." I finish my business. Then: fecal containment garment, just in case, and undergarments, and then out into the living room, where my blue pressure suit floats like a headless ghost.

Bob helps me pull it back on. "We need to get started on the powerup."

"Yeah. Schedule change threw off my internal clock," I say by way of explanation. A look at the real clock: alarm. "Crap! We really do need to get a move on."

Hasselblad in hand, I pull myself back into the spindle, stopping for a brief moment to get one last look around. It is time.

In the cockpit I stow the camera beneath my feet and don the pressure suit helmet and strap on the spaceplane. Get started on the kneeboard checklist: power up the A.P.U.s, verify current is steady and within guidelines, switch from station power to internal, push the breakers to activate the hydrogen peroxide thrusters, monitor pressure in the system to ensure it is within guidelines...despite weeks in space everything is functioning smoothly.

I'm triple-checking the comms panel: we don't want to tip off the Soviets. "Comm check. Please confirm your settings."

"Internal only," Bob replies. "Safe to talk."

"OK. Powered up here. All gauges nominal. Flight mode to AERO...and we're ready for aerodynamic control test."

"Go ahead." Bob's above me in the spindle, watching my spaceplane as it stretches its wings before flight.

"All right, left and right rudder..." I pump the pedals.

"Looks good."

"And ailerons...roll right, roll left."

"You are ready to fly, my friend. Let's close the hatches."

"Sounds good." Flip the switch back. "Flight mode: SPACE."

A knock on my helmet: I crane my head up to the limits of the servos and catch a glimpse of Bob's smile over an extended hand. Awkwardly I reach up; with the shoulder belts on it's all I can do to give him a weak overhead handshake. We close the first hatch and I work the latches and verify on the panel that the lights are good. "Spacecraft hatch is sealed."

"Closing the spindle hatch."

At last I remember the two-headed dollar. Too late. So much for new traditions. "Congrats on the new command," I say, as if that's enough. I crane my head upward to gauge his reaction. Remembering Hank's departure: on the other side of the looking glass now. I can't quit get a good angle to see him now, just an edge of distorted double-glass.

"Thank you, Falcon-1. Spindle hatch is sealed."

Back to the gauges. "Cabin pressure's good. Ready to depress the interhatch."

"Interhatch depress."

"Cabin pressure steady."

"Looking good here, too."

A scan of the kneeboard, the procedures I know, but still need to read. "All right. Attitude control to standby. Ready to undock."

I wait for the jiggle, the feeling that it's truly coming to an end, my time up here.

"Hold one." Bob says.

A sigh. What now? "Holding."

And then there it is. No comms now.

Thruster-pulse the spacecraft backwards. My arrival in reverse, film of memory rolling backwards through the camera. Down below: clouds over the Arctic, one or two patches of sunlit ice.

"Thule, this is Watchman. Normal pass up here. We are getting ready for bed and…" Bob is transmitting in the clear, a script agreed to via teletype transmissions with our earthly masters. On the off chance the Reds have a trawler listening with a hotline to their control center, we want it to sound like we're lazily fumbling through our daily routine.

A fake reminder: "Watchman, this is Thule. Please set your scramblers. Over."

Bob's phony reply: "Oh! Ahhh...Thule, Watchman. Setting scramblers now. Over."

Meanwhile I am reading a printout from my kneeboard, plugging in burn times for a rendezvous. Prearranged, pushed up through the printer, no ground monitoring: if all goes well, by the time we're back over the Soviet Union it will be too late for them to maneuver away. With a pulse of the thruster I rotate onto the dorsal side, ready for the retrograde burn that will let me catch up with my fellow traveler. Back to AUTO and commit. No need for a countdown. When it is time, I settle into my seat as the engines gently push the spacecraft into my back.

It all happens perfectly, and when it's over I check the gauges: still fat on fuel, thank God. We are high over the wide cold waters of Hudson Bay, and everything is light and beautiful; I turn the spacecraft back around, nose first, to feel like I'm flying.

We are in pursuit. But up here pursuit means to wait.

The waters fall behind, far below. And now: pale patchy green of northern Ontario clinging to folds of glacier-sculpted stone. As we fly, the bright satellite is growing, in front of me and above, getting to the point where again I can see it for what it is, a false star.

Down over the Upper Midwest, vast swaths of corn and wheat, amber waves flattened by altitude. No risk of Soviet trawlers now. I glance at the clock. Right on schedule, the radio comes on. "Falcon-1, Cheyenne. Perfect so far." I detect a drawl: Hank's Alabama antagonist again? But warm in tone. With an enemy in front of us, we're all friends. "Final approach burn as follows: GMT, that's M as in Mike, of one-eight plus two-eight plus three-zero. Duration two-three seconds. Posigrade with the transtage. Zero pitch. Over."

"Cheyenne, Falcon-1. Copy burn at Golf-Mike-Tango one-eight plus two-eight plus three-zero. Posigrade transtage burn, two-three seconds. Zero pitch. Over." Perfect: Cheyenne's praise echoes in my ears. A perfect mission: is that an unreasonable goal?

Again I key the commands. Again the engine pushes the spacecraft firmly into me, a dim facsimile of afterburners kicking in.

"Cheyenne, Falcon-1. Successful burn. Over."

"Copy that, Falcon-1. Reentry will be as follows: GMT of one-nine plus four-three plus zero-zero. Retrograde burn, two minutes, twenty-three seconds. Zero pitch. Over."

I copy methodically and read back. Meanwhile the Zenit is floating above, drawing closer, visible and known: a fat metal balloon, hanging bright in the sunlight.

"All right, Falcon-1. Go get him. Cheyenne out."

"Thanks for your help. Falcon-1 out."

LOS and I'm alone again, drawing near to what we fear. Perhaps a hundred feet now. The object of our obsession: a metal sphere hammered and sickled into shape, joined to an equipment module that's shaped...like a cone, I guess, or two cones, a fat one with its point pushed into the sphere and its round base covered by another one facing the other way, flat like a Chinese peasant's hat. Antennas and thrusters and electrical conduits all over, and smaller spherical structures at the juncture of the two modules. Are those all normal? I wait for any indication it's responding to my presence, either pivoting by radio signal, or auto-arming a booby trap. But: nothing.

Down below: Mexico. Exactly according to schedule. Still the satellite slumbers: a siesta of sorts. With a flick of the wrist I close in, just a little more, then stop.

I am here.

We are here, we have done it—for it is a team effort, like all of this—but I cannot share our triumph. Not yet.

And now I am unstowing the Hasselblad, checking aperture and shutter speed, guesstimating distance, raising the camera to my eye, shooting frame after frame after frame of Kodak Ektachrome. Dimly I sense the change of scenery below, the slow Mexico scroll abruptly flashing away to featureless ocean. My world is through the viewfinder, my world is this bright crude foreign contraption, this new thing now snagged in snippets, small tidy squares of image.

The first roll finishes. Now: fly or change the film? I pulse the thrusters, translate sideways and rotate a bit, a new angle for the spooks. Come *very* close to opening the camera without rewinding the film, but catch myself just in time, sidestepping that stab of anger and embarrassment.

New roll, squares on sprockets, close and wind. More pictures, more pictures. Still the satellite floats, mute and inert.

Rewind film, rewind film, rewind film. NOW open camera to pocket the canister…except my fingers fumble and it spins up forward in weightless space, end over end and away from my clumsy hands, into the out-of-reach place between cockpit glass and dash. It ricochets just the wrong way; it stays up there, a tumbling satellite just out of reach.

Fuck.

A deep breath. First things first. Finish the photography.

A slow film reload. Snap two pictures. Translate and rotate, just a little. Raise the camera again as the terminator swoops towards us. No way to slow it down. Two more frames and darkness, a curtain on the day's proceedings.

•••

I can relax a bit, at least, now that it is night. There is a slight bit of glow on the inside of the cockpit glass, reflections from the luminescent instruments, and their dim light on my flight suit. Still if I lean forward most of it falls away and I can see the great dazzling endless universe. All the mysteries revealed again. Except for the dark void, the spot next to me that's blocked by my orbiting companion.

We fly over black Antarctica and the empty Indian Ocean. Up towards civilization, friendly Iran, and then again our dark enemy. On the other side of the planet I may have time to finish the film before the burn.

Still, the fumbled canister floats just out of reach, mocking me. Can I leave it there until we're on the ground? Possibly. But gravity will grab it during reentry. And if it falls to the cockpit floor, rolls somewhere unreachable, somewhere with a little bit of heating...then what? Flames, catastrophe.

I check the time: enough, I think. Unlock glove, undo ejection seat harness, reach, grasp, trap the canister against the top of the panel, bring it back to my pocket and...

From the corner of my eye I catch the satellite at the last second, a black mass moving in on me now, far bigger than it should be, and I don't have time to strap back in, just a quick fumble for the thrusters, but still: too late, too late, too late.

Impact.

The collision knocks my X-20 sideways, and my head and torso strike the side of the cockpit hard enough to rattle me, and outside the stars and the black blank planet are spinning now, moving mostly sideways, yaw with a little pitch and roll, and there comes a black bloom of anger in my heart, covering a thought: I have fucked this up completely.

Then, fast after: Stop the spin or strap back in? Where is the Zenit? How bad is the damage? Can I reenter?

Breathe. Don't panic. Fix the problems, one at a time.

I spy the spy satellite sweeping around and around, still far far too close: above my cockpit now, blotting out a swath of starry sky—close enough to impact again? In the darkness I can't see details; there's just enough lighting from my cockpit windows to see it's tumbling, too. A pulse of the thrusters to stabilize myself: ideally I am my spacecraft and my spacecraft is me, but not with the harness off. My body bumps around, and it all feels unnatural after the hours I've spent firmly strapped in. I have to wedge myself back into place to use the thrusters again, to get more stability and some separation, and I can tell I am burning too much fuel, getting sloppy, taking too long to do this. Then at last the stars are still and the satellite is far off, tiny and receding.

My pulse pounds. Breathing heavy. A quick scan of the cabin pressure gauges: now that the motion is nulled back out, everything looks...well, normal. Granted, it *felt* catastrophic, but maybe since I wasn't strapped in, it seemed worse than it was. I look over my shoulder as if I can see through metal. Nothing. All looks as usual.

Where did it hit? If it damaged the leading edge of the wing I could be dead if I try to reenter. Higher, on the fuselage behind the cockpit—well, I could still be dead, but it would take much more damage. What part of it hit? That could make the difference between a puncture or a dent or (God willing) nothing at all; after all, this is a spacecraft designed to slam into the atmosphere at Mach 25, to buffet and rattle and plummet through the fiery furnace. Still, I have no way of knowing. Not yet.

I make sure the film canister is firmly in my flight suit pocket—might as well chalk up a win there, whether or not it will matter in the end. (A grim image: my charred body lying sprawled next to a river in some remote stretch of the

Northwest Territories, a lump of melted plastic in my burned and shredded clothes.) Then I strap back in.

A sensible plan: radio down to Thule, get the burn info that will send me back to the station, try to fly close to the spindle window so Bob can visually inspect for damage, dock for a day, retry the reentry tomorrow if everything looks good. If not, they'll have to delay Fullerton's launch while they schedule a Gemini flight, which does bother me: the ignominy of having someone else fly up here, not for a mission of their own, but simply for my sake. An unglorified chaperoned capsule reentry, like when your parents insist on picking you up at the airport when you're a grown man with money for car fare. Only this *won't* save anyone any money—will, in fact, cost the good ol' U.S. taxpayer tens of millions of dollars, maybe a hundred million when you factor in all the costs. Long story short, I am not looking forward to the grief I'll get around the office if I go back to the station, even though it is, objectively, the only reasonable course of action.

Then I look again at the gauges. The thrusters are low on peroxide, far lower than I'd realized. Between my flying around the satellite to shoot it from multiple angles like some hyperenergetic fashion photographer—between that and my sloppy post-impact flying—I am down in the red. Enough for a retrograde burn, but not much more than that.

The decision has been made for me. One way or another, I'm coming down today.

Flying now into daytime, high above the northern Soviet Union, blotchy browns and greens getting darker where they join the rivers that flow north to the Barents Sea. The satellite is in the distance now, almost another star again, but in the sunlight I can confirm that it is in fact still tumbling. Was it simply a plane change? An evasive maneuver? A deliberate impact? What I see offers no answers.

I rotate back around, engines in place to push me backwards: to fall out of space and into the atmosphere's unloving embrace. Key in the commands: the burn will happen soon after Thule AOS. If I tell them what happened, they'll want to wait, wrap a hundred minds around the matter. But if I initiate it according to plan…

"Thule, Falcon-1. Come in, over."

"Falcon-1, Thule. We copy…" (Static swallows the words.) "…over."

"Thule, Falcon-1. Read you five by two. Over." Another reason to stick to the plan.

"Falcon-1, Thu…" Garbledy-garbledy-goo.

Pulse pounds. I watch as my finger makes its way to the console. In a second it will be too late to stop this, too late for any choice other than to ride the bird down, watch the angles and the temps, wait as the nose and the wings glow orange and then white, pray it holds together…

I push against the button, and the button pushes back for just a second. And then it is done.

•••

There are two-odd minutes of simulated gravity, deceleration that feels like acceleration, the spacecraft pushing into me and me pushing into it: one again at last.

When that stops, it feels like we are back to normal. Feels like, only.

I jettison the transtage, pulse the thrusters so I'm above, free and clear, no chance of a collision on the way in. (The gauges are low, low low low, and I know I will need the thrusters until *I'm* low.) Then: nose up, flying forward, waiting. I remember to close and lock the pressure suit visor: if we depressurize but the spacecraft maintains its integrity, I want a fighting chance. And now there's only one set of choices that will allow me to live through the next thirty minutes. (Or: I've already made the choices that have doomed me.)

Wisps of plasma whip past the windows. I am falling into the pink light. Hands on the controls, feeling now the slight buffet, watching the angle of attack and the temperature gauge, saying goodbye to this place beyond the blues, the alien islands of rock and ice, the black space above, all of it soon hidden by the bright neon colors outside.

Orange now, the glow. More hellish. With every bump and bobble my heart rate spikes and I wonder if this is it, if this is it. Maybe it is not hell but an antechamber, a negative purgatory, an awful torture of a wait, punctuated by the loud pounding of the thrusters as they fire. And yet the inferno is beautiful. Or maybe just so strange and bizarre that with all the adrenalin everything's all the more real...

I fly, and eye the gauges, and the glow fades. We are on aerodynamic controls now. Coming up is the high-speed roll-reversal portion of the flight profile, the most dangerous part. I watch the timer, and then bank right, eyes on the gauges, watching the yaw so it doesn't get too high so we won't slip and roll and rip the wings off, and now I am feeling gravity more strongly than the instruments tell me, and for a second my head gets light but I fight, and I fly, and hold the bank and sweep back left, and right and left again, and right and left again. And still the spacecraft buffets, plummets, and my heart skips with every bump. And then it is the last of the fast roll reversals, and I am leveling out, nose down now, still at Mach 10, sky darker than normal, high above barren Nevada.

The gamble has paid off.

"Edwards, Falcon-1, we are down through the worst of it. Angels 188. Over."

"Falcon-1, Edwards. Is that a royal 'we,' over?"

More chatter than I'd expect, but I'm happy enough that I don't mind. "Sorry, Edwards. Just me. Over."

"Falcon-1, chase planes orbiting at Angels 10. Over."

"Copy, Edwards. Coming up on S-turns. Over."

Carefully I bank again, watch the speed bleed away. Mach 7. Wings level and back left. Yaw a little high but OK. Mach 6. Wings level and back right. Eyes on the gauges, all the memorized angles. Mach 5. Altimeter unwinding at a steady measured rate. Mach 4. Wings level and reverse and then I relax for just a second too long and then a whip-violent tumble and crack.

A moment of black.

I open my eyes and I am slow and the sky spins fast. Sky ground sky ground sky ground sky ground sky ground sky ground sky ground sky ground sky ground sky ground sky ground.

Distant headset voice: "Falcon-1, come in, over."

"Edwards, uhh…" Hands on the controls. Fighting the spin. Between my legs I see the ejection handle, yellow and black. No chance to use it yet. Too fast, too rough.

"Falcon-1, repeat your last. Over."

"I…uhhh…" The spin is winning. I am in trouble. I need to admit it, call it out.

"Falcon-1, Edwards. Comm check. Over."

"Mayday, Mayday, Mayday. Falcon-1 spinning in all axes. Over."

The altimeter unwinds. Faster than I've ever seen. I am a tumbling triangular mass of metal. Falling from the sky.

"Hands off the controls, Falcon-1."

"Edwards, I…" The altimeter keeps spinning. Guesstimating the difference between sea level and here: I'm in trouble.

"Hands off the controls."

I take my hands off. The spin slows down. Just yaw now. Inverted flat spin. Hands back on. Rudder and stick, and I am out of it, diving, low now, low low low.

"I'm out of it now. Too low for Edwards." A silent glider now. Mind spinning through options. "I'll take a heading for Groom Lake. Over."

"Falcon-1, uhh…wait one." Then: "Too far. We'll set you up for China Lake, Runway Two-One. Turn right two-hundred and descend at discretion. Three-zero miles. Over."

Descend at discretion. No shit. My glide ratio is better than a brick, but not by much.

Ahead, a jagged ridgeline rises in my path. "Uhh, Edwards, we are not going to make China Lake. Over."

"Uhhh…copy, Falcon-1. There's a field at Stovepipe Wells. Left turn zero-one-zero. One-zero miles, Runway Zero-Five. Over."

"Copy, Edwards." Carving through the silent sky. The lack of noise is chilling. I turn.

Mountain ridges ahead. Rising. Almost higher than my cockpit.

"Edwards, we've got terrain, over."

"Copy, Falcon-1. Punch out if you have to. Chase planes on the way. Over."

I can eject. I will have to eject. So much for a perfect mission. I press myself back into the seat, prepare to pull the handles…

A thought intrudes: the film. A week's worth of pictures in the can, latched in behind me, attached to the aircraft. Plus the camera at my feet.

Below: bottom of a valley. Ahead: a narrow road. Possibly doable. I look for a straight stretch. Not quite. Drop the skids? Not yet. I raise the nose a little, too much, feel the stall buffet, can't risk that. Nose back down to build up speed, and I drop the skids, but I am low, too low to land where I want.

The ground rushes up too fast, too fast, too fast.

Slamming down and the harness feels like it's going to rip my arms and shoulders off and the skids are tearing off and I slide onto the road, skidding, skidding, skidding, bumping and scraping, high desert around, truck on the road headed toward me, rounding a curve, and my feet are pushing the rudder pedals as if it will make a difference, hands on controls through sheer force of habit, and of course the spacecraft does not obey but the truck swerves the right way and we slide back off the road half-sideways and there is a wrenching of metal as the spacecraft surrenders to the ground and tumbles, tumbles, tumbles, sky and desert, sky and desert, body hard against the harness, pressing the flesh between my bones and the straps, and a last slow tumble and is it going to stop is it going to stop is it going to stop and a long slow last tilt and it stops upside-down with me hanging from the seat and dazed and bruised and damaged and looking out the window at the earth up close and above me now I hear the turbine scream of the chase plane on a low pass and I key the mike but the power's out and I feel the desperate need to tell them I am alive.

I am alive.

Whites

Our hero—or, if you prefer, our protagonist—is spending Saturday morning at home, stripping caulk from between the master bathroom tiles in a modest Los Angeles bungalow.

It's been a week since his return from space. Debriefings have concluded and leave has been granted and bruises have started to fade; the physical symptoms of life after space have abated, and all seems to be more or less back to normal. The world was spread beneath him in all of its beauty and grandeur: intricate cloudscapes, swaths of desolate desert, bright spiderweb cities at night, the sun's reflection moving across the mottled ocean before being eclipsed by verdant tropical islands.

And now: the world is this tedious task. Ramming the scraper into the gap between the tiles until a small tail of caulk comes up, angling it just right so it can travel smoothly up the corner seam, taking a deep patient breath and pushing, cursing when the line of mildewed caulk breaks midway through, wiping sweat from his brow with his forearm to avoid the chemical burn of caulk remover, repositioning the scraper, stripping the rest in bits and pieces. Chunks of dead caulk piling up in the corner beneath him. The spectacle of earth from space: now just snippets and snapshots of fading memory.

Eyes on his back: he spies his wife in the bathroom mirror, watching from the bedroom.

"You can come in, you know," he smiles to the mirror.

"It's nice to watch you sometimes."

He peeks his head out of the doorway. The children are in the backyard, doing childish things. He moves towards her.

She steps back, scrunches her nose. "You've got caulk remover on you."

It probably occurs to him that he's planned his morning poorly. He looks down at his ungloved chemical-coated hands: a self-betrayal.

"Stuffy in there," he says. "You're sure the air's on?" Again he wipes forehead sweat with forearm.

"I'm sure it's on. Not sure it's working." More kindly: "I'll make you an iced tea."

"That'd be great."

She retreats to the kitchen, a faux forest, or perhaps a gentle jungle: wallpaper flowers of orange and yellow and brown, dark hardwood veneer on the cabinets. Also a window above the sink where she can watch the kids in the swimming pool while she does the dishes. She grabs the carafe of tea from the fridge, and two glasses from the cabinet: more yellow flowers on each. But just enough tea for one. Ice in the glass, cold tea: beads of drink sweat to match her husband's. She's just about to bring it to him when the phone rings.

It's on the far side of the kitchen, the wall nearest the bathroom, but she grabs it before the second ring. "Hello?"

"This is Bennie Schreiver." General Schreiver. "Sorry to call on the weekend. Is your husband there?"

"Yes, one moment."

He is in the doorway now, hands still unwiped; she places the phone in the crook between shoulder and ear, and he holds it there handlessly while she looks for a rag.

"Yes, sir," he says. "Yes, sir." He stares across the kitchen at the glistening glass of tea, out of range of the phone cord; he's a leashed animal.

She picks up the tea, pantomimes taking a drink, smiles like a pixie; his eyebrows furrow in frustration.

The conversation continues. "Uhhh…yes, sir, I do have a set." Then: "No, not much chance to use them yet this summer." Forced laughter. "Uhhh, that shouldn't be a big deal, sir. Couple bruises, nothing serious."

She plucks a straw from a box in the drawer, puts it in the drink, holds it up for him to take a sip. His eyes say thanks while his mouth drinks and waits to talk.

He spits out the straw. "That sounds great, sir. All right. I'll see you in twenty minutes."

She waits for a second to make sure the conversation's over; he gives an OK nod, and she returns the phone to the receiver.

He grabs the glass at last, takes a long pull, sets it down. "Looks like I gotta go golfing."

"Today?"

"He got a late tee time."

"You're on leave. You've been gone all summer."

"I was here for dinner."

Muttered words. He hears something like: *Your body was here*. A nod towards pool/children. "They're back to school in a week. Which I'm already a little...I mean, I thought the plan was to list the house before you flew. Get started at Vandenberg."

"That was the plan. Work still hasn't moved yet. General Schriever says another six months."

"The middle of the school year?"

He shrugs. "We're all in the same boat. Talk to Hank and Judy, you'll hear the same thing."

No response beyond an eye roll.

"Look," he says. "We can get out tomorrow. Go to Santa Monica, hit the beach. Maybe play some putt-putt golf."

She mutters something like: *Air Force bullshit*.

"Look, this is the same in any job. The civilian world, anywhere. When the boss calls to go golfing..."

She picks up the iced tea, stares him in the eyes, and drains the last of it.

•••

Twenty minutes are up. He has rummaged in the garage for his twice-used set of clubs, beaten the dust from the club head cover, dipped into the hallway bathroom for a quick shower (avoiding the unfinished caulk work in the master bathroom), agonized over the choice of shorts or pants (finally opting for the latter, despite the heat), and the color of collared shirt.

"You're gonna melt in those pants," his wife tells him.

He looks at his watch and anxiously changes into the shorts.

"All right," she kisses him when he emerges from the bedroom. "Make sure you let your boss win."

And at last he is hefting his clubs and walking out the front door, looking anxious and thirsty and somewhat discombobulated.

The car is already parked outside, a late-model Ford Thunderbird convertible, red. The general is tanned and lean and fashionably golf-attired: slim-fit Ban-Lon shirt, sunglasses. He and the other two members of the foursome are wearing pants.

"He can't wear shorts there," one of them says.

A head-shake from the general. "No, he can't."

"I'm new to the country club scene, sir."

"Well, here. We'll put your clubs in the trunk. Go get some pants on."

From one of the foursome, a mild sigh of exasperation, and a glance at the watch: we're going to miss our tee time.

In short order he has changed and returned to the car. The foursome has rearranged itself so as to leave the passenger seat open. He searches his mental files but still cannot recall meeting either of the other two. Do they outrank him? It's entirely possible. No one makes introductions: they are in a hurry.

A few blocks of driving, then the 405. Traffic is heavy, a gleaming metal river flowing improbably uphill; they move at a steady clip until close to Sunset, where comes a rippling flicker of tail lights.

The general brakes as smoothly as possible for a quick stop. To our protagonist: "Busier than it was up there, I'm sure."

"I still managed to get into a fender bender, sir."

There are disappointed noises from the backseat, and a wry look from the general: "Yes. Yes you did."

Exit down Sunset: palms and magnolias under bright noonday sun. A gate guard at Bel-Air waves them through, and improbably they are pulling into the parking lot on time, exiting the vehicle, hoisting golf bags onto shoulders and handing out straw hats, one each. Our recent space traveler still doesn't know the identities of the mysterious half of the foursome, but knows he can talk to his boss, at least: "I'm sorry, sir, these gentlemen are..."

"...here as observers," one of them says.

"Sorry, it was rude of me not to introduce you at least," the general says, but makes no introductions; he nods towards the men like: you take care of it.

"Jeff," Jeff says.

"Jerry," Jerry says.

All exchange handshakes but not smiles.

"They're here as observers," the general reiterates, as if from a pre-rehearsed script. "You can talk freely in front of them."

"He's gonna need a hat," Jeff or Jerry says.

"And suntan lotion," Jerry or Jeff says.

"Yes, you didn't get much sun this summer, did you?" the general asks. "We'll stop in the clubhouse. Get you a hat. And suntan lotion."

And at last they are piling in to two golf carts, our protagonist now hatted and Coppertone-slathered and scarcely wiser than he had been at the start of the journey. Still it cannot escape his notice that 1) the general paid for everything, and 2) they are going without caddies.

"My mom ran a concession stand for years at a course back in Texas," the general says, wheeling the cart to the first tee. "And I just fell in love with it. It's the least...animalistic sport. Less about brute force, more about patient repetition. Smarts. Precision. I thought about going pro, but...well..." A shrug towards the invisible stars on his shoulders, as if his career was some inevitable force beyond even his control. "You seem like you haven't played much."

"I was a city kid, sir. Never had much chance. I've been meaning to get to the driving range. Maybe get some lessons. So, apologies if I'm a little rusty."

Smirks from the observers. They pile out at the first tee. The general gracefully loosens up, takes a practice swing or two, and lines up on the ball. But our protagonist is transfixed by the view: the fairway dropping off before them to a magnificent panorama beyond. The whole Los Angeles basin spread out, all of it beneath them, with downtown in the hazy distance.

Our man: "It looks like a beautiful course, sir."

Jerry or Jeff makes a noise like: *hup*, as if to say: Stop talking now.

From the general: a slightly dirty look, the first negative thing he's done or said. But he shakes it off and winds up smoothly and uncoils magnificently, like a limber lion, and the club makes smooth contact and the ball sails off into the wild blue yonder, bright and straight and true.

"It is a *fantastic* course," he says at last.

"Must've been quite a view during the riots," Jerry or Jeff says.

"Indeed," Jeff or Jerry says.

The observers take their shots: decent drives, although both fall short of the general's.

Then at last, the recent spacefarer. Stiff swing, a body recently battered. The ball slices wickedly and bounces off the fairway. Jerry and Jeff trade looks and noises as if to say: it's going to be *that* kind of game.

They zip off to his ball, careening downhill with the general's hand on the tiller, gasoline combustion odor mingling with the natural scent of magnolia and freshly cut grass. Pull up to it, and our man gets another whack: the club tears a huge divot that travels almost as far as the abysmally hit ball. Dirty looks from Jeff and Jerry, who have pulled up behind, rather than jetting off to hit their own golf balls.

"Let's try that again," the general says.

"You do have to replace the divot, though," one of the others adds.

Our spaceman stuffs torn turf back into the scar in the earth. He then walks ahead to his ball, which is slightly further off the fairway now, uncomfortably close to a tree; he gives the others a look and they remain impassive. He steps up to play it where it lays.

The general gives a slight nod. Then: "Would you care for some pointers?"

"I think it'll be a long game otherwise, sir."

A slight smile. "You're bending your back. And trying to swing too hard. Here." He places a club against his subordinate's spine and gently adjusts the latter until it's equally straight. "That's what it feels like when your back is straight."

Our neophyte takes a slow practice swing while the general holds the club in place. "Wow. Well, that doesn't feel normal. Sir."

"It's like…saluting. I'm sure whoever it was that had to instruct you at the academy…I'm sure they had to correct your salute a few times. It felt strange for all of us at first. Unnatural. But after some repeated and consistent corrections…the strange feels normal, and the natural feels…"

"Wrong," Jeff or Jerry says.

Our hero takes a slow practice swing. "Well…feel free to keep correcting me, sir."

The observers nod appreciatively.

His shot somehow clears the tree and bounces a ways down the fairway, and at last it's someone else's turn. The observers silently line up, each in turn making no sound at all until the crisp efficient *whack* of metal on ball. At last the first hole flag is visible as something other than a distant dream, but on the way, there are bunkers, and a stream.

Only now does the general need to hit again: a perfect iron shot that arcs confidently over obstacles and drops precisely onto the green with scarcely a bounce.

Our hero loses a ball in the stream, and drops his next one into a bunker. The general gives a helpful suggestion—hit the sand behind the ball, don't hit the ball—and at last the laggard's joined the others on the green. A flurry of putting and he's at ten strokes. The others both pull off sixes. The general single-puts for an eagle.

Everything goes more smoothly at the second tee. Still our protagonist knows they are not here for recreation or lessons, and it is up to the general to make that purpose manifest.

"It must've been neat, seeing all this from up there," the older man finally says as they get into the cart.

"It was incredible, sir. Really looking forward to getting back up there."

"Uh-huh." Noncommittal. They zip off to the first ball. Then, as the astronaut gets out of the cart, he's pulled back by a question, sheathed in a general's genial oh-by-the-way tone: "I have to say, I'm curious. Did you talk to anyone this summer when you were up there? I mean, other than the personnel at the tracking stations, of course…"

Our hero probably feels a pang of panic, and surely the sense that his answer might have real career implications, possibly even beyond whether or not he'll get another chance to fly in space. Still, he surely senses this is one of those situations where the questioner already knows the answer. At any rate, he is not a liar. "Yes, sir, I did."

A slight nod, like the honesty is appreciated. "Was there a reason you neglected to mention it in your debriefing?"

"With all due respect, sir, I was in a bit of a quandary." A stiffening and straightening of the spine, perhaps involuntary. "My commander had been…personally briefed for an important bit of information gathering. A target that wasn't on any lists."

"Personally briefed...by whom?" Jeff or Jerry says from the other cart.

"Individuals at the highest echelons of the national security apparatus." Perhaps our protagonist is unsure he can speak freely in front of them; perhaps he at least likes feeling he has something they want, some bit of valuable information, *their* currency in *his* wallet. He turns back to the game, faking coolness, but his golf stroke betrays him: an ungraceful *whack* and another slice. All the lessons unlearned, or unapplied.

"LeMay," the general says.

The younger man gives him a look that lets him know the shot's hit home. He slumps slightly. "That was one. I don't know the other. I only talked to LeMay. Sir."

The general gives a nod and they pull off in the cart, and it is clear many wheels are turning.

For the end of that hole and the start of the next, there is no talk of secrets or briefings; the next foursome is gaining on them, and the general offers some quick lessons to help our hero focus and settle in. Our man, for his part, seems intent on studying the other two men, perhaps trying to determine again which one is which, and where they're from: FBI? CIA? NSA? Something even more secret? He studies their apparel: not quite identical, slightly different shades of khaki pants, a yellow shirt on one and orange on the other. Sunglasses and hats: both slightly different. The man in the yellow shirt appears slightly older, although perhaps he's just spent more time outside. Still, they are not saying much.

Perhaps our hero is thinking of his wife's admonishment to let the boss win; perhaps he's wondering if the others are doing the same. Soon it is surely clear that it is not in his power to do anything else. But our spaceman is trying; he has a moment of seeming presence and focus, where everything else has fallen away except the dimpled ball standing there serenely on the tee above the sunlit grass; he swings smoothly at last and the ball sails cleanly away, arcing off into the clear sky.

He finishes the hole two over par. And the fifth is a short one; they're all on the green soon again. "I suppose I can speak freely," the general says between putts. "You've put me in a quandary as well."

"How so? Sir."

"Well, the accident. And the activities that preceded it. Obviously we've kept newspaper coverage of the program to the absolute minimum. If you'd landed smoothly, we could have continued to do so. Not that it was *necessarily* your fault things happened the way they did. But it does leave us with a limited set of options. We can't really punish you. Or we *could*, but that would just whet their appetites..." He effortlessly sinks his putt.

"Whose appetites, sir?"

"The press. We need to feed them something."

"Sir, with all due respect, I don't see why we'd..."

"They're hungry," the general says. "Despite the cover story, we've started to get inquiries. Even in this town, nice conservative paper like the *Times*, they get hungry. Ordinarily we could fend them off, but...they're like wolves. They prey on the stragglers. The weak, the injured, the ones falling out of the pack. The programs where everything clearly isn't going according to plan."

"Like the Chrome Dome flights," says one of the others after sinking his last putt.

"Like the Chrome Dome flights," the general echoes. "And like us."

"Sir, with the X-20 production schedule, I was under the impression we'd be able to maintain..."

"We will. Still...it's human nature. When one thing doesn't go as expected, people start to assume everything's off. And the way the political stuff is going...I mean, it is possible we'll have a new administration soon. We need to protect ourselves against every possible outcome. Obviously everything we've ever done is on a need-to-know basis, but in an election year, the public needs to know, too. Not much, but something. They need to know that these...mysterious rocket launches, these...expensive fireworks displays that they're spending their tax dollars on, are actually keeping them safe, making their lives better, allowing them to go to the grocery store and buy their cereal and watch their TV in peace and security. Because accidents are red meat to the press."

Our spaceman purses his lips, nods. He bobbles what should have been his last putt, then fucks it up again, remembering, perhaps: hanging upside-down in the cockpit, hearing the helicopters landing around his broken spaceplane, straining down to the window to catch a glimpse of airmen with M-16s establishing their security perimeter. And the long and hungry wait, the crane arriving at last to right his craft, the weary extraction and quick examination before he was whisked back to Edwards by helicopter. Then, soon: newspaper photographs of a tarpaulin-covered spaceplane on the back of a flatbed truck. And questions, questions, questions.

"We've had phone calls this week," the general continues. "We have to give them something so they don't start…questioning the whole arrangement." He walks everyone off the green; they wait by the carts for the next foursome to pass. "And we have to give them something that doesn't compromise the core mission. Because we are keeping the public safe. But the less they know, the safer they are." A pause, a glance. "Because the more the Soviets know, the more likely they are to take countermeasures. If we can finish mapping their ICBM fields, the American public will be a lot better off than if the Soviets start…playing hide-and-go-seek with every warhead. Camouflaging their silos, rolling their rockets around the country on railcars. Which they will start to do, if they know what we're up to."

"Very well, sir." The spaceman gives a look as if still quite unsure what's expected of him.

"In other words, we need to make you a hero."

An uncertain pause. "I'm not sure I've done anything that qualifies, sir."

"I mean…that was a hell of a flying job, to get down in one piece after what happened. Without losing a week's worth of pictures, OR the photos of the satellite. That was really something."

The course has wrapped around to the end of a small canyon and back: now there's a tunnel leading to the next hole, an actual stone-lined tunnel cut into the terrain. The foursome that was behind them finishes the hole and precedes them into it.

The spaceman nods towards the back of a chubby bald man. "That looks like Alfred Hitchcock."

The general says, "That's probably because it's Alfred Hitchcock."

"He has a house near the course," Jerry or Jeff says. "On Bellagio. This is basically his back yard."

They drive through the tunnel, watch on the other side as the others get started.

"So, sir...uhhh, what will..."

"What will that entail? Well, that's been the subject of some discussion. Because if we talk about you saving the film...well, obviously we'd be compromising the reconnaissance mission. So it may be necessary to disclose the satellite incident in a way that makes us look good. So...what happened to you in orbit...was that hostile enemy action?" A direct stare, somewhat more intense than anything that had come before.

"I honestly don't know, sir. I mean, at the debriefing, we discussed..."

"Yes, yes, yes. I know what we discussed. If it wasn't, there was certainly a fuckup on your part in not anticipating a routine orbital maneuver on their part. But if it *was* hostile enemy action, well…it's certainly a little easier to present you as a hero. Get you flying again."

A deep breath. "Understood, sir."

"Still, that presents us with another dilemma. If it *was* hostile enemy action, do we want to present it to the world that way? Or would there be…geopolitical ramifications? If we recommend you for the big one, how would that be perceived on the other side of the globe? Because they haven't acknowledged the incident yet. So obviously they could perceive this as…"

"Belligerent," Orange Shirt says.

"Belligerent. And embarrassing to them, if their satellite was in fact knocked out."

"Which we still don't know," Yellow Shirt says.

"Which we still don't know," the general echoes. The Hitchcock foursome has finished and driven off; our subjects now approach the tee. "We don't know if the satellite's still operational; we don't know if they're going to recover film from it. And if they do, we have no way of knowing if they have any film of the incident itself. We don't know for sure if they saw you on radar, or what they could prove if they did. But there's certainly a danger. Like the U-2 incident. We could disclose a certain set of facts, and they could release evidence that contradicts those facts." The general stops talking, takes his swing: another beautiful shot. "So there are certainly unknown…"

"Implications," Orange Shirt says, as he rotates up to the tee.

"Unknown implications. Yes, that's a good way of putting it. Unknown implications for granting you an award whose criteria includes enemy action. Medal of Honor, Air Force Cross…"

Orange Shirt addresses the ball, takes a competent swing, watches the ball fall, speaks: "Medal of Honor would be a stretch anyway."

"It would be." The general looks back. "I mean, it's not like you were…alone in the sky, fending off a fleet of bombers. But still, an award might deflect a lot of attention away from the secret aspects of station operations. And away from any…mistakes made during the satellite rendezvous."

"There was a saying, during the war," Yellow Shirt adds. "The bigger the fuckup, the bigger the medal."

The general gives him an unpleasant look. "Because if we focus on the decision you made to stay with the ship instead of ejecting…well, that's only significant because you were carrying pictures. Which, again, is not necessarily an operational detail we want to call attention to. Plus, we have no evidence there was anything intrinsically wrong with the design of the craft that might have contributed to the spin. So if we do start talking more about the crash-landing, it may also be necessary, for the sake of the program, to talk about pilot error. And that could certainly have implications for the flight manifest. Depending on how you're willing to talk about these things."

"Are you saying you want me to lie, sir?"

"Did we say anything about lying?" The general looks to the observers. "We didn't say anything about lying. It's more about…being able to steer the public discussion in a certain direction. Telling the truth in a way that covers many possibilities. I need freedom to maneuver, you see." The general smiles: a razor-thin smile. "So…was this hostile enemy action?"

Our spaceman: "I honestly can't say, sir." He steps up to the tee, swings: tops the ball, which shoots off through the grass like a hissing snake and stops a pathetically short distance away.

"Let's try that again." The general tosses him a fresh ball. "Was this hostile enemy action?"

The spaceman gives a look and purses his lips. Then: a flash flickers across his face. "It certainly felt hostile, sir." He tees up, takes a breath, relaxes, swings again: the ball rockets off into the blue, impossibly high and far and straight and true.

•••

Ahead of them, the director and the rest of his foursome—a newspaperman, two neighbors—are approaching the green. The director is a portly man, past his prime not only physically but professionally, although of course no one is willing to tell him so.

"It helps to let the camera wander," the director says to the newsman as his neighbor addresses the ball. "Not aimlessly, of course. You need a protagonist. Someone relatable. Someone that the audience can identify with. Either someone they could be, or someone they'd like to *think* they could be. And you need to spend most of your time on that person. We're...selfish. Human beings. We're narcissistic."

His neighbor gives a look like: stop talking.

"We care more about people if we can imagine ourselves in their shoes. I don't know if I could spend a movie focused on the villain. Cutting to the villain from time to time does build suspense. But you need to keep coming back to someone the audience can relate to. Someone who...embodies their hopes and dreams." He stops talking, lets his neighbor swing: a choppy chip shot that doesn't quite hold the green but rather rolls off the edge. The neighbor gives him a slightly dirty look, pulls a putter from his bag.

"Filming for an American audience," the director continues, "the studios would never let me have a protagonist who was...Negro. Asian. You can have characters who...putt from the rough. So to speak. But not the protagonist."

The neighbor hits the ball solidly; the ball breaks right, then left, and ends up within five feet of the cup.

"But you can't tell the whole movie through that person's eyes. You can't use the first person singular. The audience needs to know more than the character. That's what makes it suspenseful. If you show two people...talking in a pizza parlor, and a bomb goes off, that's a few seconds where things are interesting. But if the camera shows them talking, and then goes down under the table, and you see a timer on a bomb counting down, that makes the whole scene interesting."

The newsman puts his notepad down, lines up his own putt. "Yes, I've heard you say that before." He putts gently, too gently: the ball only makes it half the distance to the cup. "So the camera's God, then?"

"Well, the camera only goes where the director tells it," the director says. He putts the ball, a lovely putt that effortlessly finds the hole. "So perhaps the director is God. But God sees everything. And you can't show everything and tell a story."

"The director's doing what he thinks the audience wants. So maybe the audience..."

"The audience isn't God," the director says. "There's still that distance. The distance of the screen. The audience has more information than the characters, but not much more. So they're not quite omniscient, and also quite impotent. In the pizza parlor scenario, it's that tension that makes it an interesting viewing experience. You have information gleaned through observation, and you can't use it. You want to shout at the characters: 'Get out of there!' But you are completely unable to influence the course of events. You can't make the characters choose one path or another."

"What if you could?" The newsman sinks his putt.

"How do you mean?"

"If there was some sort of...interactive decision process. At every decision point, the audience takes a vote. Decides how to proceed. You could have different reels of film the projectionist could select, depending on the decision. A first-person plural, an editorial *we*."

The others finish the hole, pencil in their scores; they start walking towards the carts.

"I don't think that would be a workable solution, artistically. Every audience would have a different experience. The people who voted one way would be disappointed. It would cost a lot more to film. Some outcomes would be…artistically unsatisfying. It sounds more like a…game than an…artistic statement."

"Well, it might be interesting."

"We don't want the audience thinking they're God," the director smiles. "If they think every option is open to them…"

"Well, it wouldn't be every option. Just the ones you pick."

"I'm old, I'm set in my ways," the director says. They throw their bags in the cart, climb in. "Something for the next generation, perhaps. The interactive experience."

On the next tee, the director's next ball slices right, off the fairway and towards a gap in the vegetation. When he gets off the cart to play it, he notices a car parked on the road fronting the course. The driver has headphones on, and is holding something with a round parabolic dish on it, pointed towards the course; he's cocking his head as if listening to something.

The director waddles back to rejoin his foursome. "Well, that's strange," he says.

"What?"

"There was a man with some sort of...listening device, parked on the road. I do believe he was eavesdropping." An impish smile. "Spying on someone."

The newspaperman laughs. "You've been watching too many movies."

•••

Behind them now, the other foursome plays: general, spaceman, and two mystery observers. Up and down this beautiful canyon course, the tree-lined fairways and immaculate greens all perfectly maintained; occasionally they glimpse, in the shadows or at the fringes, one of the patient silent Negroes of the maintenance crew; they see but do not interact.

The general maintains his machinelike consistency; the others are solid, but not on his level; our hero struggles to keep up. And when it's over, the others insist on rehydrating with martinis at the clubhouse before sitting down for steaks. They all proceed to get elegantly toasted while the general tells tales of procurement deals and development discussions, games played with executives from Convair and TRW and the like. Our man politely plays along. He still cannot tell which one is Jeff and which one's Jerry; he's half-convinced they've switched shirts.

When at last they drop him off at home there is another dinner waiting for him under wax paper in the refrigerator. Everyone is asleep.

He ignores the food. Heads to the bedroom, slips off his clothing, throws on his swimming trunks, steps out into the perfect Los Angeles night. Drops into the pool feet-first with nary a splash. Tucks himself into a ball and floats suspended. Surfaces and rolls over on his back and opens his eyes, ignoring the sting of chlorinated water lapping at the corners so he can stare up at the unsatisfying smattering of stars in the light-polluted sky.

Climbing out of the pool, he towels himself off, heads inside. All of the home repair accoutrements—caulk and scraper and edging tool—are still laid out inside the bathroom; he wipes down the corner seam and lays down an immaculate line of caulk.

•••

Morning starts hungry and anxious: herding the children through the dress-up routine, everyone observing the pre-Eucharist fast. They make it to Mass exactly on time. Listen to the reading: Elijah calling down fire from heaven to destroy the priests of Baal. Watch as the man in gold-and-white robes steps through the elegant rituals: swinging censers of incense, intoning chants in Latin.

After that: coffee and donuts in the church social hall, a new bright place with big windows and shiny tile floors. The Knights of Columbus are serving; once the first rush has died down, they wander out among the families.

"Rumor has it you were on a little mission." A middle-aged man with salt-and-pepper hair has wandered up to say hello. He claps the spaceman on the back, not quite open-handed; ring and pinky finger curled tightly into his palm. "Good to see you made it back in one piece."

Our protagonist wipes powdered sugar from his hands and awkwardly stands. "Charlie, right?" He offers his hands for a shake.

"That's right. How was it up there?"

The spaceman smiles. "It was something."

"I bet it was. I bet it was." A nod. "Beautiful, I bet."

"It was. Not too much I can say about it...secret program and all. But...it was really something."

"I bet it was. Lovely family you've got here. Gonna get that guy in the service someday?" A nod towards the son.

"We'll see if he's up for it."

Talking down to the youngster now: "Well, son, I don't blame you if you want to follow in your dad's footsteps. But I'm sure you'd make a helluva Marine, too."

"That's right," the spaceman says. "You served, didn't you?"

"Yep. Made it the whole way. Guadalcanal, Cape Gloucester. Wounded at Peleliu, made it back for Okinawa. Wounded there, made it back for Operation Coronet. The Kantō Plain. The ruins of Tokyo." Another glance towards the boy. "Little bit...messier than what your father's doing, I'm sure."

"I'm sure it was." He looks towards the older man, expecting, perhaps, a war story of some sort, although he surely knows better.

The older man purses his lips. Winces with remembered pain. "Little bit messier." He claps the boy on the back and walks away.

The boy finishes his doughnut and wanders up to the front of the hall. There is a small stage with two flags: a resplendent American one, and one for the Knights of Columbus, both bordered in golden fringe. The Knights' seal is visible: a diagonal cross with a shield, on which are an anchor, a sword, and an axe in a bundle of sticks. Next to the stage: a table with pamphlets. He picks one up and reads about the symbolism of the American flag, how the red stands for courage and valor and heroism, and the white means innocence and purity of intention, and the blue represents vigilance and perseverance and justice, but also heaven, and God watching over the world.

•••

In a small and impossibly neat efficiency apartment in West Hollywood, the investigator wakes up. A severe-faced man with a crew cut and dead eyes. He checks his watch, rubs his stubbly face, reaches onto his nightstand for cigarettes, realizes the pack is empty. Shakes his head.

Before he goes anywhere, he climbs in the shower. Scrapes the stubble from his face with a pristine razor. Then: downstairs onto the bright asphalt grit. Quick pack at the corner store. On the way out he sees a horizontal chalk mark on a lamppost. Shakes his head, takes a deep breath.

He goes back to the parking lot behind his building, gets in his car, lights a cigarette, pulls out into the empty Sunday street, drives to his office. Retrieves a satchel with a parabolic microphone and a tape recorder from his trunk, and carries it upstairs. Sits down at the typewriter, puts headphones on. Listens and transcribes, page after page of transcript. Starts looking down strangely at the words that his fingers have summoned forth. Plays back the tape and listens again.

• • •

"We do really need to get started on the painting."

The family is home from church and everyone has piled out of the car, but the man is standing there staring at their bungalow, which looks a little less immaculate than he'd like.

"Today?" His wife looks skeptical.

"Might as well. I can get changed, swing by the hardware store…"

"You've been gone all summer."

"I know. Lot to catch up on."

"It's Sunday. What happened to going to Santa Monica? Putt-putt golf?"

"I had a club in my hands all day yesterday…"

"Well, go talk to the kids. If you're the one deciding not to take them, you get to tell them."

The spaceman walks inside, where he is greeted by his son. "Dad, come look at my terrarium."

"Terrarium?"

"I helped him put it together yesterday," the wife says from behind. "He was trying to tell you about it before Mass."

The spaceman follows the boy into his room, where he sees a large glass box with earth and rocks and a long branch and a ceramic bowl of water. "It has frogs in it," the boy says. "It's an open terrarium. The guy at the store said you can do a closed one where you seal it up and all the water circulates and you never have to water the plants, but it's hard to do with animals."

One of the frogs hops into the water and just sits there, breathing.

"Well that's pretty neat. What do they eat?"

"Crickets. I fed them before Mass. But it's fun to kind of sit here and watch them." The boy stares through the glass at the breathing frog. He watches for about thirty seconds and then turns away.

"Dad." The daughter walks in from the hallway. "What time are we gonna go play putt-putt?"

"Yes, what time are we going to play putt-putt?" the mother asks, and the spaceman gives her a dirty look.

"Oh!" the boy chimes in: "Putt-putt!"

The spaceman sighs, rubs the raw spot on his hand where yesterday's clubs have chafed him. "OK, get changed. Let's go play some putt-putt."

They pile into the car and head out. There is news on the radio, something about Czechoslovakia; he switches it to a classical station. The kids groan, his daughter in particular. "Dad, this makes my ears hurt." He smiles and turns it up.

At the course, they all pick up their putters from a small painted shack that looks like a barn. While Dad pays, the boy picks up his club and attacks the girl like he's a swordsman.

They fence and parry back and forth before the spaceman says, "All right, knock it off."

They take their turns at the first hole. "This is a game of silence and concentration," Dad says. The boy's shot goes wild, ricochets off rocks, rolls into a stream. "Lemme give you some pointers." Dad shows him how to stand, how to hold his shoulders.

"Dad, what's going on in Czechoslovakia?" the boy asks.

"Well, there are people there that want to be free. But the bad guys are trying to stop them from being free. They killed a bunch of people with tanks."

"Who are the bad guys?"

"They're from the Soviet Union. There's a guy named Chairman Beria, who's the ruler. He's the worst one."

"Is he going to start a nuclear war?" the girl asks.

"I don't think so," the spaceman says.

They play on, hitting balls up ramps and through tunnels and across bridges and between the blades of slowly spinning windmills. Around the ninth hole, the kids get a case of the giggles, which eventually proves contagious. Despite dad's best efforts, they play sloppily, with the kids sometimes scooping the ball around tricky bends in the green, and mom penciling in the scores somewhat arbitrarily.

At last they are on the final hole. Dad looks intense.

"This is fun, right?" Mom says. "Aren't you glad we came out?"

"I am." Dad smiles. "I may not be the best golfer in the world, but in this family…"

"I'm only two strokes behind you, Dad."

"Because your mother isn't counting every stroke."

Mom shrugs. "The kids have a handicap." She's just behind the boy in the standings.

"All right, this hole," the boy says. "I'm going to beat you on this hole."

The daughter plays first; she's out of contention anyway. She takes a ridiculous number of strokes, eight or so.

"All right, all right," the boy says, as if to say: out of the way. He hits a perfect first shot that banks correctly into the middle of a tricky set of tunnels. He then misses, in succession, four short putts, then collapses on the green in mock frustration.

"Six. Not exactly Jack Nicklaus," Dad says. Then he muffs his first shot, and his second, and his third, the ball ricocheting off the lip of the tunnel each time. Finally he hits the correct tunnel and the ball drops onto the lower final part of the green. "OK, here we go." But sure enough, the ball loops around the inner edge of the cup without dropping and then shoots off like a comet that's just rounded the sun.

"Not exactly Jack Nicklaus," the boy smiles as Dad finishes with six.

Mom steps up and quietly gets a hole-in-one for the win. "Let your clubs do the talking, boys," she says.

Dad shakes his head, makes a face that can't decide whether it's amused or annoyed.

"Oh, come on," she says. "Aren't you glad we came out?"

Dad is smiling at last. But as they walk to the car a look comes over him. He looks off and above like he's remembering something serious: maybe a conversation from the day before, or maybe just the sight of a perfectly hit ball rapidly becoming a speck as it sails off into blue space.

• • •

"You never explained what happened with all the radio stuff," the wife says.

They are lying in bed, holding one another, spent. Close and quiet, their worlds reduced to this relationship, this room, this bed.

"I was...concerned about something," he says; he looks from her upwards, perhaps remembering the sight of the planet beneath him on a peaceful Sunday morning, the relief of seeing everything exactly the way it had been the day before. "I get that way a lot. In case you haven't noticed."

"I'm used to you being concerned," she says. "But you were afraid. And that, I'm not used to." The unspoken question: What was it?

"It was nothing."

• • •

Monday in New York.

The TV studio couch, the same couch used for interviews with presidents and senators, generals and admirals, athletes and movie stars, now sits surrounded by accoutrements of science: a telescope, a microscope, a chalkboard with equations; on the wall behind it are pictures of comets and nebulae. Two massive Norelco cameras sit several feet away, their fields of view interlocking on the couch; two scientists stand at the foot of the couch, awaiting instructions.

"Does the telescope work?" The younger scientist: clearly the calmer and more confident of the two.

"Probably not." The newsman's speaking voice is more or less the same as his on-air one: a luxuriant fatherly baritone. Trustworthy. "I'm sure some…production intern went and bought it at a thrift store down in the Village. It makes for a good visual, though."

"So for everybody that comes in here, CBS just buys…" The older scientist doesn't quite finish the thought.

"I'm sure we reuse props when we can. But…yes, there is a prop budget for each show."

An eye roll from the scientists: the extravagance of it all.

"It's money well-spent!" the newsman says. "This is how the mind makes meaning. Viewers see a telescope, they assume you've been…hard at work in the lab all day. It gives context. Credibility. Which is good! You're the voice of…scientific authority!"

"There's no room for authority in science," the younger man says.

"You're not an authority?" the newsman smiles. "A Harvard professorship, don't you think that confers a certain level of authority? If it doesn't, I better get on the phone...get someone from Yale or Princeton. Columbia, maybe."

"Arguments from authority, I should say." A chatty, friendly tone. "Science isn't a hierarchy that...issues dictates. It's a system, a self-correcting system."

"Einstein wasn't an authority?"

"Einstein wasn't Einstein! Not at first. He was a...crazy young patent clerk with outlandish ideas. If you'd interviewed the more established physicists *about* him, they'd have said he was a kook. But sometimes the so-called authorities are wrong."

"Well, viewers like to think they're hearing from an authority. An older wiser voice." He smiles. "Until they're so old that the authorities are younger than them. Then they get cranky and complain about us putting...idiots on TV. We do want to satisfy the average viewer, though. If we had a...ten-year-old child on here, saying what you're going to say, would they believe it? The truth of the statements would be unchanged, but would they believe it?"

The older scientist, a bearded man with a serious-looking eyepatch, smiles thinly. "Is that why I'm here? Rather than just having a younger-looking guy?"

The newsman smiles, sphinxlike. "Let's get started, shall we?" He gestures towards the couch; the two scientists settle in, and there is a brief flurry of activity. Production assistants appear now next to the men; one holds a test card next to the younger scientist's face. Behind the large cameras, the operators peer through their viewfinders and make miniscule adjustments. At last they nod to another assistant, who holds up a clapper board with a name—Cronkite—and a chalked-in title: UFOS: FRIEND, FOE OR FANTASY? And two more names: Page and Sagan.

"All right. Rolling. And…three…two…" The assistant flashes fingers for the countdown, mouths a silent "one."

Off camera, the newsman speaks, a twinkle in his eye: "Do you believe in UFOs?"

"I'm glad you used that word." The younger man speaks: perfectly at ease on-camera. "Belief. When it comes to something like UFOs, the appropriate scientific attitude is one of healthy skepticism. Extraordinary claims require extraordinary proof. Right now, we have no proof. When I was in high school, flying saucer hysteria was in full swing. And…well, you have to look at what else was happening at the time. The Soviets had just detonated an atomic bomb, something more powerful than anything that was ever used in the war. We found out our country, too, had been developing these things, in secret, without any public discussion. We'd just survived the most destructive war in human history, and even *more* destructive weapons were being built. So there was a lot of fear. And it was comforting to believe that there were creatures out there that were smarter than us, that would come to earth and save us from ourselves."

"So no UFOs."

"The speed of light is a cosmic speed limit. Given the distances involved, it's hard to believe anyone would just come visit us out of the blue. They'd probably signal us first."

"They'd call before they came over."

"Well, you'd want to see if anyone was home before coming all that way. So I'm much more interested in listening for signals from the sky, so we can see if anyone's out there trying to get in touch with us. If they've been observing us."

"So you do believe in aliens?"

"Again, I don't think belief is the right word. But there has to be more to science than just skepticism. You also need an…eagerness to discover. A sense of wonder about the sheer scale of the cosmos. When I realized the sun was just another star, when I realized every star was another sun, it was almost a religious experience. And it certainly seems likely there's someone out there. With billions of stars in our galaxy, and the billions of galaxies…you might not know this, but there are more galaxies in the cosmos than there are people on planet Earth. More galaxies than people! And in each one of those galaxies, *each one*, there are far more stars than people. It stands to reason there's intelligent life out there somewhere, that somewhere else the same chemical reactions took place that happened here.

"Still, one has to be skeptical. Scientists recently discovered very regular radio signals that were clearly not man-made. Repeating every 1.33 seconds. It seemed like a sure sign of intelligent life! But then another similar source was discovered. And another. And apparently we've simply discovered a new type of star. A pulsar. But we do have to keep watching the sky. And sending out signals. So that anyone out there knows we're here."

The older scientist: "Tell him about the Drake equation." To the newsman he turns, somewhat nervously. "Are you familiar with the Drake equation?"

"Why don't you tell us?"

"It's...uhh, it's an attempt to quantify...I guess you'd call it a way of thinking about the possibility of extraterrestrial life. It's not a fixed known verifiable equation like...$E = mc^2$ or Newton's Second Law. It's...well, more of a back-of-the-envelope Fermi problem type of a thing. N equals R∗ times f_p times n_e times f_1 times f_i times f_c times L." He gives a self-satisfied look, as if the meaning of the letters is self-evident.

"Can you walk us through what all those letters mean?"

"I...uhh..." The older scientist nods towards his companion.

"It's a way to estimate the number of civilizations trying to contact us at any one time. If you look at the number of stars in the galaxy, and the rate they're formed, you have a pretty large number. But you have to estimate what percentage of those stars form planets. And what percentage of the planets in a system would be habitable. And how many of those planets actually *do* develop life...how often does that soup of molecules start developing into organic molecules, and then self-replicating molecules? Then: What percentage of life evolves into intelligent life? And what percentage of *that* life sends detectable signals into space? There's a big difference between...whales sending songs across the ocean, versus humans beaming radio waves out into space."

"I don't know how you'd estimate those percentages," the newsman says.

"It is very speculative," the younger scientist admits. "But the last one, *L*, brings up interesting issues. When you think of life sending signals into space, well...you spend part of life as a child, part as a grown-up. Surely it's the same for our species. We're *just* old enough to pat ourselves on the back for sending signals into space. But the percentage of time we've been able to do so is...miniscule, compared to the amount of time our species has been on the planet, which is in turn miniscule next to the amount of time our planet's hosted life. And we don't know how much *more* time we've got. The way the arms race is going...we could destroy ourselves in ten years. Or five."

"Or one," the newsman says.

"Are you concerned about that?" A twinkle in the scientist's eye, like: I'd like to ask a few questions.

A reluctant breath: "I think anyone in my shoes would be."

"I wouldn't know it from your broadcasts. The programs you've done, about Minuteman, the B-70, the X-20 program..."

"We barely know anything about the X-20 program!"

"Exactly. There was a crash-landing last week, out in the desert. The Air Force tried to play it off like a normal aircraft accident. But someone got photographs of the truck hauling the wreckage, and figured out it was an X-20! Still, there's barely been any news about it. For all we know it was carrying a nuclear weapon." He leans back.

"We have to report news," the newsman says. "Credibly sourced information. When there's no new credibly sourced information, there's no news."

"Well, we need some. Your so-called exposés seem like...commercials. Between your bits about...Air Force technology, and your broadcasts about...Berlin and Czechoslovakia, you sometimes seem like a...spokesman for the Cold War. Working for the government, reading their press releases..."

"It's every newsman's job to be on the side of freedom, rather than the side of...totalitarianism," Cronkite says.

"If there's a war that nobody survives, will it matter what form of government we have?"

"Let's get back to UFOs," the newsman says.

"Are you uncomfortable questioning the government?"

"We'll have to edit it out. If only for time."

"Ahh, yes. You have to make room in the broadcast for the cultists."

"We do try to present all the sides of an issue. Let the viewers make up their own minds."

"Not all information is equal. The credible and informed skeptic is more reliable than the person who's...fallen for a hoax, and is trying to rationalize it."

"Well, we do choose what order we present everyone," the newsman points out. "If your...credible skepticism is more compelling than the cultists, well...you might just get the last word."

The scientist nods, as if to say: fair enough.

"Getting back to this...Drake equation," the newsman continues. "It sounds like there's some uncertainty to it."

"Well, there is. You can keep the same numbers in for every other factor, and plug in different numbers for L, and get vastly different numbers. Once a society gets advanced technology, does it grow and prosper and start reaching towards the stars? Or does it destroy itself in a few decades? You plug different numbers in for L and you realize, there could be a couple dozen civilizations out there already in the galaxy. Or $N = 1$. Meaning everyone else hasn't evolved yet. Or they *have* evolved, and they've killed each other off."

"Fascinating," the newsman says.

"That's the Fermi paradox," the older man says. "Named, of course, for one of the great scientists of our age, the man who first split the atom. He looked up at the sky and said, 'If the universe is so full, where is everybody?' Which is ironic, of course, because the powers he helped unleash..."

The newsman gives a look like: You need to finish your thoughts. Our viewers aren't mind readers.

"The powers Fermi unleashed mean we might destroy ourselves before we can make it to the stars."

"Fascinating."

"Of course, we don't know how different life is elsewhere," the younger man interjects. "Elements like gold and uranium...they can only be created in a supernova, but they're plentiful here on earth. Why? Well, long ago, in this arm of the Milky Way, there must have been a supernova that sent this collection of materials spinning together. Other star systems were shaped by a different set of random chances. A different set of elements that came together at a single place in the sky. And we don't know what that's like. Are there planets where people wear gallium and indium and niobium and ytterbium instead of gold? Is uranium more plentiful on other planets? Or...is it far more plentiful here? Only some nuclei are suitable for a fission nuclear weapon, and it's impossible to create a fusion bomb without one. Are there planets where nuclear war is impossible because there isn't enough uranium? The universe could be teeming with life that's chosen to ignore us, because of our self-destructive tendencies, and abilities. For all we know, we're the Sentinel Islands of the galaxy."

"You're really eager to talk about nuclear war."

"Nobody else is."

"Getting back to UFOs...there have been a rash of sightings recently. We're interviewing people in Dexter, in eastern Michigan...there was a very compelling sighting."

An exasperated sigh. "Where's the evidence? You have...what, some hunter, lost in the woods, seeing lights?"

"There were multiple people that saw this. A dozen or so. This...disc they saw, it appeared over a marsh and hovered for over four hours. The man who initially reported it called several neighbors."

"Where are the pictures?"

"Nobody took pictures."

"How convenient. Seems strange, doesn't it? All those people?"

"It does seem strange. But stranger still that all these people would see the same bizarre thing and describe it in exactly the same way."

"A mass delusion."

"One of them was a sheriff. He drew a picture of a round silvery disc, hovering above the marsh."

"Swamp gas," the scientist says.

"Swamp gas?"

"Are you the arbiter of truth? Do you have a mechanism for correcting your errors?"

"Every respectable media organization publishes corrections when it's wrong!"

"Ahhh, the 'No true Scotsman' argument."

"How do you mean?"

"When you say, 'Well, no true Scotsman would ever spend money extravagantly,' and then...Stuart McLeod buys an expensive car, and you say, 'Well, he's no true Scotsman.' Tell me, who decides who constitutes a respectable media organization?"

"Who decides what constitutes a respectable scientist?"

"There's a peer review mechanism. What is the mechanism in media? You can put us on, and then put on these...hunters in Michigan, spouting their bizarre theories, and just the fact that you've presented us both gives the different points of view an equal footing, even though there may be no rigor or objectivity or honesty whatsoever to their observations. We are totally at the mercy of your decision to play up or play down or edit whatever we say. So who's a respectable organization? NBC? ABC? Are they respectable?"

"They're not bad. I do respect them. But we have an organizational ethos that..."

"An organizational ethos?"

"Well, look at NBC. What's their corporate logo? A peacock. But at CBS, it's an eye. Two different cultures. NBC, it's about being proud, looking good. Showing off. It's harder to...issue a correction when you're a peacock. But CBS...the eye. It's not about being seen, being on TV. It's about seeing. Being the objective eye that sees..."

"And passes judgment. Like some...Space Age God, determining what people ought to think."

"We try not to. It's hard sometimes. We try to let the facts speak for themselves."

"Is that what you've done with Goldwater?" A smile.

A smirk. "I didn't take you for a Goldwater man."

"Oh, I'm anything but. But your coverage of him this summer does...undermine your claims about your own objectivity."

"So is this going to be a...dick measuring contest about who can be more objective?"

The scientist blinks. He looks moderately surprised, but also pleased by the vulgarity.

"They're going to edit that out...obviously," the newsman adds.

"How convenient."

"Senator Goldwater...is a tough case."

"He is a tough case."

"He's far more popular than we would have imagined. If you portray him in a negative light, or...hell, if you present the negative things he *actually says*, there is some...perverse subset of the population that likes him more. 'He tells it like it is!' 'He shoots from the hip!' It's the most...baffling political phenomenon I have ever seen."

"This...elevation of ignorance. He's a dangerous man."

"Just between you and me, he is a dangerous man."

"Well, I'm glad we see eye to eye on that, at least. But to trust a government, when the presidency might well end up in the hands of a man like that..." The scientist leans forward. "Speaking of politics, how come you're not in Chicago covering the Democratic convention?"

A cold look. The newsman leans back in his seat. "Let's get back to UFOs. You both have done work on this issue...for the government." (He lets those words hang in the air. Self-satisfied now.) "You both were on government panels charged with investigating the UFO phenomenon. One Air Force...Project Blue Book, I believe...one CIA."

"We were," the older scientist says.

"How did you come up with your findings? Did you do that in a scientific manner? Obviously you seem a little...predisposed to not believe this stuff."

The older scientist speaks: "Our panel was expected to be objective in its approach, in trying to evaluate all the reports, without saying in advance that they were ridiculous. And Carl Sagan here was on a similar panel."

"Can you...summarize your...informed opinion on UFOs? As a credible skeptic?"

The younger man: "There's not a single verified or checked out report which is at all connectable with the possibility of extraterrestrial life. That's not to say extraterrestrial life is impossible...quite the contrary. I think many of the stars in the sky have planetary systems. It seems likely that life arises naturally on the vast bulk of these planets. It's possible, but by no means certain, that life on many of these planets has evolved into beings that are more advanced than us. And it's entirely possible there are civilizations thousands or millions of years more advanced than ourselves, capable of technical feats that we can hardly imagine. But if we would believe, as the flying saucer cultists would have us believe, that the majority of saucer reports are due to visitations, you have a very strange situation! That means several spaceships are coming to the earth over interstellar distances every day, as if all the anthropologists in the world would have converged on one of the Sentinel Islands in the Indian Ocean, because they'd just invented the fishnet there, or something. It's much more reasonable to speculate that there are very rare visits by extraterrestrials to the earth. There's no evidence for this, but it's not implausible. But to have frequent visits, I think it strains credulity.

"The bottom line is: we have to be concerned, any time we're just latching on to ideas that make us feel good. Because then it becomes, basically, another religion. And that's what UFOism can be. A belief that we latch onto without any proof because it makes us feel good. When you look at a lot of these sightings, they have some peculiar things in common. The creatures that inhabit these flying saucers are...creatures in long white robes who are benevolent, concerned with our well-being; they are omnipotent, extremely powerful; they are omniscient. It used to be possible to believe in a personal, powerful, all-knowing God. And now there's very few people who really believe that. So that's what flying saucerism is about, filling that void. We want to believe that there are...powerful beings up there who care about us. Sky gods who are going to step in and save us from ourselves. And we're the only ones who can do that."

The newsman nods. "Well, I think we have more than enough material."

•••

Outside the windshield: an average LA residential street. Lower-middle class, predominantly white. A child in the streets, lazily circling on a bicycle. Two others chalking a hopscotch grid on the sidewalk.

The investigator tunes out the children, looks resolutely for anyone his own age, anyone watching him. Sits for several minutes. Gets out, grabs his briefcase, looks quickly inside and sees: typewritten transcripts, and the dull metal glint of the .45. Walks two blocks, rounds a corner, heads into the alley, stops. Waits. Doubles back, all the way past his car, and another block down. Takes a quick look around: still nothing but kids. Satisfied at last, he looks back up at the house, double-checks the number: 459.

The front door is open. He enters cautiously, looks around, hand rattling his briefcase ever so slightly as if to feel the weight of what's inside. In the living room, on the couch: a man, middle-aged, white. Dress slacks, tie, short-sleeve collared shirt.

He smiles. "You found the place."

"I found the place."

"Were you followed?"

A head shake: no.

"I apologize for all these...extra precautions. Probably more than you get with most clients. Were you able to get a recording?"

"I was."

"Well, let's have it. Tapes. Transcripts."

The investigator takes a deep breath. "There's nothing in there of use to you."

"You can let me be the judge of that."

"Your story's a...load of crap." The investigator flinches slightly as he says the last word. "You're saying you need this Air Force guy on tape because...what? He's cheating on his wife? Something about an inheritance?"

A slender smile. "It is a rather substantial sum of money."

"He's a four-star general. This is all defense stuff. Space stuff."

"Do you always question your clients' motives?"

"Only when I want to stay out of trouble. Suppose I went and told the FBI I was hired to...spy on this guy?"

A pause. A shift. A change in attitude. "You haven't."

"Says who?"

"We've been...keeping an eye on you."

"Bullshit. If you had those kind of resources, you'd spy on this guy yourself."

"We have our reasons for how we've done things."

"Well, I'd like to know more about your reasons."

"I...don't think this is how the client relationship is supposed to work. We give you money, you do your job, you give us the product, we give you more money, the job is over." A tight little smile. "So then...the product."

"All right, if that's how we're gonna do this..." The investigator reaches into his briefcase; when his hand comes out it's holding the .45.

The other man laughs: a deep, unconcerned laugh. "You've been watching too many movies."

"What's that supposed to mean?"

"I wouldn't do it this way, if I were you." Then: "Victor, come in here. Slowly. Our friend is a little jumpy. We don't want to startle him."

From the kitchen, another man, also in a tie and short sleeves. He's carrying a briefcase. The investigator's attention (and handgun) both flicker between the two.

"Calm down, nobody's going to shoot you," the seated man smiles. "But you might want to wait and see what we have here. Show him what's in the briefcase, Victor."

"Slowly," the investigator says, with a nudge of the gun for emphasis.

Victor clicks the latches on the briefcase.

"Again, I don't think you understand the nature of the client relationship," the seated man says. "When I came to this country, about...oh, fifteen years ago now...there had been a lot of executions. A lot of people murdered, just for trying to keep an eye on things. I needed to learn a lot to blend in. To stay alive. A lot about...American customs. Capitalism. Learning about business, I heard a saying: 'The person who signs the front of the check gets to make the rules. And the person who signs the back of the check has to listen to the person who signs the front of the check.' And even though we're working on a cash basis, well..." He smiles. "I still think we're in charge. But in case you have doubts..."

Victor pulls from the suitcase a manila envelope. Takes from it a large black-and-white photograph, places it on the coffee table. And another, and another, and another. (We do not need to see what is on the photographs, but you can use your imagination. Suffice it to say there is a look of shame and horror on the investigator. He deflates.)

"We have a friend with similar packets. Sealed, stamped, ready to be dropped in the mailbox, should anything happen to us. Or should the job not be completed to our satisfaction. Addressed to your business partner. The Los Angeles Police Department. To your parents...they live in Glendale, yes? Very nice house. Not too different from this one. I would have put in an offer on it, except then I would have had to track them down again once they moved." The seated man smiles. "There is always someone watching. If not God, then...somebody."

The private eye is sweating now; he looks uncomfortable. Possibly ill. He sits, forearms on knees, gun no longer pointed at anyone.

"Did you think we picked you at random?" the seated man asks. "Did you think we just...let our fingers do the walking through the Yellow Pages? No. We don't work with people we can't control." He eases the .45 from the investigator's hands; the other man doesn't stop him. "Here. I'll hold onto that until we're done."

The investigator just sits there. Eyes distant, blinking heavily.

"Now," the other continues. "I suppose if I were a good capitalist, that it would be time to negotiate a reduction in our rate. A discount for...poor customer service." A smile. "But then again, I've never been a good capitalist."

•••

The New York threesome—newsman and scientists—have now left the studio and ventured up the block to the 21 Club. The waiter has deposited glasses of ice water that are leaving rings of condensation on the thick linen tablecloth.

"I'm still not sure the microscope was necessary," the younger scientist says.

"The microscope?"

"The props. We had a picture of a nebula, a picture of a comet. A telescope and a microscope..."

"I do have a bit of fondness for the latter two devices," the newsman says.

"You really are a company man, huh? The whole 'eye' thing..."

"Oh! I hadn't thought of that," he chuckles. "No, my ancestors are Dutch. We're responsible for both."

"Well, there's some dispute about that..."

"You should like the Dutch! A country with a history of commerce, scientific inquiry..."

"It's not about liking or disliking! It's about truth. Besides, my ancestors are Jewish. Every nationality, it's the same. People looking for...evidence that their own people are somehow chosen. A unique source of good."

"The Dutch were historically very friendly to the Jews."

"Until the Holocaust."

The waiter comes back, takes their drink orders: martinis all around.

"You were a war correspondent, right?" Page speaks up, interviewing the newsman.

"I was. Covering the 8th Air Force."

"Did you just...observe them objectively?"

The newsman purses his lips. "I flew a mission, actually."

A look like: really?

"Yes. To understand what they were doing. I flew a mission over Wilhelmshaven."

A pause for the waiter to deposit the drinks, take the orders. Then: "What was that like?"

"Terrible. Exciting, but terrible." A sigh as if to say: war story time. "It was early in 1943, long before we owned the skies. I was in a B-17, with...Bugs Bunny painted on the nose and a bunch of kids behind the controls. Not that I was old. But at 27, I had four years on everyone on the plane." He leans forward. "We had no fighter escort. Which at first seemed like no big deal. All the machine guns we had. We took off, started navigating across the North Sea. Flying Fortresses and Liberators. And it was boring at first, fantastically boring. That's what they say about war: hours of boredom, then moments of sheer terror. But then the attacks started. And we'd been trained, we'd been trained to perform some of the functions of the enlisted aircrew..."

From Sagan: "Wait. You were...participating?"

The newsman sputters. "I mean, they didn't want to just have an extra body up there, taking up space, dead weight. There was no room! So they'd trained us to be waist gunners..."

"Waist gunners?" The younger scientist exclaims. "What kind of...objective journalism is that?"

"Well, that was our ticket to ride," the newsman says. "It was either that or...keep doing what we had been doing. Staying safe on the ground all day, asking for interviews with twenty-year-old kids who'd...just seen aircraft full of their friends exploding before their eyes! Guys who'd had...best friends die in their arms when their own plane got shot up. When you haven't shared those dangers, when you're looking in from the outside, people tend to clam up. So we'd made that decision, to fly. A bunch of us were on that mission, one per plane. Andy Rooney. Bob Post, from the *New York Times*..."

"So you were manning a machine gun." Sagan again.

"Starboard waist gun, .50 caliber. The Luftwaffe started attacking us over the North Sea. Focke-Wulfs and Messerschmitts."

"And you shot at them."

"I shot at them. I am not sure if I hit anyone. Maybe a Liberator." A grim thin smile. "But I shot at the Germans. And then came the flak. So thick you could walk on it, these...ugly little puffs of black cotton candy. And the fighters, still..." A pained look. "Bob Post's plane, the fighters got it over Oldenburg. It was on fire. We saw a few of them bailing out, those little gentle parachutes like...dandelion seeds on the wind. But then...they started drifting towards the flak. And...well, none of them made it. Tremendous talent, Bob Post. Better writer than me. You would have known his name if he'd survived; he would have been the biggest name in the business. Didn't make it back. I thought after that mission we'd all be...filing great stories, filling in the missing pieces. But for a good hour all we could do was talk about what happened to him. What almost happened to us."

Steaks arrive. They eat. The young scientist glances up at the newsman, questions unspoken.

"You do try to lean back afterwards," the newsman says. "Get some distance, some perspective. We understood things a lot better after being up there, I can tell you that."

"But the mission probably went a little differently than if they'd had someone else as a waist gunner."

"Now, I'm no physicist..." the newsman leans back. "But when you do an experiment to observe the wave nature of light, or the particle nature of light, you observe different properties, depending on the type of experiment, right? Observing things changes them for you, too."

Sagan smiles. "I'm just saying, these Air Force stories...the X-20 crash, that B-70 that crashed in Greenland, this...orbiting space platform that could have nuclear weapons on it, for all we know..."

"What about them?"

"Well, I'm sure you ran into these people during the war, LeMay and all these...nuclear Neanderthals. Can you ask these people tough questions about what they're doing with our tax dollars, if you've been part of that system?"

"Well, we're all paying our taxes, I assume."

"What's your point?"

"You're in the system, too. The only observer that's outside it is...God."

Again a smile from the scientist, and a slight head shake: "So there's no observer that's outside the system."

"We lean back afterwards," the newsman says. "Try to get a healthy distance. And we look at things from different angles. I covered Nuremberg, too, after the war. The trials. I saw the results of the bombing raids. The destruction we'd inflicted from the air."

"Did it change your mind about what you'd participated in?"

The newsman leans forward, clutching knife and fork in his tightening fists. "I also saw film from the camps. From Dachau. I almost vomited, seeing the bodies on film. I still have nightmares. The men who'd perpetrated that, I saw their faces when they saw the film. They cried. I don't think they cared about the Jews though, even then! They cried for themselves, knowing they were going to be executed! So am I biased towards the side of freedom, against the side of totalitarianism? As a reporter, I think I have to be. If anything, it made me...more committed to this work. I realized that the German people had signed away their right to know what their government was doing with their tax dollars. And when you give away your right to know what the government is doing in your name, you sign your name to everything the government does."

Sagan and Page nod appreciatively. They finish their lunch, talking of other things while the Negro busboy cleans their table. But on the way out, the younger scientist shakes his head one last time. "Waist gunner on a B-17..."

Cronkite cocks an eye.

"I do believe we've won the objectivity dick-measuring contest."

The newsman guffaws, slaps the scientist on the back, and they step out into the summer sunlight.

•••

"My frog's not happy."

It's Monday morning and the spaceman is outside, holding up paint swatches to the side of the house, contrasting the shutters and the walls. "Your frog?" He answers his son without looking away from his task.

"We need to go back to the pet shop."

"Maybe he's hungry."

"I've been feeding him. I'm feeding him what the pet shop guy told me to feed him."

"Then what do we need from the pet shop?"

"I think we need a Mr."

"A Mr.?" Finally the spaceman looks down.

"For mist. A mister. And a hydro-thingy. For the humanity."

"Hygrometer? Who says you need that?"

"The pet shop guy."

"Why didn't you get it Saturday?"

"Mom didn't want to."

The spaceman sighs. Walks inside and goes and looks at the frog, which does indeed look listless.

"Mom gave him a name," the boy says. "Edward Hopper."

"Edward Hopper." The spaceman walks back into the living room, where his wife's reading on the sofa. "Why didn't you get a mister for Edward Hopper?"

"With all the grief you've been giving me about money?" An incredulous look. "You know how it is at a store like that. You get one thing, and they're like 'You really oughta have...' and 'He might be a lot happier if you get...' I was trying to escape without breaking the bank."

He purses his lips as if envisioning: a smooth-talking and clean-cut salesman trying to con his wife into purchasing armloads of unnecessary accoutrements, and her, stubborn, resisting. "But now we've got a live frog on our hands."

"Well if you think he needs one," she adds, "go get it yourself."

"I was going to head back to the hardware store. But you still need to look at the paint swatches."

"Just…do that after." She gives a look as if to say: go spend time with your son.

"All right." To the son: "Let's go. Quick. In and out."

Into the car they go.

Fifteen minutes later, they pull into a parking space in front of a glass storefront in a nondescript strip mall: new, like everything in LA. A barrage of smells assails them as they pull open the door: an earthy fishy smell, and…incense? Covering for something else? The boy starts looking at fish and frogs and lizards; the spaceman finds himself browsing the empty glass containers, massive tanks and jars and flasks. There's music playing, folk music, a voice of tortured angst.

"Can I help you find something, sir?" The salesman is a greasy longhaired fellow; the 'sir' sounds reluctant.

"What is this music?" The spaceman scrunches his face.

"Bob Dylan."

"Bob Dylan."

The voice screeches higher, awful on the store's small speakers: "…and it's a hard, and it's a hard, and it's a hard, and it's a hard…a hard rain's a gonna fall."

"He wrote this during the Berlin Crisis. Trying to give us a little idea of what was in store for us if we went to war." A warm glow. "Sort of a modern-day prophet."

"He sounds like a strangled cat."

The salesman disappears, lowers the music, returns. There is a corresponding dip and rise in the level of body odor in the vicinity of the spaceman's nose.

"There," the salesman says. "A sacrifice to Mercury."

"Mercury?"

"The god of commerce."

A smirk from the spaceman. "How hard is it to set up a closed terrarium?"

"Are you trying to keep it completely closed?"

"Maybe, yeah. Like a separate environment."

"In a lot of ways the open one's easier. Just having that ability to crack it open, make adjustments to the system, put different stuff in there. Then again, a closed one can be good, especially here in California. Especially if you're growing moist plants. With the right plants, and not too many animals..."

"Can you have insects?"

"Really depends..."

"Like, in a big flask?"

"Is this your first terrarium?"

"Well, he's got one." A nod to the boy, who walks over as if summoned.

"Oh, he...he came in Saturday, right? With your wife! And a little girl! Beautiful family."

There's a gleam in the salesman's eye the spaceman doesn't seem to like. "Yes, thanks."

The salesman hunches down to the son's level. "How's the frog?"

"He's OK. He's a little sad."

"Maybe he needs a lady friend." A smile as he stands. "A little lovin' to get him through the night."

From the spaceman, a dirty look. "I think we're OK with just the one. Don't want him asking too many questions..."

"It's a beautiful natural thing! They get on top of each other..." He does something which could be interpreted as an imitation of frog pelvic thrusts.

"I think we're OK. How much for the big flask?"

"Well, uh...if you're just getting into this, you may want to start a little smaller..."

The salesman helps him pick out a jar and some gravel, and describes the plants he'll need to look for at the nursery: ferns, moss, baby's tears, African violets. There is talk of Venus flytraps, at which point the boy's eyes light up, but the salesman explains that this would make the closed terrarium a bit more difficult.

"I do appreciate that," the spaceman says when they're ringing up the items. "You didn't sell me the big flask."

"Well, we'd rather you have a successful small project before you move to bigger things." The man pushes cash register buttons, methodical and deliberate. "The customers who jump head-first into a big project don't always come back."

The boy is next to his father, trying to get his attention; the father's looking at a paperback sitting next to the register, a slender paperback with a rising sun behind a Japanese pagoda. "What's that?"

"Oh. Man, it's scary. This journalist, John Hersey...he was on Guadalcanal, and then he ended up in the occupation forces in Japan, after the war. He saw the cities we'd incinerated. Just...all these desolate places. Burned survivors wandering the ruins. But it's a funny thing, there were four cities we left completely untouched. In all of Japan, four cities. Do you know why we didn't bomb them?"

The spaceman shakes his head.

"They were working on the atom bomb. They thought it would be ready before the end of the war. But they didn't want to just...drop it on a city that had already been burned down. So they kept four cities intact, so they could see how destructive the bomb was on its own. Almost like an experiment. Hiroshima, Nagasaki, Kyoto, and..." He nods towards the book, on which is written the final city. "...Kokura."

"Hmm," the spaceman says. Again the son is tapping, trying to get his attention.

"So he kept imagining," the salesman continues, "what it would have been like in a city that got hit by the big one. And this idea kept bothering him over the years. What it would have been like for the Japanese civilians. So he did a lot of research, and he wrote this." He presses the last button on the register. "Seven dollars and sixty-three cents."

"Dad…" the son says, but he's ignored.

Dad pulls out his wallet. "What kind of…uhh, what kind of research did he do?"

"Well, he found people who knew about the tests here. It was hard getting them to talk. I mean, early MacArthur years…all the executions…people were afraid. But he found some classified medical literature about people who'd died from radiation, in experiments that went bad. There were…mishaps with nuclear cores, plus some…reactor in Idaho that melted down. And it also turned out…we'd done some experiments with pigs."

"Pigs?"

"Pigs. When they started testing in the Nevada desert, they would tie up pigs at different distances from a blast. Because pig skin is closest to people skin. So these tests, they had pigs at all different distances. Pigs in houses, pigs in cars, pigs in streetcars, pigs in pens. They tattooed them, in case they got loose, they'd know how far they'd been from the blast. And pigs can't look up, so they couldn't see what was coming. They were just stuck there, milling about, waiting for the bomb. Which of course, I keep thinking about. I mean, obviously, me and animals…" A nod towards the store. "Anyway, afterwards the scientists looked at which ones were incinerated, singed, blinded, whatever. Figuring out what would happen to a city. And…anyway, John Hersey, he talks about it a little in the foreword, but he obtained some of those studies, and wrote this novel, like an alternate history. It just came out this summer. Really chilling stuff."

The spaceman picks up the book, gives it a quick glance, wallet still unopened in his other hand. He flips through it, sees flashes of words: vomiting, third-degree burns, flesh falling from bones...

"Dad!"

A flash of anger. "What do you want?"

"We still need the mister."

"Oh!" A sheepish look. "Yes. We still need a mister."

• • •

Outside the house now: a ladder, buckets of paint, paintbrushes, a roller, a tray.

The spaceman has purchased everything and spread it all out and now climbs the ladder, roller in hand, but realizes there are cobwebs clinging to the corners under the eaves; he sets the roller down and picks up an old shirt and climbs the ladder again and starts swatting at the offending filaments. He returns to the top of the ladder, dips the roller in the tray, lays down several long swaths with the roller; he reaches to get a patch above the window, but he can't quite get there.

"Dad, can we go to the bookstore?"

He turns around. Both children now, standing expectantly, squinting up at him in the bright morning sun. "I'm painting."

The daughter: "Mom's gonna take us. She told us to ask you if it's OK."

"Well, what do you need me for?"

The son: "We only need you for money."

"You're never supposed to tell someone you only need them for money." He climbs down from the ladder. "Especially when you only need them for money."

"Well, can we have some?"

"Don't you guys have library cards?"

"Yes."

"Go to the library, use your library cards. We've spent enough the past couple days."

The girl: "We've earned some allowance."

"Well you're free to spend it at the bookstore." He gives a look like: What do you need me for?

The girl: "Mom hasn't paid us yet. She said you owe us the money."

The boy: "You did tell us it's bad to owe people money."

"I did tell you that, didn't I?" The spaceman grimaces. "You guys are more reliable than a tape recorder."

"So can we have our allowance?"

"I'll go to the bank tomorrow. Have mom take you to the library."

The kids dart back inside. The spaceman looks up at the paint tray sitting on the folding work platform near the top of the ladder. He picks up the ladder without moving the paint tray, moves it very carefully with an eye on every wobble of the tray, sets the ladder down within arm's reach of the window, puts a foot on the bottom rung. And now the ladder wobbles: a leg sinks into the dirt and it topples, sends paint tray flying to the earth, flinging yellow paint on the ground, and on the spaceman and the shutters, which are supposed to be white. He collects everything up, surveys the mess as if unsure what to clean up first: the paint-spattered shutters, his yellow-stained clothing, or the empty paint-wet tray, now caked with dirt.

He has moved to the side of the house and is rinsing out the tray with the garden hose when his wife pokes her head around the corner. "What happened out front?"

"I moved the ladder without taking the paint tray down."

"You never move the ladder without taking the paint tray down." She smiles as if it will take the sting away. "Everybody knows that."

"Well, now I do, too." He surveys the cleaned-out tray, the paint-ruined shirt. "I moved it fine, I just planted it wrong."

"The kids were looking forward to the bookstore. And I need some books, too. I've burned through all my summer reading."

He wipes paint-water hands on his now-ruined shirt. "You've got a library card…"

"All right," she says. "Have fun painting."

•••

After a couple hours, he steps back to survey his handiwork. He moves back and forth, observing from different angles; he moves up close and finds spots where the white paint from the shutters has dripped or spattered on the yellow stucco. He looks like he is trying to convince himself he's done a decent job. But after a few reluctant moments he cracks open another bucket and pours it into the tray.

Behind him: car pulls up on the driveway. Engine noises stop, the door slams. "You're just starting now?"

"Just starting the second coat."

"Shouldn't you let the first coat dry?"

"It doesn't look right."

"It'll look worse if you start a second coat right now." The kids are piling out of the car.

"I just poured more paint in the tray."

"You can put it back in the bucket, you know." She smiles: a hint of mischief. "I promise, if you take care of it, it'll stay wet."

The kids, now swarming around her, are peering in her tote bag for their library books. "Don't be…" Dirty. "They're gonna…" Hear you.

She shrugs. "At least, I think it'll stay wet. You never know."

The kids pluck their books from the bag and run inside.

"It's…" He surveys the disappointing house.

"Seriously, honey," she says, more kindly now. "Relax for a bit. Help me take the groceries inside."

"You got groceries?"

"We do need to eat. I got used to three mouths in the house this summer, but now we're back to four. And they're not all the same size."

"But which one's biggest?"

She nods towards the open paint can. "You might want to put a lid on it. So it doesn't dry up entirely."

He chuckles and shakes his head as she walks inside. Then he does a modicum of cleanup before unloading the car.

When he sets the groceries on the kitchen table there are three library books sitting out: Michener's *Tales of the South Pacific*, something called *Alas, Babylon*, and Hersey's *Kokura*.

"Are these yours?"

"I hope so. Little heavy for the kids." She starts filling the pantry with cans. "Well, two of them, at least. I figured I'd need a breather with the Michener."

He scans the cover of *Alas, Babylon*. Something about a Florida town in the aftermath of a nuclear war. And, again, *Kokura*.

"The guy at the pet store told me about that," she said. "Interesting guy."

"Sort of a beatnik. Coulda used a bath."

"We had quite a conversation. He's really hopped up about this nuke stuff. Did you know there was a nuclear accident in Greenland this summer? Like, they lost a bomb in the glaciers or something. And they haven't found it yet! Can you believe that? They can just *lose* an H-bomb. You gotta wonder what would happen if someone found it."

"Huh," he says.

"But, like, did you even hear about that? I mean, I know you were...otherwise occupied. But I don't even remember hearing about that."

He shrugs, something like a no.

"You're gonna do a terrarium, too?" she asks.

"Yeah. I've still gotta get the plants."

"You were at the hardware store, right? I thought they had a nursery."

"I forgot." He stares absently at the book about the city that might have been destroyed. "I might want to read this."

She smiles. "You've got a library card."

He glares.

"Come on, that was funny. Go ahead, I'll start one of the other ones."

He's just settled in on the recliner when the phone starts ringing.

She interrupts her grocery storage to pick it up. Then gives a look like she's tempted to "accidentally" hang up. But she knows what's expected of her. "Yes, General Schreiver." Then "OK, Bennie." And "I'll get him. Just a second."

She listens to his end of the conversation with some disdain.

"Yes...uhh, yes, sir." And: "I understand, sir. Obviously. Yes, these are people we have to keep happy." Finally: "Quite all right, sir. I am looking forward to it." And: "You too, sir."

As soon as he hangs up the phone, she speaks: "I should know better than to expect anything from the Air Force at this point, but...whatever that was, it couldn't wait until you're back at work?"

"I have to go to Washington next week," he says.

"Says who? You're supposed to get two full weeks of leave. We'd talked about your parents coming out."

He shrugs. "The Chairman of the Joint Chiefs of Staff."

At last he settles in to the recliner. Reads about Kokura, a destruction that never happened: imagined scenes of unspeakable horror.

●●●

On Tuesday the investigator is back at his office, drinking coffee, perusing the file from an insurance fraud case and making notes for a report, but slowly, absently.

"So you met that client." The investigator's business partner stands in the open doorway.

"Uhhh, which one?"

"The one you kept talking about? 'I've got this big client, asked for me specifically, should be a lot of money.' The one you recorded, and ended up thinking he mighta been a spy? Sound familiar?"

"Oh, that."

"Oh, that." Mocking smirk. "Past couple weeks you wouldn't shut up, now you've clammed up."

"I wouldn't say 'Clammed up.'"

"You said you were gonna call me yesterday. After you met up."

He shrugs. "Wasn't worth a call."

"Well, what did they say?"

"It was...just a misunderstanding."

"You're not gonna...I dunno, talk to the FBI or anything?"

The investigator shakes his head no.

The business partner's eyes narrow. "So, what. You asked him if he was a spy, he said no, and you were fine with that?"

"Well, it was a little more...intense than that."

"What'd you do?" he snickers. "Pull a gun on the guy or something?"

"Well, I...uhh..."

"Jesus Christ." He shakes his head. "You watch too many movies. This is a client relationship. Word of mouth gets around."

"We straightened it out."

"You straightened it out."

"He understands it was a misunderstanding."

"He understands."

"The guy's a…Japan veteran. Wounded in Tokyo. He's patriotic. He was…glad I was being vigilant."

The partner shakes his head. "That's the least-convincing explanation in the history of explanations. Can I see the transcript?"

"I…uhhh…don't have it."

"You don't have it?"

A shrug. "That's how capitalism works. He paid me for the product, I gave him the product."

"You didn't keep a copy?"

A head shake: no.

The business partner shakes his head. "Always keep a copy. Especially when they tell you not to."

A smirk. "You've been watching too many movies."

●●●

"Are we out of milk already?" It is Thursday and the spaceman's pouring a post-dinner glass, but it's only a third full, and the jug is *drip…drip… drip…*

"Is that jug empty?"

"Yes."

"Then we're out of milk. I'll get some tomorrow. Unless you want to go out tonight."

"Well, not right yet." The spaceman glances at the clock. Takes his unsatisfyingly empty milk glass into the living room. Turns the TV on with paint-spattered fingers. Watches the set warm up.

"So when are you going to get started on this?" The spaceman's wife looks down at the terrarium flask, sitting empty on the kitchen table.

"You say that like it's been sitting around forever."

"It feels like forever."

"I had to finish up outside." The TV flickers. "The house is painted. Bathroom's done." He adjusts the rabbit ears and there it is, the convention hall filled with delegates, Kennedy on the rostrum. A handsome tanned man with a thick head of hair, just over fifty.

"...accept the nomination of the Democratic Party. I accept it without reservation, and with only one obligation: to lead our party to victory, and our nation back to greatness." The Boston accent, chowder-thick. "The rights of man, the civil and economic rights, have been under assault, both at home and abroad. We cannot afford even four more years of such assaults."

The spaceman settles back in the easy chair, drains his small milk glass, frowns, gets up, turns up the volume.

"Our task is not one of merely itemizing Republican failures, nor is that wholly necessary. For the families forced from the farm, the unemployed miners and textile workers, the old people without decent medical care: they all know that it's time for a change. We are not here to curse the darkness; we are here to light a candle. As Winston Churchill said when taking office, 'If we open a quarrel between the present and the past, we run the risk of losing the future.' Today our concern must be with that future. With bringing light to the world, and helping it burn brighter here at home. As president, I pledge to you, those will be my goals.

"First, the world. One third of it may be free, but one third is under a terrible repression, and one third is rocked by poverty and hunger and disease. The entirety of the Asian continent suffers under communist rule. The city of Berlin stands divided by a physical wall as a result of the failures of the Nixon administration. The country of Czechoslovakia, after taking tentative steps towards freedom, has been dragged backwards into darkness as a result of the failures of the Nixon administration. The forces of tyranny and repression are doing all they can to prevent their citizens from seeing the light.

"The peace and security of our great nation demands that we spread that light to every corner of the globe. And we cannot do that while cloaking our own efforts in darkness and secrecy. We cannot do it while relying on weapons and belligerency. We have, for the past several years, kept nuclear-armed bombers in the air around Soviet Russia at all hours, ready to destroy them on command. Our adversary cannot help but view us with suspicion when constantly surrounded by a swarm of B-70s. As president, I will seek a better path."

Kennedy leans forward, hands on the podium. "We must work towards peace. Our adversary, like us, was the victim of a surprise attack at the beginning of the last war. Unlike us, they suffered great destruction. The occupation of a large swath of their country by mechanized hordes, the burning of their fields, the bombardment of their factories. To imagine something similar in our country, we must imagine all of America laid waste to the east of where we are now, in Chicago. The Soviet memory is scarred by those experiences, and they have every right to be afraid. To understand their foreign policy, we have to understand their experience. And we must work with them to bring the forces of nuclear destruction under international control, because it will only be then, free from the threat of a new and more horrible devastation, that their people will be willing to look at us with open eyes and open hearts. I have it on good authority that Chairman Beria, when he took office, was willing to institute reforms that might have allowed us to end the Cold War. But President MacArthur did not respond to his overtures. The result of this failure was more repression, more tyranny, and the ongoing threat of war. We must work with the Soviet Union for peace.

"What kind of a peace will I seek as president? Not a Pax Americana, enforced on the world by weapons of war. Not the peace of the grave, or the security of the slave. I'm talking about the kind of genuine peace that makes life on earth worth living, the kind of peace that enables men and nations to grow and to hope, and to build a better life for their children. Not just a peace for Americans, but for all men and women. Not merely peace in our time, but peace for all time."

A nod and a noise from the spaceman's wife, who is standing next to the recliner now. He eyes her skeptically.

"It may seem foolish to speak of peace after recent events in Eastern Europe. But it is even more foolish to threaten total war. Total war makes no sense. In an age where great powers maintain large nuclear forces, and refuse to surrender without resort to those forces, it makes no sense. It makes no sense in a world where one large nuclear weapon contains more explosive force than all the weapons used by all the allied forces in the Second World War. It makes no sense in an age where the deadly poisons produced by a nuclear exchange would be carried by wind and water and soil and seed to the far corners of the globe, and to generations yet unborn."

On Kennedy speaks: "I realize the pursuit of peace is not as dramatic as the pursuit of war. But we have no more urgent task. Some say that it is useless to even speak of peace, or world law, or world disarmament until the leaders of the Soviet Union adopt a more enlightened attitude. I believe they will. I believe we can help them do it. But we must reexamine our own attitudes. Far too many of us think peace is impossible. But that is a dangerous, defeatist belief. It leads to the conclusion that war is inevitable, that mankind is doomed, that we are gripped by forces beyond our control. We need not accept that view. Our problems are man-made. Therefore they can be solved by man. And man can be as big as he wants. No problem of human destiny is beyond human beings. Peace does not require that each man love his neighbor. It only requires that we submit our disputes to international arbitration, and to seek a just and peaceful settlement. Peace need not be impractical. And war need not be inevitable."

The spaceman's wife mutters: "Well, that's…"

"Shhh!" He leans forward in his chair.

"It is an ironic fact that the two largest powers are the ones most at risk of devastation. Should we go to war, all we have built, and all we have worked for, will be destroyed in the first twenty-four hours. So let us not be blind to our common interest. If we cannot resolve all of our disputes, at least we can help make the world safe for diversity. For in the final analysis, our most basic common link, is that we all inhabit this same small planet. We all breathe the same air and drink the same water. We all cherish our children's futures. And we are all mortal."

The spaceman catches himself nodding along.

"We know Soviet attitudes towards us need to change as well. It is depressing to read their propaganda. But it is a warning for us not to view them in the same distorted fashion that they see us. Not to see conflict as inevitable, and communication as nothing more than an exchange of threats. It is discouraging to think that their leaders may actually believe what their propagandists write. Wholly baseless and incredible claims: according to their propaganda, quote, American imperialist types are preparing to launch a preventative nuclear war against the Soviet Union, unquote."

The spaceman shifts in his chair: uncomfortable, perhaps. Glances down at the library book, the one he just finished the previous night: Hersey's *Kokura*.

Kennedy continues: "...do not seek such a war. And I pledge that when I am president, we will not be the first nation to use nuclear weapons in anger. Their propaganda says that, quote, the political goal of the American imperialists is to dominate the planet through the means of aggressive war, unquote. I pledge that my goal will be not to dominate the planet, but to avoid the war that will destroy it.

"To do that, we must look at our own behavior. We have placed, into orbit, a reconnaissance platform about which very little is known, even by our own citizens. A platform which overflies their country several times a day to observe their nation and their military preparations."

A silent nudge from the wife: the spaceman nods with a mysterious smile.

"...ch vigilance is necessary for our own security, but we must show the Soviets that we are only up there to keep a peaceful watch. Not to create, as some have called for, an armed platform to bombard them at will, and without warning.

"We have better uses of our technology than to arouse fear and suspicion in our enemies. So I am proposing, here at this convention, that we redirect our efforts in space towards goals that will inspire, rather than cause fear. If the American people elect me as their leader in November, I pledge to take us towards a new goal, a new frontier. I believe that we should go to the moon. It will be a proper outlet for our nation's great energies, to direct them towards exploration rather than war; it will inspire the people of the world to see what great things can come from our capitalist system of government. With proper effort and national leadership, with leaders that are bold rather than fearful, we can land a man on the moon, and return him safely to earth in time for our great nation's bicentennial in 1976.

"Why the moon? Why choose this, and not some other goal, while our cities have been racked with violence? One might as well have asked, five hundred years ago, why cross the Atlantic? Or sixty-five years ago, why take to the air? We should do this not because it is easy, but because it is hard. Because that goal will serve to organize the best of our talents. This will be the most hazardous and dangerous and greatest adventure on which man can embark."

The wife speaks: "Well, that sounds more fun than...spinning around the earth, spying on the Soviets."

The spaceman catches himself smiling: "No comment."

On TV: "...to build a world where the weak are safe, and the strong are just, we must pay attention to problems here at home. In too many of our cities today, the peace is not secure, because freedom is not complete. Our nation may have launched a Negro into space, but too many of that race do not have the same opportunities for peace and freedom and career advancement..."

The spaceman turns his attention away from the TV. Back towards the book on the table, as if thinking of the scenes within.

"I...uhh...I'm gonna run out and get the milk."

●●●

A short drive. And now the spaceman is knocking on a door. No answer.

The spaceman knows someone's home. From the porch he can just make out the bluish TV glow, the sounds of Kennedy's speech, still on, and raucous applause. He knocks again, louder.

Judy opens the door. "Oh! Didn't know you were coming over."

"Nice to see you too, Judy."

"It's nice to see you too, I just..."

An awkward sigh. "Sorry. Hank is home, right? I didn't mean to be rude, I just..."

"Yes, of course. He just..." A quick head turn. "You have a visitor from outer space!"

"It's a lot less impressive when I saw him at work last week!" Hank materializes. "Space visitors are always welcome, though. As long as they're human. Come on in." A smile and a firm handshake. "What brings you here?"

"Well, uhhh...you know." He surveys the living room, sees the ham radio set up on a cabinet behind the table, the patient microphone. "Work stuff."

"Ahhh." A nod to Judy. "Hon, we need to talk about work stuff."

A tight smile and a nod from Judy. "I'll go check on the girls."

They sit down. The dining room table's covered with stockbooks full of stamps; the TV has been turned to face it. On screen, the same scene he'd seen: crowded convention hall, cheering Democrats. "I didn't think you'd be watching this!"

"Gotta know your enemy," Hank glares. "Neville Chamberlain Jr., here. Spilling our secrets to the Soviets on live TV. Heard a rumor you're flying to Washington next week."

"News travels fast." The spaceman grimaces. "I've been summoned by our friend."

"Our friend?"

"LeMay."

A nod. Inscrutable. Hank looks back over to the TV.

His visitor speaks again. "We never did talk about the contingency plan."

"What's there to talk about?"

"After you left, I…I thought they were actually gonna do it…"

"They were never gonna do it." Hank looks down at the stamp books, the tweezers.

"You weren't up there! I really thought…I mean, it was…I was climbing the walls up there. I thought I needed to get word down, or else…"

"What do you want me to say?"

"Well, I just…"

"It was just a plan! An operational plan. They're not maniacs. Nobody wants a nuclear war. But we damn sure don't want to lose one if it happens. If we can finish a war as quickly as possible, with as few casualties as possible...I mean, that's the only moral outcome in *any* war. It was a plan to do that. They wanted to see if it was doable. That's all."

"You weren't up there. You didn't talk to him when I did."

"It was just a plan." A glance at the TV: Kennedy wrapping up his speech. Next to it: a slender blue book with white titling. "Hell, sometimes I wish they had done it. Might never have the chance again. We could be celebrating a win, rather than..."

"A win?"

"The Iron Curtain got taller on our watch. Stronger. Who knows? Maybe we could have knocked it down."

"You're saying we should have gone to war."

"I'm saying we had a job. To keep watch. And we told what we saw, and nobody did anything. Doesn't exactly give you...confidence in our current political leadership. To say nothing of the opposition."

"What do you think Nixon should have done?"

"He could have done something! He had options. Hell, I don't know if we'll have options next year. Or next week, even. He's killing the Chrome Dome flights."

"He is?"

"Fallout from that...B-70 crash. The press has been up everyone's ass about 'em. And there were rumors Kennedy was gonna make an issue of it, so Nixon decided to...out peacenik him."

"I didn't know that."

"He's in a bind. All this happened on his watch. He's getting squeezed from both sides. And frankly, he deserves it! He didn't do anything."

"Well...you weren't up there. It's easy to say this stuff when you're...watching it on TV. It's different when it's your call."

Hank purses his lips. There is a look, not quite a nod. Again he looks down at the stamps.

His visitor speaks again. "Got a lot to do?"

"Reorganizing. I was doing it a little more thematically, but...gotta go chronological."

"I'm starting a little hobby myself. Putting together a terrarium."

"Seems a little messy for your tastes."

"Well, once you get everything in the jar you can seal it up. Forget about it. I'll tell you, though. This guy at the pet store...quite the character. He was reading some book about if we'd dropped the bomb on the Japanese."

"The Hersey book."

"You've heard about it."

"Of course. Ever since I landed, the *media*..." (Said as if a dirty word) "...has been...*fawning all over* the guy." A nod towards the screen, the convention scene: Roger Mudd and Robert Trout are on the air, providing some inane banter.

"It's quite a read. Did you hear about the pig experiments?"

"Pig experiments?"

"Yeah. Really horrific stuff. Apparently we nuked a bunch of pigs in the desert. To see what would happen to people, because our skin is so similar. Just tied up a bunch of pigs at different distances and then...boom. Just...devastating effcts."

"Mmmmmm." A noise as if hungry.

"Mmmmmm?"

Hank smiles. "Nuclear bacon."

●●●

In New York the newsman has just returned home, slightly buzzed, and is finishing up in the bathroom, drying his hands with a plush towel when the phone rings.

Rrrring. He keeps drying.

His wife, from the bedroom: "The phone's ringing."

Rrrring. "I'll get it."

Shoes click on the hardwood floor.

Rrring. He is next to the phone now, but he waits a couple seconds.

Rring. At last he picks up the receiver. "Cronkite."

"Walter, it's Bill." Paley, network president, his boss's boss.

"Oh! How can I help you?" As if it were a random phone call.

"Fred and I were thinking about having you fly to Miami in a couple weeks."

"Did you have issues with the Chicago coverage?"

"Walter. You know I wouldn't be calling if we didn't."

"What seems to be the problem?"

"Mudd and Trout just…didn't get it done. Ratings are still coming in, but from what I saw, we just…we need you out there."

"As long as I'm anchoring solo."

"Walter…" A sigh.

"It should be quite a battle. I mean, I'm sure Nixon's going to hold off Goldwater, but still…it should be quite a battle…"

"I don't want to hear any complaints about the Goldwater coverage."

"I'm a responsible newsman."

"You aired a piece implying he's a Nazi!"

"I have to report what I see."

"There is more at stake here than what you see, Walter."

"If we don't do our jobs, this man's finger could be on the nuclear button! In January, next year!"

"Walter, I have to look at the big picture. You know that."

"What bigger picture is there?"

"Walter. You're not making it easy for yourself. I have to look at next year, and the year after that, and the year after *that*. What if he *does* win? We can't throw out our credibility over one election. All this Ed Murrow, tell-the-truth-and-go-clean-out-your-desk stuff sounds noble, but..."

"I'm not Ed Murrow." A long sigh. "For better or worse, I am not Ed Murrow."

"Do you really understand that, though? Do you really understand that? I mean, this company is a machine now. It's a money-making *machine*, and it's a hell of a lot bigger than any one person. But if someone throws a wrench in the works...FCC rules, licensing...these people can really fuck with us if they win! I mean, really, really, really fuck with us!"

"They're not gonna win."

"Walter, we have to prepare for every eventuality. If we cover the election and can't keep covering the presidency afterwards...as I said, we don't want any complaints. You understand, right?"

A sigh. "I know who signs my paychecks."

●●●

Los Angeles, the next morning. The detective agency is empty when the business partner arrives. He goes into his office and shuts his door and pulls the cord to drop the blinds before opening the phone book, picking up the phone, dialing.

"FBI, Los Angeles office." A chipper female.

A blink of surprise and a small smile. "Well you're a cheerful one."

"How may I help you, sir?"

"Well…uhh…I'm a local private investigator. A private dick…in the parlance of the trade…" He listens for a reaction: none. "And…uhh, you investigate spying on U.S. soil, correct?"

"That's correct, sir."

"Well, my business partner has been talking to someone that…well, I think this client might be a Soviet spy. Like, they're having us do work under false pretenses because they're using us as a…what's the word?"

"Sir, I…"

"Cutout! That's the word. Anyway, I…"

"Sir! I'm a receptionist. Would you like to speak to an agent?"

An embarrassed sigh. "Uhhh, yeah. That'd be great."

•••

It is Monday morning, a sticky northern Virginia August morning. The spaceman ascends the short stone stepway to the Pentagon's river entrance. Squat square columns on the portico, imposing vertical rectangular windows: he catches a glimpse of his glistening face as he pulls open the heavy door.

Inside: air-conditioned relief. Flags and portraits and gold letters, walls of burnished wood and polished stone floors in the Hall of Heroes. He presents identification to a guard at a desk, hears: "Do you know where you're going?"

"Uhhh...5E315?"

A blink, and he is directed to the elevators.

Upstairs, seeing stars, in a general sense. He finds the appointed room, peers inside: massive mahogany conference table, projector, side table with coffee urn and pitchers of ice water. Enters it tentatively. Sees: a full bird colonel, waiting.

An air of annoyance. "Excuse me, you are..."

"Sir, I was told to be in room 5E315 at 9:00 a.m."

"Oh! You're early." A nod of respect. "I'll let him know you're here."

The spaceman looks like he doesn't know whether to sit or stand, or what to do with his hands. He waits in the empty room, thinking, perhaps, of LeMay stories he's heard: legendary ass-chewings, angry verbal bombardments that obliterated careers and sent shockwaves echoing throughout the Air Force.

In less than a minute, his wait is over. A gruff bulldog of a man barges in alone, a man with gray wavy hair and ribbons on his uniform jacket stacked almost to his four-star shoulder boards. A scowl on his face, one side pulled down by Bell's palsy.

"General LeMay. Sir."

Handshakes exchanged. "Have a seat. Pleasure to meet you."

The spaceman sits, tentative and tense, perhaps thinking: this man doesn't look like he spends much time thinking about pleasure.

"Relax," LeMay says. "I'm not here to chew your ass. You need anything before we get started? Bathroom? Coffee?"

The spaceman blinks. "Coffee…uhh, might be nice, sir."

LeMay nods. "Cream? Sugar?"

"Uhh…both, sir. That'd be great."

Another quick nod. Next to the coffee urn: a field of immaculate ceramic mugs adorned with the Department of Defense seal. The Chairman of the Joint Chiefs of Staff prepares two, and serves his visitor before sitting down.

"Good flight?"

"Not bad, sir."

"Get in this morning?"

"No, sir. I…uh…flew into Andrews last night. Stayed at the BOQ."

A nod. The general sips his coffee.

The spaceman tries to sip, tries to relax. Thinking, perhaps: Did I fly out here for coffee?

"We have a VIP joining us shortly."

The spaceman nods.

"Before he gets here, though: I heard about a…recommendation for a decoration making its way through the Air Force bureaucracy. Supposedly it was to be presented publicly. Your boss and I don't see eye to eye on that. As well as some other things." Unpleasant pause.

"Yes, sir."

"He's carved out...quite the little empire for himself. 40 percent of the Air Force budget. And he is an effective administrator. I will give him that. But this is an operational Air Force. All that...Hollywood bullshit, mad-scientists-in-the-lab stuff, it doesn't mean anything unless you use it to win wars." LeMay takes a breath. His eyes don't waver. "Which is what that was all about. Those extra photographs we had you do."

"Yes, sir."

"Based on what you told me from up there, we had positive confirmation of the location of the Soviet leadership. Is that correct?"

"Yes, sir."

The general's lips curl: the barest hint of amusement. "I'm not used to being the talkative one in the room."

"What would you like to know, sir?"

"The gentleman you were up there with, the Negro...does he know about the plan?"

"He knows the name of the town, sir. It's hard to keep a secret on a two-man crew. Especially when you've got to work together to make it happen."

LeMay nods. "He's still up there, right?"

"He is, sir. Until next week."

"Is he...reliable?"

"He's as good an officer as I've served with, sir. Negro or not."

Again, a nod. "I'm not...hung up on those things. So you were able to identify the target. No issues."

"No major issues, sir."

"So we did at least have the means to do something, if we wanted to. And the politicians, the ones who...don't understand the nature of modern warfare, they threw it away. The only question is...do we want to get it back?" The door opens. "Speaking of politicians."

In walks a familiar-looking civilian: black suit, mostly white hair, tanned rugged Western face, familiar horn-rimmed glasses. The spaceman gasps.

"Barry," the general says.

"Curt." An enthusiastic handshake. To the spaceman, another handshake: "Pleasure to meet you. Thanks for coming out. You probably thought I'd be...off on the campaign trail or something."

"Sir, I..."

"Even if it wasn't an election year, most of us do escape Washington in August. Many of my colleagues are not...eager to get reacquainted with the people who sent us here, but they still want a break from the DC humidity. For me it's out of the broiler, into the fire. I usually get out, too, though. Except this year. This year's different." A breath. "Obviously,

351

the election. Convention coming up. And I am still, of course, Chairman of the Senate Armed Services Committee. Although we're out of session, I have a very active interest in your program. It gives us…capabilities. Capabilities that may well prove vital to the survival of our nation, and the defense of our way of life. Do you understand?"

"Yes, sir."

"We're faced with an enemy that is bound and determined to undermine that way of life. And not through direct conflict! Not through direct conflict, if they can avoid it. This is an enemy of…insidious ideas. Ideas that can undermine our democracy. Ideas that, if left unchecked, will grow. Like an infection, they will…poison our national discourse. These ideas are already manifesting themselves in all sorts of…fevered rhetoric. We need to be able to stop that, if necessary. Not that we want to! These are…horrible weapons. We don't want to use them. But we need to be able to. The more we prepare for it, the less likely it is."

"Yes, sir."

"We need to be able to make…credible threats. Not just…setting off a bomb on some atoll, but a real, credible threat. You know, the threat is one of the great instruments of warfare. If you make a threat, and they know you can— and will—back it up, they will back down. Whereas if we rule out direct conflict, they will have an advantage. If they know we will not go to any lengths, they will be…emboldened. They need to know that we will go to any lengths. That we *can* go to any lengths. You do understand, don't you?"

"Yes, sir."

"Collectivism…it's an insidious poison," the senator continues. "I don't know if you were watching my colleague Senator Kennedy the other night, but…those ideas. World government, world law. International control of nuclear weapons. Leaving us no way to secure the peace and the freedom of the American people. The notion that you could have some…United Nations diplomat in a turban telling us what to do with our nuclear weapons, it's just…" He shudders.

The spaceman nods, as if on the verge of agreement.

"Of course, the thing they don't tell you, the thing the liberals and the news media never tell you is, the way to maximize peace and maximize freedom is to leave people alone. No more government than is necessary. I mean, obviously we need to promote the common defense, but beyond that…the rights of the individual come from God. It's not man's right to restrict that."

"Yes, sir."

"The communists don't get that. And their…unwitting allies in the Democratic Party don't get that. They claim to want peace, but you can't achieve it through world government. Not without spilling a lot of blood! That's been the case throughout history. The more people you want to rule, the more you have to kill." He sighs. "Sometimes I think they don't mind, though. They are the bloodthirsty ones. I mean, look at our presidents, this century. Have any of them shed more blood than Franklin Delano Roosevelt? Or Harry S. Truman?"

LeMay shifts in his chair. Looks elsewhere.

"Wilson, too. Whereas conservatives...I mean, for all the eggheads prattling on about the dangers of a President MacArthur, look at his record. Peace! We built a bulwark against communism. The Asian continent, it had already fallen under the sway of the collectivists. We lost China, Korea, Vietnam by the time Truman was out of office, but under MacArthur we built a bulwark. Japan, Taiwan, the Philippines. Australia, Singapore, Indonesia. A strong fence. You need a strong fence to have any sort of peace."

"Yes, sir."

"But again, the collectivist strategy is an insidious strategy. They know if they can weaken the wall, they can continue to expand. So they'll do whatever they can to...poison us with those ideas. Get us to drop our defenses. Their ideas, these...foolish notions of utopia. Every tyrant who has ever spilled the blood of millions was trying to build a utopia. Every one. Do you understand that?"

"Yes, sir."

"We need the means to avoid that, if we do find ourselves with our backs against the wall. We don't want...surrender to be the only option. Your...former crewmember, Hartsfield, he understood that. I just wanted to make sure you feel the same way."

"Yes, sir."

"There's been talk of...relaxing the publicity restrictions. Advertising..." (A sneer.) "...some of what we're doing up there. And I say there's no need. Your funding is secure. Unless Kennedy wins in November, which he isn't going to.

And even if he did…which he won't…no leader gives up a capability like this, once it's in their hands. So…no need to talk about it. We don't want…Walter Cronkite blathering about our capabilities on the Communist Broadcasting Service."

"Of course not, sir."

"They likened me to a Nazi. On his show! I'm half-Jewish, for crying out loud! That's the kind of falsehood they are willing to perpetrate. To further their agenda."

A head nod from the spaceman. Somewhere between contemplation and agreement.

"We do plan on recognizing what you did," LeMay says. "In a way that's…appropriate."

"Thank you, sir."

The senator says: "Do you have any questions of us?"

"Questions, sir?"

"Anything," LeMay pipes up. "You've seen the operational side. Anything. Feedback, comments…"

"Well, sir…isn't this sort of academic at this point? Trying to make sure the contingency plan is workable? I mean, if we've ended the Chrome Dome flights…"

The senator smiles. "You let us worry about that."

LeMay: "You'd like to get back up there, wouldn't you?"

"I would, sir."

"We'd like to get you back up there. That can happen, as long as you're with us. Are you with us?"

A deep breath: "Yes, sir."

Nods and glances. There are no papers to clean up, no records of the meeting; the two senior men just look at each other as if to say: that's it.

But Goldwater seems reluctant to leave. "It must've been neat, being up there."

"It was, sir."

"There's nothing I love like flying. Nothing like it at all. That feeling of...pure individualism. Pure freedom."

"Well, we are...set in our courses up there, sir. Orbital mechanics and what-not. It's not like we can just...swoop around at will."

"Of course. Still...flying and photography. Two of my passions. We've built quite the setup for both."

"Yes, sir."

"Tell me, did you...see anything?"

"Anything?"

He stares at the younger man. "Any...UFOs?"

An eye roll from the general.

The spaceman gives a look like he's choosing his words carefully. "The only unidentified object I saw turned out to be a Soviet satellite. Sir."

The senator chuckles, shakes his head. LeMay stands, straightens his uniform, checks his watch. "Gentlemen..."

"I can walk him out, Curt, if you've got stuff to do."

A nod from the general. "We do need to..."

A knowing nod in return. "I'll swing back by your office."

"I'm at your service." A returned nod, and the general steps out, oddly deferential.

The senator smiles, alone now with his quarry. "So, tell me. What did the universe look like from up there?"

"It was...incredible, sir. Especially outside, on the dark side."

"I bet. That's one of my favorite things about getting back to Arizona, getting away from the *city*." (He says it as if it's a dirty word.) "Being alone in the desert, looking up and seeing the sky at night..."

"It's even better from up there, sir. There's just...so much out there. More than we can comprehend."

"Indeed." A hesitation. Then: "I've asked our friend here to see the room."

The spaceman looks as if he's misheard. "The...room?"

"The aliens. Whatever they've recovered at...Roswell, or whatever. That Project Blue Book stuff. I know you came down in Nevada, close to Nevada. I know we have...facilities out there that even I'm not authorized to know all the details of. Black budget stuff. Groom Lake. I wasn't sure if they'd taken you there afterwards."

A perplexed look from the spaceman. "I...don't know what you're talking about, sir."

"No." He smiles. "Of course not."

"Sir, I'm sure there are still...secrets I'm not privy to in this Air Force. Rooms I haven't been to yet. If there is some sort of place where...I mean, it seems like you have a good relationship with General LeMay..."

"Well, as I said, I asked him to see the room. And he gave me holy hell. He said, 'Not only can you not see the room, I am not authorized to talk to you about the room. Don't ever ask me again.' So you see, I am in a bit of a quandary. I'm not sure what else I'd have to do to know more. Maybe in November..."

The spaceman nods. Smiles. "Now you've got me curious. Sir."

•••

When the spy gets into his car he looks at the back seat, runs his hands along the front and edges of the vinyl, tugs on everything to make sure it's secure. Then he turns the car on, turns on the radio, bops his head as Herman's Hermits sing: Something tells me I'm into something good. He backs out of his driveway and is soon on wider streets, in thicker traffic. But he doesn't seem to mind. Every time someone cuts him off, or tries to squeeze in in front of him, he ushers them in with a magnanimous hand gesture. He's in no hurry.

Before he leaves town he drives to random alleys, pulls in, waits, listens to a song or two, smokes, watches. Dry cleaning, in his organization's parlance. After a good hour of this, he at last gets on the interstate heading south.

The morning congestion's clearing up, and as he rides the river of cars he sticks to the right lane, travelling with the speed of traffic, careful not to stick out. America, a land of lawbreakers: and as long as you're breaking the law in exactly the same way as everyone, you're fine. He watches cars enter and exit the expressway, eyes the occupants, presumably looking for men with crewcuts, men travelling alone. If they are tailing him they will probably have two behind and one in front, and they will rotate periodically. But they are not tailing him.

South of town the road opens up; there are rumpled brown hills off to the left flecked with green. To the right, over the undulating tops of trees and scrub, he can see endless Pacific blue.

It is a couple hours to the border. He'll have to repeat the dry-cleaning process once he crosses, on the off chance one of the Mexican border guards IDs him, but he doesn't appear terribly concerned, nor does he look at the rear seat.

Underneath it is a roll of microfilm, full of transcripts.

•••

A lonely midday flight home for our spaceman: Clear Air, Visibility Unlimited. Rugged rumpled Appalachian mountains flattening out, land turning into geometric shapes, tamed and made regular. It is all beneath him; it is all distant; it all makes sense. The great American heartland, the endless fields of the Republic, peaceful and inviolate for a century,

now. It is all just *there*, naked and vulnerable, and perhaps it is easier to imagine the destruction of the nation from this height: every city and town just a blotch on the earth. The spaceman finds himself scanning the countryside, presumably thinking of camera calibration passes a few short weeks ago, in another life. Or thinking of the Soviets, and what they've seen.

The land dries out, crumples upwards again: all the order and regularity is, after all, an illusion, a temporary interlude, not the normal state of earthly affairs. It all seems perhaps less majestic than it would on a cross-country drive: the plains less fruited, the mountains not as purple. Although he does gaze in wonder at the mystery of the vast Nevada desert. So much space: how much could be hidden?

An uneventful landing at Vandenberg. All the usual forms and checklists, and then he's back in civilian clothes, his service dress uniform on a hangar and ready for the dry cleaners, his overnight bag on his shoulder. Back at his car in the POV lot: everything the way he left it twenty-four hours ago.

On the drive down the PCH: more time for quiet contemplation on that narrow shelf of asphalt, a man-made platform perched precariously between the infinite Pacific and the unsculptable hills.

Down near Malibu, a crown of flame on the dry hillside. He sees an old PBY Catalina banking over the terrain in front of him, unloading a torrent of water on the distant inferno. Imagines, perhaps, the workday: landing on the ocean, scooping seawater into hull tanks, throttling up for the takeoff run, feeling the pounding of the water on the ancient aluminum rivets before the aircraft lurches skyward. Then: droning along towards today's blaze, calculating terrain shapes and wind speed and fire propagation patterns before making a final approach, unloading a deluge on the conflagration: man-made rain, the opposite of firebombing.

Before long he's back in LA, the same aggravations, the same traffic. Lazy airliners above floating in to LAX. Another day like every day, it's all the same.

•••

"Kids are out back," his wife says when he comes in. "I was just about to put dinner away."

"Oh. Sorry, I should have called from Vandenberg."

"How was the trip?"

"Good." He serves himself: meatloaf, mashed potatoes, green beans.

"Just good?" She smiles. "I know I can't expect much in the way of detail. But I wouldn't mind *something*."

"Well, the flight out was pretty smooth. The time transition usually screws me up, but I slept pretty well. I had to swing by the Pentagon. Talk to the powers-that-be. And then it was back in the plane." First forkful of food.

"Do they appreciate what you're doing for them? I mean, do they appreciate what it does to a man's family to keep having these...dislocations?"

"We've had it OK these past couple years."

"*You've* had it OK. *We've* had plenty of late nights. Lost weekends."

"A program like this, it takes work to make it happen."

"And we're glad it came together! We're proud you're doing such...great things. But we don't know what they are. And...well, it's nerve-wracking. Knowing everything that could happen."

A pause before eating more. "Imagine how it is for me. Knowing everything I know."

"You enjoy it."

"It's...what I know how to do. It's...I mean, you go to the academy, and people complain about the workload, but it's...comfortable. It's comfortable to get a calendar and know what's due, and when. You know what your Tuesday's gonna look a month from now, what your Friday's gonna look like in two months' time. It's nice to have it all planned out, to have your time...tamed. To know what you need to do, and when you need to do it. And then...you get out, and you're on a staircase. You see the steps, and you know what it takes to get up to the next one. You see all the forms and checklists. You know what's being asked of you. There's a...structure. A regularity. And...I like that. You know me...I like it when everything's in its right place."

"It's OK," she says, "if every day is not the same day."

He shrugs. Finishes his dinner.

In the bedroom he is putting things away, deconstructing his overnight bag, when he sees it: glass flask, soil and plants, a stopper on top.

"Your parents called yesterday, after you left," she says as she walks in. "I thought you'd have called them already."

"Yeah, I keep forgetting. You finished my terrarium?"

"I was tired of seeing it sitting around."

"I was gonna do it."

"That's what you kept saying."

He moves behind her to hold her. Kisses her hair, revels in the smell. "Thanks for taking care of it, sweetie."

"Uhh-huh." She shrugs him off.

•••

In the morning when he wakes, she is in the kitchen in her bathrobe, drinking coffee and reading: *Alas, Babylon*.

"Remind me never to survive a nuclear war," she says.

"Huh?"

"This book, it's all…post-apocalyptic. Society falling apart after World War III. They're in this small town in Florida, and the cities have been destroyed, and they're trying to survive without electricity or money. Shotguns and machetes, dealing with…marauding packs of criminals. It doesn't sound very fun."

"Well, not with that attitude."

A sour look. "I keep thinking about when you were up there. That message. I mean, if something like that did happen…"

"Nobody wants that."

"Sometimes things happen that nobody wants."

"The more we prepare for it," he says, "the less likely it is."

"If you say so."

He pours himself a coffee, grabs a magazine, sits down.

She smiles. "Are you gonna make breakfast?"

"Am I?"

"Well, I just thought…you're not always here for it. I'm usually doing it. I figured it might be nice…"

"I don't even know what…"

"There's pancake mix in the cupboard. Bacon in the fridge."

"OK, then." He roots around for frying pan, bacon, mix, mixing bowl. Spends the next few minutes watching the bacon curling and sizzling in the pan, spearing it with a fork, feeling the burn as grease pops onto his bare knuckles. Soon the kids have awoken and are hovering, curious; he keeps shooing them away from the spattering pan before reluctantly picking each one up in turn for a quick glimpse of the proceedings.

After breakfast his wife leaves for the post office, and the kids head out back to play. He sits down to read, but can't seem to focus. He gets up, paces, picks up the telephone, dials "0," asks—hesitantly—for a number for the Forest Service. The operator gives him a number up in Vallejo, long distance.

Two rings and a bored female voice. "Forest Service, Pacific Southwest office."

"Uhhh…hello. I'm…ahh…this is probably an odd question, but…I'm a pilot, and I'm a little curious about jobs there. The…uhh, firefighting planes, or whatever."

"Let me connect you to personnel."

"OK."

More rings. "Personnel."

"Yes, hello…I'm…uhh, I'm a pilot, and I was wondering about…well, jobs. Flying the firefighting planes."

"Well, we're not hiring at the moment. In a few months we may have slots, once the fire season's over…"

"That's fine. I'm…I'm in the service now, so there'd have to be a bit of a transition. I was actually kind of hoping to talk to one of the pilots, maybe. See what the flying's like…"

"They're all…this is an administrative office. It's not like they're sitting around. Especially this time of year. They're off at the local command posts, whatever little local airport they're at. Flying all day, putting out whatever fires they can, snatching a few hours of sleep on a cot in a hangar at night, getting up to do it all over again."

"That…sounds kinda fun, actually."

"It's very busy in the fire season. Months away from family and friends. And then pretty slow for the rest of the year. At least for the few pilots that work directly for us. Some of it's contract work, little aviation companies that do other things in the off season...it helps us be a little more flexible with the firefighting. It's pretty demanding flying. Low altitudes, rugged terrain. We're really only interested in very experienced pilots."

"I'm pretty experienced."

"Well, with all due respect, we get calls from experienced pilots all the time. I mean, low-level flying around terrain, it's very demanding."

"I'm very experienced. I've...uhh, I've actually been in space. I mean, not much terrain avoidance up there, but..."

A pause at the other end: "Is this a prank call?"

●●●

In the low light of the evening bedroom he sees her back turned towards him as he climbs into bed. Admires the rise and fall of hips and torso. Moves up behind her, snakes an arm over her body to hold her.

She looks over her shoulder: "If there was a war, would you know about it before?"

A sigh: "You know I can't talk about this stuff."

"I just want to know if you'd know."

"I don't know if anybody would know."

"Somebody would know."

"Nobody I know."

Now she rolls all the way toward him, out from under his arm. "You just got back from the Pentagon. You met the Chairman of the Joint Chiefs of Staff. Who's it? LeMay?"

"I don't really know him."

An incredulous head shake. "You did know something! When you were up there."

A sigh. "When I was up there, there was...something that could have been something. But it ended up being nothing."

"So you would know something the next time." She turns back away. "In the book, there was a character in the service. He sent his family away to Florida. And he had to send them a signal, that the war was coming. I can't help wondering if you'd even send a signal. Something more substantial than 'You might want to go camping.'"

A reluctant sigh. "If I was up there, I *might* know something ahead of time. In certain scenarios. Down here...I probably wouldn't know much more than the average man on the street."

"But you'd be part of it. I mean, just being in uniform, you'd be a part of it. Is that something you want to be a part of?"

"Well, obviously, it depends on the outcome."

A huff. She pulls the bedsheet tighter around her.

"I mean, the Air Force is important to me...it's been a helluva place to launch a career."

No reaction.

He speaks again: "Look, if I'm ever in a position where it's in my power to let you know anything, I'll let you know. Secret or no. We'll get a radio if we have to, like Hank. We'll do whatever we have to do."

He can see her torso rise and fall: a deep heavy breath.

He takes a deep breath of his own, puts his hand on her hip, starts to caress.

"If you think I'm in the mood right now," she says, "you're nuts."

•••

"It's my turn to play with teddy!" The son's voice spikes, plaintive and insistent, the first loud sounds in the house all morning.

"You put him down. You weren't playing with him."

"I just put him down for a second so I could look at my frog."

"It's my turn."

"Kids, don't fight over teddy," the mom calls from the living room. But she hears a bump and a crash, and by the time she makes it to the bedroom, they are engaged in a full-on tug of war, whirling about and bumping into bed and dresser, drawing uncomfortably close to the glass terrarium.

"Give him back!"

"Stop!" The mom pulls them apart. She is in her Sunday best even though it's Thursday; the kids are still in their pajamas. "No fighting! You're gonna break the terrarium."

"He started it."

"She took teddy."

"I don't care who started it!"

The spaceman appears. "Kids, listen to your mother. Don't fight. You've gotta get ready for church anyway."

"Get them ready," Mom says. "I have to finish up in the bathroom."

"Do we have to go?" the son groans. "It's not even Sunday."

"It's the Feast of the Assumption. It's a Holy Day of Obligation. They taught you about that in school, right?"

A sigh. "Ugggghh. Yes."

His daughter: "What's the feats of the assunscion?"

"Well, Jesus' mother Mary, at the end of her life, she went straight up to heaven. Body and soul."

"Did she go on a rocket?"

"They didn't have rockets back then."

"Did you see her when you were up there?"

The spaceman chuckles. "No. I think she went really high."

"Like to the moon?"

"Past the moon, even."

The son: "I want to go to the beach."

"We can go to the beach afterwards." Dad picks up the clothes his wife has set out on the bed for the boy: collared shirt and pants. "Here, put this on."

Soon they are clothed and outside and belted and in the car, rolling through bright sunny Los Angeles streets: no smog today, blinding sun on car chrome, trees and lawns somehow simultaneously green and golden. There's news on the radio: Dr. Martin Luther King speaking in Chicago. "Our society is transfixed by dreams of space. But the crosses we have to bear are here on this earth..." The spaceman changes the channel, puts on classical music.

"Oh, man!" The son plugs his ears.

"We can turn it off," the wife says.

"Thanks, mommy. You're a great mommy."

"Today's all about great mommies," the dad says. "The reason the Virgin Mary went straight up to heaven is because Jesus loved her so much. She was a perfect mommy."

Daughter: "What's a virgin?"

"It's...uhh, it's somebody who's really good."

"So mommy's a virgin?"

Stifled chuckles from the parents.

"Mommy's not that good," Mom says.

"She's trying to be, this week," the spaceman says, and his wife whacks him hard on the shoulder.

Son: "Hey, no fighting!"

"Yes, no fighting," the spaceman echoes.

"Was she better than our mommy?" the daughter asks.

"Good question," the mom says. "Was she better?"

The spaceman grimaces. "Your mommy's a wonderful mommy. She cares about you very much. She works very hard to feed you guys. To keep you from fighting."

"But she's not better than Mary."

"Mary was perfect. She's our mother too, in a way."

"So she doesn't want us to fight?"

"Probably not."

"But you fight, daddy."

"I don't fight."

"You used to fly fighter planes."

"Uhhh…I trained to fight. I trained to fight the bad guys. But I never had to fight."

"But we're not supposed to fight. Why would you train to do something we're not supposed to do?"

"Uhhh, if you train to do it, sometimes it means you don't have to do it. But it's OK if it's bad guys. The bad guys don't believe in God. They don't want anyone to believe in God."

At last they are pulling in to the parking lot. He glances down at the dashboard clock anxiously, spies a tight spot close to the entrance, pulls in unevenly, opens the car door to look at the yellow painted line on sunbaked asphalt, pulls the car out, pulls it back in again: still uneven. Back and forth again.

"Remind me again," the wife says, "what it is you do for a living?"

"Nobody parks that close on the tarmac," he says. "Come on, we're late."

A quick march across the lot and they are pulling open the doors, filing humbly into the pews.

"A great sign appeared in the sky," the reader pronounces from the lectern. "A woman clothed in the sun, with the moon at her feet, and on her head a crown of twelve stars. She was with child and wailed aloud in pain as she labored to give birth. Then another sign appeared in the sky; it was a huge red dragon, with seven heads and ten horns, and on its heads were seven diadems. Its tail swept away a third of the stars in the sky and hurled them down to earth..."

The girl whispers: "Dad..."

"Shhhh. No talking in church."

"Did you see a red dragon in the sky?"

"No," he whispers. "Not really."

Psalms and responses. The spaceman shifts uncomfortably.

Another speaker, another reading: "For since death came through man, the resurrection of the dead also came through man. For just as in Adam all die, so too in Christ shall all be brought to life, but each one in proper order; Christ the firstfruits; then, at his coming, those who belong to Christ;

then comes the end, when he hands over the Kingdom to his God and Father, when he has destroyed every sovereignty and every authority and power…"

He excuses himself, goes to the bathroom. Stands and relieves himself while examining the poster showing the Los Angeles Archdiocese's seminarians for the current year. It's been disconcertingly placed on the wall above the urinal: forty eyes of future priests staring at him while he pees.

Back inside, the priest begins his homily. "We are offered a dramatic reading today from Revelation. Indelible imagery. A woman, Mary, threatened by a red dragon. It is comforting in today's political climate to think that we know who the dragon is, to think that we are the ones defending Mary. In past times the dragon was taken to be Babylon, or Rome; now there are those who say it's Moscow. The third Rome. But when we look at our culture, I'm not so sure we can be comfortable. We are presented with an image of perfection in Mary, a woman modest and chaste; we are seduced by other images: women in Technicolor bikinis, Gingers and Mary Anns…the CBS eye giving satisfaction for our lust as it gleams in hunger for the almighty dollar. Babylon has nothing on us…"

The priest drones on. The rituals unfold. Stand, kneel, sit. Sit, kneel, stand. Incense and bells and Communion.

•••

After Mass they linger in the church. The kids are hanging off the pews, sagging as if the force of gravity has suddenly increased threefold. A short queue forms outside the wooden confessional doors: priest booth in the center, and a booth for penitents on either side. There's a reddish-orange light over one of those booths.

"I'm gonna go to confession," the wife says to the spaceman.

"Do they have it?"

"People are lining up."

"The light's not on…"

"Sure it is."

"No, the…priest indicator."

"Priest indicator?" She smiles. On the booth, the green center light comes on at last. "There you go."

A parishioner enters the vacant booth, and the light above that door comes on.

"What's that red light called, then?"

"Sin warning!" he says. "Sin warning!"

"Very funny." She does not laugh.

"You know what? I'm gonna go, too."

"Good!"

"Are you saying I need it?"

She shrugs.

A parishioner emerges from the first booth, and the wife takes her place. The kids silently slump, crushed by boredom. The spaceman is staring off into the middle distance, perhaps performing an examination of conscience, perhaps avoiding.

When it is the spaceman's turn, he enters the booth, closes the door, kneels, hears the switch in the kneeler that triggers the light above the door. "Bless me, Father, for I have sinned. It has been two months since my last confession."

Through the screen: a pixelated anonymized image of the priest. "Tell me your sins."

"Well, the thing is, Father...my job is...well, secret. I'm in the service. I've sworn oaths. I'm not sure how much I can..."

"You can trust the seal of the confessional."

"I'm not sure how comfortable I feel..."

"God knows all. God watches everything; nothing is hidden. God is both a part of everything, and above it, observing. Immanent and transcendent. Every thought, every action, God sees it. If we pretend otherwise, we are fooling ourselves."

The spaceman takes a deep breath: thinking, perhaps, of his mission, the petty lies and evasions necessary for operational secrecy. Or perhaps bigger things: contingency plans, decapitation strikes, threats of war. He opens his mouth and starts to speak.

•••

"How may I help you, sir?" Again the chipper voice, but now there's a face to it: a blonde, stunning, sitting behind the front desk under the FBI seal.

"Oh! I spoke to you on the phone the other day," the business partner says. "I have an appointment with Agent Truax."

She nods, picks up the phone, presses a button. "Agent Truax, your 9:30 is here."

He nods, smiles. Leans on the desk. Gazes at the woman.

"You can have a seat, sir," she says.

"But then I'd be farther away."

She gives a nod that could be interpreted as: well, yeah.

The private dick does not interpret it that way. "I'm sorry, it's just...I called expecting G-men. I didn't think I'd meet a G-woman."

"Well, gee whiz," she says, with a tight smile. "Aren't you original? I'm going to mark my calendar. 45 consecutive workdays with a G-woman joke." There is a touch of angst in her voice.

He responds to the smile. "I guess that would make this the G-spot then, huh?"

She looks up. "Sir, you're not going to find that here."

"Well, not if you don't let me look."

"Ahem." To his left now: a crew-cutted man in a dark suit, who has apparently been standing there for a few moments.

"Oh," the private dick says. "Agent Truax, I presume."

They retire to his office.

"She's a little frosty, huh?" the dick says, with a nod towards the reception area.

"She's my sister-in-law," Agent Truax says. "We're Mormons."

"Oh." An awkward smile. "Well, don't I feel like a moron!"

"You're just...full of original jokes," Agent Truax says, unsmiling. "This...incident with your business partner. Tell me about it..."

The dick starts explaining: vague secondhand reminiscences. The G-man listens.

"We'd like to get some evidence, if possible," he says at last. "So far, this is just hearsay."

"Well, he's clammed up," the dick says.

"There's always evidence."

•••

"You were praying for a while there," the wife says. "After confession."

They are on the sand at Venice Beach, shielded by an umbrella from the midday sun, watching their children stand in the stretch of sand that keeps getting re-wetted by the remnants of each wave.

"It was a good solid penance. Ten Our Fathers, ten Hail Marys, ten Glory Bes."

"Wow, I got, like, two of each." A knot of bikini-clad women walk past; the wife glances down at her one-piece. "After that homily, when I see women like that, I keep thinking of...Babylon."

"What women?"

"The ones over there in the bikinis."

"Sorry, can't look."

"What?"

"I'm sin-free! Gotta see how long it can last. I don't know if you noticed, I haven't gotten angry at all since church. I drove peacefully, I didn't yell at anybody...gotta keep up the streak."

"So the bikini women are gonna give you lustful thoughts?"

"Well, it's a possibility..."

She hits him on the shoulder.

"Uh-oh," he says. "Anger. Seven deadly sins."

"Oh, Lord," she shakes her head.

"I think I told you about my uncle, my mom's youngest brother, the one I never met..."

"A little."

"Well, he was hit by a truck walking home from confession. My mom and her siblings, they always ask him for intercession. The assumption is he just went straight to heaven."

A smirk. "So you've got a death wish now? Maybe I should drive us home."

"I wouldn't say that. It's just...on my mind sometimes. I went the day before my first solo flight. I went before I launched this summer."

"I didn't realize that."

"Dad." The son's returned from the fringes of the ocean. "I have to go to the bathroom."

"Is it a number one or a number two?" Mom asks. "If it's number one, you can just go in the ocean."

"Ewww."

"The fish do it," Mom points out. "Your legs are covered in fish pee."

"Gross!"

"It is kinda gross, actually," the spaceman says. "Let's go."

The boardwalk is well-worn and spattered with pelican shit, thick with all the cataclysmic trappings of civilization: t-shirt shops selling tie-dyed weirdness, tattoo parlors; dirty couples in tattered jean-shorts walking hand in hand, the hair on the men only marginally shorter than the women; clean-cut Beach Boy wannabes, tanned and disdainful; a knife juggler; a woman with a python around her neck; another woman spewing fire into the afternoon sky; a clot of shirtless men watching a glistening strongman lift weights; a young man in a suit and tie passing out flyers. The spaceman takes one. ARE YOU AWAKE TO THE DANGER OF WORLD GOVERNMENT? it asks. It's from the John Birch Society; there are passages about various plots against the American people: an army of Chinese Communists massing in Mexico to attack across the undefended border, a UN project to train an army of Negroes in the swamps of Georgia so they can mount an armed insurrection. ARE YOU GOING TO DO NOTHING?

The spaceman folds it, puts it in his pocket.

"But the Lord is the true God!" Near the bathroom, an older Negro waves arm and hand and index finger skyward. "He is the living God, and an everlasting king: at his wrath the earth shall tremble, and the nations shall not be able to abide his indignation!" The boy looks over, curious; the spaceman ushers him along.

In the beachhouse their nostrils are assailed by the scent of warm stale urine mixed with smokable narcotics. Flickering lights, rusty stalls, cracked concrete floor with puddles of unknown provenance. One stall is choked with wet toilet paper. Another is closed. The spaceman makes the mistake of touching the door without checking underneath it; it swings open to reveal a Negro passed out on the toilet, sprawled out, a hand wrapped around his erect penis.

"Jesus!" the spaceman recoils.

"Dad, what's..."

"Don't look, there's something gross in there." He turns, shields his son's eyes, turns back to the stall, tries to pull the door closed. The rusty hinges give way and the door falls over with a clatter; the spaceman feels a light splash on his bare shins from the unknown puddled liquid on the floor.

"Oh, Jesus Fucking Christ!" the spaceman erupts. Shoes his son over to the side of the bathroom, looks again at the Negro, who has stirred slightly but remained in place, dirty shorts around his ankles, soaking in the filthy floor fluid. He pulls his leg back as if to kick the man, thinks better of it, yells: "Wake up...man."

The Negro stirs, heavy lidded, and then slumps back again against the side of the stall.

"Dad, I have to..."

"We'll...we gotta..." He drags his son out of the bathroom, frantically scans the horde of humanity, walks fast down the boardwalk until he sees two cops, trim and muscled, in immaculate dark blue uniforms. "Officers, there's a man in the bathroom in a state of...lewdness."

"Lewdness?" A bemused smile on the slightly shorter cop.

The spaceman plugs his son's ears. "He's in there holding his cock."

The cop sighs; the other shakes his head in disgust. "Where is it?"

The spaceman leads them to the beachhouse, parks his son outside the door with a stay-right-there admonition, leads the cops inside as if needing to gauge their reaction, or maybe just confirm that he'd seen what he'd seen. Amazingly enough, the man is still in the stall, still passed out in the corner, still undressed and obscene.

"I'm sorry you had to see this, sir," the taller cop says apologetically.

"You're gonna arrest him, right?"

"Oh, yeah," the cop says. "Gotta funny feeling he's gonna resist. In the meantime you might wanna find another bathroom. We're gonna have to close this one for cleaning."

The spaceman backs off. Lingers for a moment before rounding the corner.

"Boy, get up!" the taller cop says. "This is a family fucking bathroom."

"Don't make me get my nightstick dirty." The shorter officer kicks him hard on the leg and this time the man stirs, shakes his head, eyes wide in alarm; he scrambles to his feet and starts pulling up his shorts; the cop reaches in, grabs him by the upper arm, extracts him from the stall; he slams him into the cinderblock wall between the urinals.

The spaceman turns to leave at last. Hears, on the way out the door, a sickening crack of cartilage and bone.

Outside, his boy is standing obediently.

"Come on. Let's go find another bathroom."

"Uhh, I don't have to go anymore."

"Let's find you a bathroom." The spaceman shakes his head. "I'm sorry you had to see that."

"It's OK. He had the door closed."

"What?"

"He had the door closed. He wasn't bothering anyone."

"Well, he was bothering me."

• • •

When they return to their beach umbrella the spaceman is anxious and irritable. He settles in on the blanket, sighing and shaking his head.

"Still sin-free?" His wife puts down *Alas, Babylon*.

"I...uhh..."

"Too many bikinis on the boardwalk?"

"I'll tell you about it later." He settles down on the blanket; his son scampers off to where his sister's building a sandcastle. "We do need to move to Vandenberg. The city is..." He shakes his head, leaves it at that.

"OK." She picks the book back up.

"It's weird, being here. On the beach." He nods towards the infinite ocean. "You look out there, you realize it looks the same as it did fifty years ago. A hundred years ago, five hundred years ago. It still looks...clean. Like God made it. But back there..." (A nod towards the boardwalk.) "...that's all on us. All the filth."

"You think things are filthier than they were fifty years ago? The silent film age? You had...morals committees trying to police everything up. Fatty Arbuckle getting arrested for...rape and manslaughter."

"Fine. A hundred years ago. Before Mulholland brought the water. When it was all...cowboys or whatever."

A snort. "They still had...you name it. Liquor. Gambling. Prostitutes."

"A thousand years ago, then. Two thousand years ago. Five thousand years ago."

"Well, I don't know what was here, but on the other side of the globe you had Rome...Babylon...Sodom and Gomorrah. And the ocean, nature. How clean is that? There's still...death, decay. Corruption."

"It all gets cleaned, though," he says. "It all gets washed away." He glances over. "When you read about Sodom and Gomorrah, you read about how Abraham argued with the Lord to spare them. For the sake of fifty righteous people. For the sake of ten. But you keep reading, and...well, God destroys Sodom. God destroys Gomorrah. Burning sulfur from the heavens. Dense smoke rising from the land. You wonder...God or man, which one is merciful? Which one is just?"

She furrows her brow, props herself up on an elbow.

"The thing I didn't tell you about," he goes on. "When we were talking about confession earlier. During the Berlin Crisis...I mean, we were ready to go. They had loaded up the aircraft. They staged us from Libya up to Turkey."

"I remember you telling me about that."

"Well, the thing..." A heavy sigh. "The thing I never told you is, I had a weapon to deliver."

"Well, I assumed you had weapons."

"No...a weapon."

"Oh."

"And we…I mean, we had been briefed. When things get that serious, they're strapping something to every aircraft, every fighter that can fit a nuke on its belly. And as far as we knew, we were launching. I mean, we were taxiing down the apron. Lining up to take off. I was going to fly across the Black Sea, to Odessa. And all I could think of, was that I hadn't gone to confession. And whether or not it would have mattered, given what I was about to do. I mean, you tell yourself, 'They're worse than us.' Godless Communism and all that. But you come back here and see…peep shows in Times Square, half-naked women on Venice Beach. And then you think, well, it goes both ways, right? Surely there are people there raising kids. Raising families. Teaching them to be honest, teaching them not to steal…"

She says nothing, just sits there listening.

"Anyway, we were going. We were taxiing down the apron. We lined up to take off. And we just never got the order. And word came that the Soviets had backed down." He looks back towards her. "I mean, I signed up to fly fighters. To defend. The nuclear stuff…you tell yourself it's necessary, to keep the country safe. You tell yourself it's not on you, if anything awful happens. Decisions beyond your pay grade, and all that. But then at some point you think, does anyone's decision matter, then, below the president? Are the systems just too big and too complicated for anyone else to stop it? I mean, in the whole history of humanity, we've never developed a weapon and then *not* used it in anger, once the stakes got high enough. So you have to wonder, does it matter, what you decide? If you don't deliver your weapon, that's one less bomb, out of 30,000, so what does it matter?" He sighs. "But then you get older, you move a little up the pay grade, high enough to see the people who are making the decisions, and you realize, you really realize, they're just people. They're not…gods handing down decisions from Mount Olympus, they're people. And you realize you *do* have decisions to make, too. You're their eyes, you can decide what they see. You can interpret something one way or another. Now, if you're unreliable, if you do it poorly for a long period of time, you'll be replaced, so you might still wonder if it matters. And maybe the same set of circumstances will happen again for the next guy, but then again…maybe they won't. And even then…once your commitment is up, you have a decision, whether or not to stay with the organization. So sometimes…sometimes that's it, that's your decision. Do you know what I'm saying? I mean, what do you think?"

He turns towards her and waits for an answer.

•••

Saturday night, alone in the kitchen, kids in bed. The spaceman dials the number: the sixth time in the past three days. It's written on a notepad next to the phone, but he almost has it memorized now.

Three rings, then an unexpected: "Yell-o?"

"Hey. Long time no talk."

Instant recognition, and a shift in tone. "Wow. Didn't expect to hear from you." The voice on the other end of the line is familiar, a roommate from the academy: not his favorite roommate, perhaps, but a useful one at the present moment.

"Yeah, it's been…what, since graduation probably, right?"

"Yeah, since graduation."

"Ever…settle down? Kids or anything?"

"Not that I know of." A drunken chuckle. "How about you?"

"Oh, yeah. Wife, two kids. Boring old me."

"I heard you were…doing some hush-hush space thing."

"I can neither confirm nor deny." But his tone does.

"Wow, I can't even…that's really something."

"Yeah."

"Two of you up there at a time, right?"

"Yep. Living in a can for six weeks."

"Do you hassle your crewmate about cleaning?"

"Well, I…"

"I mean, you don't have to worry about…surprise inspections."

"No, not exactly." A forced chuckle. "Look, I…I wanted to ask a favor."

"From me?"

"Well, it's just that I…heard through the grapevine that you got out. Flying for…Pan Am, is it?"

"Pan Am it is."

"Well, I'm just…exploring career options. What I've been doing has been…amazing, but I just…I mean, for the sake of the family, I figure it might be worth looking at something less...nerve-wracking."

"Less nerve-wracking."

"Look, I know we weren't...the best of roommates. I know that wasn't all your fault, I just...I'd appreciate your help."

Another shift in tone. "Well, it's a hell of an airline. Very profitable. Flying to every continent but Antarctica. 'The World's Most Experienced Airline.' I'm actually...pretty low on the totem pole here. Which is something to consider. I mean, I'm still not married, I don't entirely mind. Actually, truth be told, I am enjoying the hell out of it. Every day I'm...flying to the best bars in the world. But for the guys with families...until you have a little seniority, it's rough. Lots of nights and weekends away. No normal holidays. Constant jet lag, never able to get straightened out. A short-haul carrier might be better."

"Yeah."

"I love it, though. Not the most exciting flying job in the world, but the view from up there never gets old."

"I hear you." The spaceman smiles. "So...flying to every continent. Does that mean you have a girl on every continent?"

A chuckle. "I can neither confirm nor deny."

From the boy's room: a crash.

His wife calls from the far end of the house: "Can you see what that was?"

"I…thanks for your help, I gotta go." An awkward hang-up.

Inside the room, he turns on the lights: catastrophe. The terrarium on the ground, its sides shattered in big glass shards, dirt and plants and water spilling out onto the carpet. His son frozen in fear.

"Don't move!"

"I'm not moving." But he takes a step.

"Don't move! There's glass." The spaceman runs up front, grabs a pair of low quarters, darts back to the bedroom, picks up his son, evacuates him to the hallway, looks his feet over for glass. "What happened?"

"I don't know."

"Don't lie. What happened?"

The son cries. "I don't know."

"Were you asleep? Were you sleepwalking?"

"I…don't…know." Tears. Heavy breaths. "Edward Hopper."

"What?"

"The frog. We gotta look for the frog."

"Wait here." Back in the room the spaceman looks at the wreckage. Expecting, perhaps, to see a bloody amphibian carcass in the midst of it. But no. He looks everywhere, high and low; he opens the closet and peers under the bed and looks behind the dresser. Nothing.

"Did you find him?" The son is in the doorway.

"Not yet. Just…" He picks up his son, scans frantically for his wife. She is emerging from their bedroom, wrapped in a towel, hair wet.

"What ha…"

"He broke the terrarium."

"I don't know how it happened."

"Just…take him." He hands off his son, turns back to the mess. Grabs the mop bucket, spends the next fifteen minutes gingerly scooping up glass and dirt and plants into it. He vacuums the floor, vacuums it over and over and over, moving his head back and forth to catch little glints of light between the loops of carpet fiber, bending over and teasing out wayward shards with his fingertips.

When at last he has deposited the contents of the bucket into the trash, his wife and son are asleep on the couch, son nestled close under her: peaceful, vulnerable.

●●●

Late in the day on Sunday, the son is watching TV and the spaceman's leaving the hallway bathroom. Right before putting his foot down he looks down all of the sudden and sees: Edward Hopper.

"I found the frog!"

The son bolts over. "Where was he?"

"I almost stepped on him."

"Where did you go?" the son asks the frog.

"Ribbit."

To the father: "What are we gonna do with him?"

"I guess I can put him in my terrarium."

"He can't breathe in there."

"I'll leave the lid off."

"It's too small."

The spaceman sighs. Looks frantically around the house. Finally grabs the mop bucket, rinses it and rinses it, looking in the corners of the galvanized metal for miniscule shards of glass. At last they set the frog inside with a bowl of water; the son drops in a couple dead flies and they wrap the top in a piece of window screen, secured on all sides with duct tape.

•••

Monday morning drive to El Segundo: the spaceman is wearing his Air Force blues, uniform jacket hanging in the back so it won't get wrinkled while he drives. The morning smog hasn't burned off yet, and the city streets are choked with cars; soon he is in that part of the city with low anonymous aerospace industry buildings, and it all looks grey and futuristic and depressing.

But once he turns off Douglas, he can tell it isn't a routine morning: airmen are policing up the landscaping under the expansive palms around the gate, picking up every stray cigarette butt and candy bar wrapper, and the one standing guard is in his full uniform, with jacket. The kid salutes perfunctorily, his mind clearly elsewhere, on the bigger visitor who's apparently coming soon.

The spaceman parks, puts on his jacket and hat while still sitting, checks himself off briefly in the rearview mirror, gets out, smooths over his uniform, checks himself off in the distorted gleam of the car window, and finally walks across the parking lot. At the front door, more preparations: airmen in polished helmets, a carpet, velvet ropes.

He bumps into General Schreiver just inside. Risks a thin joke: "I'm just coming back from leave, sir. You didn't have to roll out the red carpet."

"He surprised us with this. I didn't even know he was coming when I talked to you."

"Who?"

"LeMay." A thin look of displeasure, still well within the bounds of professionalism.

"Well, sir...as much as you two are...philosophically different when it comes to this stuff, operationally we have been...I mean, despite my incident, you have been getting results..."

"I don't think he's here to talk to me."

"Me? Sir, I just...I just flew out there."

"I was told to make sure you were here. And to make sure I had set aside a secure room. That was all they told me. They should be here in twenty minutes."

"Well, sir, I will...let me...I mean, I need to...uhh..." The spaceman's eyes dart off in the direction of the bathroom.

"Crap. Here he is."

Outside now: a drab anonymous government-issue staff car pulls up, with Neubeck at the wheel. LeMay and another major get out of the back, a briefcase in the latter man's hand. They compose themselves, return the salutes from the airmen standing guard, and stride inside.

Schreiver and the spaceman snap to attention.

"As you were, as you were." Their visitor's gruff, impatient.

Schreiver extends a hand: "You made it in OK, sir."

"Obviously."

"We built in a heavy time budget for LA morning traffic," LeMay's aide says.

"I don't trust any air force installation that doesn't have its own fucking runway," LeMay explains.

The aide: "Your staff duty officer got us out of LAX much quicker than we'd anticipated."

"We'll put him up for a medal," Schreiver jokes.

A nervous chuckle from the spaceman. The others remain stone-faced.

"The room's set up?" LeMay says.

Schreiver: "Yes, sir."

"All right. Let's go."

A quick walk down the hallway, heel-tapped shoes clicking on the gleaming white tile. LeMay's aide stations himself outside the door and hands off the briefcase to his boss.

"0930 for the other thing," LeMay says to him.

"Yes, sir."

To Schreiver: "My aide has some instructions for you. We'll do a quick inspection before I leave, for appearances sake. That's all for now."

The spaceman casts a wistful glance as his boss disappears. The door closes and he takes a deep breath.

"Good to see you again," the older man says. There's an odd twist to his face, but something like warmth in the eyes now. A mask removed. "You need to get coffee? Bathroom?"

"Uhhh, that'd be great, sir." Hand on the doorknob, he turns back. "Coffee for you, sir?"

"Black."

Our hero darts down the hallway. In the bathroom he tends to his business, then looks himself over: uniform, teeth, smile. Then to the pantry: two Styrofoam cups, powdered creamer and sugar in one, although someone apparently forgot to restock the lids, so it is perhaps not that simple; the spaceman's face looks as if there's a mainframe in a room behind it, whirling through punch cards so as to calculate the optimum amount of coffee necessary to avoid spillage on the return trip while also not offending the general with a too-small cup. Then back down the hall, where the spaceman stops short, looking down at the doorknob and the two cups in his hands as if trying to solve a difficult operational problem. The aide is chatting with General Schreiver, back turned to the door; without so much as a glance he deftly reaches behind himself and opens it for the spaceman.

LeMay gives a nod of thanks as they settle in. The general sips his coffee, and the spaceman follows suit, and there are moments of silence like minutes like hours like eons.

"I have something for you," the senior man says at last. Spins the locks and opens the suitcase to reveal: almost nothing. A small jewelry box and a piece of paper. He slides the box across the table. "Congratulations. Welcome to the club."

The spaceman opens it to find: a familiar medal. Its ribbon: mostly blue, with three white stripes and a red stripe in the middlemost one. A flared cross with a radiant square behind it, and in front, a four-bladed propeller.

"Obviously the propeller's a bit…anachronistic," the general says.

The spaceman smiles, but there's a hint of pain. "I'm not sure I deserve this, sir."

"I like to recognize people for a job well done. And you've proven yourself to be…reliable. Dependable."

"Yes, sir."

"We'll have a few of your coworkers in here to present it properly. It's important for them to know you've done a good job. But other than the people who will be in this room…that's it." LeMay glances up at the clock. "All right. Let's get the others in here." He sticks his head out the door, gives a nod.

In short order a handful of the Air Force's other astronauts have started trickling in, followed by General Schreiver.

"Just...arrange yourselves along that back wall, gentlemen," LeMay says. He grabs the paper from the briefcase and reads: "In accordance with Public Law 446, enacted 2 July 1926, and in recognition of his extraordinary achievements in the realm of aerial flight, the recipient is hereby awarded the Distinguished Flying Cross for heroic actions on or about 29 July of this year. Given the sensitive nature of these exploits, and the national security concerns related to his mission, this medal is not authorized for public wear, and this citation is classified as Top Secret. This citation will remain in the secret portion of the recipient's personnel file until such time as his mission is declassified. Signed, etc., etc." He puts the paper down and picks the medal back up and now he hands it back again to the spaceman; they shake hands. There is a smattering of applause.

"This is an...odd town," LeMay continues. "People come here from all over the world to work in the movies. To be seen. But there's another side to it. Defense. Aerospace. Working in secret to defeat our nation's enemies. That's what makes the rest of it possible. You've done an admirable job of avoiding the spotlight. We need to keep it that way.

"Now," he goes on. "Some of you have been briefed on this already, but we are expanding the capabilities of this program. Our nation faces an existential threat unlike any in its history. And there's no faster way to deliver a deadly blow to our nation's enemies than from your orbital platform. Our nation's leaders need that capability. Some of them don't know it yet, but they need it. And whoever the American people choose in November will have it.

"Americans are a peaceful people. We go to war reluctantly. Usually we get our asses kicked early on because of it. Lose for a few months, maybe a year, until our head's in the game. Bull Run, Bataan, you name it. But we won't have a year in the next war. We won't have a few months. We won't have weeks, or days, or hours. If we don't win in the first half hour, we've lost.

"This platform is our best chance to do that. The...ICBM..." (A sneer.) "...flies in a high trajectory, and would be visible to Soviet radars for a full half hour before impact. Allowing their leadership plenty of time to launch a retaliatory strike. But with this system, if we launched while we were overhead, the Soviet leaders would have less than five minutes to formulate a response. Before they're vaporized.

"Now. The new module has been built. The team that's going to install it has been chosen and briefed. And the launch has been scheduled for December, prior to the inauguration of our nation's next president. Every subsequent crew that flies to the station will have the means to deliver ten nuclear warheads, anywhere on the globe. Orbital mechanics being what they are, it might take you a few hours to put you in a position to launch over any particular target. But still, you will be the tip of the nation's nuclear spear.

"For reasons that will soon be apparent, this will be among the last duties of my Air Force career. It's been my great honor to ensure that our nation has the means to win its next war. Beyond that, there are few things I enjoy more than recognizing a job well done. So, please, join me again in offering congratulations to your coworker." Again, a smattering of applause. "As you..."

General Schreiver makes an impatient motion. "Sir, if I may…"

LeMay glares: "I'm sorry, general. Did you have something to add?"

"Yes. Since everyone's here. We got a call on Friday afternoon from the FBI's Los Angeles field office warning us about…possible espionage activity, related to this program. You've all been chosen, in no small part, for your discretion. I know I don't need to impress on you how important it is that we keep a tight lid on everything we do here."

Nods and uneasy glances from the assembled men, and one from Schreiver towards his boss.

"Thank you for your time. As you were," LeMay says.

There is a subtle relaxing of poses and a sudden burst of murmurs; the spaceman's coworkers line up to shake his hand.

LeMay leans over to speak in his ear. Glances down at the medal. "I'll have to take that back to Washington with me."

"Yes, sir."

●●●

End of the workday. Late commute home. Plus, an errand.

The spaceman parks in front of the pet store. Checks his watch, not sure if the place is closed; through the glass storefront he can see no customers, no employees. Looks for posted hours, doesn't see them. Takes a breath, suddenly somewhat self-conscious of his uniform. Goes inside.

On the speakers, intricate guitars. "Sitting on a hill...siiiide. Watching all the peo...ple die. I'll feel much better on the other side..." The spaceman scrunches his nose: a strange herbal odor, one he rarely smells, although perhaps he subconsciously remembers catching a residual whiff in a public bathroom a few days ago.

"Uhhh...hey...uhh..." The salesman emerges from a doorway of hanging beads, trailed by wisps of smoke. When he glimpses the other man's uniform, he's instantly anxious. "Sorry about the smell...uhhh...we had a little...uhh, dog vomit in the back, and my...uhhh...boss wanted me to burn some incense before I closed up..."

"Incense?" the spaceman asks.

"Yeah. But now...uhh...I think I gotta...do something *else*, to get the incense smell out."

"I'm Catholic, I know what incense smells like. That's...not incense."

"Well, officer, I don't know what to tell you. Like, my coworker was here earlier, and it smelled weird to me too, so I said something about it, like, 'What's that smell, man?' and then he got, like, really paranoid, officer, and..."

"I'm not a police officer."

"...thinking maybe he *made* the dog vomit. Like maybe *he* needed the awful dog vomit smell, to cover up that *other* smell, whatever it is. But I don't know what it is. It smells weird to me, too, officer."

"I'm not a police officer!"

"OK, Mr. Not-an-officer. Next you're gonna tell me you're not in uniform."

"I mean, I'm an officer, I just…"

"Oh, man! I knew it! I saw the uniform and I was like…"

"I'm not a police officer, though, I…

"…doesn't look like an L.A.P.D. uniform, so he's not *under* cover, but maybe it's a totally *different* cover…"

"…in here the other day! I was in civilian clothes and…"

"…or like, *first* undercover, *then* different cover, like…"

"…buying a terrarium, as a customer, not a police officer, but I…"

"…these guys are switching up the whole *cover strategy*, like a way for the squares to *confuse* us, and…"

"…am not a law enforcement officer! I'm not here to get you in trouble. I just don't want to get that smell on my uniform. I'm an air force officer. An air force officer. Air. Force. Officer. Do you understand what that means?"

"Oh! Oh. Ohhhhhhhh. Oh." The employee takes a step back as if struck by the revelation. "Oh." Then he reaches beneath the counter, grabs an electrical fan, sets it up and plugs it in, turns it on, full blast: straight in his customer's face. "It's like…you need the air forced off you, sir."

"I'm not sure that's better." (His voice, fan-distorted.) "Can you turn that around?"

"Sure, sure." The salesman grabs the fan, turns it 180 degrees, so it's straight in his own face; his hair is flowing in the artificial breeze. "How's that, officer?" (Voice chopped.)

"Better. I'm here...well, I'm here as a customer. I was here a week ago with my boy. Buying a mister for the frog. But we..." (A nod at the fan.) "...you know, that's not a lot better."

"Oh!" His bloodshot eyes widen. "OK, man." He turns the fan sideways, directly onto a caged parrot. (Air ruffles feathers; bird squawks in complaint.)

"My son had a frog in a terrarium. And something happened, and the terrarium fell, it shattered..."

"Oh no! Oh, man, that's..." The salesman's voice breaks; his eyes go from dry to the verge of tears.

"Well, I mean, yeah, it was a little...traumatic, I mean..."

"Oh, I'm sure. I mean, can you imagine? I mean, like, you're a frog, and you're just sitting in there minding your own business, and all of the sudden your whole world's, like, in freefall, and it just *falls apart*, and you die!"

"Well, he didn't die, he just...I mean, the glass broke all around him, but somehow he was OK."

"Oh, wow!" Wide-eyed astonishment. "That would have been...I mean, wow! Your *whole world* shatters, and you're, like, face-to-face with this...*god*, this huge *being* that you can't comprehend that's been feeding you flies, like a lord of the flies..."

"Yes. But the frog escaped, and..."

"Oh! So it was, like, this mind-blowing *expansion* of his *world*, and he was *free* from the *tyranny*…"

"Well, I don't know about…"

"And now you need a new frog…one you can control…like a *mind control experiment*, like one of these military…"

"No, the frog…we found him! He didn't leave. We're not trying to *control* him, we just want to keep an eye on him and…"

"Oh, man, it's all about control, isn't it? Like, what am I *doing* here, selling *animals* for people to *control*, man? I mean…" An anxious glance around at the store.

"No, I just…he was free! And he stuck around! We took good care of him…"

"Except for *destroying* his *world*…"

"I'm not…I don't…we're trying to keep the world *safe*, man…" The spaceman blinks, perhaps surprised to find the salesman's speech pattern cropping up in his own words, perhaps feeling slightly funny in the head from the lingering effects of a hotboxed pet shop. "We're trying to make a *safe environment* so the delicate little frogs of the world can be *safe* from the *predators*…"

"Except that frog! You destroyed his world…"

"We created it, too! The destruction part, that was just…an accident. But he's OK! We put him in a bucket, with a screen on top, and…we don't need a new frog, we need a new terrarium. It's not a big deal."

"It is a big deal for the frog, though," the salesman says. "You've gotta, like, make a new *world* for him."

The spaceman nods, takes a step back. "Well, I guess...yeah, we've gotta make a new world."

•••

Home. The spaceman unloads from his car a bigger terrarium than he had before, and a new extra frog, female. But before setting it up he takes off his uniform and sits down to eat. He eats ravenously, serving after serving of meatloaf and mashed potatoes, effusively praising his wife's cooking.

After dinner, he finds himself in the bathroom, looking in the mirror. "I'm an air force officer," he says. "Air. Force. Officer."

•••

"Chase-1 and -2, cleared for takeoff, Runway Zero-Four." The voice in the helmet: clear and precise and professional.

Outside the Plexiglass: beautiful clear blue high desert sky, Hank's T-38 ahead and to the right. The spaceman glances across the tarmac: red and white control tower in the distance. Hank's voice: "Cleared for takeoff, Runway Zero-Four, Chase-1 and -2."

The spaceman pushes the throttle forward, and the aircraft presses into his back. Runway rushing, endless runway, white centerline marks coming faster and faster, the other airplane fixed in place as it accelerates at the same pace. The rumble of the takeoff roll and that familiar disorienting feeling of the world now tilting backwards. A reassuring glance down at the instruments to verify horizontality and watch the airspeed indicator climb. Then Hank's voice: "Rotating." Both aircraft, back stick. "Wheels up." An end of the rumbling and a little shimmy as both planes settle in, now in the hands of God, or Bernoulli.

"Off to a good start." Adams, in the back, speaking up for the first time, intercom only.

And now the desert is falling away, everything getting smaller and slower as the T-38s climb into the dry sky, fold their spindly legs into their metal bellies, and turn north towards empty wilderness.

"Fingers crossed for the rest of it," the spaceman replies.

A chuckle. "I'll handle the finger-crossing. Keep your hands on the stick."

After the crash-landing, there had been talk of interrupting the normal schedule to investigate. And the next launch—Herres—had been delayed for two days to allow for debriefings, determinations, evaluations. But the determination had been: minimal changes. A slightly altered flight profile on the next reentry to mitigate the risks. And the unspoken prayers: that it will all go back to normal.

Beneath, a small line of desert road inches past. California-58. The altimeter steadily winds upwards. Hank's aircraft is fixed in place: above and ahead and to the right. His voice in the helmet: "Edwards, we're at Angels 10."

"Chase units, Edwards, copy Angels 10. Come left two-seven-zero. Over."

"Edwards, Chase-1. Left two-seven-zero. Over." The spaceman eyes his flight leader's wings and banks at the same time, and now they are flying parallel to the road, a few miles north.

"Good formation flying. You should audition for the Thunderbirds." Again, Adams on the intercom.

"I'll settle for another trip up there." It is not his first flight since the crash—there was, of course, the solo trip to DC—but there are many more eyes on him now, and surely he is conscious of that; anything less than perfection is a failure.

"Chase units, Edwards, come left one-eight-zero and start your orbits when you're crossing the road. Over."

"Edwards, Chase-1. Copy left one-eight-zero. Over."

The clock ticks upwards and they cross CA-58 headed south now, and bank away from one another, Hank starting a clockwise orbit on the right and our protagonist in a counterclockwise one on the left. A steady sweep of the desert landscape, a mild amount of bank, a medium amount of throttle. Then depending on the instructions from the ground, they can tighten or loosen the circle and end up in the right place when Bob Lawrence's X-20 returns from space. (Assuming, of course, that everything happens more smoothly than it did the last time.)

Outside the spaceman's canopy, a couple miles away now, Hank's aircraft comes back into view, arcing through its own lonely circle; they point directly towards each other, but just for an instant. Curve towards each other, more or less out of sight. An act of faith, or mathematics.

"Chase units, Edwards. Relay from Thule: Falcon-1 is in comms blackout. Descent looks nominal. Estimated rendezvous 12 minutes, 15 seconds. Over."

"Edwards, Chase-1, copy 12:15. We'll loosen our loops. Over."

Six more laps. Enough time for the spaceman to settle in. Ragged mountains in the distance panning smoothly left to right, artificial horizon smoothly tilted, eyes constantly on the clock. Around and around and around.

"He's probably passing overhead right now," the spaceman says, on intercom.

"Who is?"

"Herres."

"You think he's listening?"

"I did." They of course cannot see the station in daylight but it is up there, zipping ahead of its decelerated and departed passenger. "Right up to LOS."

"...con-1, comms check, over." Bob's voice, relaxing as a late night DJ.

"Falcon-1, Edwards, we copy comms. Over."

"Edwards, Falcon-1, looks like I'm coming out of it. Smooth ride now. Starting roll program. Over."

"Falcon-1, Edwards, copy roll program. Chase-1 and-2 orbiting Angels 10. We'll give a five-minute mark for rendezvous. And...mark."

The spaceman glances down at his instruments: another slight adjustment. Smooth and perfect and boring, life reduced to lazy orbits. Around and around and around.

"All units, Edwards. Two-minute mark. And…mark."

"Edwards, Chase-1. Copy two minutes."

And the last lonely sweep above the sterile desert landscape. Sand and dust and Joshua trees. One more glimpse of Hank in the distance.

"All units, Falcon-1. Chase planes in sight. Over."

"Falcon-1, Chase-1. We have visual. Looking good."

And then they are coming out of the last lap and there it is, the small black spaceplane, slightly charred by its fiery passage but otherwise no worse for wear, and it grows larger in the canopy, above and to the right, as the last arcs end and the two T-38s come together: safe distance, safe separation, the X-20 slightly above and ahead and between them, all now angled steeply downward towards the dry lake and the long desert runway.

"Camera is out." Adams on the intercom.

Hank's drawl: "Falcon-1, Chase-1. Underbelly looks good. Backseaters are taking pictures. Over."

Larger and larger the runway looms, wide and inviting, looking from this angle not like a slender long strip of concrete, but a fat trapezoid, widening.

"All units, Falcon-1. Dropping the skids. Over."

From the spaceplane now, three slender appendages extend in unison. The chase aircrew can see the colored indicator panels that flip into place when everything's extended normally.

"Falcon-1, Chase-1. Looks good down here. Moving high. Over."

Our protagonist eases his aircraft up simultaneously with the white T-38 on the other side. Glances now at instruments and the other aircraft. Levels off at a hundred feet, everything rushing by again, and the spaceplane continues to drift downward, downward, downward until there are gentle puffs of dust and smoke and it starts to fall behind.

They scream low across the tarmac, waiting for the call, although it is out of their hands now, invisible to them.

Then: "Falcon-1 stopped. Safing the spacecraft and waiting on ground. Over."

From Hank: "Falcon-1, Chase-1. Congratulations on a successful mission. Over."

"Good to have it in the books. Thank you all. Shutting down the spacecraft. Falcon-1 out."

"Now that's what I call coordination." Someone, not our spaceman, says. "Even got all the pilots the same color as their planes."

Guilty tentative chuckles in the cockpits as they turn back north.

•••

They have time for a little proficiency flying, so they head up to China Lake, a few quick minutes away. Arrange a few head-to-head passes that devolve into turning mock-dogfights, the twin T-38s circling and looping and scrambling to wax one another's tail, which Hank does in the end, two times out of three.

Then at last, return to base. Everyone quiet now except the routine chatter. Though there are other options, the main runway is clear now, and they touch down gently and uneventfully.

Taxi and park. Climb down from the aircraft. Walk back to flight ops to close out the paperwork.

When all that's done our protagonist wanders back outside into the blistering afternoon heat. Makes his way to an out-of-the-way hangar. There is an air policeman with an M-16 standing guard outside the door.

"Sir, this is a restricted area."

"I've...uhh...flown this thing. In space."

"Sir, I need to see some ID."

Our man produces his program badge.

"Sorry, sir. I...uhh...don't think I've seen you before."

"I didn't quite...uhh...make it this far last time."

The airman gives a nod, steps aside.

Inside, again, the spaceplane. It doesn't look as impressive it did in flight: sickly, now. Helpless. There are hoses and cords from generators and pumps connected to various ports and access points on the upper rear portion of the fuselage: interior plumbing to be purged and safed. And still...

Next to the cockpit, a yellow metal ladder. The spaceman climbs it, stares inside: all the familiar sights.

"Smells a little funny in there, huh?" From the ground on the other side of the craft, a tech of some sort, out of sight.

"How's that?"

"Dumbass turned off the environmental systems too early. Takes a little while to cool the plane off after riding it through a furnace. Desert in August, no A/C, I do believe that boy passed out. And their sweat, I swear it smells..." The tech has wandered around the nose of the aircraft, and now at last he sees the flight suit, the rank. An oh-shit look settles in on his face.

"You gonna put a sir on that?" The spaceman climbs down from the ladder. "That *man* is an officer in the United States Air Force."

"Sir, I..."

"He did a helluva job today." Better than I did, he doesn't say.

●●●

When at last he tracks down Bob, the other man is resting comfortably in a private room at the base clinic, watching the evening news on TV.

"Doing all right?"

"Can't complain. Any landing you can walk away from, right? Although I did need some help getting out..."

"Not as much as I did." A smirk. "Congratulations. Helluva job. Just what the program needed."

"Just trying to do my part."

"Well, still. Helluva job. I know we've got…debriefings scheduled for the rest of the week, all that fun stuff. But when I heard you were here…"

"I do appreciate it."

"Hank and them didn't…"

A smile. "You were the last one to swing by, actually."

"Oh."

"They didn't stay long. Just popped in and chatted for a bit. I think the shuttle flight to LAX might be leaving soon, so you may want to…"

"We should still be good." The spaceman looks at his watch. "I didn't want to leave if you were still here."

"I should be out soon. You know how it is. Observations. Cover-your-ass by the flight surgeons." A smile. "I heard a rumor you were decorated while I was gone."

"Ha. Yeah. A decoration I can't wear. Or talk about outside the program. Or look at."

"Well, still. That's gotta be a record, to get a DFC that fast. I mean, usually the paperwork…"

"You flew a better mission."

Bob shrugs.

Our protagonist sighs. "I've been...I haven't told anybody in the program about this, but I have been...contemplating my options, career-wise. Depending on how the election goes, I mean...Kennedy made a helluva speech at the convention. There's talk of a moon program. Which presumably would be civilian, but I'm sure experienced astronauts would be..."

Bob listens impassively.

"Still," our man continues. "Even without that, it sounds like they're taking the program in a new direction..." Another sigh. "As in, they're launching the bombardment module."

"Well..." A long pause. "That is what the Air Force does."

Our protagonist gives him a perplexed look.

"I mean, it's nice to think we're knights in the sky. Single combatants, only doing battle with other brave flyers who've chosen to do battle. But if that ever was the case, it hasn't been for a while now."

"No."

"And it's not like we can feign ignorance. We grew up reading about the firebombing of Japan. We signed up knowing about the a-bomb. But...I mean, maybe it does keep the peace. Maybe it is *stopping* another world war. Making it clear how destructive it would be. I mean, conventional weapons, it's a little easier to blunder into it. But this...in their heart of hearts, nobody wants to let that genie out of the bottle. Even on the other side of the globe. Maybe that's enough to stop it."

"You sounded a little different, last time we talked about this. Up there."

"Yeah, well...I've given it some thought. And talking to Herres up there...he had some good perspectives."

"Herres."

He shrugs. "People do rub off on you. More than you think."

"Well. I'm not one to go with the crowd."

"...he says, while wearing his uniform." Bob raises a skeptical eyebrow, smirks.

"Apart from that."

A head shake. "The national disease. We all like to think we're...cowboys. Rugged individualists, ready to buck the system." He smirks. "Even John Wayne isn't John Wayne. Most of what we know is learned from others. Language. Behavior. Especially us, in the service. Every organization has its norms. Stick around long enough, they become your norms."

The spaceman looks off at the grainy TV eye. "What if the organization's wrong?"

Bob takes a long deep breath. "The organization's a tool. A tool isn't right or wrong. A tool isn't guilty or innocent. We have civilian control of the military for a reason. We're not doing our own will, we're doing the bidding of the American citizen. The American taxpayer. I know it seems like the Air Force has a mind of its own, but it is really just...doing what the people want."

On the TV now: pictures of Dr. King. Counter-protestors yelling, angry. "What if the people are wrong?"

"Well, you'd like to think the right ideas will win out in the end. The right politicians. I mean, Lord knows we're not perfect, but we've got ideals, at least. Goals to aim for. The system can correct itself over time. But, yes...Lord knows it can take a while." He shifts in his bed. "Speaking of time..."

Our protagonist glances down at his watch. "Yeah, I should see about the shuttle. You want I should check on the flight surgeon, too?"

"Yeah, if you don't mind."

Our protagonist steps out into the tiled antiseptic hallway. Sees no one. Walks past gurneys, IV stands, closed doors with charts outside, a nurse's station: empty. Looks around and around. Glances anxiously at his watch. And at last hears a flush from the women's room. Hears, after a tedious interval, water in the sink, a pump of the soap. A long anxious pause. Paper towels being pulled from the dispenser. More paper towels. A pause. More paper towels. Sink again. Soap again. More paper towels. A pause. Sink, once more. Soap, once more. Paper towels.

At last the nurse emerges. Stands taken aback at the strange officer ambushing her outside the door.

"Excuse me...I'm with Major Lawrence in Room 205. Is the flight surgeon coming back around? We're looking to get out of here."

"We're keeping Major Lawrence overnight for observation, sir. New protocol for your program."

"Says who?"

"You'll…probably want to talk to your program manager. He and his aide were here earlier…they should be back soon."

"OK." A guilty glance back towards Room 205. "As for getting back to the flight line…"

A glance at the bland wall clock. "The duty driver should be making the rounds. You probably want to get downstairs."

"Oh." He turns towards the elevator, turns back to 205, turns back towards the elevator, almost pushes the button, heads back to 205.

"Look," he pokes his head in to the room. "They're keeping you overnight."

A chuckle and a head shake. "Good thing nobody told me."

"The nurse said Schreiver's around somewhere."

"I haven't seen him since they checked me in."

"I gotta…" A look down at his watch.

"Oh. OK. Yeah, go, go."

At last, the elevator. Downstairs at the front desk, he finds out that the duty driver just left, and won't be back for another half hour. He asks for a phone, calls base ops, waits while the duty officer tracks down Hank Hartsfield.

At last, the familiar drawl: "Where are you?"

"Back at the clinic, with Bob. We thought he was getting released tonight."

"No, they're keeping him overnight. New protocol for the program." A tone like: doesn't everyone know that?

"Well, nobody told us."

"Well, they should have."

"Evidently."

"How soon are you gonna be here? We were trying to wait on you."

"I missed the duty driver."

"Crap."

"Yeah."

"The Herc driver's getting antsy. The schedule did say…"

"I know what it said. Look, I…" A glance at the watch yet again, resigned this time. "I don't wanna hold you guys up. Schriever's still out here, right?"

"Well, he's not with us."

"He's gotta be here still…I'll RON. Get a room in the BOQ, ride back with him tomorrow."

"All right, suit yourself."

He makes two more calls: one to the BOQ to secure a room for the night, one to his wife.

"I told the kids you were gonna be back tonight," she says.

"The Air Force has a mind of its own."

Over the long distance line, a sigh. "Oh. Your parents called. Again. They want to talk to you."

"Yeah, I was gonna call them back tonight."

"I don't know how much I can tell them."

"I'll call them when I get back."

At last our protagonist heads back upstairs. Pops his head back in the room. Bob Lawrence smiles. "Still here, huh?"

"I missed the duty driver. So if it makes you feel any better, I'll be staying the night, too."

The other man smiles. "It does, actually. Also, Schreiver swung by when you were downstairs. I guess he tried to come in and talk to me earlier, but they were running tests, so he ran off to get dinner. The Herc isn't sticking around?"

"The Air Force has a mind of its own."

They settle in to silence, bathed in the cold TV glow.

A commercial break ends, then, again, Walter Cronkite: "This is a CBS special report. We are here to talk about UFOs." Cronkite reads the words with the same grave and dignified tone he'd used to announce the death of President MacArthur. The same one he'd used at the height of the Berlin Crisis. "Unidentified Flying Objects. Flying saucers. Little green men. This is a controversial topic. Lots of speculation, and very little known truth. But the question of whether or not we are alone in the universe, and whether we've had visitors from elsewhere, is as important as any that mankind faces."

The camera cuts to a man, a hunter from Michigan. "I had just left the house when I saw it. It was hard to see it through the trees, but it was hovering over a pond. So...I walked over there. It was early in the morning and the sky was still dark. I was eager to see what it was. And it just...hovered there. This silvery disk. It was there for a few hours. I called some neighbors. They saw it, too. One of them drew this..." (He holds up a drawing of a silvery disk.) "Finally I tried to get close. And it just...accelerated upwards at a tremendous rate of speed."

They watch mindlessly.

"Did you see anything while you were up there?" our protagonist asks.

"See anything?"

"Any...UFOs?"

Bob laughs. "Not that I recall. Why do you ask?"

"Somebody asked me about that recently."

"Who?"

"Somebody...important. Someone I wouldn't have expected."

"Schreiver?"

"No. Higher up."

A curious smile. "Who?"

"Nobody. Forget I mentioned it."

On the screen now, a uniformed Air Force officer: "We have been investigating these sightings. For the past few years, we have pored over transcripts, interviewed eyewitnesses, studied radar evidence, and we can say categorically..."

"Well, I guess it could be worse," Bob says.

"Could be worse?"

He nods towards the screen. "We could be assigned to that program."

•••

A small LA office, empty in the early evening.

The business partner enters, looks around: the sad silence of a workless workplace. He walks over to the other man's office, jimmies open the locked door. Opens the typewriter, pulls out the ribbon, starts to unspool it: a line of transparent negative letters, crisp shapes in black.

He places a fresh ribbon in the machine, takes the old one back to his office, unwinds it the rest of the way, and starts writing down words.

•••

Desert morning.

The spaceman and Bob Lawrence and the general and the aide have reassembled outside the hospital and are piling into the duty driver's vehicle, a bland anonymous government-owned Ford Econoline driven by a surly technical sergeant.

Schriever and his aide have taken up position in the back. Our protagonist is sitting shotgun; the radio crackles with news: "...octor King says they are marching in response to the..." He reaches up to change the station.

"Could you turn that up a little?" Bob asks as he settles in to the middle bench.

"...of a civilian in police custody in Venice Beach last week."

"So he's in LA. Interesting."

The sergeant gives a look like he wants to say something but knows it's unwise. Once the doors are closed, he pulls away from the curb.

"What was the Chicago thing about?" our protagonist asks from the front seat.

"Fair housing, I believe."

Schreiver's aide speaks up from the back. "Do you think that was a reasonable amount of protest for that topic?"

Major Lawrence stiffens a little. "Sir, I'm not paid to have an opinion on political matters."

A slight nod.

But then Schreiver speaks. "We all know the rules. Speaking frankly, though. Man to man. I think it's fair to say the rest of us don't know much about life as a Negro. Perhaps you'd care to offer some observations."

From the radio, Doctor King: "...greatest purveyor of violence around the globe is the American government. We cannot threaten nuclear holocaust, and then act surprised when there is blood in our streets…"

"Well, to be frank, sir…" A deep breath. "It sometimes feels like being under observation. Constantly. Endless scrutiny, from people who don't trust you. As Du Bois said, there is a certain sense of…double-consciousness one can get…always looking at oneself through the eyes of others. Not just thinking, 'What do I want?' but 'How does what I want look to someone else?' He says, 'One ever feels his twoness,—an American, a Negro; two souls, two thoughts, two unreconciled strivings; two warring ideals in one dark body…'"

"Warring ideals?" The aide's gaze sharpens.

"Those were his words, sir."

The aide: "Do you feel…divided in your loyalties?"

Again Major Lawrence stiffens slightly. "Sir, I am an American, first and foremost."

"But there's that division…"

"Society itself is divided, sir. The girl who wrote *Raisin in the Sun*, she went to my high school."

A blank look from the aide.

"It's about fair housing. Housing covenants. We grew up knowing that if we moved to certain neighborhoods, if we crossed a line on some banker's map, people were going to have issues. There might be legal fights, or real fights. Her family had a legal fight. The case went all the way to the Supreme Court."

"She was a communist, wasn't she?" General Schriever interrupts. "A homophile."

"I didn't know her very well, sir. Those were the issues for all of us, though. People say America's a melting pot. But when you see neighborhoods where every face is one color, it doesn't seem like it's melted. You're scrutinized if you cross over the line. And if you stay in the community...your community is scrutinized."

Again, the aide: "I mean, certainly, the Negro community understands that if there's a certain amount of...lawlessness, that there will also be a certain amount of scrutiny."

Lawrence inhales slowly through his nose before speaking. "The places I've lived...Woodlawn, Englewood...I mean, they're working-class Chicago communities. Men working in the stockyards. Working in the steel mills. I don't recognize the...pictures I see in the public media. The things certain...politicians say about crime, and lawlessness."

"But there has been crime. There have been riots. Watts, Newark, Detroit."

"Some individuals saw fit to riot, sir. I certainly don't agree with that, and I believe those individuals should be punished. But not the group. Not the community. I think we all want to be seen as individuals, sir. To be judged on our own merits, not by the...failings of others who happen to share our skin color."

"But Dr. King..." the aide goes on. "Would he be in LA leading protests, if that dead man was of a different skin color?"

"Would the dead man be dead if he were a different skin color, sir?"

Now it is the aide's turn to take a deep breath. "Dr. King has several associates who are communists. To have a man, surrounded by communists, leading a protest movement, promoting instability..."

"I don't speak for Dr. King, sir," Major Lawrence says. "I don't agree with everything he says. And I'm certainly concerned by those allegations. But he did set out an ideal. About being judged by the content of our character, rather than the color of our skin. And...well, we have so many...foundational ideals in other areas of public life, but nobody had ever spelled one out for race relations. And we're clearly not there yet. When you get pulled over, and you haven't been speeding, and you didn't run any red lights, and all your turn signals are in working order, you can't help but wonder if there's another reason for it."

"Well, if it is an area of high crime..." The van rolls down a desert road, heading towards base ops, and the flight line.

"This happened to me, sir. A few weeks before my flight. And...well, I was in Malibu, headed up to Vandenberg."

General Schreiver nods.

"Obviously I was concerned that it would screw things up. I knew I had to do exactly as I was instructed. React calmly and politely, whatever the policeman's demeanor. I handed him my military ID along with my license. Which always seems to help. But still, sir, you can't help wondering, why the higher standard?"

"But don't you think," the aide persists, "that if there's a higher incidence of something among a certain population, that it's normal you're going to be...watched a little more closely?"

"It could be, sir," Major Lawrence says, "that watching closely leads us to believe there's a higher incidence of something. The more...Negroes you pull over, the more you're going to bust for carrying reefer, for instance. But the same goes for...white peacenik college kids. Any group. You name it. If a certain percentage of that group is criminal, then the more you pull over, the more criminals you find. It becomes self-perpetuating. Especially if someone doesn't look like you, it's easy to assume they...want different things. God help us if we ever make contact with aliens. We have a hard enough time with people who look different. And it's fear. That's all it is."

"So you're not afraid of anyone?"

Major Lawrence chuckles. "People who don't sound like us, sir. To me, that's a more legitimate cause for fear. I mean, hearing Hitler ranting in German, or Beria blustering away in...Russian or Georgian, to me that's scarier than someone who doesn't share my skin color. When you don't even know what someone's saying..."

"There's speculation that Chairman Beria is...mounting a disinformation campaign. To exacerbate those racial tensions in our society. Providing false propaganda to the associates of men like Dr. King and Malcolm X. In addition to the normal spying, MVD agents and what-not. Turning groups against each other. Does that...concern you, at all?"

"Are you familiar with set theory, sir?"

"Set theory?"

"Yes, mathematics. Set theory? Zermelo-Fraenkel, any of that?"

The aide blinks, shakes his head no.

"So you can have something that's infinite. And you can have subsets of infinity. Say, for instance, you take all integers. You have an infinite number of them, stretching off into both directions, positive and negative. The number of positive integers is itself infinite. And so, too, the number of negative. You take only the even numbers, that, too, is an infinite set. And so, too, the odd numbers. And when I think of race, and all the differences between individuals, that's what it feels like. An infinite subset of an infinite set. There's a world of difference between myself and Doctor King. There's a world of difference between Doctor King and Malcolm X. There's a world of difference between Malcolm X and Miles Davis, or between Miles Davis and the...jazz saxophonist I saw playing at the club three months ago. There's a world of difference between *him* and the college football player from USC, or the one going to law school, or the man peddling reefer in Chicago, or the guy working in the stockyards, or the one who's taken an assembly-line job in Detroit to feed his family, or his neighbor who's starting a bank. You look at odd numbers, you can have an odd number that's prime, a number that's not prime, a number that's big, a number that's small. If I say I'm picking an odd number, at random, all you know for certain is that it's an odd number. If I'm picking a Negro, at random, all you know for certain is that he's a Negro. An infinite subset of an infinite set."

The aide says nothing. They pull up to base ops, start collecting their effects. Major Lawrence and General Schreiver head inside; the aide lingers outside to talk to our protagonist.

"You've flown with him," the aide asks. "What kind of person is he?"

"He's...as good of an officer as I've served with, sir." Our protagonist eyes the aide suspiciously. "Are you...concerned about his loyalties?"

"Well, like the general said the other day...we've had credible reports of Soviet espionage activities. We want to make sure everyone's...reliable. No unauthorized communications."

"Sir, if there's one person you can rule out. I mean...you do realize he's been in space all that time, right?"

The aide smirks. "That didn't stop you."

●●●

Back in LA that night the spaceman is settling down for dinner (glistening pork chops, steaming mashed potatoes) when there's a knock on the door.

His family looks up at him expectantly as he hovers over his chair. Again, the insistent knock. He lets out a huff and walks up front.

"Excuse me, sir." The man on the doorstep seems oddly surprised someone's answered. "I'm sorry to bother you at home, but...well, I've been trying to get ahold of you via Air Force channels, and...well, we have reason to believe you were involved in an incident in the desert, a crash-land..."

"I'm sorry," the spaceman interjects. "Who are you?"

"I'm a reporter for the *Los Angeles Times*, and..."

The spaceman shuts the door in his face.

From the other side of the door, a muffled voice: "The public has a right to know what's going on with your program!"

"We have the right to eat dinner in peace!"

Muffled: "I can wait until after dinner."

He opens the door. "If you don't go away, I shall be forced to call the police." Closes the door again.

On the way back to the dining room, the spaceman walks tentatively, as if expecting more door disturbance. But: nothing. He settles in at the head of the table. Sign of the cross, grace.

His wife: "Who was that?"

"News guy."

"What did you tell him?"

"That I'd call the cops if he didn't leave."

"Seems a bit harsh."

"I..." (Exasperated sigh.) "You know the rules. I can't even tell *you* anything. Just that I've been up there. As for everyone else..."

"Well, I mean...just to play devil's advocate. You're spending a lot of tax dollars. There is a certain public interest in..."

"We're keeping the public safe. That's what the public needs to know. I need you on my side on this."

Her look says defiance.

"If I talk to him," the spaceman says, "I may as well be...talking to Moscow."

After dinner he settles in to his easy chair. Hand poised over the stack of library books. Touches *Alas, Babylon* for a second, sets it down, picks up *Tales of the South Pacific*.

• • •

Headed to work the next morning, the spaceman is pulling the front door closed when he notices it. Wedged in to the top of the door knocker, a reporter's business card, letterhead from the *Los Angeles Times*.

There is a name and an address and a phone number on the front of the card, and on the back, in a hasty pen scrawl: YOU CAN TALK ANONYMOUSLY. He flexes his hand as if about to crumple it, then stops. Slips it into his pocket and heads off to work.

• • •

"I barely spoke to him at all, sir," the spaceman says. Shifts in his chair. Glances at the walls of the windowless office.

"And you still have the card," General Schreiver asks.

"Yes, sir." The spaceman hands it over.

The general nods, as if to say: this could be useful.

"Anything else, sir?"

"No, I think that's it. Any weekend plans?"

"Nothing much, sir. Yardwork, call my folks. The usual. You?"

"Might go golfing."

•••

Tuesday morning, the office is buzzing. Our protagonist barely has time to set down his briefcase before Hank walks in, tosses the *Los Angeles Times* on his desk. "You see this shit?"

SECRET SPACE PROGRAM REVEALS SOVIET NUKE WEAKNESS, the headline blares.

"What the hell?" our man replies. He grabs the paper, frantically reads. Sentence after classified sentence, all anonymously attributed. Alarming phrases to see in print: reconnaissance platform, sun-synchronous orbit, photographs of Soviet ICBM fields.

There is a bit about a minor collision between a space plane and a Soviet satellite, and a crash-landing in the high desert, and it is more or less accurate.

The spaceman shakes his head in disbelief.

General Schreiver's aide summons the spaceman a few minutes later.

"I'm going to ask you a question," the general says. "I want you to answer honestly. And the correct answer is 'No, sir.'"

The spaceman nods.

"Have you spoken to any member of the press, any newsgathering organization, or anyone outside this organization about anything that happened during your flight?"

"No, sir."

• • •

On the floor of the convention center, all is chaos: chants and counterchants, rivers of delegates flowing one way and another, smaller currents eddying off this way and that, a swirling churning cauldron of angry humanity. Signs and placards: ILLINOIS FOR NIXON and GEORGIA FOR GOLDWATER.

Above it in the booth: a bank of TV monitors. Don Hewitt producing, and Cronkite on headphones, trying to make sense of it all.

"Mudd's got the head of the New York Nixon delegation," Hewitt says.

"I can hear that." Cronkite's hand is on his desk, holding a scrap of paper from the AP wire.

"We can cut to him after the break…"

"We already know Nixon's got New York. Where is the story there?"

"The president's support among East Coast moderates is…"

"I don't need to cut to some…small town banker who's already a known quantity."

"It's a good visual." Behind him on the first monitor: Mudd on the floor, microphone under the would-be interviewee, both getting jostled by some placard-wielding conventioneers.

"It's not part of the visual story."

"All right...Trout's got Harold Stassen."

"Jesus Christ. Stassen? He barely had a chance in '48, he hasn't had a chance since. Stassen isn't the story. This is the story." Cronkite waves the AP paper scrap like a party streamer. "The fight is elsewhere. The fight is uncommitted delegates. What are you hearing about that?"

"Apparently the Texas credentialing committee met earlier today. Goldwater's people had access to the meeting room early. Filled it up. There was a...scuffle of some sort when Nixon's people arrived and couldn't get a seat."

"A fistfight?"

"That's the rumor."

"Well, this is TV news. Where's the fucking visuals?" A nod towards the clock. "Break's almost up. Get me visuals. Get me Reagan."

"Don't tell me how to do my job."

Hewitt drops back and there is a quick flurry of activity and then the red camera light and Cronkite is on. "The last few Republican conventions have been stately affairs. The ascension of Douglas MacArthur in 1952 saw remarkably little opposition. After the loss of China and Korea and Vietnam, the surprise of the Soviet A-bomb, and the first trials of atomic spies, it was clear we were facing a new totalitarian ideology every bit as terrifying as the one we'd just defeated. So it was no surprise that the party turned to a general who had given us victory in the last war, and built up Japan as a bulwark against communist Asia afterwards. Given the extensive...one might call it a preparatory bombardment by Henry Booth Luce and *Time* magazine...the few Taft supporters who dared to raise their heads were quickly driven underground, and MacArthur landed on the American political scene practically unopposed..."

Hewitt rolls his eyes, as if to say: enough with the history lesson.

"1956 offered even less drama. An administration that had learned to manage the flow of news, and was willing to clamp down on labor unrest, faced little opposition during that period of peace and prosperity. After twenty years of depression and war and atomic angst, most Americans didn't mind the lack of government transparency; they were happy enough with a full fridge, two cars in the driveway, and a TV. The 1956 Republican convention was practically a coronation. In 1960, there were complaints from conservatives about the process by which the 22nd Amendment was repealed, displeasure in the South at the president's willingness to use troops to enforce school integration, but in general Republicans seemed happy to have a long presidency of their own to balance out the lengthy term of F.D.R. An imperial presidency, a *Pax MacArthur*, and a party more than willing to move the clock forward on civil rights, and roll it back everywhere else."

An ugly glance from Hewitt, and mouthed words: Paley's not gonna like that.

"Then of course, 1964. A decrease in public appearances. Rumors of mental decline. Then the dramatic death during the primaries of our nation's second-longest-serving president. The Berlin Crisis, coming soon afterwards, gave the newly minted President Nixon a chance to prove his mettle. He won election in his own right by promising a return to normalcy and a two-term presidency. But the subsequent years have been anything but normal. Southern conflict over civil rights mandates, riots in Northern cities, crime and chaos and new nuclear angst: it remains to be seen whether President Nixon will even win his party's re-nomination, and the chance for a second full term. And now we are hearing from the Associated Press that the number of uncommitted delegates has risen to one-hundred and sixty-four, many of whom are from the president's own home state—California. More than enough to swing the nomination either way."

A nod from Hewitt towards the clock: it will be time for commercials soon. He signals a controller, and they switch to footage from downstairs: signs bouncing up and down, waves of emotion rising and cresting all over the convention floor.

Cronkite gives a dirty look and keeps talking: "This is the story, here in Miami: a party in chaos. How will that play out? Who will be the party's nominee—Nixon, or the insurgent Goldwater? How battered will they be heading in to the final months of the campaign? And, of course, the ultimate question...after 16 years of Republican rule, will the

American people finally hand the Oval Office back to a Democrat?"

Hewitt signals for commercial, and once it's on, he blurts out: "Lens hog."

"Grow up," Cronkite says.

"Trout wants to talk to you."

"Do I need to talk to him?"

"Forget the revolt in the party. You're gonna have one from your own floor crew."

"All right, put him on."

Trout, in the headset: "Walter, it's a madhouse down here."

"I can see that."

"The viewers can't, if you don't put us on."

"I have to make order out of that. Be the eye of the storm."

"I've been grabbing people for interviews and letting them go without talking to them. It's embarrassing."

Hewitt interrupts: "Break's almost over."

"If they control us, we don't control the story. Get me somebody worth talking to, and I'll put you on. Get me Reagan."

Again, Hewitt: "Headphones off. We're on in ten, Walter! No floor, again?"

Cronkite shakes his head: an incredulous, forceful NO.

Silence and composure. Then: "So the story for the past few days: two commanders marshalling their forces for the final showdown…."

Hewitt rolls his eyes. Mouths: we have no visuals for this. Then: cocks his head, listening to the headset. Scrawls a message on a scrap of paper.

"…the beleaguered president coming to town early, taking delegates for rides on Air Force One, using every lever of the office…"

And now, the note: MUDD HAS REAGAN.

Cronkite nods. "…in the hopes of quashing the conservative insurgency. The only question: will it be enough?"

On the console, a clear picture now: Roger Mudd and the Gipper, handsome and smiling.

"And now, from the convention floor, Roger Mudd with one of this story's key players, California Governor Ronald Reagan."

Mudd: "Governor Reagan, the California primary is over. The state's Republicans have spoken. They preferred the president to Senator Goldwater. Why now is there talk of a shift among the at-large delegates?"

"Our president has a basic duty to preserve freedom and peace wherever they are threatened. The Soviets today are the greatest threat to that peace. We had an opportunity to stand up to them, to stand on the side of freedom and support the Czechoslovakian people. And we failed. The California voters spoke before that happened. Senator

Goldwater has a level of...moral clarity on Soviet aggression that's refreshing, compared to the muddled response from the White House."

"What of those who say the American people have no tolerance for nuclear brinksmanship?"

"We won't have brinksmanship with a strong leader in the White House. It's a weak leader that invites aggression. We saw that with Nixon this summer. And if we had, God forbid, John F. Kennedy..." He shudders. "The specter of nuclear war is horrible. But it's less likely with a strong leader. If we tell the Soviets what we're not going to do, that encourages them to act with impunity. The weak leaders, the ones who seek peace at any cost, eventually get pushed too far. Before long they have to go to war, to have any credibility. World War II started under Neville Chamberlain. It didn't start under Winston Churchill."

"A story broke in the *Los Angeles Times* today about a secret space reconnaissance program. This story claims that we are, in fact, already far stronger than the Soviets, that we have a good handle on their capabilities, that we have nothing to be afraid of."

"With all due respect, the media is wrong. The media has consistently underestimated the Soviet threat. We know Chairman Beria has been doing everything he can to divide and weaken us. Everything he can to spy on us. During the Roosevelt and Truman years it was American members of the Communist Party. The atomic spies. Now it's sleeper agents, arriving under deep cover to live among us and steal our defense secrets. But they've also been mounting a

disinformation campaign. Spreading racial strife to weaken us from within, and undermine our resolve at this critical hour."

"One more thing, Governor. It sounds like you've chosen sides in the Goldwater/Nixon split. Is there something in it for you? A spot on the national ticket, perhaps?"

The governor smiles, sphinxlike. "I am prepared to do my part in whatever way the party asks."

"Thank you, Governor Reagan." A smile and a handshake and he's gone.

•••

In front of the TV, the spaceman watches as the vote tally comes in.

"And with that, it's official," Cronkite intones. "The crowd here, the conservative members now energized by this result: the impossible is now a reality. Senator Barry M. Goldwater has defeated the incumbent president to capture his party's nomination for president of the United States. As California goes, so goes the nation. And it appears that the California delegation has abandoned the first president from their home state, and gone with the senator from Arizona. And now from the convention floor, Roger Mudd..."

"Yes, we're here with one of the California delegates whose vote was so crucial in bringing out this...historic outcome, this...repudiation of a sitting president by members of his own party. So tell us, what was behind this seismic shift?"

"Well, I think a lot of us simply don't trust this president anymore," the delegate says. "He never says what he means, he never does what he says. But Senator Goldwater, he tells it like it is. People say he shoots from the hip, but a lot of us like that out West."

"Indeed."

"President Nixon, I don't think he'd shoot if you had a burglar coming through the front door. Just talk, talk, talk, talk, about 'evaluating our options' and 'appropriate responses' and all that. Which is why the Russians have been so belligerent lately. But Goldwater...I trust him to put them in their place."

"A lot of Americans think he's too extreme to win the presidency in November. Do you think he can beat Senator Kennedy?"

"Oh, absolutely. He's a tough guy and a straight shooter. I talked to him about Kennedy, and he said, 'I don't want to shoot missiles at the moon. I want to lob one into the men's room of the Kremlin. And I'll make sure I hit it!'"

Mudd gives a nod, the look of a newsman who has a golden quote and knows it. "And there you have it, folks."

From Cronkite, a head shake. "And there you have it."

The spaceman turns off the TV, picks up *Tales of the South Pacific*. Eager, it seems, to get back to the scenes: tropical moon rising over placid volcanoes, young lovers eating papaya on the beach. A safe war: one in the past.

"Good Lord," the wife says. "What a nut."

"The delegate?"

"Goldwater."

The spaceman responds slowly, in a tone that suggests contemplation more than agreement. "He is a character."

•••

In the convention hall now, the fervor of the victorious, the eager, those who have done the impossible. Voices roar and reverberate off metal and concrete; signs and placards bounce in their separate rhythms. From the rafters now, a rain of balloons: red, white, blue. The crowd's roar now punctuated by the occasional *pop*.

Senator Goldwater ascends to the podium, stern and unsmiling: an angry prophet in tortoiseshell glasses, oddly unmoved by the energy.

"Thank you," he says, stern and booming on the PA system. "Thank you." And at last the crowd noise dims. "It is my great honor to accept this party's nomination for president, and I'm looking forward to leading us to victory in November."

Up with the noise again: a fervid animal roar, full-throated and passionate.

"Thomas Jefferson reportedly said, 'Eternal vigilance is the price of liberty.' Eternal. Vigilance. And we are heading towards a choice in November, a choice between a vigilant defense of our liberty, and the relaxation that will allow the enemies of liberty to triumph.

"Too often in recent years, our party has stood against the cause of liberty. Our government has taken it upon itself to tell private businesses whom they must serve, to tell private citizens whom they must associate with. The government has no business making these decisions for business, and as president I pledge that I will take the government out of your business."

Again a roar from the convention floor: faces contorted with passion, signs bobbing up and down with emotion, the human ocean surging. MISSISSIPPI FOR GOLDWATER and SOUTH CAROLINA FOR GOLDWATER.

"But by far the most deadly and dangerous threat to liberty is the leadership of the Soviet Union. They have continued to impose their will on the Soviet people; they have continued to deprive the people of Eastern Europe of their freedom, and to crush all dissent under their tyrannical heel. We need to tell the Soviet leadership that if they continue to infringe on liberty, if they continue to oppress the peoples of Eastern Europe who are longing to be free, they will be called to judgment! We will soon have the means to swiftly and decisively do so. As president, I pledge that we will work to develop and maintain those capabilities: to strike with overwhelming force anywhere on the globe at a moment's notice, anywhere tyrants are gathered to deprive people of their freedom!"

Again the crowd roars: intense, passionate. The senator gives them a few moments, then ushers calm.

"There are those who call me an extremist," the senator says. "But I would say to that...extremism in the defense of liberty is no vice. And moderation in the pursuit of justice is no virtue!"

The crowd takes over, unrestrained and chaotic at first, but then gradually synchronizing into a chant: GOLD-WA-TER! GOLD-WA-TER! GOLD-WA-TER!

•••

The key is silvery, and non-functional, with a code on the blade—M 5463—and a famous logo on the end: a rabbit wearing a bowtie, set against a black background. The man holding it happens to be a reporter from the *Miami Herald*, but he is not here professionally; he is here drunkenly, and he dangles the key suggestively.

The door bunny, an ample-chested brunette in a tight pink corset teddy, gives him a nod and a smile; her ears bob cutely. "You can put that away now, sir."

"I like to show it off sometimes."

"I'm sure you do." Another smile, forced now, and a nod towards his party. "How many?"

"Four. We'll sit in the living room."

"Right this way, sir." She leads them off; the newsmen, already slightly drunk, stare at her rhythmic derriere, the round white cottontail bobbing back and forth.

The room is dim and red, a pleasant vision of hell; the newsmen unbutton their jackets and loosen their ties and take seats on the plush chairs arrayed around the table. The second man is a first-timer, another reporter, but from the *Los Angeles Times*; as he moves past the bunny, he grabs a handful of ass. Her face registers a brief moment of shock and pain, masked quickly by an angsty smile. She wags her finger, speaks as if reading from a script. "Please, sir. You are not allowed to touch the bunnies."

"Yes. No touching," Cronkite intones. "You can only look."

"That's a gyp. Lemme see that key," LA says to Miami as they settle in.

The local newsman holds the keys up, jangles them. The other man reaches, but the Miami reporter whisks them away. "You can only look."

"Supposedly there's a special key," LA explains. "One that gets you...access."

"The Number One key," the anchorman says.

"Well, I don't have that key," Miami says. "Yet."

Waiter bunny, a blonde named Marie, arrives. They order: martinis and Manhattans and an old-fashioned.

"So..." the local man says. "Goldwater."

"Jesus Christ!" the anchorman says. "Can we take a night off? We're going to be talking about Goldwater for the next...two and a half months."

"Or more." A sly smile from LA.

"Two and a half months," the anchorman says. "The public-at-large is not going to vote for that...nut. Everyone I've ever talked to is just..." He shudders.

"You should get out of New York sometime," LA says. "Orange County, they love the tough talk."

"Really?"

"You have no idea."

"Two and a half months," the anchorman says: a reassuring mantra.

"Are you going to take him down?"

"His own words are going to take him down. That quote from tonight. A nuclear missile in the Kremlin men's room…"

"They love it in Orange County," LA says. "They're building the missiles as we speak."

The anchorman shakes his head. "The Chandlers must be thrilled."

"Nobody gets rich pissing off their readers," Miami interjects.

"Nobody says to piss them off," the anchorman says. "Just…stop feeding their…paranoia and prejudice…" A head shake. "If you want to do right in this business, you need to be willing to speak truth to power. Not be the propaganda for the power."

Miami laughs. "Are you kidding me? Your network spent twelve years…fellating Douglas MacArthur."

A burst of laughter from the table. "We asked tough questions!" the anchorman protests.

"After he was dead."

The anchorman shakes his head. "We speak truth to power."

His producer, who's been silent until now, chortles. "That piece you did on the Minuteman was practically a commercial for Boeing."

"Well, the people need to know what the government is doing with their tax dollars," the anchorman says. "They need to see it. Sometimes you do need to get…access."

The bunny returns, delivers their drinks with a dip; LA stares at her bare high hip. "Here you go, Marie," the anchorman says: a generous tip.

"Into the vault," she smiles, and deposits the cash in her bra.

"I'd like to get into the vault," Miami says, staring at her departing pristine white cottontail. "What a piece."

"We had a good piece this week," LA says. "On that secret space station thing."

"Oh, really?" The anchorman's ears perk up.

"There he goes," Miami says. "You know how TV newsmen get their story ideas, right?" He asks the table but doesn't wait to deliver the punchline. "Reading the morning paper." Both newspapermen laugh.

"If we can deliver an important local story to a national audience…" the anchorman says.

LA nods. "It is an important story. We're up there…ramming into Soviet satellites. Someone's gonna start World War III…" He shakes his head. "And there's still more to it than we know."

"Might be something for our local affiliate to look at," the anchorman says.

"Rumor is Goldwater's got a real hard-on for that program."

"Goldwater never met an Air Force program he didn't like."

"You really don't like him, do you?" Miami asks.

"We do have a little bit in common, actually," Cronkite says philosophically. "We're both ham radio operators. I made contact with him earlier this summer. When he realized it was me, he didn't want to talk. I sent a QSL card and he never sent one back. Strange fellow." He sips his Manhattan. "Two and a half months."

"Or more," LA says.

"Unless there are...new race riots, or something, I don't think he stands a chance," the anchorman says. "Two and a half months."

Miami stands up to go to the bathroom; there's a clatter of metal. LA lunges, grabs the keys from the floor. "A-ha!"

"Congratulations," Miami says. "You finally got your hands on something."

LA turns the key over, inspecting it. "It's such a...crude phallic symbol."

"Not everything is a phallic symbol, Dr. Freud," the producer says. "Is your penis short and metal and serrated?"

"Well, actually..." LA says as the others laugh.

"Non-functional?" the anchorman smiles. "Only for show? Stamped with a serial number?"

"All right, all right…"

"When you take it out," the producer chimes in, "does the woman tell you, 'You can put that away now, sir?'"

More laughter. LA probably blushes, though in the lights it's impossible to tell. Still he looks at the key. "Seriously, though…I mean…"

"For fuck's sake," Miami swipes for the keys but misses.

"NOT EVERYTHING IS A PHALLIC SYMBOL," the producer says.

"Reminds me of a joke," the anchorman says. "This drunk, he goes up to a cop. Says, 'Officer, you gotta help me find my car.' And this drunk, he's wobbling. The cop says, 'You're in no condition to drive.' Drunk says, 'I'm not trying to drive, I just wanna know what happened to my car.' Cop says, 'Well, where was it when you saw it last?' And the drunk, he pulls something out of his pocket, says, 'Right on the end of this key.'"

The others chuckle.

"No, that's not it," the anchorman says. "So the cop, he starts talking, but he looks down and does a double-take, 'Well, I'd love to help you, but…before we fill out a report, you better zip up your fly.' And the drunk looks down and says, 'Aww, man, they got my girl, too!'"

Everyone laughs. LA fingers the notches on the shaft of the bunny key. "No greater phallic symbol."

Miami swipes again, finally grabs the key. "Well get your hands off it, then!"

•••

Out on Biscayne, inebriated, they wobble and sway like sailors at sea, under palm trees lit by warm sodium lights.

"I can drive," Miami says, and fumbles in his pockets for his keys.

"We'll get a cab," the anchorman says.

"No, I'm good." He drops the keys, bends to pick them up, falls.

"You can't walk!" the producer observes as Miami rolls over onto his back.

"It's a different set of muscles." Wearily he picks himself up.

"We'll get a cab, we can expense it."

"I can't."

"We'll drop you off."

"No, really, I'm good." He heads toward the car, key primed for insertion; he stabs clumsily at the lock.

LA body checks him to the side, pries the keys from his hands. "My God, man! You're going to kill us all!"

•••

The key is brass, smaller than a house key, apparently no different from one that might be used for, say, a padlock assigned to some insignificant task: preventing the theft of your clothes while you work out in the gym, or securing the gate on some seldom-used ranch road in the middle of Montana.

"Doesn't look like much, does it?" Hank asks as he dangles it.

The spaceman looks up from his work. "What is it?"

"Training material. For after they install the OB module." A slight pursing of the lips, some inscrutable emotion. "It's a launch key."

•••

That night, the commercial airs: a young girl in a country field, plucking petals from a daisy. The camera zooms in as she counts with sloppy cuteness: "One...two...three...four...five...seven...six...six...eight...nine... nine..." Offscreen, an emotionless voice starts counting down with military precision. Her dark eyes look up as if she hears; they betray a note of fear. "Ten...nine...eight...seven...six...five..." The image is frozen now but the camera keeps zooming: into her eye's dark void. The voice, vaguely Southern, counts down: "...four...three...two...one." In the black of her eye now: a bright white flash. The roar of explosion, a roiling mushroom cloud. Senator Kennedy's Boston tones: "These are the stakes. To make a world in which all of God's children can live...or to go into the dark. We must either love each other, or we must die." Then a calm male voice, devoid of accent: "Vote for Senator Kennedy on November 5th. The stakes are too high for you to stay home."

The spaceman's wife takes a deep breath, shakes her head. "Do you think he's going to win?"

"Kennedy?"

"Goldwater."

"They say he's a long shot."

"He shouldn't have any shot."

"Well..."

"Lord knows, the Berlin Crisis was scary enough. You were gone, I was home. The kids were so young. You think you can defend them against anything, for a while at least, and then you realize..."

"We could have a war with either one of them. Either one. The Berlin Crisis, I mean, that happened under Nixon..."

"Well, I don't like it." She sits there for a minute, her gaze unfocused, looking at the blank wall just above the television. "Do you think they're going to send you back up there?"

"Well, I hope so."

"How soon?"

"Might be a few months."

"So it could be after that...yahoo is in the White House."

He shrugs.

Again she speaks. "I want us to get a ham radio. Like Hank has. If something's gonna happen, I want to know about it. Before you go back up there, I want a radio."

"What would you do, if you knew something was gonna happen?"

"I'd take the kids. Get us out of town."

"Where would you go?"

"Mexico."

Incredulous: "Mexico?"

"Nobody's gonna shoot nuclear weapons at Mexico."

He shakes his head. "It'd be...chaos. You don't speak Spanish. You wouldn't be safe."

"Safer than here."

"Nothing's going to happen. Nobody wants to start World War III."

"Nobody wanted to start World War II, or World War I."

"Sure they did."

"They wanted to do something. They didn't want to do that."

He sighs. "There are...missiles around LA. Defensive missiles, to shoot down anything that comes our way. I'll take you up there sometime and show you."

"It only takes one to get through."

•••

A morning meeting on the other side of the globe. A fat bald leader sits behind a stately desk in a large wood-paneled office.

Calmly he scans the report that's been prepared to accompany his briefing. At last he looks up at the man standing on the other side of his desk, a severe spymaster in an austere suit. "Where did you get this information?"

"A mix of sources, comrade chairman. Some public, some private." The spymaster's suit is modestly adorned with two tasteful medals pinned on his lapels. "You have my assurances, it's reliable."

The leader leans back. Reads. "And it will be launched in four months."

"Yes, four months, comrade chairman."

"All right, you're dismissed. Send in Grechko."

The severe man takes a step backward, makes an informal nod, turns and heads out. In moments, the defense chief comes in. His uniform jacket is bedecked with decorations, an absurd amount: red ribbons and gold medals; discs, stars, hammer and sickles, and crosses in myriad combinations—so many medals that when he stops in front of the chairman's desk there is a brief dull clatter as they continue moving for a fraction of an inch and then fall back to his chest.

The leader speaks calmly. "I've received interesting information about this...American space platform."

The defense chief inhales anxiously; the chest full of ribbons rises and falls.

The leader continues. "They overfly us several times a day. We already know they've been taking pictures, good pictures. But they are developing the ability to drop bombs, too. From up there."

"You know my position on all of this, comrade chairman. If anything starts, we have to launch everything."

"Yes, yes. But would we have time? With these other methods, we'd have warning if something started. Radar alerts as their missiles climb above the horizon, things of that sort. An hour, half an hour. Not much, but...something. Time to issue the orders. But if they bombed us from this...platform of theirs, how much warning would we have?"

"It depends, comrade chairman. They overfly Moscow twice a day. There are long periods where they could not attack. But when they are about to overfly us..." He shrugs. "Five minutes, comrade chairman."

"Five minutes. And now this...cowboy is talking about...shooting missiles into our men's room." He leans back. "There's no way we could strike their cities with less than five minutes' warning, is there?"

"Not unless we..." Grechko snorts, shakes his head. "We'd have to do something truly crazy."

"Such as?"

"Smuggle nuclear warheads into their country, perhaps. Something like that."

"Smuggle...weapons." A smile. "It would be possible, would it not?"

"It would be very risky, comrade chairman."

"As risky as doing nothing?"

"It would take some work. You'd have to…set up some sort of phony industrial shipments, perhaps. From a place with strong business ties to America. Japan, say. You'd have to talk to Andropov about that."

"Five minutes." The leader nods in calm contemplation. "We do have a similar platform of our own in development, do we not?"

"A reconnaissance platform, comrade chairman, yes. Not for bombing."

"How long until it's up there?"

"Six months."

"Get it up there in three."

An anxious nod from the other man.

The leader makes a tent with his fingers, an airy prayer to a God he doesn't believe in. "Will it have weapons?"

"Weapons, comrade chairman?"

"Yes, for defense. In case they try to approach it. Disable it. Like what happened with that satellite."

"Our approach with that satellite was, perhaps, provocative. We…we can launch this one in a different orbit, comrade chairman. So they can't just…leave their station and fly to it."

"But if they launched one of their space planes on a solo mission, they could still reach it, yes?"

"Yes, comrade chairman."

"Make sure it has weapons. An…automatic cannon or something." A simple nod, as if this is a simple task.

"We've never fired an automatic cannon in space, comrade chairman. I'm…not sure if it's possible."

"You boys are clever. I'm sure you'll figure something out. Make sure it has an automatic cannon."

Another anxious nod.

"As for their platform," the leader continues. "We do have…rockets. Radars. Warheads. Surely there are…capabilities we can develop. In case we need to…neutralize it."

A deep breath. Not quite a smile. "We have in fact started developing those capabilities, comrade chairman. But there have been…difficulties."

"Difficulties?"

"We want to have a platform with some flexibility. Rather than a rocket from a launch pad that must be prepared for weeks, we think we can launch something from an aircraft. One that could take off from any runway, anywhere in the country, on short notice. That part is easy. But…you want to be able to neutralize this station. As in destroy, or render inoperable?"

The leader smiles, shrugs.

"Either way," the defense chief says. "It is hard to launch a missile like that and get it close enough to do what you want. Unless we use a nuclear warhead."

"Well I guess you'll have to use a nuclear warhead, then."

•••

A calm moonless night. A quiet airfield nestled in a silent Russian forest.

Inside a hangar, a general stands near the tail of a large aircraft, a prototype of an interceptor. Twin engines, twin tails, a stainless steel beast with red stars on wings and fins.

He is admiring the craft when a test pilot walks up from behind. Checks his watch: quick verification of timeliness before he says, "Good evening, comrade general."

"Evening, morning, I'm not sure which is the better greeting!" The general turns, smiles. "Either way, thank you for coming out at this...ungodly hour. There's something I need to show you, and unfortunately this is the only time we can see it." Again he looks admiringly at the large steel aircraft. "You've been involved in flight testing since the beginning, have you not?"

"Yes, sir." The pilot rubs his bleary eyes. "It's...quite an aircraft."

The general places a hand on one of the huge nacelles, scans the stainless steel welds, smiles. "You flew it...close to 30,000 meters, correct?"

"Yes, sir. In a zoom climb, not sustained."

"It can probably carry a payload to that height, correct?"

"Possibly, comrade general. If we cut weight elsewhere. What kind of payload?"

"A missile."

"It depends on the missile, sir." The pilot fights a yawn. "I mean, a full combat load, it would be…"

"Just one."

"Well, it's possible, sir." A tired pause. "Again, it depends on the missile. Obviously, the lighter the weight…do you know the weight, sir?"

"Not yet. It wouldn't just be some…off-the-shelf R-4. We still have some development work to do." He checks his watch. "Possibly a two-stage missile."

"A two-stage air-to-air missile…"

"Well, not exactly air-to-*air*…" The general smiles again, checks his watch. "Have you shot at anyone before?"

"I was, of course, too young for the Great Patriotic War, sir." The test pilot purses his lips. "There were a few incidents with the Americans when I was at Severomorsk-3…we downed a B-47 once. But I was away on leave. Then when they started with the U-2…I was scrambled a few times. Never in a position to shoot."

"It is…exhilarating," the general says. "I must admit, there is nothing quite like it. Having a target in your sights, knowing there's a man in there every bit as smart as you, who has done all he can to avoid being shot at…and especially when that man has the ability to shoot back. All that adrenalin...it is something. Images that haunt your dreams: that sight of the target as you pull the trigger. Would you like to see your target?"

"My target, sir?"

"Yes. We should be able to see it tonight. We should get outside now, though. Give our eyes time to adjust."

The test pilot's look: pure confusion. "Lead the way, sir."

Out the hangar door and into the summer night. All is quiet and dark. Peaceful. They walk across the apron, away from the blurry trapezoid glow of the light shadows from the hangar windows and down the side of the runway, away from everything, on the border of grass and concrete. Dim expanse all around, and beyond that, the dark splotchy line of the silent birch forest.

"The Americans have an orbital platform. It's been overflying us several times a day. Spies, trying to photograph and count our strategic rockets so that if a war starts, they can destroy them and leave us defenseless," the general says over his shoulder, calling into the darkness. As their eyes adjust, the universe comes into view: an infinite array of stars, the uneven Milky Way. A couple meteors hitting from random directions, flickering bright and dying.

"I haven't heard of this. Sir."

"We've kept quiet about it. Just like we kept quiet about the B-47s, just like we kept quiet about the U-2s, before we downed one. We don't want the people to feel...vulnerable."

"It's...understandable, comrade general."

"Yes. But it seems we are more at risk than we knew. They're putting bombs up there. This...cowboy that's running for president, he sounds like he wants to use them. We have to be able to prevent that."

The test pilot says nothing. They stop.

"It will be coming out of the south," the general says. "They fly over twice a day. Once in daylight, coming out of the north. Taking pictures, presumably. And once again at night." He checks his watch: soft radium glow. "So right now they are, most likely, asleep."

Silently they scan the heavens. Then from the pilot: "There it is, sir!" Dim arm against the starry sky. And up there, fast and smooth and steady against the firmament, a moving point of light.

•••

Morning flight to Tucson, a two-ship formation of T-38s. On final approach into Davis-Monthan the pilots and backseaters can see, off to the east, rows and rows of mothballed B-47s gleaming in the morning sun: aluminum aircraft arranged repetitively across the desert floor.

They land, touching down nearly simultaneously; they taxi to a designated spot on the apron and open their canopies to the Arizona heat. The four men—Mike Adams, Bob Lawrence, Hank Hartsfield, and our protagonist—climb out of their aircraft; each one retrieves a bag with a change of clothing from a pod underneath the aircraft. They go inside to change and await their ground transport.

"Quite a sight," Adams says. "The boneyard."

"Our predecessors," Hank chimes in.

Bob: "How do you figure?"

"Well, they had the mission, before us. Or before the U-2s, I should say. The B-47s were the ones doing overflights."

"There were shootdowns, right?" our protagonist says. "Before the U-2."

"There were shootdowns," Hank says.

"We would have gone...ape shit, if Soviet bombers were overflying us," Bob says.

"They didn't have to," Hank smiles. "They had the American press on their side. Read anything they wanted to about us, damn near."

Soon they are changed, and piling into a van driven by a young missile officer, one Lieutenant Ostrowski. He wheels them down US-89 into the Green Valley: a wide beautiful expanse of desert spread out before them, tinged with verdant brush, dotted with saguaros standing sentinel like rockets.

"Odd to have ICBMs out here," Adams says.

"Not at all," Hartsfield says. "Soviets pop a nuke out here, all they kill is rattlesnakes and rabbits. Maybe a few ranchers. Not the end of the world."

"And then the silo guys come out a month later," our protagonist says. "And this has all been turned to...radioactive glass."

"No big loss," Hank says.

"No, but down here, in Arizona," Adams says. "You'd think they'd put the missiles a little closer to their targets."

"They did with Minuteman, sir," Lieutenant Ostrowski says. "North Dakota. Montana. Wyoming. But Titan, well...if you have a senator heading the Armed Services Committee, and a missile that requires a lot of support personnel, guess what? You're probably gonna get some missiles in your state."

Off the highway now. A lonely mine road, empty. And after a couple minutes, they turn off *that*. Wheels crunching on gravel, scrub and cactus on both sides of the road. And at last, a chain link fence, with a gate. "Here we are, gentlemen," Ostrowski says. "The middle of nowhere."

Hank: "If nowhere had a middle."

The driver speaks into a squawk box next to the gate. "Lieutenant Ostrowski here with four visitors. Planned visit for operational orientation. Daily authentication code: 3-4-6-2-1-3."

A chain-link rattle as the gate rolls open, motors transmitting signals from hidden sources. On the other side: desert, but cleared of brush, dotted with a few ugly functional structures and a low heavy silo door. The van rolls through and parks.

"All right, gentlemen, watch out for rattlesnakes," Ostrowski says as they disembark. "Here you have a standard Titan command and silo facility. Hard stands for fueling operations, access building for the Launch Control Center. And of course, silo door, with intrusion alarms, and air shaft, also with intrusion alarms." He gestures towards the silo door: objects on each corner that look like air horns.

"You ever get any intrusions?" Hank asks.

"Rattlesnakes," he says. "Once we had a deer. Must've snuck through when the gate was closing. We never have to deal with intruders, it's not our mission. We're buttoned up downstairs, our job is to stay that way. We call the security detachment. Let them come shoot Bambi's mother."

They walk down a concrete stairwell to a door and another squawk box. "Lieutenant Ostrowski at the inner access point. 3-4-6-2-1-3."

An electric buzz, and the door is released. Inside, they descend several flights of metal-grating stairs to a pale green room. Ostrowski presses a button and there is a sharp quick klaxon sound and the massive blast door swings open.

"Good morning, gentlemen." A captain on the other side. Name tape: BANNER. "We are here to walk you through a tour of an active ICBM site, to familiarize you with issues related to the operational deployment of nuclear weapons. Obviously this is the blast door. Which you can probably guess what it's here to protect us from. You will notice that everything on the other side is suspended on springs from the ceiling, for added protection in the event of a nearby nuclear detonation."

They file on through, a short hallway whose walls are lined with pale green pipes and equipment boxes. Signs all around: NO LONE ZONE. TWO-MAN POLICY IN EFFECT.

The control center itself is a round space filled with computers: pale green housings, aluminum panels, a console in the center with a green chair. And a red safe with two brass padlocks. The space is circular, but not quite a room: all around the edges, there is a gap between the floor and the wall, several inches wide.

"Now we are in the Launch Control Center itself. This entire room, plus the living quarters above and the power center below, are all on springs so as to offer further isolation from the shockwaves of a nuclear attack. We have four-man crews on duty at all times, 24/7, because you never know when a nuclear war is going to start. In fact, we might have one this morning." He leans on the console, expectant. "This very morning." Several slow seconds pass, and a look of mild annoyance flickers across the captain's face. "I said, we might have a nuclear war this morni…"

A warbling klaxon sounds. From a speaker on the console: "Emergency Action Message Follows. I repeat. Emergency Action Message Follows."

"In real life, this message," the captain explains, "will come via SAC Headquarters in Omaha, Nebraska, or from the 15th Air Force in Riverside California, after a launch decision by the president, or his duly appointed successor in the National Command Authority." He pulls out two red binders and passes one to Lieutenant Ostrowski; both men grab grease pencils and open their books.

"Emergency Action Message," the speaker announces. "Tango-Romeo-Alpha-India-November."

The men fill in the blanks in their books: T-R-A-I-N.

"Message follows: Yankee-Oscar-Uniform-Lima-Oscar-Sierra-Echo-Romeo-Sierra," the speaker intones in a metallic but vaguely Southern voice. "Alpha-Romeo-Echo-Sierra-Tango-Uniform-Charlie-Kilo-Uniform-November-Delta-Echo-Romeo-Golf-Romeo-Oscar-Uniform-November-Delta-Foxtrot-Oscar-Romeo-Echo-Victor-Echo-Romeo."

"We then copy the EAM into our books, and swap books when the message repeats," Captain Banner says; they do so. Our protagonist glances at the writing and snickers. His coworkers do the same.

"Repeat message: Yankee-Oscar-Uniform…"

Both officers follow blank-by-blank with the grease pencil: Y-O-U-L-O-S-E-R-S-A-R-E-S-T-U-C-K-U-N-D-E-R-G-R-O-U-N-D-F-O-R-E-V-E-R.

"Always a 35-character message," the captain explains. "And sometimes it's a stupid message, because the training officer thinks they're a comedian. But for purposes of this demonstration, I see a valid message."

Lieutenant Ostrowski: "I agree. On all counts."

"Go to step one on the checklist," Banner says. "Launch keys inserted." There is, beneath the key on the console, a wallet-sized picture of a mother and child.

"Key inserted," Ostrowski echoes.

"And now, the Emergency War Order safe. Two locks, one each for the commander and deputy, and each only knows the combination to their own lock." The two men walk over to the red safe, open their locks. Captain Banner retrieves several envelopes. "We look through the envelopes. In a real launch situation we find the envelope with a two-letter code that matches the beginning of the EAM. Which, fortunately, we don't have. But if we did, inside each envelope is a plastic case with a piece of paper inside. We call that 'the fortune cookie.' Break it open, pull out the paper, read the message. In this case, a five-character code which will match the end of the EAM. Further verification that the EAM is correct. And there is a target string in the envelope which we will enter in the console. Here we will enter the training sequence: Papa-Seven-Papa-Seven-Papa-Seven."

Both men go to their respective positions: Banner in the center console, Ostrowski in front and to the left, at the deputy's station. Each dials in the code. The junior man says, "I concur: Papa-Seven-Papa-Seven-Papa-Seven."

"We could be launching immediately, we could be launching an hour later," Banner says. "We could be launching up to twenty-four hours later. Depending on our taskings in the Single Integrated Operations Plan, and the option chosen by the president, both of which are unknown to us. Our launch time, in GMT, will be in the EAM. For purposes of this demonstration, because I don't want to bore all of you with a leisurely nuclear war, we'll assume immediate launch. You'll notice the keys are 87 inches apart. Not that I've measured it or anything. But too far for one man to turn both keys simultaneously, unless his arms are substantially longer than the normal Air Force medical standard." Dry deadpan delivery. "Each key is spring-loaded into the OFF position. They must be turned within two seconds of one another, and they must be held for five simultaneous seconds. But I have my deputy here, and we're ready to turn on my mark. So…"

(He glances at Ostrowski, who nods.) "…Three-two-one…and turn."

Both men turn their keys in unison.

"And hold," Banner says. A light on the console goes on: LAUNCH ENABLE. "And release. Now we have pulled the trigger. It's out of our hands."

"Oh my God, what have you done?" From a staircase behind the console, another captain is ascending from the lower level, a crooked grin on his face.

Captain Banner shoots him a dirty look. "Now the batteries charge for 28 seconds. After BATTERIES ACTIVATED, we get an APS light. And you will hear…"

BERRRR-BERRRR-BERRRR! A loud klaxon, red lights.

"…a klaxon as we go silo soft. Oh no! That means the door upstairs has moved through the intrusion alarms."

The visitors trade uncertain looks.

"And then GUIDANCE GO, followed by FIRE ENGINE and LIFT-OFF. If this were an actual war, or if we had royally fucked up this training exercise, you would now be hearing a very loud roar from the other end of the cableway, and our missile would be on its way to its target, presumably somewhere in the Soviet Union. And we would be second-guessing our life choices for the very brief remainder of our military careers." A grim look. "The missile would be in flight for the next 30 to 35 minutes, reaching an apogee of about 450 miles in the middle of its flight. Around that time, the Soviets would presumably launch a retaliatory strike. But of course they might have launched first, so their missiles might already be in flight. At any rate, we would have an uncertain amount of time to get right with God." Another pause to survey the expectant faces. "There would be fires to extinguish at the other end of the cableway, because the silo would be ignited by the missile's departure, so that would keep our minds off the big picture. Although, fires underground, that might be a more literal reminder of hell than most of us would like at that point in our lives." (Grim pause.) "And other than that, the binder says, last item on the checklist: Await instructions. Which, who knows what authority would be issuing them? We have food and water in here for thirty days. After that, that hole behind you..." (A nod to a round hatch.) "...leads out to the emergency exit, a ladder through the air shaft to the surface. So assuming we've survived and the tunnel's not obstructed, we can see if there's anything left up there."

Low grim nods from the men.

"Any questions?"

Our protagonist: "Yeah. Uhhh, is there a bathroom?"

"Upstairs in the crew quarters. Only place you can go alone."

"Uhhh, thanks."

Up the steel staircase he goes: a small kitchenette (stove, refrigerator), bunk beds, a bathroom.

In the kitchenette he notices a small shelf with reading material. James Bond novels, *Atlas Shrugged*, the Bible, some Hemingway, and a plastic box, magazine-size but thick as a book, with red plastic letter tape on the spine that says SOLO TARGETING OF YOUR TITAN MISSILE. Taped to the side: a typewritten memo. SITE SOP: YOUR TITAN MISSILE IS A POWERFUL WEAPON WITH A MAXIMUM RANGE OF ONE METER. USE THE ENCLOSED TARGET INFORMATION TO FIRE IT QUICKLY AND EFFECTIVELY, WITH A MINIMUM OF DISTURBANCE TO YOUR FELLOW CREWMEMBERS. Inside: four back issues of Playboy. He puts the material back, shakes his head.

Back downstairs the others are talking: stories from the missile crew about their routines, shifts underground, cooking, sleeping, eating.

"So I have a question," Adams asks. "The launch order system, it seems to be dedicated to preventing one person from just…unilaterally going crazy and firing a missile. Rigid chain of authentication for launch orders. Two-man rule and all that. So there's no single point of failure…except at the top. The president has sole authority to issue a launch order. How do we know that a launch order is coming from a sane president?"

"Are you worried about Senator Goldwater?" the training officer asks with a sly smile.

"Some of us are worried about Senator Kennedy," Hartsfield smiles.

"Kennedy?" Lawrence asks.

"I heard a rumor the guy's on uppers. Amphetamines. For 'energy' or 'pep' or whatever. Which, I don't know how healthy that is for anyone, long-term. People get paranoid."

Bob Lawrence shakes his head.

"No, really. I'm serious," Hartsfield goes on. "You know who else was on uppers? The Nazis."

"Let's…" Captain Banner makes a hand motion as if to still the waters. "Gentlemen, we all know we need to be apolitical here. We have to trust that whomever the American people select will be a steady and wise leader. We have no right to second-guess the will of the people, just because we're wearing a uniform." A nod towards Adams. A grim look. "So as to your question: that, sir, is a question beyond our pay grade."

Nods from around the room: not agreement, but understanding.

"All right, now that our friend has returned, we can verify that our Titan missile is, in fact, safe and sound in its silo. Have you men seen one before?"

Hank: "Uhhh…we've all ridden one. Into space."

A nod. "Very well, gentlemen. Right this way."

Out of the launch control center, past the blast door, down a corridor of steel girders and fluorescent lights, a single-point-perspective drawing stretched out to infinity.

Finally, a pale green access door.

Captain Banner smiles. "And behind Door Number 1, you have our friend the Titan. Nine-megaton fission-fusion-fission warhead, largest in the U.S. inventory. And now, without further ado…"

On the other side: the vertical cavern of the silo, steel access platforms folded up against the walls. Enough large quiet emptiness that it feels like a Space-Age church. And in the center, the delicate aluminum missile, fat from this angle, sides neatly stitched with rivets, and the letters US AIR FORCE stretching vertically down the side. Nose cone like a black dunce cap with the point rounded off. A sleeping beast, resting in its silent space.

•••

By early evening they have flown back to Vandenberg. A collective no more, four men climbing into their separate cars for the lonely drive home under darkening skies and the fading glory of a Pacific sunset.

Our protagonist participates in the rituals: collecting his still-warm leftovers from the fridge, putting the kids to bed, chatting with his wife. But his mind appears to be elsewhere. They go to bed, and she is out immediately, and he lies there, eyes open.

He gets up and walks to the living room and turns the TV down low. Ayn Rand, talking to a host about the tyranny of collectivism: a proud angry woman. He changes the channel to a nighttime movie, Cecil B. DeMille's *Samson and Delilah*. Comfortable and familiar: the tyranny of the Philistines contrasted with the freedom of the Israelites. "You like to have people bow to the will of spears," Samson says. "I like to have spears bow to people." At last he starts drifting in and out of sleep. Scenes flicker. "For all that I do to you now, I'll be blameless," Samson says. "I'll give you fire for fire, and death for death." Samson blinded, between the pillars of the temple of Dagon. "Mine eyes have seen thy glory, Oh God.

Now let me die with thine enemies." The temple toppling, death and destruction.

•••

As the spaceman walks out his front door on his way to work, he turns to lock it and sees something falling from the door knocker, fluttering to the ground: another business card. The CBS eye stares blindly at him.

He picks it up, turns it over. THE AMERICAN PUBLIC NEEDS TO KNOW WHAT YOU ARE DOING. He slides it into his pocket, turns back to the driveway.

In the car, on the radio: "Arrests were made yesterday in protests related to Dr. Martin Luther King's Los Angeles visit. The..." With a click he turns it off, drives to work in silence, a blank look on his face.

Across the parking lot, aluminum and glass doors, an air-conditioned blast: the banal routine.

The group secretary flags him down on the way in to his office. "Sir, we have...visitors this morning. You'll be receiving a solo briefing at ten-hundred hours in Conference Room B."

"A briefing about what?"

"Sir, I'm not privy to that information."

He keeps busy until then, and once the appointed hour is near, he gets up, grabs a pen and notepad, uses the bathroom, gets coffee, and walks to Conference Room B.

"Good morning, sir." The instructor is in civilian clothes but looks vaguely familiar; the spaceman squints as if unsure whether or not he's ever seen the other man. "Please, have a seat."

The spaceman complies.

"Since you're here," the briefer continues, "I guess we can get started. Some of this material may be familiar to you, some of it may be new. We've briefed a couple of your fellow astronauts already, but we need to make sure everyone in your program is on the same page."

A nod from the spaceman.

And on it goes. "As you already know, we are expanding the capabilities of the orbital platform with the installation of a special weapons module. Yesterday you received a familiarization tour of a Titan missile site, to acquaint you with operational procedures related to deployed nuclear weapons. Today we will discuss in more detail some of the procedures related to your particular program, with training activities and practical exercises to follow. Should you be assigned to another flight on or after mid-December of this year, you and your fellow crewmember will, under the orders of the National Command Authority, be able to launch nuclear weapons against select targets at various locations across the globe. These targets will be unknown to you, even at launch time; we have determined that it is best for all concerned if you do not have that information. Various options will be programmed in to the warheads, and depending on your orbital position in relation to our nation's adversaries, and your tasking in the Single Integrated Operations Plan, the warheads will be released over the next several minutes or hours. Launch procedures will, of course be subject to the two-man rule, and will require simultaneous key turns by each crewmember at separate consoles that will be installed at opposite ends of the orbital platform. We will cover those procedures in detail shortly." A pause for air. "But before we go any further, we need to discuss your attitude towards nuclear weapons. We need to ensure that all personnel entrusted with the operational care and deployment of such weapons are reliable and mentally fit; we also need to ensure that each one has a positive attitude about nuclear weapons. A positive attitude does not mean that you are eager to use nuclear weapons, or that you want to use nuclear weapons. A positive attitude simply means you understand the importance of nuclear weapons, and their necessary role in the defense of the United States of America; it means you are willing to use them if necessary. So, please tell me: Do you have a positive attitude about nuclear weapons?"

The spaceman takes a deep breath and begins to speak.

•••

New York, early evening.

A lawyer—part of the rush-hour crowd—heads through the brass and wood and glass doors of Grand Central Station and walks down the marble stairs—worn in particular spots by decades of feet each choosing the same path—to the main floor. A river of humans branching out to various trains, decisions all made. Only small choices for most: whether to stop and buy a magazine, or cigarettes, or a pack of gum; whether to look up at the clock, or check a wristwatch. They know their destinations, and so does the lawyer; in theory each of them could choose any train, but no one deviates from their set path.

Since the lawyer is in-house, rather than at a firm, he has the advantage of a fixed schedule; he hasn't missed a train on a workday in two years and ninety-three days, although of course he does not know that is the interval. In that time he has boarded the New York Central 5:23 Hudson Line to Poughkeepsie five hundred and forty-two times, with an average boarding time of four minutes and fifty-three seconds before scheduled departure. (Although given financial and management issues with the New York Central, the actual and scheduled departures have sometimes been at variance.) With the exception of one December evening— when he was head-cold addled and fell asleep and missed the station and had to call his wife to pick him up in Ossining— he's gotten off the train in Tarrytown every single one of those times. This is presumably his plan for today as well.

The train transits much of Manhattan underground before emerging at 97th Street, then continuing on via viaduct, crossing the Harlem River, and traversing the Bronx, meanwhile making all scheduled stops. The lawyer does not give more than a cursory glance out of the windows until well north of the city, when the train is running along the east bank of the Hudson and he can gaze across the silvery river at the silent green highlands beyond.

It is a short ride from the train station parking lot to the family home, a lovely little colonial with white shutters. Inside it is slightly messy, strewn with dolls, doll clothing, piles of opened and unopened mail (birthday cards, bills for electricity and car insurance, advertisements, grocery store flyers, etc.), piles of laundry. The husband doesn't seem to mind the clutter.

The family eats, and everyone chats for a bit about their day, and soon it's time for the two girls to brush their teeth and go to bed. But first:

Elder daughter: "Daddy, can you tell us a story?"

"Sure. Pick out a book."

Younger daughter: "We've read all the books. We know how they end."

"We can get a couple more. This weekend, maybe."

Elder daughter: "How about you tell us a story without a book?"

"OK, how about Goldilocks?"

Younger daughter: "We know how that ends, too. Plus I'm scared of the bears."

"They never eat Goldilocks, they just scare her."

Elder daughter: "I always think she's dumb for going to sleep in the bed. She should have left the house after she broke the chair."

"Well, stories have endings. They have lessons. If you change the ending, someone might not learn the lesson."

"I always want to tell Goldilocks to do something else."

"OK, I'll make up a story." He smiles patiently. An idea is born. "And we'll let you decide how it goes. Where do you want this story to happen?"

"How about on an island?"

"OK, what's the island called?"

"Sugarcane Island."

"That's a nice name for an island." To the younger daughter: "Do you like that name?"

"Yes."

"OK, you're on Sugarcane Island. What kind of island is it?"

"A tropical island."

"OK, it's a tropical island, with palm trees and coconuts, and wide sandy beaches. You were shipwrecked and you had to swim there, and you don't know what happened to everyone else, but you're on this island, and it's so nice that you kind of like it! So you walk down the sandy beach, and you look at all the trees, and you see mountains, because it's a big island. And you realize, you have to decide: Are you going to try and get off the island right away, or try and live there until somebody comes to rescue you? So you have to decide: Do you build a raft? Or start a fire?"

"Build a raft!" the older girl says. And the younger: "Start a fire!"

• • •

"The pilot, he must have hit every patch of turbulence between New York and here." The spaceman's parents are visiting Los Angeles at last; they took a drive to Point Fermin Park and are setting out a picnic on a beautiful patch of grass near a bluff overlooking the vast Pacific. "I mean, don't they see that turbulence? Can't they steer around it?"

"They can't see it," the spaceman says. "Clear air turbulence."

"Well. Anyway. Your mother was about to get sick. And I pulled out that bag, that little bag they put in the seat in front of you. And it had dried vomit on it! Like someone had used it! And they hadn't thrown it away, or cleaned it off, or anything! It was so gross that I got sick!"

"That's...awful," the spaceman's wife says. She opens the picnic basket, starts passing out sandwiches. Ham and cheese for the adults, peanut butter and jelly for the kids.

"It was awful! And there wasn't another bag! So we were both getting sick in the same bag!"

"It was awful," the mother says.

"I gave them a piece of my mind, I did," the father says. "They were standing by the front of the plane, when we went down the stairs. And I told them, 'My son's a pilot, he's been in space. He would have been a much better pilot for this flight. Very unprofessional, to have that much turbulence.'"

"Very unprofessional," the mother says.

"Very unprofessional," the spaceman echoes. Takes a bite of sandwich.

"You should fly for the airlines," the father says. "You'd be a much better pilot than those...jokers. Getting everyone sick, all that turbulence. Have you thought about that? Flying for the airlines? You should think about that."

"Yes, you should think about that," the mother says.

The spaceman swallows. "I'll think about it."

"You've been in space already. You've seen all there is to see. Put yourself in danger. Very brave. And that's great, we're very proud of you. But you should leave the service, become an airline pilot. You wouldn't have to be gone from your family for forty days at a time. You could be based out of New York, we could see you more often. See the kids. It would be nice to see you more often, without having to...fly across the country, through all this turbulence."

"It would be nice to see you more often," the mother says.

The spaceman takes a deep breath, as if trying to relax. Says, "I'll think about it." Takes another bite of sandwich.

Eyeing his discomfort, the spaceman's wife speaks up. "Isn't this is a beautiful spot here?"

"It is beautiful."

Below them on the water, a massive freighter crawls through the water, heading towards the port at Long Beach.

"This is a good spot for a fort," the father says. "You could see anyone coming. Anyone trying to approach the city. Like if the Japs had tried to invade. Be a good place for...cannons, or something."

"They did have cannons here, back in the day," the spaceman says. "Behind us on the hill, at Fort MacArthur. There's missiles there now."

"Why would they have missiles in a city?" the father says. "If the bad guys shoot at the missiles and miss, they hit the city."

"They're air defense missiles," the spaceman says. "They're here to protect the city."

"We should have a look at these missiles," the father says.

"It's an Army installation."

"You're in the Air Force. You've got that sticker on your car. Department of Defense. We should have a look at those missiles."

After they finish eating, and the picnic is picked up, they pile into the car—men in front, with the boy sandwiched between them on the bench seat, bare skin sticking to the vinyl; women and the girl in the back. It's a quick drive up the hill to the installation.

The missiles are, objectively, beautiful: clean white Spartans aimed up at the empty sky. Small trapezoidal fins up front, a larger set of triangular fins in the middle, and at the end, trapezoidal fins, larger still.

"It's an Army system," the spaceman says. "So I have to dislike it, officially. But it is interesting. These ones, the Spartans, are designed to hit Soviet missiles outside of the atmosphere."

"That's gotta be hard, to hit a missile," his father says.

"There's a nuclear warhead on them. A five-megaton warhead. Which on earth would destroy most of a large city, but doesn't have as big of an effective range in space. Still, they'd launch a few of these, try to destroy a bunch of warheads. Then there's a smaller missile called Sprint that goes very fast, that would try to hit anything that got through. And those have warheads, too. The system on the whole is called Sentinel."

"Shooting nukes at nukes?" the father says.

"Yes, shooting nukes at nukes."

"That seems dangerous, all those nukes. Why have I never heard about this system?"

"It's been in the papers."

"I've never heard about it."

"It's been in the papers. Your tax dollars paid for it, you should know about it. It's a big expensive system. They built it to keep us safe."

"I've never heard about it."

"I saw a magazine article the other week," the spaceman's mother says. "About the safest places to be, in a nuclear war. The top one's actually here in California."

"Really?" the wife says.

"Yeah. It's pretty far north, along the coast. Miles away from any targets. Hundreds of miles north of San Francisco, even. I guess the winds are usually out of the west. So you wouldn't have fallout."

"What's it called?"

"I think it was…Eureka. Yes, that's it. Eureka, California."

"That'd be a good place to go," the wife says to the spaceman. "If anything started, and we had a warning."

"Assuming we'd have a warning," the spaceman says. "We wouldn't necessarily have a warning."

"Yes, but if we did, that'd be a good place to go."

They pile back into the car, start it up, start driving north, out of the installation. There is a radio bulletin on; the spaceman moves to turn the knob so they can drive home in silence.

"Wait." The wife places her hand on his.

From the radio, crackly: "…received word that civil rights leader Dr. Martin Luther King, Jr. has been shot and killed today, at a rally in downtown Los Angeles. Police said Dr. King was struck in the upper chest by a bullet from a high-powered rifle. He was taken to Good Samaritan Hospital, where he was pronounced dead on arrival. Police say no arrests have been made…"

"There's gonna be riots," the father says. "The blacks, I know how they think, there's gonna be riots."

"They're not a 'they,'" the wife says.

"They're a 'they,'" the father says. "I know how they think."

"They're not a 'they,' they're a bunch of individuals. Just like…us."

"They're a 'they.' Animals. A pack of animals," the father says. "Inglewood, do we have to drive through Inglewood to get home? Or Watts? That's where they live, right? Inglewood. Watts. We might wanna pick another route. I know how they think. There's gonna be riots."

"We'll be fine," the spaceman says.

And the father, again: "There's gonna be riots."

They are on Osgood Farley Road heading north into San Pedro and they are on a little bit of a rise and can see west across a dip to some high terrain beyond, and the father looks ahead out the windshield as if expecting to see something: riots, fires, plumes of smoke. Imagining the city already in ruins.

A football game, late November. Blue LA sky up high, low fog rolling in from the Pacific. On the gridiron, a tangle of bodies: gold pants and helmets on both sides, dark red jerseys on one, pale blue on the other. Crowd noise crescendoing after major plays for one side or the other (for this stadium is home to both) and then returning to a dull ocean roar.

The president is smiling, relaxed: clean teeth emerging from the famous jowly cheeks. Around him in the stands, a handful of men, also in suits, some dividing their attention between the action and the crowd.

A reporter comes down the steps from the press booth, notepad tucked under his arm; when he is abreast of the chief executive he stops, as if to plan his approach: so focused on the famous faces that it takes him a second to notice the anonymous one right in front of him.

"Can I help you, sir?" the lead agent yells over the noise.

"We wanted to see if the president had changed his mind about press availability. We're curious to hear his thoughts on the incoming administration."

A few seats down, Nixon glances over, distracted finally from the action on the field. The smile disappears. Dark angry eyes.

The agent glances back, catches the look. "The president is here to watch the football game, sir."

Nixon turns back to the field. Takes a sip from a thermos. Shudders, relaxes.

"They do really like to bother you, sir," his chief of staff says. "Everything that's happened these past few months...it's all their fault. And they're still trying to blame it on you. I don't blame you for not wanting to talk to them."

"It'll be over soon enough, thank God." UCLA has the ball, near the goal line. A succession of pounding short runs, and at last on 4th and goal, a sweep around to the right to score. Another eager sip from the thermos. "There is a guilty feeling, though. To be walking away from it all." The president glances back at the lonely reporter, who is still trudging back up the stairs. "You know, in another life that could have been me."

"A reporter?"

"A sportswriter. I'm sure I've told you, I was...awful on the field. Two left feet. But I'll tell you...the lessons. How to take a pounding and hang in there. How to keep going, never quit. My parents named me after Richard the Lion-Hearted, you know." Again he drinks. Words liquid and loose. "I knew early on I would never be good on the gridiron. The other guys were twenty pounds heavier than me. But I hung in there. And still, even now, there's something about...just being around the game." He appears relaxed, but the smile hasn't returned. Eyes now distant, wistful. "In another life I could have been a sportswriter. Just...chronicling it all. I might have been happier as a sportswriter. But there is that call, to be in the arena..."

USC is driving now, steadily chewing up the field, feebly resisted by the ineffectual blue shirts. "Did you ever think of coaching, sir? I mean, the action on the field...it's not a closed system. The coaches are part of it, too."

"I...couldn't do that. How can you tell someone to do something you can't do yourself? My coach, the Chief, he was a hell of a guy. All-American here at USC. He could tell us what to do because he'd been there. I think that's what made me want to be in the arena myself. Just seeing that...a man who could speak with authority, because he'd been there. That's what I loved about MacArthur, that's what the people loved. He'd been there. A tough act to follow..."

"You have a lot to be proud of, sir. I'm sure the new administration will end up saying the same about you."

"You can't help but wonder." Another drink, another shudder. "I was ready to go to war over Berlin. I was. And they...I mean, thank God they backed down. But I don't know, maybe I lost my nerve, too. Czechoslovakia, maybe I should have been tougher. But you know...it's different. When you're the one making the call. MacArthur, for all the tough talk during the election about losing China, arming Chiang Kai-shek to retake it, when he was in office, it was..." Again he drinks. "He had people urging him to attack. When Beria took over, when we had those...squabbles over the Chinese islands. And I was one of those people. But once I was in office..." Drinks again. "It's different when it's you. When it's all on you. When you're in uniform and things go south, you can always blame it on the man upstairs. But when you're that man..."

The chief of staff nods: possibly understanding, possibly acknowledging that he will never understand.

"Anyway, MacArthur. He was a man...immune to pressure."

On the field, a lovely little run by USC, #32. The crowd around them roars: so, too, does the president.

"Quite a run, that man. Quite a run."

"Uhhh, yes, sir."

Next play, 2nd and 4, #32 plunges in: battered by collisions but he falls forward, picks up a few hard-earned yards.

"He is something, isn't he? Even on a short play, he falls the right way. Really something."

"He certainly is, sir."

"He had that run last year...sixty-four yards to tie it up, set up the win. I remember watching that on TV and thinking, 'What a hell of a run.'"

"He's a lock for the Heisman this year."

"He is. But last year...that game. My God, I wish I could have caught that game."

#32 again...with a little leap he darts deftly through a hole in the lines, and by the time the sky blue jerseys close in, he is plunging across the goal line. 13-10, USC. The crowd roars, surges: feet stomping on stands, rolls of toilet paper flying through the air.

The chief of staff shakes his head.

"Tough break for you guys," the president says.

"You're taking sides, sir?"

"Every politician has to, eventually. If I cheer with you and Haldeman, I get the cold shoulder from Pat. And I see the Chief in my mind, shaking his head at me." Down on the field, fresh-faced cheerleaders are hopping and clapping; cheerful clean-cut pep squad types, clad in white, are pumping their fists. Extra point: good. "This energy. It's really something, isn't it?"

"It is, sir."

"You know, this is America's national pastime. Not baseball. We don't want to admit it, though."

"How do you figure, sir?"

"We're a violent nation. An energetic nation, born of violence. Most other countries, their origin stories are so boring they're lost to history. Some group of people started...living and fucking in the same patch of earth for centuries. So long that they started speaking the same language. But no, not us. Born of violence and rebellion. Reborn through civil war. It's who we are. There's violence in baseball, but it's incidental. Two outfielders bumping into one another while fielding a fly. A collision at home plate now and then. It's possible to make it through a whole game without...resorting to physical force. And it's a lazy game. No clock, no sense of urgency. More appropriate for...South America, maybe. You can take a siesta while you wait for your turn at bat." Again the president drinks. "We're violent. But we're ashamed of it."

On the field, UCLA tries helplessly to make a final drive before the half runs out. A few rows down, a supporter catches the president's eye; Nixon smiles, waves, points an acknowledging finger.

"Caesar in the Coliseum," his chief of staff smiles.

"Except I won't be Caesar much longer." Still no smile.

"There were legal options available, sir."

"I fought, I tried to fight. I never quit."

"There still are options, sir."

"There are still options."

"And you're still president, sir."

"I am still president." He surveys the field. The final seconds of the half tick down. The players depart, the USC marching band takes the field. "The crowd is part of it, too, you know. They want it to be violent, they want the spectacle. Blood lust. All of the caesars understood that, they understood the need. The crowds weren't observers, they were participants. Voting up or down. Decisions of life or death. And maybe here, too. The players, they want to see that someone's watching. Proud parents, cheering them on. A young girl, hoping for a date. They feel that, they feed off that energy. They hit harder when there's a crowd. The crowds cheer the hard hits, and the players hit harder." The president wobbles, possibly drunk. "The crowd is always a part of it. They pretend otherwise, but they're a part of it. They were part of it when Jesus was crucified. When I lost the nomination…" Another mournful drink.

The chief of staff looks over at him. Observation, no judgment.

"Maybe I wasn't hitting hard enough for them," the president continues. "My parents were Quakers, I'm sure some of that rubbed off. Maybe I wasn't hitting hard enough. But I can hit hard." The president leans in to the chief of staff, speaks in low tones; he nods toward another aide a few seats away, one in uniform, with a leather briefcase attached to his wrist. "People talk about Caesar. Caesar had nothing, by comparison. I could go under the stands with my aide. I could go under the stands, and in half an hour, a hundred million people would be dead."

The chief of staff says nothing.

The president wobbles, ever so slightly. Out on the field, the USC marching band lines up with military precision—a rank on the 15-yard line, a rank on the 10, a rank on the 5, a rank on the goal line, uniforms red, gleaming brass instruments: they step off with a blast of energetic horns.

Blues

We are waiting for launch. We are waiting for the beginning of the end.

The missile, a silvery Titan III, stands on its coastal California launch pad in the cool of a winter morning. All around, seabirds: gulls, cormorants, pelicans, guillemots, auklets. Atop the missile, a black spaceplane pointed skyward. And inside, our spaceman.

We haven't mentioned his name. You may think you know who he is, based on certain biographical details, but you'd be wrong. There is an American flag on the pressure suit shoulder. The tax dollars that have placed him on this temporary aluminum pedestal: Where do they come from? They come from you and me. He is us. We are him.

(Plus, we're eager to see how this ends. We're in this together, awaiting the kickoff.)

We see what our spaceman sees. Morning sun streaking in: a bright patch of cockpit with a few miniscule threads of lint highlighted. We feel his discomfort: the unnatural feeling of laying on one's back at a slight downward angle, shoulders squeezed against straps, blood flowing strangely, pressure and tension and angst. Through the trapezoidal windows, a boring swath of sky: the mild blue yonder. Occasionally a bird drifts into view. Easy to ignore, until one pelican swoops in low and somehow perches precariously on the rounded nose cone; we see him (her?) beat wings for balance at the edge of our field of vision, and improbably maintain the precarious perch.

Let's key the mike: "Ummm, LCC, Falcon-2. There is a bird on the spacecraft."

Voice, vaguely southern: "Falcon-2, LCC. You said a bird, over?"

"Affirmative, LCC. He is sitting on the nose cone. Over."

"I'm sure he can't hurt it, Falcon-2."

"Looks like he doesn't want to leave. Over."

"Well, he will in a minute. Give us a status, over."

A quick glance at the kneeboard checklist. Every silvery switch is set in position. Pressure in the transtage hypergolic tanks: good. APUs, hydraulics: good. If there's a reason not to launch, we don't see it. "LCC, Falcon-2. GO for launch."

"Copy all systems go. Range is clear. T-minus two minutes. Instrumentation, Page 94, Step Three, LC, Step Four. T-minus 1:55."

Another voice: "Verified."

Everything is armed. We are ready. Down goes the count.

"T-minus one minute. Launch sequence is started."

Computers in control. The Titan now on internal power. At the edge of the window: the feathers of the seabird. Distracting. So many things to imagine: if he's stunned at launch and falls against, say, the fairing on the transtage, would that cause problems? Probably not. But what will happen is seldom as interesting as what might happen.

In the headphones: "T-minus fifteen seconds. Automatic sequence engaged. Ten...nine...eight..."

Far below, a dim shudder. Valves opening? No, the solids fire first.

"...seven...six...five..."

Tension: bones pressing the flesh against the ejection seat, straps tight against the tops of the shoulders, arms pressed firmly into lap. There is nothing to do.

"...four...three...two...one...." The noise and shudder: familiar but not routine. The seabird disappears. "...and liftoff!" Rising, one with the rocket: the tension washed out in a flush of adrenalin. "We have cleared the tower."

Shudders and rattles and an overwhelming roar: the visuals have not changed at all—same instrument panel, same bland blue through the trapezoid windows—but all is energy and excitement, noise and controlled fury.

A quick transmission: "Everything is looking good!"

Back comes our capcom: "Roll program initiated. Pitch program initiated." Through the shuddering windows, the sun angle changes as the booster nozzles gimbal.

Ears popping. Flexing of the jaw. Still the clean steady push from the solids, the overwhelming roar, the jarring and relentless ascent. A moment of thought for the pelican: unconscious, dead, roasted by the boosters? Or: flying home traumatized, with a story for the family.

The buffeting increases.

"Max-Q," our LCC calls out. "Still a good steady burn from the solids. We are through the sound barrier. Coming up on staging."

Arcing upside-down out over the empty ocean: there is a very slight dip in the thrust, and then the indicator lights. The rockets are, in fact, burning out. And shudders of fuel valves opening and boosters being discarded and the kick of the ullage motors and then the bigger kick of the first stage, the hypergolics, and looking up, which is down, we can see the Pacific falling away now, and ahead the sky seems slightly darker, the slow steady fade out of the blue and into the black.

We are thinking now of the mission.

What is our mission? First we need to figure out: who's president? You may have a preference, depending on which political party you support, or your comfort with the whole nuclear war thing. (To quote Major Kong in *Dr. Strangelove*, "Heck, I reckon you wouldn't even be human beings if you didn't have some pretty strong personal feelings about nuclear combat.") BUT the author gets a little indecisive, so he hasn't even made up his mind about whether or not we're launching before Inauguration Day. So it could still be Nixon.

We're in this together, though. So, pick:

If we are launching before Inauguration Day, go to page 496.

If we are launching after Inauguration Day, go to page 497.

(CONTINUED)

OK, cool. Nixon it is.

Now let's go to page 498.

(CONTINUED)

All right, it's after Election Day. So who won, Kennedy or Goldwater? You, being a keen observer of American politics, doubtless have a party preference that echoes your own choice in the present day. So, let's flip a coin. Heads means your party lost; tails means they won. So:

Heads: go to page 498.

Tails: go to page 500.

(CONTINUED)

The roar and the rumble continue: a full-throated rippling rocket loudness pushing the sky apart, toxic chemicals exploding on contact and thrusting the shuddering aluminum tube through the thinning air, faster and faster as the resistance drops and the fuel is depleted.

Now the sky is nearly black, now the first stage is nearly spent; through the vibrations we can see the accelerometer showing 6 gs, an elephant squeeze. Then there's a slight dip and *BOOM!* And a burst of flame all around, but only for a moment, and again the rocket slaps us in the back.

"Fire in the hole."

From the headphones: "Staging looks good."

Acceleration, acceleration, always and relentless: the Titan is a kick in the pants, a souped-up hot rod, a star-spangled pulsing mass of Yankee Doodle POWER. 6 gs, creeping up to 7 now, the noise diminishing as the air thins, but still the giant pressure, so much so that it feels like forever.

When is it going to end?

In the headphones: "Coming up on SECO."

And at last, there it is: body surging against the straps, violent. A flash of panic, perhaps the memory of a crash-landing, the fear of being ripped apart.

And: weightlessness. Arms now drifting up. Again the planet is spread out beneath us, the infinite blue Pacific, the hazy atmospheric glow clinging to the horizon beyond our inverted cockpit.

Key the mike: "SECO. Everything is looking good. Twenty seconds to SEP."

"Copy SECO," the ground says. "Altitude and trajectory are looking good. Five hundred fifty miles downrange."

An upward reach, towards the button: SEP SPCFT. There is nothing to decide: this must come next; there's no scenario where we don't make this choice.

A gentle push with gloved fingers. Behind us, small guillotines fire, cutting the electrical and umbilical connections with the remainder of the rocket; the explosive charge around the base of the transtage combusts with a noiseless shudder. All around now, a cloud, flecks of metal, bolts and washers and tiny scraps, the machines now torn apart, the spaceplane once more flying free.

We are in space—beholden to the whims of our earthly masters, and the mission they have chosen. But what is that mission?

It's up to you, dear reader.

If the Soviets launched their station, the Almaz, and we'd like to get some pictures, then let's go to page 501.

If we are going directly to our station, we can go to page 658.

Or, heck, maybe this is a bombing mission. No trip back to the station, just a nuclear warhead in the payload bay. If so, let's go to page 706.

(CONTINUED)

The coin has two heads. (Sorry!)

Let's go to page 498.

(CONTINUED)

On we fly, in the empty silence. The route's familiar—down across the bottom of the earth—but the calendar promises something new, daylight views of the southern continent.

Our attention is elsewhere, though: on the bright foreign light just above the horizon.

Down below in the open ocean there is a tracking ship; our launch and their course have been choreographed so they can support us in this task. A scan of the kneeboard: eyes on the acquisition time. The clock counts upwards, and at last it is time to transmit: "Range Tracker, Falcon-2. Come in, over."

No response.

Again: "Range Tracker, Falcon-2. Come in, over."

Crackly answer. "Falcon-2, Range Tracker. We have you on scope. Excellent launch. Slight wedge angle with your target, but you should get a few pictures if you play it right. Over."

"Copy, Range Tracker. Waiting on burn instructions. Over."

"Falcon-2, Range Tracker. Burn instructions as follows: GET of zero-zero plus two-one plus one-two. Burn duration two-zero seconds. Posigrade burn with the transtage. Two degrees pitch."

"Range Tracker, Falcon-2. Copy GET zero-zero, two-one, one-two. Posigrade transtage burn, two-zero seconds. Two degrees pitch. Over."

The Soviets are not orbiting in the same plane as our station—that would be far too easy and convenient and weird. So a long drawn-out rendezvous is impossible; there can be no leisurely snapping of pictures. But their inclination is similar enough that it was possible to plan a close conjunction and still have enough transtage fuel—just barely—to rendezvous.

"Falcon-2, when you get up there, they should be moving slowly across your orbital path, left to right. Closest point of approach should be under a quarter mile."

"Copy, Range Tracker."

"Godspeed, Falcon-2."

"Enjoy your voyage, Range Tracker. Preparing for the burn. Over."

It is time to reorient the spacecraft, key in the commands. Exciting, is it not? There is a smoothness to it all; when one moves quickly and stays busy, there is no time for any worry, any angst.

Horizon right-side-up now. Down below: still the relentless blue.

When the timer counts down there is the soft urgent push of the ejection seat into the back. None of the violence of launch, but a calmer burn, gentle and insistent: come now, friends, it is time to do this.

And now, next tasks. Stowed at the base of the ejection seat, another Hasselblad. It only takes a slight loosening of the straps to retrieve the bag. With the action come more memories of collision, the dramatic end of the last flight. Best not to think about it.

Ahead and below, Antarctica scrolls into view, the ragged white coastline, an unknown mountain range. But of course there is no time to take it all in. We'll have plenty of time to do that later: of that we are quite sure.

Open the bag, assemble camera and telephoto lens. There is a smooth precision in the way they fit together.

Ahead now, their station.

Through the camera viewfinder: a metal cylinder, thicker and fatter than our station, flanked by squarish solar panels.

We don't have much time.

We snap away, shot after shot after shot, pausing to change rolls, interrupted here and there by the frame of the cockpit as the station transits left to right. A flicker through a window—a person moving inside? Closer now. Closer.

Small puffs: thruster gas? Their station pivots: aware of our presence?

THUD!

Everything is spinning. Space-ice-space-ice-space-ice-space-ice. An instinctive grasp for the thrusters to stabilize everything; the camera, floating free, rattles against the sides of the cockpit. At last we are right-side up. Outside the helmet faceplate: shards of broken glass glint suspended in the air. One thought: what happened?

Our orientation: nose down now. A glance "up" at their station, still slowly moving left to right. We are close enough to see a slender metal protuberance. It is pointed directly at us. It looks like a...

THUD-THUD!

Again all is chaos: endless black and blinding white, and the horizon's blurred blue band spinning. Nausea rising now. Glimpses of a smear of bright metal: our hostile enemy. And something else catching the sunlight...pieces of our spacecraft? The instinct, the mindless instinct of memorized training, is to reach for the controls once more. But: a thought. Two thoughts. They are still watching. And we have no weapons.

Outside, the universe spins. A wave of nausea swells inside. And an animal fury about this crime. Fight or flight: the first was never an option; the second may no longer be.

Still the relentless spinning. A stomach convulsion. Swallow, choke down the bile.

Frantic evaluation of options. No way to safely vomit in the helmet. Outside the pressure-suit visor: is the cockpit still intact? No sure way to tell: the pressure indicator and two other gauges are cracked and broken. Still: must hold it in.

No luck.

At the last possible second, flip up the visor. A convulsive heave. The spinning cockpit is full now with chunks of half-digested steak and eggs, globules of bile which form and float and travel in a straight line like some sick Newtonian experiment; they quiver before hitting the instrument panel, the inside of the cockpit glass. With the relentless logic of weightless fluids they cling to the surfaces: no dripping, nothing but viscosity and surface tension. These now-flattened globules cling to whatever they land on, and stay there.

But: a deep breath. The cockpit is still pressurized.

From the swirling view outside we can see flashes of blue now with the ice. Crossing the Antarctic coast again. A distant bright metal spot still intermittently visible as it sweeps across the black sky. Close enough to keep shooting?

THUD-THUD-THUD!

Breathe. Don't panic. Glimpse through the windows a shadow on the waters of the spinning world.

A thought: flip switches, turn off exterior lights, turn off most cockpit lights, dim the instrument panel to its lowest possible setting.

We flash into darkness. We are dark.

At last, tentatively, it is time to grab the controls, with no certainty the spacecraft will respond.

But it does. Mostly.

Thruster response is mushy. It takes some effort to arrest the rotation, stabilize the spacecraft. Invisible now, at least.

•••

In the eerie darkened cockpit, it is time to half-heartedly wipe the glass surface of the dim gauges with the pressure suit gloves. Looking around, it seems the back of the Hasselblad ricocheted off the instrument panel during the chaos: hence the broken glass.

Stow the camera. Re-spool the mental film.

There was nothing to see: no spurt of flame, no obvious indication of what was happening; we of course heard nothing, no roar of gunfire. Just that dull noise transmitted through the frame of the spacecraft with every impact.

Attempted murder. This was attempted murder.

Again, the fury. But: no point. Orbital mechanics being what it is, the Soviets are drawing further away.

Below, the great blackness. Then: familiar sickly lights rotate into view.

Tananarive.

"Tananarive, Falcon-2. Tananarive, Falcon-2. Emergency situation, we need to speak secure, over."

Nothing. Are we transmitting? Who knows what's damaged.

A deep breath. On go the cockpit lights. A mess of vomit and broken glass. But: power gauges look normal.

In the headphones now, a stranger: "Falcon-2, Tananarive. Going secure. Over."

Relief. We explain the situation.

"Falcon-2...Tananarive." Uncertainty. "Are you saying they shot at you, over?"

A deep breath. Let's keep it professional. "Affirmative, Tananarive."

Another pause. "Falcon-2, there isn't some...alternate explanation? Over."

"Tananarive, we..." (Pause to choke rage.) "This was a hostile attack. Over."

Still one more hesitation, longer now. "Falcon-2, can you re-enter? What is the condition of your spacecraft? Over."

A breath. "Unsure, Tananarive. There may have been some damage. No way to tell if it's on the transtage or on the spaceplane itself."

"Can you still rendezvous with Watchman, over?"

"We'll have to find out, over."

"Say again, Falcon-2."

"We'll have to find out, Tananarive. We have no other choice."

•••

Again come the nighttime lights: the Horn of Africa, the Middle East, Turkey, the Soviet Union, Scandinavia, a slow depressing progression of winter cities, sad and distant, half obscured by clouds.

And now all is darkness, and the darkness lasts and lasts and lasts.

Then comes the blinking red light. Ahead and slightly above. Our only hope.

Over blackened winter Greenland it is time to talk: "Thule, Falcon-2. Come in, over."

"Falcon-2, Thule." A familiar voice, at least. "We received a secure call from Tananarive. Any changes to your status, over?"

"Negative, Thule. Roll response somewhat mushy. Unsure about the condition of the spacecraft. Anything happening down there, over?"

"Falcon-2, say again, over."

"Thule, this was a hostile act. For all we know they could be…trying to start World War III. Over."

"Falcon-2, we'll certainly keep an eye on things. First things first, let's take care of you. Can you do the burns? Over."

"Thule, we will need to. We'll need a visual inspection to verify the condition of the spacecraft. Over."

"Copy, Falcon-2. We'll need to drop you down to catch up a little faster. We'll have instructions for you shortly. Over."

"Thank you, Thule." (A pause to shift gears.) "Glad you're still down there. Over."

"Say again, Falcon-2."

"Thule, we talked over the summer. You filled us in on the glories of northern Greenland. You were talking about putting in a packet to leave."

"Ahh, yes. Any day now, Falcon-2."

"Well, there are more depressing places to be, Thule."

"We'll get you down, Falcon-2. No use feeling blue." A pause, then: "Burn as follows: GET of zero-zero plus five-zero plus one-nine. Burn duration one-five seconds. Retrograde burn with the transtage. Zero degrees pitch. That'll catch you up. Rendezvous on the next rev. Over."

Time for a readback. Then comes LOS, and we fall into silence over the winter Arctic dark.

•••

When at last it is time for the burn we are over the empty blue Pacific once more. Visor closed against the vomit smell. Gauges cleaned as best as possible. Upside-down and backwards, watching our past fly away through the spattered cockpit glass. Hickam is on the line, but we are alone with the consequences of whatever will happen next.

"And...commit." There is a blessed relief a second later when comes the gentle push. And yet there's something unfamiliar in it: a pulsing shudder.

At last the engine cuts out, on schedule. Registers read normal.

"Hickam, Falcon-2. Burn is complete. It didn't feel quite right...but everything looks OK. Over."

"Falcon-2, data is coming in now...and our telemetry looks good. One more burn and you'll be where you're supposed to be. We'll have another comms window next rev. Over."

"Copy, Hickam." Always the reassurances. But outside now there is something new, something black outside that summons a dark angst. Out there, tumbling slowly in the airless space: the starboard winglet, plus a ragged corner of wing.

Disbelief at the totality and finality of it all. Everything we took for granted has now come undone; all the choices we thought we'd have, now gone. But it is time to choke down feelings and work. The winglet floats on, its torn edge bright and twisted. They must have been firing an automatic cannon. Apparently it nearly severed the winglet, which then came off during the transtage firing.

A reflex grab for the Hasselblad to snap a few pictures documenting the evidence, although of course no one will ever develop them without a rendezvous.

There will be no reentry in this spacecraft.

In a dead mechanical haze we fly the next rev, chat with Thule, push the buttons for the final burn.

•••

Now again the station draws close, but our bright weightless memories have been replaced by grim reality. We have changed, and so has it: no longer a slender metal baton, it now has a large boxy appendage bolted on the far end, down by the telescope opening: the orbital bombardment module. It grows larger as we approach, then disappears behind the rest of the structure as the station pivots. Out of sight, not out of mind.

"Hickam, Watchman." Our companion's voice: calm and reassuring in the headset. "We're going to bring him in to about 200 feet. Over."

"Watchman, Hickam, we are monitoring. Send a damage update when you have it. Over."

"Falcon-2, Watchman. Hold at 200 feet. Over."

"Copy, Watchman." A few final sloppy pulses from the thrusters, and it's time for stationkeeping.

Our companion is visible now, floating in the window. A joyless rendezvous. He gives a nod, and his face disappears behind the camera. There is a deathless wait for his assessment. Then at last: "Hickam, we've got quite a bit of damage. Starboard winglet is completely gone. Starboard aileron and wing, heavily damaged. And there is a...crease along the transtage. Looks like they grazed you there, Falcon-2. Over." He changes film, then gazes down at the passing ocean, headset on. "Hickam, Watchman. Do you copy? Over."

From Hawaii: "Watchman, Hickam. Copy winglet gone, wing and aileron damage, crease on the transtage. Over."

Our turn: "That explains the pulsing. Must've knocked something out of alignment." Contemplation of possibilities: a dud shell, or one that was just a hair's breadth away from detonating the contact fuse.

From the ground: "Falcon-2, you're lucky you could even do the burn. Coulda been a lot worse. Over."

On our end, a grim smile. "Wouldn't call it 'luck,' Hickam."

Our companion speaks: "Falcon-2, wing damage is close to the starboard roll thruster. That explains your control issues. May want to disable that thruster."

"Copy, Watchman. Disabling the thruster." Reach down, flip switches. Contemplation of the difficulties: rendezvous in a damaged spacecraft.

"All units, Hickam. Coming up on LOS. Thank you for the status. Kanton Island should have you on the home stretch. Over."

"Thank you, Hickam," our companion says. Moments pass. Then: "Falcon-2, can you translate down safely? Might be better to photograph you against the planet. Over."

Exasperation seems appropriate. "Watchman, that doesn't seem useful at this time." The need to document everything is, of course, understandable. Still it is time to bring this part of the mission to a close. There is a weariness settling in.

"All right," our companion says at last. "Let's get you in."

Line up for the terminal phase, keeping an eye on the thruster fuel. It's far lower than budgeted: nearly gone, in fact. A few pulses and we are closing in on the trapeze contraption. Easing in slowly, smoothly. Then...

"All units, Kanton Island. Give a status when ready, over."

A flash of frustration. Then, no *click*: we are too far forward.

Angry exhale: "No trap, no trap. Backing off to try again. Over." Gingerly we translate down and away. No point rushing this.

From our commander: "Kanton, Watchman. We are on final here. Falcon-2, you've got this. Over."

Except we don't. Again we position ourselves. Again we ease forward. Again: no luck.

A thought, one worth sharing: "Watchman, was there any damage forward? Over."

"Falcon-2, didn't see any. Over."

"Watchman, how close were you looking? Over." The horrifying, worrying thought: if there's something wrong with the docking apparatus, the assumption always was that the docking craft would just fly home. But obviously that's impossible now.

"Falcon-2, there was no damage forward. If you want to back up a little, we can get a closer look. Over."

Staticky voice: "All units, Kanton Island. What seems to be the issue, over?"

Contemplate the unprofessional response, much desired: What *isn't* the issue? "Kanton, we are working through it. Over." Could we do a pressure suit EVA? A dicey proposition—the oxygen hoses are far too short. There's an emergency oxygen bottle under the console. But: no tethers. So: possible to float off, get lost in space. Unless...if our commander suited up solo somehow, cracked the hatch, came out halfway, hands ready to pull us together...

"Falcon-2, translate back a little farther. Over."

A glance at the gauges: damn near empty. "We're pretty low here. Over."

"I need to see the probe."

"Copy, Watchman." Retrograde thrusters.

"Falcon-2. Uhh...can you confirm your probe is deployed? Over."

A glance at the panel. "Oh, Christ. We missed the checklist entirely, didn't we?"

"We need a checklist for the checklists," our commander chuckles. "It's all right, Falcon-2. Lot on your mind."

"All right. Ejection seat is safe. Attitude mode: AUTO. Probe: deployed."

Again: line up on the target disc at the far side of the trapeze. Slow steady approach. Thruster gauges tickling empty. It has to happen this time. Of course there is the thought: what if it doesn't?

But all the finely milled machinery comes together with a smooth *click*, and somewhere above us our companion flips another switch and there is the familiar long metallic noise, almost a sigh this time. We are docked, but there is no joy in it, only momentarily relief, soon eclipsed again by anger: this was an attempted murder.

•••

Floating in the living room, all around are familiar sights: storage lockers, sleeping gear, large window. Only now everything seems a little older, a little dingier. What was heaven now feels like prison.

"Quite a mess in there, huh?"

Our commander is floating back through the spindle and we are figuring out how to adapt our normal procedures for this insane deviation: removing the pressure suit, inspecting it for flecks of vomit, contemplating how best to stow it so we can't smell it.

"Indeed."

His face: a tight smile. "All's well that ends well, huh?"

Our mood: grim. "That's easy for you to say. You've got a plane to fly home in."

"I guarantee you," he says, "they're gonna work 24/7 for however long it takes to put a Gemini on the pad."

Noncommittal grunt. "Where is their station?"

"We'll have to call down. Talk to Cheyenne, see if there are conjunctions coming up."

"If we can wait that long."

"You don't think they're gonna attack *us*, do you?"

"We have to be prepared. Anything's possible now."

Pursed lips, a reluctant nod. "Is it possible they were just...running a test of some sort with that...cannon, or whatever?"

"They knew we were there. They had to aim the whole station to fire at us. They aimed it."

"You think this was an act of war."

"War." (A snort.) "War is fair. War, you know someone's going to try to kill you. You get a warning. There was no warning." (And now, perhaps, hesitation.) "Tell you what, when the plane was spinning...that was the only course of action, turning off all the lights. Going dark."

On our companion's face: some strange look. Heavy inhale, slight head shake. "Well," he says at last. "If you ever thought you didn't deserve that DFC, this should put that to rest."

"Not sure if wearing it'll be an option any time soon."

A glance around at our prison. There is something new, and it's taken far too long to pay attention to it. Down at the far end of the living room, riveted to the side of the storage locker, with conduit running the length of the module to an identical device bolted near the lip of the observation module that's been deliberately placed more than an arm span apart: a launch console. Hand to chest. Under pressure suit and cooling garment, between t-shirt and skin, close to angry heart: the key.

Our commander is gazing down through the window. "Well, cheer up," he says. "It's not the end of the world."

•••

The family now has a ham set, back at home; we discussed having a comms session on Saturday after the launch. But given everything that's happened, it seems wise not to wait. So: time for a trusty telegram.

BEGIN TRANSMISSION

BEGIN PERSONAL MESSAGE FALCON 2 FAMILY

BUMPY RIDE TO MY HOME ON HIGH BUT I AM HERE SAFE AND SOUND STOP

MAY BE SOME CHANGES TO MY SCHEDULE IN THE INTEREST OF MISSION SAFETY STOP

LOOKING FORWARD TO TALKING ABOUT THIS GREAT ADVENTURE AND SEEING YOU ALL AGAIN STOP

LOVE DAD

END PERSONAL MESSAGE

END TRANSMISSION

•••

A restless night. Unknown hours go by avoiding the clock, pursuing sleep with a vengeance that assures we won't catch it.

What else is there to do but watch the world go by? Perch at the end of the spindle and float, and brood. On the far side of the glass, untouchable, the planet scrolls by; we are conscious, as always, of the fact that we are outside the ecosystem, observing it from a distance. And we can see the tail of the disfigured spacecraft: our broken link with home.

•••

Over a sluggish breakfast of reconstituted eggs, we re-rehash the previous day's events.

"How do you feel?"

"Angry."

"I don't blame you."

"Good."

"This, too, shall pass. We'll get you home safe."

"A lot can happen in the three weeks it'll take to launch another Titan. We could be at war by then."

"There's no sign they want a war."

"Other than the fact they shot at us."

"Hate to be the devil's advocate, but this isn't the first time the Soviets have done something like this. I mean…we talked about the RB-47s. Everybody knows about the U-2…"

"If you're the devil's advocate, what does that make them?"

"They are…probably doing the same things we'd be doing, if we were in their shoes."

"Well, what the hell are we supposed to do, then? Let bygones be bygones?"

"If it's that or war…I mean, what's the alternative?"

"A proportionate response."

"My wife and I saw *The Fiddler on the Roof* last year. Someone mentioned an eye for an eye, and the main character said, 'That way the whole world goes blind.'"

"OK, a disproportionate response. Make them think twice."

"An eye for an eye, at least it's proportionate."

"And that's fine for criminal justice. Not war. Besides, the Jews didn't really believe in that. Proportionality."

"You don't think?"

"Think about Samson, in the temple. They blinded him, and what did he do? He pulled the temple down on top of them. Killed all the Philistines. That's a lot of eyes."

"Killed himself, too."

"Sacrificed himself. To stop them from doing it to anyone else."

"So you think we should kill…"

A sigh. "Just the leaders…just the guilty ones."

"Do you think everyone in that temple was guilty?"

"They chose to be there. If they were in the temple, they knew Samson had been tortured. They were there to see him suffer." A thought. "Remember, after they shot down the U-2, how they paraded the wreckage through Red Square? Big black eye for MacArthur. Imagine if, after they shot down the U-2, we'd bombed the crash site. Rather than letting their…MVD agents pick through the wreckage, imagine if we'd bombed it. Maybe there would have been a couple curious civilians, but certainly they'd be guilty, in a way. And you'd get a lot of officers…everyone who thought it was a good idea to shoot down an unarmed airplane. Make 'em think twice."

"Is that moral?"

"War is a different set of rules. A different morality. Once you're at war, the only moral thing is to end it as quickly as possible. Proportionality just...pisses your opponent off. Encourages them to keep fighting. Overwhelming force, that's the only way."

"Well, it's a good thing we're not at war."

The radio interrupts: "Watchman, Antigua. Come in, over."

"Antigua, Watchman. We read you five by five. Over."

Our ground station is clear but hesitant. "Watchman, the...uhhh...news media is picking up rumors about your incident. Over."

"How the hell is that possible, Antigua? You're saying one of our ground stations talked to the press, over?"

"Watchman, the Soviets are claiming they repelled an attack on their space station and shot down an American, quote, space fighter, end quote. Over."

Instant rage. "Space fighter."

"Their words, Watchman."

"Well if they're gonna lie like that...we're gonna have to push back. They probably don't realize we've got pictures. Over."

"Although nobody's going to see them for a few weeks," our companion mutters.

•••

Our workday: mostly routine tasks. There was a Centaur resupply during the last mission, so our orbit's fine. And resolution has been great. So we're planning on maintenance work on the blowers and an EVA tomorrow before going through the workday shift and getting back on Soviet time.

Except now everything's poisoned by the knowledge of what happened. We have finished offloading supplies from the cockpit of the damaged X-20; now there is the question: Once EVA's done and the film buckets are offloaded, how do we get rid of it? Undocking it's easy. Getting it to deorbit, however…

And of course, the acid worry: How is all this is playing out on the ground?

We find ourselves drifting over to the radio for the CONUS comms passes. Headsets on but still huddled, anxious. "Watchman," Cheyenne tells us. "Be advised, the Soviets are calling for an emergency United Nations Security Council session. They're calling this 'An illegal act of aggression by space pirates.' Over."

Bitter laughter. "Space pirates. Jesus Christ."

"Their words, Watchman. They are also claiming to have photographic evidence that the United States has developed, quote, 'Offensive weapons in space that threaten the peace and security of the planet.' Over."

To our companion: "Have they photographed us?"

"Not as close as you got to them. But there have been conjunctions."

Key the mike: "Cheyenne, if they wanna talk weapons, we've got pictures too. Close to a full roll from before the attack, so we probably have pictures of whatever...cannon or whatever they have on their station. Plus ample pictures of the damage to the spacecraft itself. Over."

"Watchman, what's your plan for getting those back to earth? If your commander's going to fly them down, that'll be a good three weeks. If you're waiting for the Gemini, probably the same. Over."

A moment of thought. Then: "We could put them in the bucket."

"Say again, Watchman."

"Tomorrow's EVA, Cheyenne. We could send down the rolls we shot during the rendezvous, and the ones showing the damage. Over."

"There wouldn't be room on top of the film canister. Over."

"We'd have to delay loading it, Cheyenne. Assuming you're sending a Gemini up, we could haul it back down then."

"Watchman, that's...that's a risky gamble with those pictures. If we don't recover that bucket, we lose that evidence. Over."

We look at each other, then speak: "Cheyenne, we do have a whole photography lab up here. Should be easy to make some duplicates."

This feels like a good plan, a solid plan. We spend the next few hours in darkroom mode, contact-printing the film to make interpositives. It feels at last like we're doing something.

Still no response to the telegram, though.

• • •

Spacewalk time.

Again the claustrophobia of the airlock, the liberation of egress. Our planet whipping past below: high winter clouds, and the bleak windswept rocky desolation of northern Quebec giving way to brown-and-white New England. This time the planet feels distant, unreachable.

The work: slow and methodical. Long stretches looking across the small airless gap between the helmet faceplate and the bright aluminum side of the station, now slightly pitted here and there from micrometeorites. But the work never stops, because then come the thoughts.

Glimpses of the planet as it passes. A brief look at the urban blight of western Long Island and New York. South across the cold Atlantic. The Bahamas: emerald dots in turquoise waters. Cuba and the Caribbean and Panama, and then the long empty Pacific, chaotic and stormy.

There is still a long gap in coverage going south across the Antarctic, but now with the season, the unfamiliar continent is brightly lit, and it's possible to work the whole way. So: not much sightseeing, just more snippets. Forbidding coast, icy mountains, long expanses of frozen emptiness. No longer our planet.

The film canisters have been wrapped in carefully cut pieces of fireproof insulation salvaged from behind a cockpit panel in the damaged X-20. The temperature inside the bucket should be fine; it's designed to protect the larger canisters from the DORIAN console. But we don't want anything rattling around, and we don't want to take any chances.

●●●

Back inside, we prepare our next meal and prepare to eject the bucket.

But the ground intrudes. "Watchman, Thule. We're getting notice of bad weather in the Pacific in the primary squadron's area of operations. Please hold on to your bucket. Over."

"Yeah, we saw that. Any options with the secondary squadron?"

"Watchman, weather is a little better in the Atlantic, but the backup ships are out of position. Either way, we'll have to wait until tomorrow. Over."

We work through packages of hot dogs, floating and waiting. No urgency now.

From Cheyenne: "Watchman, be advised, you're in the news again today. Over."

"Cheyenne, what seems to be the issue? Over."

"Watchman, the Soviets have introduced a Security Council resolution condemning the presence of offensive weapons in space. As expected, it was defeated three to two. But the Soviets put something out in the General Assembly, and the vote there was a little different."

We trade skeptical glances. "Cheyenne, wake us up when the U.N. actually means something. Or does something."

"Our thoughts exactly, Watchman. The biggest concern is: several neutral countries that used to lean our way, they are angry about this. The resolution actually expressed, quote, hope that the Soviet Union will take whatever measures might be necessary for the peace and security of the planet, end quote. Not sure what it means, but thought you oughta know. Over."

"Cheyenne, are there...conjunctions that would put us in range of their guns? Over." It feels absurd to hear these thoughts put into words. Then again, all of this is absurd.

"Watchman, no conjunctions any time soon. We'll certainly let you know if that changes. Over."

The reassurance feels artificial, forced, formulaic. Still...if there were cause for concern, they would tell us, right? "Copy, Cheyenne. Any decision on the bucket drop tomorrow?"

"Not yet, Watchman. It looks like ships will be in position if we want to do an Atlantic drop at the beginning of your workday. But the Pacific weather system is dissipating, so we could go with Hawaii. We'll get you a decision via Vandenberg on the next rev. Over."

"Copy, Cheyenne. Watchman out."

If they decide on an Atlantic drop, let's go to page 533.

If it's Pacific, we'll go to page 611.

How did we get here?

The X-20 is in level flight, the last of the roll reversals complete. Below, the blue Atlantic, day-lit. Altitude: 12,000 feet, give or take. Tropical sun high above. Everywhere else, everything familiar is gone. But here at least all looks...probably normal?

"Falcon-2, Ascension, we have you on radar." Clipped British accent in the headset. "Looking a little high. Over."

"Copy, Ascension." Better high than low. Coming down over the ocean in what is now a glider, it is best to err on the side of caution. High means the chance to circle, sideslip, eat up altitude. Low means a long swim.

"Turn left one-eight-zero and descend at discretion. Range one-zero nautical miles."

"Turning left one-eight-zero." Nudge the stick. Steepen the slope. The island is visible, brown and sunbaked with patches of green up top, a volcano sleeping under a crown of pillowy clouds. Home for...how long? Forever? Five hundred people.

"Looking good, Falcon-2."

"Might be your last landing for a while, Ascension."

"Might be." Much unsaid. "Falcon-2, come right and you are clear to land on Runway Three-One."

"First in the pattern, huh?" Every joke is a little bitter these days.

"First in the pattern."

The runway is a beautiful long strip of asphalt south of the volcano. Free and clear, although there are jetliners choking the apron and: animals nearby?

Drop the skids. Glance down at the ejection handle: better to punch out? No. One last landing.

Up comes the ground, the runway yawning to swallow us. The last time?

The X-20 makes violent contact, skidding and shuddering and rumbling, rough and awkward. Body pitched forward, terrain rushing past, a brown and bitter land.

From the right, two skittish sheep dart onto the tarmac. Collision seems inevitable. But: a snap of the first one's head, a quick puff of red. It falls dead as we skid past.

At last the spaceplane rumbles to a halt. The stillness and silence are complete. It is all over.

Shut down the spacecraft, all per the checklist, as if it matters. Wait for a moment in pressure-suited coolness. The island looks like a hardscrabble place, rough and rocky, without much in the way of vegetation, although near the top of the mountain there are patches of green, underneath the clouds.

Perhaps this was a mistake.

Crack the top hatch. Still sitting, slightly woozy. Outside, a muffled rifle *crack!* Off to the right: another fallen sheep? And now it seems urgent to crack the helmet, too, to make contact with this alien environment, to see what the hell is going on outside. Faceplate up: a warm breath of foreign air.

On the left, behind and out of sight, there is a thump and a British-accented "Fookin' hell!"

Unclip the ejection seat harness, after making sure the seat's safed. Awkwardly rotate to a kneeling position, head out of the yawning top hatch.

Out on the tarmac there are three twentysomething men in wide-brimmed hats and sunglasses, one next to the spacecraft rubbing his hand in pain, and one holding a bolt-action rifle.

Yell out: "It's hot!"

The rifleman speaks: "I tried to tell him." An American accent, familiar. Our capcom.

"It's going to take…a good twenty or thirty minutes for it to cool off enough to get out. Unless you want to hose it down."

"No chance in hell of that," the third man—slightly older and also British—says.

"Water's pretty scarce here. Even in the best of times," our capcom says. "And the population's a bit…larger than normal, these days."

"Saw the jetliners, on approach. Those have been here since…" No need to say the words: the war.

"Yes. A few days now," the older Brit says. "One of the BOAC flights was...Buenos Aires to London, I think, another from Rio to London, and another...Pan-Am, I think. Johannesburg to New York."

"Pan Am."

The Brit goes on: "Once everything started happening, it was...well, everyone figured it was best to sort things out on the ground. Wait and see what to do. We'll have to do something soon, though."

"Do something..."

"Well, this island isn't...I mean, there's not a lot of water. There's never been a native population. We're dependent for supplies on places that...probably no longer exist. Killing the livestock..." (A nod to the rifleman.) "...it'll buy some time, but...if we don't make some evacuations soon..."

"All the...uhhh...those departure cities are still...I mean, should be..." Reach behind the ejection seat to grab the small duffel bag of personal items.

"Well, yes, but...the passengers are a mixed bag. The South Americans and South Africans, they're eager to return home. The Brits and Americans, well..." A shrug that speaks volumes. "And certain of the personnel here wouldn't mind letting some of the female passengers stay, for...uhh...demographic purposes."

"Demographic purposes."

"I mean, technically, according to the Crown, there is no right of abode here, and legally no one can stay without the written permission of the Administrator. But legalities and norms are…" He shrugs: it says everything. Then, a nod towards the spaceplane: "No wheels, huh?"

"No wheels."

"Guess you can't just…taxi this thing off the runway, huh?"

"We usually have…support personnel. You don't have any vehicles that can…"

"We'll have to talk to the Administrator. Petrol's being rationed. Everything's being rationed. There's quite a few things we need to sort out in the next few days. Besides the passengers, a lot of the Saints are clamoring to go home, and…"

"Saints?"

"Support staff here from Saint Helena. It's a better place to live anyway, so we might all just…"

"Well, you've got planes, right? Seems like you could send one to South America, one to South Africa, use one to shuttle people to Saint Helena."

The three men on the tarmac chuckle. The older Brit speaks: "Ascension has a runway, but no fresh water. Saint Helena has fresh water, but no runway."

A rueful nod. "Well, that would be a problem, wouldn't it?"

Our capcom shakes his head. "Of all the places on the globe you could have come down…"

This remark cannot go unchallenged. "You said, and I quote, 'I guess there's room for one more.'"

The Brits both look at him. "It was a flip remark!" our capcom protests.

"He could have come down anywhere?" the elder Brit says.

"He could have come down anywhere! I mean, anywhere that wasn't…but, yeah! He could have come down anywhere."

"And he chose here," the elder Brit says. "And you didn't stop him."

The capcom shrugs. "A lot of people have made a lot of bad decisions this week."

The Brits start laughing. "That's…" the older one shakes his head. "I thought we were the ones known for understatement. Guess we're rubbing off, huh?"

We smile as well. Share a brief chuckle. But the good mood evaporates.

Open the small duffel bag, look down at the personal items: a Bible, toiletries. As many food packets as it was possible to fit. Still: not enough. (The horrible realization: there will never again be enough of anything.) The picture of the family, staring up with accusing eyes.

Perhaps this was a mistake.

"You flew with a carry-on," the elder Brit says, observing. "What did you bring?"

A pang of fear: not enough food. "Oh, nothing. Just…personal stuff."

Zip up the bag. The family: out of sight, not out of mind.

Perhaps this was a mistake.

(CONTINUED)

First thing Friday morning it is time for us to eject the bucket. We take turns watching from the spindle as it arcs downward over the mottled high mid-Atlantic clouds, a slow shooting star falling behind and finally dying.

We have looped around the planet and are over its darkened crown when we hear the news: "Watchman, Thule. Please switch to secure channel. Over." An unpleasant angst.

"Thule, Watchman. Going secure. Over."

"Watchman, be advised there was an incident of some sort during bucket recovery. We are at DEFCON-3. Over."

We trade alarmed glances. "Thule, Watchman. Did you say DEFCON-3? Over."

"Affirmative, Watchman."

"What kind of incident? Over."

"Watchman, Cheyenne will have details. Over."

"Thule, we...uhh...don't have comms with Cheyenne this pass. Is there anything else you can tell us? Over."

"Watchman, it sounds like the situation is still playing out. Cheyenne will fill you in. Over."

More anxious glances. "Thule, thanks for passing that along. Out."

Daylight bursts. Through the big living room window we can only see dense clouds, with the occasional high edge picking up the low winter sun. Whatever happened, it happened a rev behind us now; we have no way to get a look anyway. We do have another comms window, at least.

"Loring, Watchman. Calling secure. We have received word we are at DEFCON-3. Do you have any details for us at this time, over?"

"Watchman, Loring. No details yet. We were hoping you might know something. Over."

"Loring, Watchman, all we know is we had a bucket drop. And then all hell broke loose. Over."

"Watchman, that is more than they've told us here. There's been a lot of activity out on the flight line, and we've seen Valkyries taking off for the last ten minutes, but other than that we're out of that loop. Over."

We are concerned. A SAC base: not a good place for people to be busy. "Loring, thanks for the info. Watchman out."

Because of the bucket drop delay, we have caught up on most maintenance tasks; there is little to do but clean and do busy work. Outside, the familiar procession of oceans. And we do have a little time to sightsee, at least, as Antarctica scrolls into view, blinding and rugged and beautiful.

"That's…really something."

"Isn't it?"

"Peaceful."

"Probably because there aren't any people."

Over the night side of the planet we swoop over the Indian Ocean and India and a bit of China before slashing upwards across the Soviet Union east of the Urals. Now at least there are operational tasks. We look for clues that something is happening; we record some radio chatter and scan for air defense radars, even though it's doubtful we'll be able to pass the information along any time soon.

Again we talk to Thule. There, too, the bombers have been launching. But our ground guy still doesn't know why. As light returns to the planet below, we await Cheyenne with bated breath.

Then, at last: "Cheyenne, Watchman. Calling secure. Over."

"Watchman, Cheyenne, we have classified details on the incident in your recovery zone earlier this morning. Over."

"Go ahead, Cheyenne."

"Watchman, it appears the Soviets sent a flight of Tango-Uniform-Niner-Five aircraft to the recovery zone. NATO code-name Bear."

"In the western Atlantic?"

"Affirmative, Watchman. Apparently they staged out of western Africa. Algeria or Guinea-Bissau. We've never flown fighter cover for a recovery operation before…it was one of those things that just…never occurred to anyone. But U.S.S. *Kitty Hawk* was in the area, and once we realized where the Bears were headed, they sent up aircraft to intercept. They…uhh…were apparently trying to get the Soviets to change course when there was a collision." Long pause. "Over."

We are concerned. "Cheyenne, we copy aircraft collision in the recovery zone. Any casualties? Over."

"Affirmative, Watchman. One Phantom crewman KIA, one missing. The Soviet aircraft headed back across the Atlantic but had to ditch a couple hundred miles away. Kitty Hawk is on site attempting to recover their aircrew, but there is a Soviet task force in the area. The president will be issuing a statement shortly. Over."

"Cheyenne, any orders for us, over?"

"Watchman, we don't have anything yet. But you, uhh, might want to stand by the teletype. Over."

This is just about the last thing anyone wants to hear when entrusted with nuclear weapons. The seriousness of the words imposes silence on us; we certainly have a lot that we could talk about, but talking might make it real. We have been hoping for benign messages, family telegrams: not this.

There is, at least, more to do. We inspect the teletype, verifying that the ribbon is, in fact, fresh and well-inked; we print the test sheet and run a functionality check on the alert klaxon, which rings out hollow and loud. We look over the red EWO safe, the weightless padlocks drifting upwards towards us; one at a time, we enter our combinations, ensure that each of us can unlock our side, and then swivel the shackles back into position; we push them closed, and tug on the locks as if for reassurance. Then we drift over to the key consoles: first one, then the other. We remove keys from under our garments, press the circuit test buttons and verify that the indicator lights glow bright green, and then, one at a time, insert and turn. It feels like nothing: just the most gentle motion.

Are there options here? There is at least one choice to be made: the next rev will put us over California; we could call down on the Single Sideband. (Schreiver has turned a blind eye to the behavior, so it's become an open secret, tolerated in the general sense and…well, in the general sense.) The plan had been for a Saturday comms session, but given current events, they may well be listening Friday.

Down the globe we loop again, speeding towards an unknown future.

If we want to call down, turn to page 538.

If we don't, then let's go to page 541.

(CONTINUED)

Far below, the Northern Lights shimmer. Distant curtains of green, glowing in the darkness.

We float through the silent tunnel and through the hatch to the useless cockpit. Daylight comes on; below we see the Canadian Rockies, jagged stone mountains blanketed with winter snow. Around us, the dirty smelly cockpit, no longer new and full of anonymous potential, but rather reminders of decisions made, options that can't be undone. Patches of dried and half-cleaned vomit. The missing panel and rectangular hole behind it: a carefully excised patch of insulation. This spaceplane will never fly again, and is fit only to be cannibalized for parts. But the radio still works.

Flip the switches and on it goes. Anxious anticipation: it is almost time.

Snow below, visible under the clear mountain air. A good day for skiing? How much do they know, the people down there who are out of the loop, the ones who don't pay attention to the news? Are they still in their normal oblivious routines?

At last it is time. "Kilo-Niner-Yankee-Tango-Yankee, this is Kilo-Seven-Tango-Romeo-Victor. Come in, over."

No response. Family at Vandenberg now. Better or worse than LA, if something happens? The wife knows to go home and turn on the radio if there is news. Perhaps she has not been following the news; perhaps she's still expecting to talk tomorrow.

Patches of brown now. Snow only on the mountains. Ahead: the Pacific sweeping closer. Certainly the kids are in school;

perhaps the wife is finishing up errands, inspecting plastic-wrapped chicken drumsticks at the commissary before going home to get the kids off the bus. Or maybe they're home sick. Maybe she knows at least to listen.

"Kilo-Niner-Yankee-Tango-Yankee, Kilo-Seven-Tango-Romeo-Victor. Do you read, over."

No response.

"Kilo-Niner-Yankee-Tango-Yankee, Kilo-Seven-Tango-Romeo-Victor. Do you read, over."

Still nothing.

Below, the blue Pacific sweeps by, pushing away our past.

Back in the living room, our companion awaits, eyes wide and fearful. "Where the hell did you go?" he asks.

"Trying to talk to my family."

"I talked to Vandenberg while you were in there," he says. "The president made a statement about Soviet aggression...responding with overwhelming force. He's scheduled to address the nation tonight."

Over on the teletype, a scrap of printout drifts up weightlessly.

BEGIN TRANSMISSION

BEGIN PERSONAL MESSAGE FALCON 2

GLAD YOU ARE SAFE STOP STRANGE STORIES IN THE NEWS STOP BUSY WEEK HERE STOP LOOKING FORWARD TO SATURDAY STOP

END PERSONAL MESSAGE

END TRANSMISSION

We turn our eyes down towards the window, as if looking for reassurance that the world is still as it was. Far below there is still nothing but ocean: a relentless, monotonous blue.

Let's go to page 543.

(CONTINUED)

Things aren't that serious yet, are they? That's what we tell ourselves as we fly over the high Arctic yet again. We watch the Northern Lights, slow-dancing curtains of pale green. There is comfort in that.

Soon we are swooping down over snowy mountains, dry and cold and desolate. Eventually there is brown between the peaks.

"Watchman, Vandenberg. Understand you talked to Cheyenne last pass. Be advised the president has issued a statement that further acts of Soviet aggression will be met with overwhelming force, at a time and place of our choosing. He will be addressing the nation by television tonight."

A pang of regret. We imagine: wife hearing the news in the car, going home, turning on the radio, waiting.

A glance down as we pass overhead. We know, of course, where the launch pad is; we scan the contours of coast and mountains, mottled brown and green, slivers of beach and breakers barely visible; a distant sketch, a dream.

The teletype clatters. No klaxon, though.

BEGIN TRANSMISSION

BEGIN PERSONAL MESSAGE FALCON 2

GLAD YOU ARE SAFE STOP BUSY WEEK HERE STOP LOOKING FORWARD TO SATURDAY STOP

END PERSONAL MESSAGE

END TRANSMISSION

Perhaps the rocket will be on the pad before long. The Gemini. It can't come soon enough.

Let's go to page 543.

(CONTINUED)

Flying south over the Pacific, we trade lines. Two heads, but of one mind.

"Sounds like there's nothing for us to do yet. Operationally."

"Still dark on that side of the globe. We can listen. But until we get on Soviet time, we won't be able to do much observation."

"We're not just an observation platform nowadays."

"There's nothing for us to do yet."

There is both a comfort and a helplessness. Again we overfly Antarctica. Isolated and alone, for better or for worse. The klaxon is mercifully silent. Who knows for how long?

And now upwards again: the normal path. Malagasy Republic, Horn of Africa, Middle East, Soviet Union. City lights flicker out beneath the wispy fringes of winter weather. Then: cloud tops silvered by moonlight.

We float back towards the observation module. Our companion stays by the window, looking for a break. "That's weird," he says.

"What?"

"This…contrail above the clouds, like…"

Then it comes: a soundless bright flash.

It is the most intense light; all the metal is a punishing blinding white. And then there is nothing.

"Jesus H. Christ, what the hell was that?"

"They didn't...that wasn't..."

Blink to escape the ghosts of bright shapes. But the real things don't come back. There is a decaying whirring noise from the equipment as everything that was spinning, all the fans and gyroscopes, slowly winds down to a halt. Then: silence in the dark.

"My God, that was..." Our commander, shaken.

"I was facing the other way and still I..."

"I must've been looking straight at it."

"Did everything go offline?"

"It sounds like it. I don't know." (He takes a deep breath.) "I still can't see."

"Me...uhh, me neither."

Another long pause while the meaning and consequence of those words echoes soundlessly between us. There is no point in panic.

"That was...that had to be a nuke."

"Yeah, I think so."

We float towards the sound of each other's voices. Bump blindly into one another. Hands on shoulders, wordless reassurance: we are not alone.

•••

For endless minutes there is nothing but a blackness painted in splotches.

Slowly, sight returns. Shapes gradually reveal themselves in the darkness. Bathed in a weird pale green light.

Sight returns. For one of us.

Our commander: "How are you doing?"

"I think…it's coming back. My vision."

"Well, that's good."

His face: an impassive mask, lit by the dim green glow.

"You can't…"

"It's…uhh, it isn't coming back yet."

"Well…shit."

"How's yours?"

"Getting there. It had to be just…flash blindness or something."

"Yeah, the pigment. I think it bleaches out for a minute or two. Anything that bright."

"It might just take longer for you. Because you were looking at it."

"Maybe." Then: "We have to call this in."

"To Thule?"

"Yeah. They might not know what happened yet."

"Yeah. We have to call this in."

Everything is off. All power, dead. Gauges, indicator lights: off. Air and water pumps: silent. We drift through space in near-total darkness, the planet still black below, except: above it, the only reason we can see, dancing and free: *aurora borealis*.

"It must've been…"

"EMP, yeah. Just like in the summer, with the test."

"Except this was a lot closer. A lot closer. You're going to have to get everything back online before we can call."

"Yeah. Lemme…" Cycle the fuel cell breakers. Nothing. A breath of fear. Cycle them again. Nothing. "Well, shit."

"What?"

"The fuel cells aren't coming back up."

"Shit."

"I guess the good news is, we're not going anywhere. The hull is…nothing seems to have happened."

"Outer space…no air, no shockwave."

"We'll have to…we're probably over Thule now. I…"

"Well…I'm not going anywhere." Then: "Do you see anything?"

"Just the Northern Lights."

"I mean, if this was the start of it, the first shot, I…"

"No, there's no…" (The klaxon is silent. But then again, of course it is.) "We don't know what's going on. Do you want me to…"

"What?"

Outside the glow is dimmer now. "Well, if you still can't see. The medical locker is…"

"We'll have daylight coming up soon, right?"

"Yeah, just…"

"Well, it sounds like you'll have forty-five minutes of good light through the window to figure another way to get us back online. And there's flashlights on the side of the emergency locker if that doesn't…"

"It's…you're…I mean, the medical locker, there's…"

"I'm not going anywhere."

A pause to consider the multiple meanings of this sentence. Then: "We're gonna take care of you."

"We'll see." Our commander grimaces: maybe he won't. Then he says: "Look at it this way…you might not have to wait for the Gemini."

•••

Daylight now. High latitudes of Pacific coast, crossing from glacier-choked mountains to ice-wreathed islands and frigid waters: Alaska or Canada.

Every circuit breaker on the panel has been tripped. Cycle the fuel cell breakers one last time, hoping against hope. Still: nothing. "I don't know what's going on with the fuel cells."

"That was my subsystem." He speaks slowly: the deliberation of a man trying to think through pain. "Could be any number of things. You'll have to get us running on battery power. That'll make it easier to get the cells back up."

"OK." Pause. Then: "There's...what, two, three days' power on the batteries?"

"Depending on what we turn back on. Yeah."

"Well, if we can't get the fuel cells going, and you can't fly yourself down, and we need a Gemini for *you* instead of *me*, and a Gemini's a few weeks off..."

For moments, our companion is silent. Then: "First things first. Let's get the batteries up. Take some readings. Call down and see if they have ideas about the fuel cells."

A useless nod. Then: "Sounds like a plan."

Float over to the window with the binder. Flip through weightless plastic-covered pages to the section on battery power. When the first breakers go in, the instruments come on. "All right...28 volts...amperage looks good. We'll get the radios, lights, ECS, and the fuel cell instruments going."

"Sounds good."

More breakers. The radio comes to life. Then lights. Then ECS. But with the fuel cell breakers, the station plunges back into darkness.

"All right, let's try that again." Narrating for his benefit. "Radio, lights, ECS only."

Again through the breakers. Radio and lights back on. Fans whirring. The clock's stopped, but a glance out the window suggests we're coming up on a comms window with Hawaii.

"All right, time to call down." Key the mike. "Hickam, Watchman. Come in. Over."

No response.

"Hickam, Watchman. Come in. Over."

Anxiety. We call for what feels like minutes, with despair rising all the while. Then at last, garbled: "Watchman, Hickam. Read you three by three. Go ahead, over."

"Hickam, this is a Class 1 emergency. We had a NUCFLASH incident over the Soviet Union. One Whiskey-India-Alpha with no eyesight. We are on battery power. Over."

"Watchman, Hickam...uhh, say again all after Class 1. Over."

Exasperation. "Hickam. They shot a nuke at us. Our commander is blind and we are on battery power. Do you copy? Over."

"Watchman, did you...uhhh...call this into Thule? Over."

"Hickam, you are the first to get this news. We had EMP effects. Over."

"Say again, Watchman."

"EMP effects! Electromagnetic pulse. We lost power. We just got the radios back up before we called. Over."

"Watchman, we're...uhh...gonna have to call this in to Cheyenne. In the meantime, uhh...telemetry is showing your EWO console is off. Over."

"Uhhh...that's correct, Hickam. We just got the radios and the lights back on. Over."

"They're gonna want confirmation you're back online. That your console is turned on. Especially now. Over."

"Hickam, we'll..." A glance at our companion, who of course cannot glance back. "...we'll turn it on shortly. Over."

In the excitement, we completely forget to talk about the fuel cells.

•••

After LOS we are heading south over the Pacific. All the lights are on in the living room, and when we push the right breakers, the EWO console comes to life. Still silent, still no klaxons: we won't be in position to receive an order any time soon, so that may not mean much. We can't quite pretend things are still normal, but at least they're not as abnormal as they could be.

Still: everything is slightly quieter, running on batteries. There is the nagging knowledge: two or three more days of this and the lights will be out again, for good.

"Let's try the fuel cells again." Cycle the breakers again. Nothing.

"Are you getting temperature readings yet?"

"Oh." Drift over to the gauges. "Yeah, it's...it's off-scale high."

"Can you tell if anything's happening when you push the breakers?"

"The startup sequence is…it's like, I hear things happening, but then it stops."

"The controllers must be fried."

"The controllers?"

"Yeah, it's…integrated circuits. The auto mode. The controllers have a set sequence for the pumps and the coolant loops so everything turns on in the right order. But if the controllers are fried…"

"Well…shit." A sigh. "Is there a way to start it up manually?"

"I think…you'll have to put the system in test mode. Start the coolant pumps. Wait for the temperature to get back down to operating range. Then start the line heaters from the cryo tanks."

Flip the mode switch. Now the coolant pump breakers. Blessed noise from behind the panel. Then: wait for the temperature to drop.

We are transiting Antarctica now. Blinding white below. A guilty glance out the window.

"Wow."

"Where are we?"

"Antarctica. Is your vision…"

"Just a little light on the periphery."

"Does it hurt?"

"Yeah."

"We're gonna have to…in the medical locker there's…"

"I can manage for now. Just…keep an eye on those temps."
A thin smile from our commander, like: I am still in charge.

Over to the gauges. The needles are no longer pegged.
Drifting down towards normal range. We wait another few
minutes. Then: push the breakers for the cryo tank heaters.

All the lights go out.

Again we flash into darkness.

"Well that's not good."

"No, it is not."

• • •

The planet is moonlit but it will be quite a few minutes before
we'll be getting any real illumination from outside. So: time
to retrieve the flashlights from the locker. Before pushing the
button, there's perhaps a moment of worry, but the beam
comes on bright and strong. Same with the other one. Thank
God for regular inspections.

Floating back to the circuit breakers, the flashlight beams
dance and slice across the darkened sides of the living room
walls. The good thing about working weightless: no need to
hold the flashlight in one's mouth, or put it between head
and shoulder, or anything dumb like that. Just park it in the
air and it will stay there, pointed where it's needed.

Then: push in the battery breakers. Soft clicks, anxious inhale. Nothing.

"We didn't lose everything this time. You're gonna have to turn off the other stuff first."

"Yeah."

Sweep the bright ellipse across the breaker panel. See which breakers are still on. Glance outside as Africa slides beneath: wispy cobwebs of light on the vast silvery blackness. Back to the panel: flashlit fingers blinding white. Pull the other breakers back out. Then: battery breakers. And lights. All is renewed.

One at a time, we turn the other systems back on. Everything that was on before the lights went out. Everything but the fuel cells and the EWO console.

Below now, black Libyan desert. Coastline like a thin electric worm. Specks of light on the inky Mediterranean.

"Watchman, Lakenheath. Come in. Over."

"Lakenheath, Watchman. Go ahead. Over."

"Watchman, we have been briefed on your incident. Be advised we are at DEFCON-2. Over."

"Lakenheath, Watchman. Copy DEFCON-2."

"Watchman, please verify that your Emergency War Order console is on. Over."

Instant anger: "Lakenheath, we have a blind crewmember and we are running on batteries. Over."

"Watchman, we copy. You have enough power to run the console, corre-"

Step on them. Fuck it. "We need the fuel cells online, or we'll have to come down in a couple days. And we can't both come down until we get a Gemini up here. We tried to turn the cells back on while the console was running, and it didn't work. Now, is someone down there going to help us out, or what?"

Long pause. "Uhh, Watchman, you're going to have to talk secure to Thule. Lakenheath out."

We have a couple minutes before acquisition.

"DEFCON-2."

"DEFCON-2. It's happened before."

"But this is a lot different."

"DEFCON-2. They said all that unsecure."

"Imagine what they're gonna say secure."

"They seem...pretty fixated on the war console."

"Well...we have been attacked twice. The X-20, and this. Especially this. If that's not an act of war, then..."

"There are lines you can't cross, once you've crossed them."

"The question is, have we already crossed them?"

"*We* have been passive, through all of this. *We* haven't done anything."

"Yet."

Set the scramblers. Await our fate. Outside all is dark: we are alone.

Then: "Watchman, Thule. Transmitting secure. We have talked to Cheyenne. You are hereby ordered to power up your Emergency War Order console and await instructions. Do you copy? Over."

There is no point in exchanging glances, but still an urge to do so. Our companion—our commander—speaks: "Copy, Thule." Then, directed who knows where: "God help us."

The radio crackles. Our capcom heard. "Watchman, I get the sentiment, but…we're on the front lines down here. We're going to get hit first if this gets big. So they can take out the radars. Nobody wants this less. But we might still be able to stop it from getting big. *You* might be able to stop it. Over."

Our commander's face: impassive. "Copy, Thule."

Time to interject: "Thule, we…we would like to give ourselves a chance to get back down there. Both of us. Is there a plan for that? Over."

"Uhh, Watchman…we are working on it at this time. Has your commander's vision come back at all? Over."

"Very limited, Thule. Just some light on the periphery."

"Well that certainly complicates things. It's…if it's retinal burns, it may take some weeks to heal. Oh…that was another thing Cheyenne mentioned. That blast…sounds like it was in the upper atmosphere. If that is the case, there wasn't anything to attenuate the radiation. We are unsure of the dose you received. But you might be getting sick soon. Over."

"Thule, that's...fantastic. Any symptoms to watch out for? Over."

"Usual. Headache, fever, nausea, diarrhea. Over."

Watching our companion for clues on how to take this. Still no expression. "Understood, Thule."

"Watchman, it's a lot to digest. But we'll need confirmation when your console is back up. Over."

A glance out the windows. What would we see...rocket plumes? Not at this latitude. If there were warheads aloft, they would be a few hundred miles above us, answering gravity's silent call in the dark of outer space, arcing down to their cataclysmic end.

"Thule, we'll have it on soon. We'll confirm with Hickam. Watchman out."

Whisper the words: "You don't want to talk to Eielson?"

"Not really. In fact, turn off the radio."

A quick click on the panel. Time to talk amongst ourselves.

"They're waiting for us to get in position."

"That'll be a long wait. The bombers are already in the air."

"They can refuel. And besides, LeMay's not in charge anymore. Not sure we'd lead with the bombers."

"Still, timing-wise. I mean, we were hit over the western Soviet Union on an ascending node. Smart move on the part of the Soviets."

"Assuming we weren't going to launch on the previous pass. Then it would have been too late."

"Maybe they weren't confident of a kill. They knew if they missed it'd be quite a few passes before we'd be in position to launch again. And it still is a while. I mean, we've got far far eastern Siberia on the next descending node. If Cheyenne wants us to…hit Moscow or something, it'll be seven revs until we get there."

"That'll be a long wait."

We cross into daylight. Crystalline beauty of southwestern Alaska, brilliant under surprisingly clear skies. Pack ice clogged around the northward side of the Aleutians. An incredible sight, worth floating into the spindle to get another glimpse as it falls behind.

Above the horizon: a bright star, following us.

"Uhhh, there's a…we have a follower in orbit."

"That couldn't be their station, could it?"

"It doesn't seem to be moving, relative to us."

Our commander's brow furrows. "What do you think it is?"

"Maybe another Zenit. Or a Soyuz."

"Well."

"You think they're trying to stop us? Or just observe?"

"Your guess is as good as mine." Deep breath. "Maybe it is time to turn on the console."

If we want to power up the console, let's go to page 569.

If not, let's go to page 600.

How did we get here?

Coming down fast, the last of the roll reversals finished, the altimeter unwinding and possibly inaccurate. Terrain below, the Malagasy Republic, foreign and hot. But how high?

"Falcon-2, Tananarive, we have you on radar." Heavily accented English. A touch of French?

"Tananarive, Falcon, can we get an altimeter reading? Over."

"Say again, Falcon-2." The lack of urgency is…infuriating.

"Altimeter, Tananarive. We'd like an altimeter reading. Over."

"Altimeter here is two-niner-four-five. Over." (It sounds like alt-e-meeter.)

"Copy, Tananarive. two-niner-four-five. Over." Adjust the knob. That at least is taken care of.

"Falcon-2. Turn left. one-eight-zero. Descend at discretion and…" (Garbled.) "Range is ten miles."

Mild annoyance. "Tananarive, say again, all after 'discretion,' over." Slight bank to the new heading. The horizon moves smoothly, and in sync with its artificial counterpart.

"Discretion?" Confusion, as if the controller himself doesn't know what he said.

Scan the gauges. Altitude dropping. Annoyance spiking. There is only so much time. "Say everything again, Tananarive!"

"Falcon-2, Tananarive, we have you on radar. Turn left. One-eight-zero. Descend at discretion and…" (Static eats the words again.)

Alarm! Passing in front, closer than expected, fat and slow and oblivious: a Cessna 172. "Whoa! Traffic!"

"Yes, Falcon-2, that's what we said!" (The annoyance is now mutual, apparently.) "Watch for traffic. Over."

Breathe. Try to breathe. Relax. Try to relax. Still it's happening fast. Glance below: irregular fields of brown and green, long lazy streets. Shoddy aluminum sheds on large plots of dirt.

"Falcon-2, come right onto final. You are cleared for Runway Two-Niner, over."

Respond as a professional. "Copy, Tananarive. Runway Two-Niner."

A smooth turn onto final. Imagining, perhaps, the approval of an invisible instructor. (Absent? Dead? Living within us?) The runway is ahead, the land around its end jutting into a large irregular lake. Another complication. But altitude and speed look good. Right? Was the adjustment correct?

Drop the skids. The white lines swell and beckon…too far off? Tension and clenching over the water: anxious glances at the altimeter.

But the shore sweeps under, and the access road whips by, followed quickly by a small patch of dried-out land. Flare slightly, and at last: rough contact. Body lurching against the harness. Skidding down the tarmac in an impossibly long rough rumble, with that strange deceleration making it feel like the planet itself has tilted upwards. Shaking and rumbling and skidding forever.

At last it stops.

There is the stillness and the silence. The moment of blessed relief, of tension's release.

And now it's over.

"Tananarive, we're stopped. Please tell everyone to stay away. The spacecraft is hot." (Spacecraft? If they did not know, they know now.) "Over."

"Falcon-2, you said…stay…away? Over?"

"Yes! It's hot! We just reentered! From outer space! Over." (Where is this anger coming from?)

"Falcon-2, I know where you came from. I am familiar…" (Fa-me-lee-ar.) "…with the concept of adiabatic heating. And your fellow officer has been kind enough to refresh my understanding. Several times he's reminded all of us. Over."

(Choke down anger.) "Copy, Tananarive."

"We have instructed our ground personnel. We will leave you some time for you to cool off. And the fire truck will come by to hafeeen the protheeess."

"Sorry, Tananarive, say again, over."

"To hasten the process! To water you down with a hose. You are familiar with the cooling effects of water on hot metal, yes?"

"Copy, Tananarive."

"Now, as I said, we will leave you some time. Over."

Sit back in temporary pressure-suited coolness. Glance at the gauges and try to remember how much longer the APUs can provide power. Try to forget everything else. All things seen and unseen.

The water startles. A sudden blast like a cannon against the hot steel alloy: even with the helmet on it seems a bit much. Cascading over the cockpit windows. A violent baptism for a new life.

Still it lasts. More water, more water, more water.

Crack the faceplate, remove the helmet, unclip the harness, shimmy in the seat to allow circulation. Relief: incomplete. And the water is louder now. Damaging the spacecraft? What does it matter. It is destined for: what? Junkyard or museum, if they have them here. Mounted on a pedestal at the airport's front gate, insignia fading in the sun, on display because there's nobody left to say what's classified. Nobody from whom to hide the secrets...

It is annoying. All the water.

Transmit: "Tananarive, Falcon. Can you tell them to cut that out?"

A response, inaudible.

Outside the windows, jetliners on the apron. Insignia: mostly unfamiliar, especially blurred through sheets of water, except one: Pan-Am.

Wait and wait. Wait and wait and wait.

At last the water stops. Crack the top hatch. Safe the ejection seat. Squirm upwards, slightly woozy. Head out of the hatch. Another assault: Africa hot.

Outside now the fire engine is visible. Impassive firefighters. Skin lighter than expected. Their captain is looking towards two men in a yellow jeep, as if awaiting advice. One of them is an officer in Air Force blue: our capcom. But the other man, the driver, is clearly in charge.

"You have scraped up our runway," he says. Voice familiar from the radio. There is a thin veneer of friendliness: a glove on an angry fist. "Your fellow officer told us you were returning from space. He did not tell us you didn't have wheels."

A nod toward our capcom. "You already told him where we're coming from?"

Our man shrugs, and the other man speaks, as if he is the one to whom all questions must be addressed. "Would we not have figured it out on our own? Even they would have figured it out." A gesture towards the firemen. "When something that looks like this lands, it is not hard to figure out."

Nod and shrug. Nothing else to do.

He lifts a walkie-talkie to his mouth, says something unintelligible. Then: "We are going to have to assess the repair fees, and fine you for the damage. In addition to the landing fees."

Now, at least, is something worth chuckling about. "A fine? Landing fees?"

"Yes. And perhaps a charge for removing this...thing from the runway. Whatever else is going on in the world, we still have scheduled flights. Except for the one to Paris, all our flights are..."

Our capcom looks awkward. Uncomfortable. Antsy. We gesture in is direction: "We...don't have any money."

"Your embassy is still functioning. For the moment. The embassy I'm sure has operating accounts with local banks. To take care of everything the U.S. government normally must take care of in this part of the world. Odds and ends. Food and domestic service for the personnel at your tracking station, which will of course be not needed any more. Housing for the air police who provide security there, and the marines who guard the embassy, all of whom will soon be unemployed. In the meantime we are going to take you into custody."

But now two more jeeps are arriving. Blue with stenciled numbers, although who is there now to inventory every last piece of equipment? Air police inside, in khaki summer uniforms with billy clubs and sidearms. Our man nods at them as if relieved, and speaks at last. "We're taking him."

"With who?" the other man says. "These men?"

"Yeah, that's right."

"I think not." As the air police dismount, three more vehicles arrive. Police cars. Local gendarmeries inside, men in drab uniforms with ostentatious shoulder boards and ridiculous French-looking hats. They get out. Chat in foreign with the airport man.

Our ground man speaks to the air police: "Surround the spacecraft." Then to our capcom: "We're still taking him."

The air police exchange tentative glances. But the gendarmeries fan out, surrounding them. Everyone eyes each other warily, looking to adversaries for signs of action, looking to superiors for nods of approval.

To the other Americans, the airport man speaks. "There is nothing for you to do here. And no one to do it for. I see you're wearing sidearms. You represent a government that no longer exists. Are you going to shoot us, for the sake of this man?" He shrugs. "You would not be soldiers, but murderers. And where would you take him? You cannot take him home." He steps down from the jeep. "You are manning the outposts of a dead empire. This is the last twitch of the tail from a fish dying on a dock. A chicken with no head jerking up from the chopping block and running blindly through the marketplace." He looks around at the tentative air policemen. "It is up to you. You can live out your years here in peace. Assimilating into our society. Marrying local girls. Or live out your days being hunted. The greatest criminals in the land. It is entirely up to you."

The air police mutter amongst themselves. Some now lean against the side of their jeeps, or sit back down in them. One removes his headgear. Our capcom surveys them with dismay and shakes his head.

More vehicles are arriving now: trucks, and a set of air stairs. Their drivers exit and walk up to the airport man, who is talking to the head of the gendarmeries.

Perhaps this was a mistake.

•••

After the repositioning of the air stairs and the reluctant descent to the tarmac and the brief pause—too long, no gravity—we are in the jeep sweating, duffel bag in pressure suit lap with helmet on top of it, sitting catty-corner from our capcom while the airport man—important, head of operations, perhaps—drives, and the head of the gendarmeries occupies the other back seat. The police cars precede and follow. The blue jeeps trail at a distance.

The head of the gendarmeries is in his late 30s, perhaps. Skin the color of coffee with two creamers. "Did you expect us to be black?" he says, but does not wait for an answer. "We are Merina." There is a moment of silence. Then: "You were involved with what happened. You were involved with the war, yes?"

How to answer? So many ways to answer.

He shakes his head. "We are going to have to talk to you about that."

Our capcom turns. "You could have come down...where else could you have come down? Anywhere on earth, right?"

Shift uncomfortably. Why *did* we land here? "A lot of the normal options were...no longer options. Even Australia, a lot of it, the populated parts were..." A shrug.

"Still...South America, that was...untouched, right?"

"Pretty much."

"And you didn't want to..."

A rueful head shake. "Didn't know anyone there."

Both of the foreigners laugh.

"South Africa? New Zealand?"

"There were some...ahhh, New Zealand wasn't entirely...uhh...there were a couple spots targeted. As for South Africa...didn't really think of that." It does sound odd, saying it out loud.

"You could have come down anywhere," our capcom mutters.

We are pulling up to the terminal building: small and new and sleepy. We disembark.

"You are no longer needed here," the airport man says to our fellow American.

"What am I supposed to..."

"Talk to your ambassador. Make arrangements."

"How much will we need to..."

"We will let you know."

We make eye contact. "We'll get you out of here," he says.

And then he is gone and the foreigners are leading the way through a metal access door, down a narrow utilitarian hallway, and to a small holding cell with a desk outside. Dimly lit, bare cinderblock walls, metal bedframe, flimsy rolled-up mattress.

The foreigners speak to one another in their language. One of the gendarmeries grabs the duffel bag, puts it on the desk, starts inventorying the contents.

"You were involved with what happened, yes?" the head of the gendarmeries says again. "You had some responsibility for this war. We are going to have to talk to you about that."

Perhaps this was a mistake.

(CONTINUED)

With a few more breaker clicks, it is back on. Function tests run smoothly; we narrate for our commander, and he answers with a grim nod. Klaxons peaceful, for now.

Below, relentless blue.

"Do we have comms yet?" he asks.

"Hickam again. Other side of the coverage area."

"Call down."

"All right." Key the mike. "Hickam, Watchman, transmitting secure. We have powered up our EWO console and are standing by for instructions. Be advised it looks like we have an orbital follower. Do you see anything on radar? Over."

"Watchman, Hickam. We…ahhh…we do in fact see a follower. Range approximately five-zero miles. Any clue how long they've been there? Over."

"Hickam, we were hoping you could tell us. We've been a little preoccupied here. Over."

"Watchman, we'll have to call it in to Cheyenne. Over."

"Hickam, any ideas about their intentions? Over."

"Watchman, your guess is as good as ours. It does appear the distance is holding steady. But it's safe to assume hostile origin. Over."

"Well, it's not a UFO."

Nobody laughs. "Say again, Watchman."

"Sorry, Hickam. Bad joke."

Our commander speaks. "Hickam, that incident...maybe they weren't trying to shoot us down. Maybe they want us to evacuate. Over."

"Watchman...uhh. That's a pretty big escalation for a pretty small reward. Over."

"Well, Hickam, they did it." (Weary voice. We are both exhausted.) "Maybe it feels like a big reward to them. They can say it was a detonation over their own territory, and we just happened to be in the way. Or...claim it was a defensive act, and make...presentations to the U.N. about 'American aggression in space.' And if they are expecting war, well, we're the tip of the spear. This throws us off. Buys them some time. Over."

"Time for what?"

"Well that is the $64,000 question, isn't it."

We have no answers.

•••

Despite everything that's happened, it's still only mid-afternoon on our workday schedule.

"We need to eat," our companion says.

We are indeed famished. The type of hunger that sneaks up on you when you are busy and hollows you out so that, the moment you stop pushing on whatever's in front of you, you collapse. But: "We haven't...uhh, your eyes. The medical locker."

"Not sure what there is to be done, really."

"Are you in pain?"

"It's bearable."

"Can you see anything?"

A little head shake. "It's not getting better. Little bit of light on the edges still. That's it."

Bitter smile. "Well I guess I'm all alone on kitchen duty, huh?"

Our companion graciously chuckles. Then floats placidly as we add water to hot dog packets. Below, lots of blue.

"What's down there?"

"We're really out there now. Couple revs east of Australia, still. Empty South Pacific. Couple islands."

"Might be good places to fly down to. If something does happen. You'll be in a unique spot at the end of the world. The one man who can go anywhere."

"Nothing's gonna happen. This'll blow over. Your eyes'll get better. We'll get you down."

"We'll see. What islands?"

"I'd have to check the maps. Samoa, Tonga. Fiji, maybe. Haven't spent much time on the geography in this part of the Pacific."

"No need to, huh? Nobody's trying to kill us down there."

"Not down there. Just up here." Hands on the hot dog packets: tepid. Place one in our companion's hand. "I'm sorry, the water didn't...I think the heater must've gone out, with everything else."

"We'll get by." He works his fingers into the packet, widens the opening, slowly extracts a cool hot dog, takes a bite, thinks. Then: "Did you ever see *Operation Petticoat*?"

"The Cary Grant movie?"

"Yeah. With the pink submarine."

A chuckle at the absurdity. "Long time ago. Why?"

"Do you remember that scene? They were being depth-charged by a friendly destroyer, by mistake. And they discarded a bunch of junk through the torpedo tubes. Blankets and pillows and oil and stuff. To make the destroyer think they'd sunk them."

"Are you saying we should do that here?"

"Sure. Why not? Make 'em think they did shoot us down."

"How?"

"Get some debris. Make some homemade chaff. Anything radar reflective. Hell, we've got a whole spaceplane we can discard."

"We're gonna get you better."

A bitter chuckle. "We're not gonna get the plane better."

Drift through the hatch, glance through the spindle window. Our follower is low now, a bright spot of metal against the Antarctic whiteness. Lower orbit: trying to catch up.

"Shit. They're trying to rendezvous." To do what? Board us? Impossible. Take pictures? Ensure our destruction? Fantastic visions: a spacesuited cosmonaut outside, umbilical cord snaking back to a nearby Soyuz, attaching an explosive device to our outer hull. It all seems far-fetched. But then again, here we are.

"Well I guess we'd better do something."

•••

Upside-down in the vomit-spattered cockpit, looking for: anything discardable. Very little is: everything's been riveted together nicely by the good people at Boeing, built to endure the high gs. Silently we curse their diligence.

There is also a strange tentative feeling, an unwillingness to further damage what had been our ride home. Under the cockpit panel, next to the missing patch of insulation we cut out for the reentry bucket, we snip a few more pieces. Then: start yanking wires from behind the instruments, cautiously at first, but with increasing fury. Stuff it all into a floating bag, unsure if any of it will be noticeable in a cloud of space debris. All around, the smell of dried bile: intolerable.

Then, an idea. Back to the living room: open the trash bin. Empty meal packets. Aluminized plastic insides. It takes little effort to flatten them out, scissor them into irregular shapes.

"How's it going?" our companion asks.

"Getting there."

"What's it look like outside?"

"Not sure it's the best time to talk about the view." Tone: perhaps harsher than necessary.

"I'm only asking 'cause it might be able to do this as soon as we are back in light. If it is still dark."

"Oh. Yeah. Good thinking. There is a full moon out but...yeah, daylight would be better."

"Should we call down to...who's coming up?"

"Lakenheath again. Second window."

"Should we talk to them?"

"Tell them what?"

"That we're abandoning ship. We can transmit in the clear. Assume the Soviets have somebody listening...a trawler in the North Sea or something."

"All right. But...we want Cheyenne to know we are in fact OK."

"We can talk secure to Thule afterwards."

"OK." Finish the cutting. Float with the bag of debris back towards the spindle. Close the X-20 hatch. Kiss fingers and place them on the outer skin of the metal friend that flew us here. Then: debris from the bag, in the soon-to-be-airless interlock space. And close the station hatch before it floats away. Back to the living room.

"Lakenheath, Watchman, come in. Over."

"Watchman, Lakenheath, go ahead. Over."

"Lakenheath, battery power is failing. We believe we have sustained some…external damage of some sort. Falcon-2 is going to have to depart the station. Over."

"Uhhh, Watchman, say again, over."

Our companion repeats the transmission.

"Watchman, this is…uhh, should we be talking secure here?"

"No time to explain, Lakenheath."

"Uhhh, copy Watchman. Your ground track will be…uhh…where exactly are you going to reenter? Over."

"We'll figure that out with Thule. Could probably do eastern Australia on the next pass. Over."

"Watchman, we're gonna need to talk to Cheyenne about this. Over."

"Lakenheath, there's no time. We…"

"Watchman, this is…uhh, we can't just authorize you to…uhh…" (Crackle.) "Let's see if we can patch you through on the Autovon. Over."

Long moments of silent angst punctuated by garbled static squawks. Then: "Wchhhh mccchhhh. Tchhhh ichhhhh Chhhhhhhncccch. Gchhhhh Ahhcccchhh. Occhhhhhh."

"Cheyenne, uhh, we do not copy. Over."

More garbled awfulness. The dark planet sweeps by below, clouds and ocean silvery in the moonlight. Our orbital track is taking us towards Iceland. Soon we are at LOS.

"We'll explain it to Thule, at least."

Set the scramblers. Watch the clock as it ticks upwards towards the predicted acquisition time. Then: "Thule, this is Watchman, calling secure. Over."

No answer. And outside, nothing to see: no Northern Lights, nothing on the planet. The night is silent, devoid of clues.

Again: "Thule, Watchman. Calling secure. Over."

Still nothing.

More calls. Trying to bury the concern in our voices under layers of professionalism. At one point it sounds like there is a flicker of a transmission, but nothing intelligible. A black angst wells up. "Well that's...not good."

Glance towards the EWO console. Still silent. Still silent.

● ● ●

Coming out of darkness over the North Pacific: low-lit clouds and patches of gray ocean. Deadness.

We set the controls up for a brief sustained pulse with the cold gas thrusters, then place our companion's hand on the EXECUTE button. Float into the spindle. Wait for the thrusters to stop. Push JETTISON and watch as the spaceplane dips away and the infinite vacuum sucks our debris out into airless sunlight.

But: no time to dwell on sights we will never see again. Back to the living room. Nudge the station back in the other direction to edge it away from the derelict space plane. Once more into the spindle to confirm we've built up a little separation at least. Then: the living room yet again. Another blast with the thrusters to set us spinning. All narrated for our commander.

Then at last: "We should turn off the interior lights, too. In case they get close enough to see through the windows."

"I have no objections." A flicker of a shadow of a smile.

"Should we call down, next comms window?"

"As opposed to…"

"Well, it's just…do we want Cheyenne to think we're totally out of action, or…I mean, if *they're* listening…" (A nod towards the Soviets.) "…we don't want *them* to know we're only playing dead."

"What are the next windows?"

"Kwajalein. Ascension. Thule again."

"No Pine Gap?"

"No primary stations before Thule. We're still one rev east of Australia." So: no secure comms.

"We'll listen. See if they call us. Try again at Thule."

Outside the horizon drifts down, past the window. Airglow in blue and green. Black daylight sky, bright stars visible. A shaft of sun slicing across the darkened station interior. Then the horizon again.

Radio crackle. "Watchman, this is Kwajalein. Come in. Over."

Look to our commander for guidance. Are the Soviets listening here, too, all the way out in the central Pacific? Will we blow the ruse if we respond?

"Watchman, this is Kwajalein. Come in. Over."

A glance out the living room window as the world revolves around us. And: the enemy spacecraft is out there, is visible now. A Soyuz, drawing closer, green and white modules daylit, solar panels making it look as if it is, in fact, flying. An ugly mechanical insect silently approaching.

Again the crackle: "Watchman, this is Kwajalein. We received a...confusing phone call from Lakenheath. Picking up...several objects on radar around you. Unsure about your status at his time. Over."

Paralyzed thoughts: Should we answer?

Face against the glass, but only for a second. Then the thought: stay away from the windows. Our commander floats impassively: of course. He doesn't see what we see.

"Uhhh...they're out there."

"Who?"

"It looks like a Soyuz."

"Jesus."

"Yeah."

"Call down."

"What?"

"Call down as Falcon-2. Tell 'em you left. They won't know where it's coming from."

Deep breath. Glance out at the slowly spinning view: no sight of the X-20. Key the mike. "Uhh, Kwajalein, this is…Falcon-2." Quieter than necessary.

Our companion smiles. "I think you can speak up a little."

"Kwajalein, we had…uhh…several electrical issues following the NUCFLASH incident. Station batteries have failed. I have departed the station. Be advised, there is a…Soviet spacecraft of some sort in my vicinity. Over."

"Falcon-2, did you say Soviet spacecraft? Over."

"Roger, Kwajalein. It appears to be a Soyuz. Just…observing for now. Over." Hiding in the shadows, looking out the window: now at last the damaged X-20 comes into distant view. It has continued to drift; it's just far enough away that it's hard to tell its status. Can they see it, too?

It is evident in the long pause that this is simply a lot of information for a junior officer to process without guidance. "Falcon-2, copy, possible…observation flight. What is the status of Falcon-1, over?"

"Kwajalein, he…uhh…had some medical issues related to the NUCFLASH incident. Over."

"Falcon-2, that was our understanding as well. Your departure seems…highly irregular. Over." Professional words, but a tone that says: What the hell are you doing abandoning your crewmember? "What did Thule have to say? Over."

"Kwajalein, uhhh…Thule was offline. Over."

"Falcon-2, I'm sorry. Did you say…offline?" Incredulous tone.

"Roger, Kwajalein."

"Falcon-2, has that ever happened before? Over."

"Uhh, negative, Kwajalein. There was a…burst of…some radio transmission. But no voice comms. Over."

"Falcon-2, this seems…a matter of concern. Over."

"It does, Kwajalein. If you could call them on the Autovon…that would seem the best course of action at this time. Over."

"We agree on that, at least. Hold one, Falcon-2."

Eternity in the pause. Breathless heavy wait. Eye the clock as we tick up towards LOS and the answers we don't want.

Then: "Falcon-2, we are getting a fast busy signal. Over."

"Are you calling FLASH OVERRIDE? Over."

"We…uhhh, that's a…we have the button, I'm not sure it works for our node. We'll try again on FLASH. Over."

Another excruciating wait.

Our commander: "How soon until LOS?"

Quick look at the relentless clock: "Uhh, coming up."

"They need to call Cheyenne."

"Uhh, Kwajalein, Falcon-2. If you are not getting through you need to call Cheyenne. Over."

"Falcon-2, we called FLASH and we…" A radio crackle eats the end of the sentence.

"Shit."

The Pacific vista sweeps up again across our living room window. An emerald chain. The Solomons, green fresh hell. An anxious thought: we're at the start of something a million times worse than Guadalcanal.

Our commander: "What are they doing?"

Glance out at the Soyuz as it whirls past. Glimmer of movement through their porthole. "Probably photographing us. Planning their next move. What should we do?"

"Not sure what we can do, other than play dead."

"What if they come out?"

"Why would they?"

"To make sure."

"Not sure what we can do."

"We have…more offensive firepower than all the air forces in World War II. And we don't even have a…cap gun to defend ourselves."

Long pause. At last our commander says: "There are flares."

Again, islands below, and the view spins, and there is the Soyuz. "Flares?"

"In the survival kit, on the other X-20. There's a flare pistol, right?"

"Would that work outside?"

"Well, it's gunpowder. It doesn't burn from oxygen in the air...the saltpeter's the oxidizer. And...*they* had a cannon, and it worked on you, right?"

"But even if it hit 'em...it's low velocity."

"It'll burn. The flare, it'll burn out there."

"You think?"

"Yeah. I mean...it's got its own oxidizer, too. Potassium perchlorate. They burn underwater. Closed barrel, full of hot gasses, everything has an oxidizer. The gunpowder should ignite the flare, the flare should burn."

"That's...this sounds like a crapshoot. Can I even get outside?"

"I can help a little...I mean, EVA prep, getting the torso zipper closed. I can do that by feel. You can do the rest from in there. Dump the pressure. Watch through the hatch window."

And the view is gone, it spins back away, and there is the Soyuz. Moving into position.

Watch anxiously as the view spins away to black sky. Then again, ocean. And in the distance, Australia. The fatal shore.

"Well," our companion says. "If we're gonna do it, we should do it now."

If we want to conduct an impromptu EVA to drive off the Soviets, let's go to page 583.

If not, go to page 594.

(CONTINUED)

Frantic preparation in the half-light. Pulling the Very pistol out. Four cartridges: one in the pistol, three for the thigh pocket of the suit. Next to them: a survival knife, large serrated blade. Something we used in jungle training.

Back to the spindle. Umbilical connected. Then to the living room. Suit and helmet and gloves. Connect up the other end of the hose. Wriggle into the suit and guide our back towards our commander so he can fasten everything by touch. Everything is out of order, everything feels wrong. Voices spike in frustration. We have to turn on the environmental controls for the suit first, and *then* get helmet and gloves on.

Then: cram into the spindle and pull the umbilical in with no help. And listen to our blind companion narrate as he fumbles with the hatch latch.

At last, his voice in the headset: "I think that's it. How does it look to you?"

Glance down in the dim light past feet and umbilical. "Think it's good."

"OK, great."

"We're gonna have to…we're gonna have to wait half a rev anyway, I think. Not too much daylight left on this pass."

"No?"

"We just crossed the coast of Antarctica. We'll be crossing the terminator again pretty soon. Don't think they'll try anything while it's dark."

"Well, just...keep your eyes out."

Deep breath. Very pistol in gloved hand, held against chest, like a duelist waiting to start walking. Finger resting against the trigger guard: very little purchase. A glance through the window: the Soyuz has moved into position near our axis of rotation, and is turning more or less in sync with us, parallel to us. On the round end module, a hatch is open, and a white helmet has emerged.

"Shit."

"What's happening?"

"They've cracked their hatch."

Beyond the Soyuz: empty space and then the earth coming down from above, Antarctica now, bright painful desolation. And from the enemy spacecraft our adversary is emerging. A torso clad in a blue spacesuit. Thick white gloves. Red letters on the helmet: CCCP.

"I don't know what they're doing. It's gonna be dark in a second."

And then the white coast flashes by, and flecks of sea ice, massive bergs like chips in a drink, and then comes the terminator, the edge of night, but there is, after all, still moonlight, so once we pass out of the sun there are a few discombobulated moments while eyesight adjusts but then our spacecraft are silvery and illuminated, and our adversary is a cool shadowy blue.

And then he reaches up on his helmet and flips a switch: twin beams of light, stabbing towards us.

"Shit."

"What is it?"

"We might just have to do this."

Glance back out, and the cosmonaut is hesitating in the hatch as if judging: distance, speed of jump, where to grab a handhold. Then he pushes off, crossing the void; as he moves he passes out of sight beneath the edge of the hatch window.

With our gloved hand on the hatch handle we can feel the bare hint of vibration. Noise like a knock on the door.

"What was that?"

"That was him."

"Damnit."

And yet when we peer out, he is not on the station; he is floating at the end of his umbilical cord, a dim shape against the stars, drifting back towards the Soyuz.

"He didn't stick. I think his crewmember is...reeling him back in, or something."

"Jesus."

"The guy's got guts, I'll give him that."

"You gonna go?"

"I'm gonna wait. Until he's on. Until he's committed. Less of a chance he'll see me if he's busy."

There are a couple tedious minutes while our adversary repositions himself. Beyond, the planet spins, starry infinity and soft moonlit Atlantic all backdrop now. The moonshadows on the Soyuz angle and change and sweep around as we spin. At last the cosmonaut is in position, one hand awkwardly grabbing a railing, legs tensed beneath him like a swimmer on the starter blocks, head and helmet lights fixed straight ahead on his goal.

He springs across the void.

Again there is a tremble transmitted through the hatch handle. The soft knock of impact transmitted through the hull.

Outside the hatch window he is not quite visible, but there is a dark snake moving slowly through airless space against the starry infinite universe.

It is time.

"He's on."

"What's he doing?"

"Dunno. Gonna have to go out there."

"All right. Read through your locks before you dump the spindle."

"Helmet is locked. Gloves are locked. Suit pressure steady. Dumping the spindle." Open the valve. Watch as the pressure goes down, down, down. "Suit pressure steady."

"All right. Good luck."

Deep breath. Swing the hatch latch with the left hand while the right still clutches the flare pistol. If he sees the airlock open, can he do anything? Better to use the knife instead?

Push the hatch open. Pulse pounding. Pull head and arms and torso out to see.

On the station's aluminum hide there are two compressed circles of light, and in their reflection and the moonglow we can see the blue spacesuit and the white helmet and the gloves, one on the handrail and one positioning some shadowy shape. Pressing a keypad. Working towards some nefarious purpose. Oblivious.

Level the pistol. Line it up along the barrel. Finger on the trigger. Barely any room, with the gloves. Pull the trigger.

And there is a muffled flash and a brief recoil of arm and body, and a bright burst of smoldering flame that hits the top of the cosmonaut's helmet and ricochets off.

"Shit! Shit. Shit shit shit."

The cosmonaut's actions show confusion and then comprehension. He pivots, pulls himself along the handrail, a relentless man on a mission.

"What's going on?" Our commander's voice in the headset, distant.

"Just...shit."

Look down. Think about going for the survival knife. Fumble in the spacesuit pocket for the next cartridge instead. Look up. Helmet lights, coming towards us, blinding. Hand on a cartridge, other hand on the pistol.

Collision.

Body against body, foreign shoulder against spacesuit chest, not so much violent as disorienting. Pressed back against the edge of the hatch. Holding onto the pistol and the cartridge and the enemy is there, he is in front, and he is reaching with one gloved hand for the lip of the hatch while his weightless body swings up and away.

Struggle with gloved hands to open the breech of the pistol. Place cartridge suspended for just a second to get a second hand on the gun. Mistake.

The cosmonaut looks up and pivots and swats the floating cartridge away, off into space.

We give an angry animal shove against his torso, and his body pivots, his legs swing down and hit our helmet. And he is drifting, he is off the station, but there is a loop of umbilical in front of us and mindlessly we tug it but it does not disconnect, and we grab it with our free hand and pull him back in and we are bracing our legs against the sides of the hatch and trying to maneuver him and grab his helmet to pull him down and smash his faceplate on the edge of the hatch, and then he reaches up and starts fumbling at our helmet locks, and now he has a finger on one, and it's sliding, we can feel it starting to give, and we shudder and twist and push him off.

In the struggle we have let go of the pistol. It is drifting up, up, and is near the Soyuz. Breech open.

The Soyuz hasn't moved, but in the moonlight it is apparent that someone is pulling the umbilical cord back in. The cosmonaut drifts back towards it, arms flailing in empty space, and then his arm brushes the spacecraft and he grabs a handrail and there is a brief wave of relaxation that passes through his body. He pulls himself back inside the hatch. Retreating? Going for a weapon? A flash of memory: briefings, a story about a flight that came down in Siberia, and the crew shooting to keep wolves at bay.

Shooting: there is a shotgun in there.

Headset voice: "You OK out there?"

"Yeah, I just gotta…"

Nervous hand clasp against the thigh pocket. One cartridge left.

Push off against the lip of the spindle and fly across the gap, and with awkward bear hands, trap floating flare pistol against spacesuit chest and then hold on with one hand and raise the other to keep from smashing into the Soyuz. Awkwardly twist to insert the cartridge, and…

OOF! Our adversary has re-emerged, is grabbing, is struggling, is reaching for something, but now again the pistol is loaded, and a flash of a thought: no need to aim, no need for anything but contact.

Press the muzzle against his back and pull the trigger.

There is a brief recoil and a puff of smoke and a sun-bright ball of fire and a black burned hole now in his suit, and he wriggles, he wriggles and wriggles for longer than one would expect, and then he is still.

There is a brief horrifying glimpse of his features through the helmet visor as he drifts up. Face not distorted in anger or struggle but relaxed, peaceful. Eyes flecked with frost.

No time to savor the victory. Glance up at the Soyuz: impossibly strange to be here, to be next to it, the large round orbital module next to us. Grab a handrail. Through the porthole we can see movement in the bell-shaped descent module, a slice of foreign face, eyes excited, pressure helmet on; they must be suited up in there, they...are they coming out? Reeling their dead comrade back in?

Turn back to face the station and there, there it is still on the side, whatever it is the cosmonaut had deposited: a device, an explosive charge of some sort. Push off hastily against the Soyuz to get back there, but without enough force, and we are stuck between, are drifting slowly, and we have to pull on the umbilical cord to get back, gently, gently, gently. And at last we are in arm's reach of the spindle.

Grab the handrail. Pull ourselves back towards the spot where our dead adversary was working. And there it is, a block of plastique affixed with adhesive, connected to detonators, a timer. Counting down.

Again the headset voice: "Talk to me. What's going on?"

"Just a sec."

Pry the device off the station. Better not to deactivate it. Look back up. They have pulled the dead man in close to the station, but there is no good way to get him through the hatch without his participation. And the spacecraft is pivoting, from parallel to perpendicular. Getting ready to withdraw? Preparing to ram us? Flash memory from an intelligence briefing: the round end module, the orbital module, is discarded in space, and they return in the central module only. Maybe they still want to do what they came here for. Maybe they figure they can ram us with the orbital module and get away with it.

Push off from the station, across the void once more, and they have cut the dead man's umbilical, and the end is floating out of the hatch, and we grab the lid of the hatch and we have the device in our other hand and the timer is counting down and we look inside the Soyuz and there he is in the orbital module: another cosmonaut, head coming out of the descent module, but he can only get so far, he is connected by shorter internal hoses, they don't have another full umbilical, and so: throw the device in their module and then fumble for the survival knife, feel his arms grappling, stab and slash at his shoulders as his arms flail now with animal panic and feeble attempts to fight, and through the clear visor we can see his face contorted in shouts and screams, eyes alarmed as he tries to get back down through the hatch, and his suit resists the knife, but only a little, and then there are puffs of red mist turning to frost crystals and sublimating, just a hint of reddish residue, and then there is movement from the spacecraft itself, and the device is still in the module and we can feel the lid of their hatch scraping against the back of our suit as their third crewmember pulls away, and outside now we frantically try to swing their hatch closed, maybe it needs to be closed, but we can't quite close it before we're off the Soyuz and watching the soundless puff of thrusters as they pull away, and we stay there tethered at the limit of the umbilical as they back off, perhaps 50 yards away now, and there is a moment's hesitation and a blurt of light. A reflex reaction, to cover ourselves against debris, but we are far enough away, and the spacecraft is tumbling slightly, is drifting, is dead.

On comes the headset: "You OK out there?"

"Yeah. I think we're all right." Blinking. A spot of strange vision: the ghost of the flare.

Then: "All orbital units, this is Ascension, all orbital units this is Ascension. Be advised we have received FLASH traffic from Kwajalein. They have been unable to raise Thule or any CONUS stations. Assuming we are at DEFCON-1. I repeat. Assuming we are at DEFCON-1. Please relay any information you have received from the National Command Authority, or any visual information you might have. Over."

Our companion: "Ascension, this is..."

"Watchman."

"Ascension, this is Watchman. We have not received any war orders. We should be over the Soviet Union this rev. Not exactly sure where, but..."

Gazing down at the empty moonlit south Atlantic as it spins by. Weary. "West of Kamchatka, I think."

"West of Kamchatka. We have been a little...preoccupied up here."

"Uhhh, Watchman, we received word that there was a hostile..."

The crackle of LOS. Guilty pleasure in the silence. Float for a couple minutes as the station slowly turns. The last EVA: indescribably beautiful. Moonlight on winter clouds far below, patchy enough to see the silver calm of the equatorial night on the ocean.

Then: a clot of narrow contrails poking up from the water and angling northeast for a few dozen miles before they cut off. Dead thin smoke trails. Dread.

Then another cluster, pointing west this time. A fast flash of light as another missile joins it.

Then another cluster. Then another.

Gently pull on the umbilical. Back towards the spindle. Position ourselves in the open hatch, reluctant to end the last EVA. Look up at the full moon, the endless universe. Impossible. Impassive. Is anyone watching? Does anyone care?

The horizon swings back up as we rotate back in. In the dark distance there are bright flashes of light. A thousand miles away, just out of sight, on either shore.

"What's going on out there?"

A catch in the throat: speaking it makes it real. "You don't wanna know."

And then it's back inside. Close the EVA hatch for the last time. The dark confines make it feel like a coffin.

Let's go to page 604.

(CONTINUED)

In the darkened station we wait. Position our companion so he'll be away from the living room window, take position ourselves in the shadows. Outside the world still spins: the clear blue sea, the distant coast of Australia a mottled green. A glimpse of the impassive Soyuz.

"What are they doing?"

"They're…" (A quick peek at the silent spacecraft.) "…not doing anything yet. Just watching."

Breathless anticipation. Memories of World War II movies: sweaty submarine crewmembers casting eyes upwards towards the enemy destroyer. Except here of course we cannot slink away, invisible.

And then: movement. The hostile craft positioning itself so that it can turn in sync with us. They float parallel to us now, turning as we turn.

"Well, shit."

"What are they doing?"

"Dunno…but they're doing something."

On the round end of the Soyuz, a hatch opens. From the darkness inside emerges a helmet (white with red letters: CCCP) and then the blue shoulders of a spacesuit. In the sunlight his visor is down. The sight is chilling: an inscrutable emotionless enemy.

"Aaaand there he is."

And now he is pulling himself all the way out of the craft, awkwardly moving his body into position on the side so he can push off with his legs and cross the airless gap.

After a few moments the cosmonaut is ready. In his motions, one can see the stillness of contemplation and then: a flash of movement.

From our position there is no way to see the end of his path, just the spacesuited body moving out of sight past the edge of the window, and the umbilical trailing behind. It writhes in empty space, a dying white snake, and there is a small impact sound transmitted through the metal of the hull.

"Was that him?" our commander asks.

"That was him."

But he has not stuck the landing; he is drifting back towards the Soyuz, his umbilical disappearing inside slowly as if he's being pulled back in.

"Is he on?"

"No, he didn't do it."

Behind our adversaries now as the backdrop rotates: Antarctic whiteness, the barren strangeness of a land without people. Again the foreigner positions himself. Again he tries to cross the gap. Again, impact sound, softer now. Again he is drifting back.

"That was him?"

"Yeah. Still not on."

Then there are a few moments when our adversary stops. As if receiving a transmission, he stops. Stays motionless out there, next to the hatch, as we pass into orbital night.

"Well, it's dark now. Maybe they'll take a breather."

But he reaches up, touches his helmet: lights, one on each side. In the soft moonlight glow we can see him position himself for another attempt.

"Shit."

"What's happening?"

"He's got...uhh...helmet lights of some sort."

"Shit."

"Pretty ballsy."

"Yeah, I'll give him that."

The cosmonaut crosses the gap and again there is an impact thud. And...

"Is he on?"

"He might be."

Will ourselves to stillness. Silence, even though it doesn't matter. Imagine what he's trying to do to us, what he will do if he peeks in and sees us hiding there. Glance towards the EWO console: what would happen if that came on now? Klaxons? Lights, visible through the windows?

"Should have gone out there."

But the cosmonaut does drift back into sight, headed back towards the Soyuz. And it looks like he is holding his hand strangely.

"Oh, maybe not!"

"What happened?"

"It…looks like he…hurt his hand, maybe."

"Are you kidding me? How the fuck…"

"I dunno, but we'll take it!" A headshake, a shout to our outside adversary. "Aww, what's the matter, Ivan? You got a widdle booboo from the big spacecraft? Is mommy gonna kiss and make it better?"

In the moonlit dark it is harder to see exactly what's going on but it seems like the cosmonaut has his left hand clasped to his right palm. He removes it for a second and then puts it back.

Our commander laughs: "Really?"

"Actually, it looks like he's…he might have cut his glove or something."

"There's not a lot of sharp edges out there!"

"No, there's not!"

"Maybe on the edge of the carrier mechanism. If he couldn't see, and he grabbed that…I dunno. Couldn't have been a big cut, or he would have decompressed. But if it's little…"

"Maybe he's gotta go back inside."

And sure enough, the cosmonaut sticks his arms and head back inside the hatch and crawls back inside.

"Ahaha! Sonofabitch!" Cackle with glee.

"What's happening?"

"He's going back inside!" A surge of relief: the false bravado of the recently reprieved. To our enemy. "Ohh, Ivan, too bad! You got a widdle cut on your glovey wovey! Fuckin' moron! That's what you get!"

"Kinda anticlimactic. But we'll take it."

"Hell yeah, we'll take it...fucking morons!"

The Soyuz maneuvers away, pulls back slowly out of sight.

And then over the darkened South Atlantic comes the transmission: "All orbital units, all orbital units, this is Ascension. Come in. Over."

"Ascension, this is...Watchman. Go ahead. Over."

"Watchman, be advised we have no comms with Thule or any CONUS station. Assume we are at DEFCON-1. Repeat. Assume is we are at DEFCON-1. Please acknowledge. Over."

A squeeze of angst. "We copy DEFCON-1. Have you heard anything official? Is there a reason to assume this isn't just a...technical issue? Over."

 "Watchman, we received FLASH traffic on the Autovon from Hickam, and they went offline halfway through..."

Off-mike: "Jesus."

"...then we have no other information. Over."

"Copy, Ascension. Sounds like everyone is in the dark. Over."

"Uhhh, say again, Watchman."

"It sounds like everyone's in the dark! Over."

"Indeed. Uhhh...if you do have other info, let us know. Over."

"Well, Ascension...we're coming up on the eastern Soviet Union this rev, and we'll have passes over CONUS after that. We should have another window with you in 12 hours. On the descending node. We'll let you know what we see. Over."

"Much appreciated, Watchman. Ascension out."

In silence we wait. Fly northward, up the center of the moonlit Atlantic. An absolutely perfect night down there, it looks like: calm dark waters. We cling to the hope that nothing's really wrong, other than the comms.

And then: what looks like a pencil-thin cluster of smoke trails, arcing up from the ocean and pointing northeast.

And another set, further west in the Atlantic, and heading west; on this group we can barely see a flash of ignition as another missile joins them.

And there are more. And more.

As the station tumbles, the dark horizon comes up and we can see hundreds of miles, almost to the shore. In the airglow, just out of sight, we can see the soft echoes of blinding flashes of white.

Let's go to page 604.

(CONTINUED)

"We can turn it on later."

"They gave us an order."

"Look…if we turn it on, there's a chance we'll have to use it. If we use it…well, there's a pretty big chance nobody's ever going to be sending a Gemini up. We need to stay up here as long as possible. So we can both come down. We can turn it on later."

We turn our backs to the silent war console.

For the next two hours we orbit, attempting all manner of fixes to get the fuel cells working. Different startup sequences, pumps and cryo tank heaters and breakers. Nothing works.

Meanwhile the bright dot in orbit with us has drawn closer, has revealed itself to be: a Soviet spacecraft.

"Well, that's just great."

"What?"

"It's a Soyuz. About a hundred yards away."

"What's it doing?"

"Hard to say." The enemy spacecraft hovers out of reach, patient and sinister. "I mean, they're not doing anything aggressive. It's almost like they're…waiting for us to abandon ship."

"We should probably call it in."

"They're...probably gonna be mad that we've been offline."

A smirk. "What are they gonna do to me?"

We turn the radio back on, heading north above the peaceful moonlit Atlantic.

Then comes the call: "Watchman, this is Ascension. Come in. Over."

"Ascension, this is Watchman. Go ahead. Over."

We brace, awaiting a tongue-lashing. But instead: "Watchman, we have had some...comms difficulties with some of the other tracking stations. What was your last contact with Thule? Over."

"Ascension, it's been a couple hours. We have had...continuing electrical difficulties following the NUCFLASH incident. To be honest, our radio has been off. And we have an...orbital follower. Over."

"Watchman, we did see that, on the scope. Any evidence of hostile intent? Over."

"Nothing yet, Ascension. Just...observing for now, over."

"Copy, Watchman. And you haven't received any war orders? Over."

"No war orders, no comms. We're in survival mode up here. Over."

"Well, we are...completely in the dark as to what's going on in the rest of the world. Obviously there won't be another comms window with us until you're on a descending node.

But please, pass along any information you have at that time. Over."

"Will do, Ascension."

On we orbit, in Atlantic night. Moon on mottled clouds below, and a peaceful ocean visible between the gaps. It seems easy for a moment to believe all will stay that way, to forget about the fuel cells and pretend everything will stay as it has been.

Then: a thin straight cloud, pointing northeast like a slender tree toppled by the wind. Contrails.

Then another set, heading west, and a bright pinprick exhaust flash to remind us what this is.

Then another set. Then another.

It is hard to get a good angle out the living room window, but it seems there are distant white flashes, just over the horizon on either shore.

The scene is so distant it seems unreal. The words come reluctantly: "It started."

No follow-up questions: the tone eliminates the need. No response, but: "Jesus."

"We didn't tun on the console. It's...could we have stopped this?"

"Does it matter?"

The clouds tighten up before we cross the Greenland coast. An alien landscape, lit by the unreachable moon. We call down to Thule: nothing.

Over the high Arctic there are fewer signs of what's happening, but we know there are thousands of warheads arcing overhead, tipping over under gravity's pull, reentry vehicles plummeting down to deliver their deadly payloads. In the Northern Lights there are odd patterns, strange colors, charged particles coming from different sources than normal.

It is tempting to watch as we sweep down over the Sea of Okhotsk, tempting to look out towards the daylit Siberian shore and watch the horror spectacle, to see it all destroyed, bright bursts on every town and village, every silo and airstrip, every bridge and rail hub. But: no.

On go the goggles. The end of the world in boring monochrome: bright flashes tinted green, and no details. The lights go out, the sounds fade: EMP again. We are observers, not participants.

Let's go to page 707.

(CONTINUED)

Northward we travel, set in our course. Bisecting the warring Atlantic, then up to the cloud-cloaked coast of Greenland, and arcing across the high Canadian Arctic and the edge of the polar ice. One imagines so many warheads in the sky that one will strike us purely at random. Put us out of our misery. But they all pass silently in the night.

West of Kamchatka the nukes are still falling. It is tempting to watch the whole spectacle directly, see the technicolor flashes of light in the polar twilight. But not at the cost of our eyesight. So: on go the goggles. The end of the world in monochrome green. Bright flashes and no details.

Somewhere in there, the station lights have gone out. The gyroscopes are winding down again. We don't do anything about it. Not yet.

Around the globe we go. Pacific, east of Japan: green flashes in the distance. New Guinea, at peace. Australia, too? No: more green flashes. And Antarctica again, and back up over the dark Atlantic, further west now, ready for our first glimpses of home.

It is nighttime over the Eastern seaboard, but the warheads are still falling there, too. Enough flashes in the darkness that we know nothing will ever be the same, nothing will ever be recognizable.

Our commander's voice, disembodied in the darkness on the other side of the goggles. "It's really happening, huh?"

"It's really happening."

"Looks like you'll be flying down after all."

"No rush. Believe me."

"How long do you wanna stay up here?"

"Another day, at least."

"Another day?"

"Might as well. At least another day. Figure out where to go. See how long the batteries last. Stay as long as possible."

"Yeah." A bitter invisible chuckle. "Might as well."

We float, and wait. The EWO console is silent.

Let's go to page 707.

How did we get here?

Coming out of the last roll reversal, two miles above the vast Pacific, anxiously scanning between puffy cumulus clouds at the empty open waters below. Alone.

"Kwajalein, this is Watch...uhh, Falcon-2. Kwajalein, Falcon-2. Come in, over."

No response. No sight of land.

"Kwajalein, Falcon-2. Come in. Over."

The altimeter unwinds. Still no response. Where is everyone?

Switch to the UHF Guard frequency. "Mayday, mayday, mayday. All units, this is Falcon-2, descending unpowered. Need azimuth to the nearest runway. Over."

Overwhelming silence in the helmet.

Sweep left and then right, banking gently, scanning the empty ocean. No sight of land.

"Mayday, mayday, mayday. Falcon-2, descending unpowered. Need azimuth to nearest runway. Over."

A crackle of static. Someone calling? Some glitch of the equipment? Transmit once more. Nothing.

Switch to VHF Guard. Again: "Mayday, mayday. Falcon-2 descending unpowered. Need azimuth to the nearest runway."

The clouds rise up the way the ground does on final approach: slow, then fast. Assuming the air pressure is relatively normal and the altimeter is accurate, we are under 5,000 feet.

Time for a complete circle this time. Scanning, breathing, wondering how this happened, imagining Amelia Earhart desperately calling down to the empty Pacific…no. We are here and now. And there it is: a coral atoll like arms enfolding turquoise waters in the corner of a lagoon, as if protecting them from the deep blue beyond.

We have overshot by quite a bit; the island was directly beneath us when we were above the clouds. No matter.

Turn back towards it. Slender wave-washed beaches, palm trees. No sign of the runway.

Decision time. The waters closer now, shimmering in the tropical sun, textured and real. Closer now, closer, closer. Just ahead, lighter blue: coral formations below, and the beach just beyond. We can make it. Right?

No. Not if we're not landing. Personal effects in the duffel bag behind us: no chance to retrieve them. Buttocks clenched, back pressed against seat, spine straight, hands around the yellow and black handles: this must be perfect. Pull and *BOOM!*

Senses catch up a few hundred feet up and there is the hatch fluttering down and the spacecraft banking slightly now, and the parachute catches air and opens, full canopy, hard to survey with the helmet on, white and green and orange, risers taut with weight, and ahead now the X-20 crashes just short of the beach, no explosion, just a spray of saltwater and coral and black metal pieces flung back skyward for brief seconds. A combat documentary about World War III that no one else will see, filmed not in grainy and black-and-white, but glorious Technicolor.

No more time to take it in. Hands on the quick release. Water right below. Don't pull too high, don't pull too high, don't pull too high...pull.

A plunging whoosh of saltwater and bubbles outside the helmet visor, a frenzied chaos of nylon and water, the chute released but collapsing on top, no world beyond the parachute, air inside the helmet now stifling, water pouring in the suit valves somewhere down below, suit getting heavier.

Is this death? No, not yet.

Duck and windmill both arms in a reverse front crawl to get out from underneath as the underarm pressure suit water wings auto-inflate in a *whoosh* of CO_2.

And then: out alone in the blue Pacific, underarms buoyed by the floatation devices, the air in the helmet stifling, the chute that was essential just seconds ago and a hindrance just seconds after that now just useless flotsam.

Some lightheadedness. Too long in space. But we can't relax. Not yet. In the pressure suit there is drag on every movement, and everything is still getting heavier. Lessons from survival school, exercises repeated in the pool. Close hose valves, close neck dam, open helmet visor, breathe free at last. Awkwardly unlock the helmet. Hold it up: a souvenir? No. Discard it, watch it *plop* into the blue, gone forever.

And now senses can catch up again: time to relax, if only slightly. The island is a half-mile off. It will be a long slow swim.

Perhaps this was a mistake.

But we swim.

Slow kicks in the shimmering waters, pushed by the low ocean swells, buoyed by the underarm devices. But that is too slow, so now: front crawl with the arms. And that is too awkward with the arm devices, so: back to kicks.

Salty mouth taste. Rising and falling on the low waves. Without the pressure suit it would be a perfect tropical day. With it, it's tedious. A survival exercise with no instructor, or at least none visible. No grade but pass/fail.

Still, we swim.

The beach grows closer. The palm trees get taller. We cannot see anybody.

Tiring swim, awkward swim. Stomach unpleasant: radiation or saltwater? The X-20 is off to the right, a hundred yards away, battered, one corner of its wing sticking out of the water, re-wetted by each low wave. Eventually it will be coral-encrusted, like those forgotten Zeroes strewn in shallow waters on atolls across the Pacific. A rare wreck from a new war. But this one is ours. The small duffel bag in the cockpit: the picture of the family. Shredded? God knows. Perhaps someday we'll visit.

There will be time. There will be all the time in the world. After these last few yards.

At last, feet find the submerged sand. Not quite shallow enough to stand, not with the low waves, but a few more tired strokes and there we are, wading ashore, tired and over-encumbered, not quite MacArthur in the Philippines. No: an untriumphant slow soggy slog. Survival, not victory.

Across the wave-lapped bit of beach, and at last, dry sand. Time to strip off the soaked pressure suit. An awkward unzipping with the self-egress lanyard. Nobody in sight. Bile rising in stomach. Where is everyone?

Perhaps this was a mistake.

(CONTINUED)

Our Friday starts slowly enough: meal packets, instant coffee. Chatting and floating. We're a little less anxious today about the damage to the spaceplane, the long wait for the Gemini, and the reassurance of having a ride home on hand. After a good night's sleep, all problems seem solvable.

Morning: maintenance. Taking apart the lungs of the spacecraft, checking for leaks in the system, replacing the filters, ensuring that the new lithium hydroxide canisters are correctly seated. CO_2 levels have been slightly high; the air feels thick, headache-inducing.

Coming up on Vandenberg, with the work half-done: "Watchman, we…uhh, brought Falcon-2's family in to say hello this fine Friday. Over."

There has been a tacit acceptance of the unauthorized radio communications, but here it seems they are eager to provide an approved alternative, rather than risking us discussing an incident that's presumably highly classified.

A shuffling noise, a familiar voice. "Honey, we…uhh…got your telegram. Our liaison officer said we could talk to you directly. Over."

"Well that's…quite a relief. It was starting to feel pretty lonely up here, wondering if anyone was going to respond. Over."

"We heard they're changing your mission schedule a little. Over."

"We are probably nudging it a little bit, in the interests of…mission safety. Over."

"There were wild stories in the news this week. The Soviets claimed they were attacked by...space pirates. Our family liaison keeps saying it has nothing to do with you, though." A pause, then: "Is that true? Over."

How to respond? A smile, invisible. "Rest assured, I am not a space pirate. I don't even have an eye patch."

•••

On we wind around the globe. Our last lazy workday before the time shift: come Monday we'll be back on the DORIAN console, watching the Soviet Union one soda-straw-sized slice at a time, trying to pretend things are normal.

And yet there are worse things than routine. We reassemble the filtration system, breathe in relief as it whirs back to life. The unspoken fear: if it had broken down, and the station became unlivable, we wouldn't both be able to leave.

We have time for a breather. Time to gaze on the completed job with satisfaction, like God on the Seventh Day.

"It is amazing, isn't it?"

"What?"

"How much work it takes. Keeping us alive up here."

"You gotta wonder if there's any other place where it *wouldn't* take work. I mean, what are the odds? All the right gasses, all the right percentages. Same temperature, same pressure..."

"If there is...we're not getting there in our lifetime."

"Probably not. I want to go to the moon, but…it's never gonna be a place where you can take off your helmet and relax. Which…same goes for anywhere else in the Solar System. We can explore all we want. But we'll have to come back home eventually."

"And we're not gonna meet anyone when we get there."

"Well, that's an open question."

"Anyone like us, at least."

"That is the amazing thing…all these TV shows. You see people landing on some…faraway planet, and everyone's walking around without a helmet. If we did ever meet honest-to-God aliens, the chances we'd even be able to share the same environment are…" (Pause to ponder.) "But you never know…could be their environment's better for us than their own. Or vice versa."

"Better how?"

"Lower gravity…fewer UV rays…narrower temperature ranges…"

"Like how white people must've felt when they first went to California." A chuckle. "That could be worse. It's hard enough when it happens on our planet."

"How do you mean?"

"You know, just…invasive species, or whatever. Chicago…they opened up the Saint Lawrence Seaway in the 50s. Sounded great for commerce, but guess what? The Great Lakes had been isolated from the world's waters since the Ice Age. So all of the sudden you had alien fish, fish that had never been native, coming in. Like the alewives...they just took over the lake. Then they had a huge die-off, a couple years ago. Just...rotting fish everywhere on the shore. Or...Australia. Rabbits in Australia. They didn't have as many predators as they had elsewhere, the seasons weren't as extreme...the population just exploded. Huge problem."

"Or...colonists coming to the New World."

"I guess that's one way to look at it."

Below us, the western Soviet Union slumbers in silence. Pale streetlights of winter cities sliding by in the moonlight.

•••

Over Alaska, descending in darkness, we release the bucket. We cannot see it but there is a soft metal shudder as it ejects. And then behind us, a bright meteor chasing us, falling behind as we fly towards daylight.

It is almost a full rev later when we hear the news: "Watchman, Thule. Please switch to secure channel. Over."

Flip the switches. "Thule, Watchman. Talking secure. Go ahead, over.

"Watchman, be advised there was a...hostile incident in the bucket recovery area. Over."

"Say again, Thule." As if we hadn't heard.

"Watchman, they apparently sent a flight of Bear bombers for...reconnaissance, or something. Flew them from...must've been Kamchatka, right at the limit of their range. We intercepted the flight, attempted to turn them away from the recovery zone. Apparently there was a shootdown incident. Over."

"Thule, you said shootdown? Over."

"Watchman, that is correct. No further details at this time. Over."

"Well, did they get the bucket, at least?"

"Watchman, no further details at this time."

We float in uncomfortable silence.

•••

On the next rev, we are heating up hot dogs and watching the Northern Lights when the call comes. "Watchman, Thule, calling secure. Over."

We had been hoping, perhaps stupidly, that we would still get a leisurely Friday evening, but the tone of the call confirms that this won't be the case. "Thule, Watchman. Go ahead. Over."

"Watchman, we have some details on the bucket recovery incident. Apparently we splashed both Bears. USS *Enterprise* is conducting recovery operations in the area. Over."

"Thule, any indication if this is a prelude to wider hostilities? Over."

"Watchman, funny you should mention that. You...uhh, might be in a position to know a little better than us. Cheyenne wants you to power up your DORIAN console this evening and make some observations. Weather reports are...not terrible for this time of year. You...uhh, should be able to get obliques this pass of the Soviet naval air base at Sharomy, where this flight most likely originated. Also possibly Burevestnik in the southern Kurils. Over."

We trade disappointed glances. So much for the five o'clock whistle. "Uhh, Thule, we aren't going to be able to get this imagery down in a timely fashion. Over."

"Copy, Watchman. Cheyenne says this is an emergency contingency. They would like you to get imagery on one of the test rolls. Develop and interpret it up there. We...understand you've done that before. Over."

Our commander: "We're going to have to hustle to pull that off. Over."

"Understood, Watchman. We'll leave you to it. Thule out."

The hot dogs float forgotten as we spring into action, rushing through the sequence to pressurize the chamber and swap out the film. Memories of summer, the contingency plan: not quite the same. Or is it worse?

Finally coming out of the night we are on the scopes for the descending pass, peering across the snowy Kamchatka peninsula through light clouds, wondering: If they're planning anything, would we be able to tell? Then: snippets of the Kurils, working the spotting scope and swiveling to find the bare-bones runway at Burevestnik.

Only after that, heading back over the open Pacific, do we relax, ease back from the console, and float back in to the living room. Our hot dogs have grown tepid with the wait.

●●●

An anxious loop around the globe—calling down to Pine Gap as the hot orange Australian Outback sweeps smoothly past, briefly glimpsing the dazzling array of Antarctic ice guarding the coast of the southern continent, sliding across the terminator onto the dark side of the planet—and then we are swooping upwards across the North Atlantic in the early evening winter dark. Clouds and blackness below. "Watchman, Loring, calling secure. Over."

"Go ahead, Loring."

"Watchman, we've been eager to contact you. Be advised we are at DEFCON-2. Over."

Disappointed head shakes as we absorb the news. "Loring, we copy DEFCON-2. Anything else you're eager to tell us? Over."

"Watchman, we're busy here. They're scrambling bombers. The president is set to address the nation in an hour. I was...uhhh...actually hoping you might know something. Over."

"Loring, they should have already told you about the shootdown. We don't know much more than that. Not sure what else you'd want to know. Over."

"Watchman, uhhh...I can see your EWO console is on. You...uhh...haven't received orders yet, have you?" There's a tentativeness to the question that suggests the asker knows it's out of bounds. "I...uhh...called my wife on break half an hour before acquisition and...well, she can hear the bombers taking off. She's no idiot, she knows something's going on. We've talked about if there was a war. Now she's thinking about...packing up the car, taking the kids. I mean, we're...fifteen minutes from the Canadian border, there's a lot of empty New Brunswick forest after that that. Podunk towns a few hours away that probably aren't on Ivan's target list. So depending on the winds, depending on the fallout... But it's...the weather isn't great, there's a storm coming in. So I don't know what to tell her. I know we haven't transmitted any orders, but...I know you'd probably be getting them from Thule anyway. Over."

A glance over at the Emergency War Order console. The mute teletype, the silent klaxon. "Loring, we're...not sure what we can tell you. Over."

"Anything you can, Watchman." (An undercurrent of anxiety. Unprofessional, but relatable.) "Anything you can. Over."

"Loring...we've been told to take extra pictures. But that's it. Over."

"Appreciate it, Watchman. Loring out."

On this ascending node, the acquisitions line up; the invisible circles of line-of-sight radio coverage are practically touching. So: within a few seconds of flying out of Loring's coverage, far above the invisible empty Labrador coast, we are in range of our Greenland station, our most frequent contact with Planet Earth.

"Thule, this is Watchman, calling secure. Over." Anxious now ourselves. Emotions transmitted from a junior officer at a lonely SAC base in the Maine woods, relayed back down to the next station.

"Watchman, Thule. Glad to talk to you again on this fine winter evening. Over."

"Thule, understand we are now at DEFCON-2. Over."

"Watchman, that is correct. Over."

"Thule, is anything happening...operationally? Over."

"Watchman, the weather's bad but...well, everything's in the air. Over."

"Thule...there aren't...uhh...further orders, are there? Over."

"Cheyenne does want some more pictures. The SS-11 site at Svobodny, the strategic air base at Seryshevo..."

An anxious glance towards the silent console. After all the drills, the conditioning: so easy to imagine it springing to life. "Thule, did Cheyenne say anything else? Over."

"Watchman, we have no further information at this time. Over."

•••

Over daylit Siberia now, a jarring low morning on what, to our bodies, feels like Friday night. Binders prepared, targets circled in grease pencil on the transparencies.

"You wanna spot or shoot?"

"Shoot." Our commander is already taking up position at that console; he nods toward it. "Of course."

"You shot the last pass."

A smile: "I'm good at it." Then: "You wanna flip for it?" He produces a MacArthur dollar. Smiles again. Shows the other side, the second head.

"Didn't expect to see that up here."

"Some traditions refuse to die. Despite your best efforts."

We settle in at the console. Scrolling through slices of snowy Siberia to see: what? "Not sure how much time we wanna spend on Svobodny."

"How do you mean?"

"The sites are close together. Seryshevo, there may be empty revetments if they've got...planes in the air heading for Japan. But Svobodny...the SS-11...there might not be much to see. If we wait too long to switch over..."

"All right. Well, look at the approaches. Let's come up with a plan." He puts his head back to his scope.

A glance away to look again at the approach map, analyzing again the scant landmarks. "It looks like we can..."

Everything goes white.

Even without eyes on the scope, even looking away from the living room window, the flash is blinding: all shapes etched in light for one impossible moment. Then: nothing.

"Jesus, what the hell was that?" Blinking against pain.

"Oh my God."

"Was that a nuke?"

"Oh my God."

"That had to be a nuke."

In the sense-confusion chaos it takes a moment to take stock: sight gone, sounds...fading out?

"I think I'm..." Our commander's voice, touched with fear. "I can't...my eyes are..."

Deep breath. "Maybe it's...flash-blindness, or something..."

"My eyes were on the scope."

"But the sounds are fading, like..."

"Your voice is fine, it's...I'm just...my eyes were on the scope." A horror in his voice now.

"It's...it's gonna be OK." Still the background noises are turning down, down, down. Still no sight. "It sounds like we've lost power."

"Where are you?"

Blind hands towards the disembodied voice. A reassuring clasp of the shoulders. "Right here. Right here."

Sight slowly returns. For one of us.

There are no lights on in the station interior, no gauges, nothing except a blue ocean glow—the Yellow Sea, maybe?—diffused now through the station, and in it, our commander's face: a mask of pain, fluid pooling strangely in his empty eye sockets.

A gasp of shock.

His hand moves towards his face.

"Don't! Don't touch it..."

"Is it..."

"It's..." (Speechless.)

"We're...we should probably call this in."

"Well...obviously, but...first things first. You're..."

"I'm..."

"Are you in pain?"

"There's..." A deep sigh. Stress in his voice. "Yeah. I'm not sure how much we can do about it, but..."

"There's gotta be something in the medical locker."

"I don't know what's in there but...aspirin and antibiotics and gauze."

"There's more than that." Float over to the medical locker. Flip through the slender binder. "Demerol. We've got...three injectors of Demerol." Try to read the impossible fine print. Float back towards our commander. "Here, let's..." Find the vein in his arm. Tentatively jab the needle, reluctant to cause more pain. Depress the plunger: "There you go."

"OK, that's..." A softening. "What else is in there?"

Another glance through the contents. Eye drops. Not even worth joking about. Various other meds: Darvon, Seconal, tetracycline, ampicillin. Skin cream and ointment and band-aids and gauze. "We'll get some gauze on your eyes."

"OK."

Below now, Western Australia, rugged rusty brown angling out into the ocean. No time to sightsee. Gently we place the gauze pads into position, secure them with loops of medical tape around our companion's head.

The world scrolls by below, unaware.

●●●

Over Antarctica now. The jagged icy mountains slide by below, brighter by contrast with the dead station interior.

Thinking out loud. "We're gonna be dark soon."

Our masked commander's lips curl: a tight smile. "You are."

"The flashlights are…"

"Somewhere. Sorry I can't…" On his face, beadlets of sweat.

"How are you feeling? Is that kicking in?"

"Yeah, it's…better."

The flashlights: clipped on the side of the storage locker. Both working. Everyone's been doing the end-of-shift inspections: thank God.

The end of Antarctica—high above the Weddell Sea, ice shelf flaking at the edges in the southern summer. The rocky snowy islands of the Antarctic Peninsula strewn across our flight path. Then: darkness.

With the flashlights floating suspended in the air and carefully positioned above both shoulders it is possible to work at the breaker panel. Several of the push-pull buttons have been tripped, but when we reset them, nothing happens.

To our commander: "The fuel cells aren't coming back on."

"That's...too bad." His tone: an opioid dream. We'll have to fix this without him.

Page through the binder, scan the typewritten page headers in the hazy ovals of light to find the startup sequence for the fuel cells. Push the breakers to get battery power going to the panel. The indicator lights come on: a small victory. Voltage and amperage good. Again the fuel cell breakers: nothing. We should hear pumps starting up to push reactants through the stack, but they remain silent. And then the panel breaker trips and the indicators go back off.

A glance back at our commander, dimly visible in the flashlight backscatter. He is calmly floating, sweating just a little, bent slightly at the waist.

"Are you OK?"

"Yeah. Much better. I'm..." A reluctant vomit convulsion.

"Oh, shit." A scramble to get out of the way. Flashlights sent spinning. Chaos and confusion, lights slashing through the darkness, small bile globules spreading outwards, awful scent everywhere.

"Sorry about that. It does still feel...pretty good."

"Well...that's great." What is there to do? Grab for the closest flashlight, track down a washcloth to clean the floating catastrophe.

"Do you think they're gonna miss us?"

"What kinda question is that?" Cloth in hand, ready to clean. "We're gonna get back."

"You can fly. I can't fly."

"They'll send the Gemini." Back to the panel. Where the vomit has struck, it clings—no gravity to make it drip. "They'll send it for you instead of me. It'll be fine."

"They're gonna miss us. Loring's gonna miss us."

"Loring." Adjust the flashlight. Clean another vomit patch. "Loring."

"That guy sounded worried. The one that was thinking about...driving. We're already...missing comms windows, probably."

And it is true. Antigua, Cape Canaveral...are they calling us while we're offline? What will they do if they can't get ahold of us? Call in to Cheyenne? And what will *they* do if they don't hear from us? Or, for that matter, if they do—if they figure out we were attacked?

Quick glance towards the living room window. Not much visible in the darkness: peaceful moonlit cloudtops, sleeping ocean. If it starts, will we see anything?

A twinge of the stomach: are we going to add to the sickness? It does feel that way. Everything is awful, everything smells horrid. But: time to choke it down and work.

Back to the panel at last. Scan every breaker, make sure everything is pulled. Then push the panel breaker again. Again the blessed indicator lights.

Narrating: "Gonna turn on the interior lights."

"I have no objection."

Push in the breakers and everything's illuminated: a sad echo of what it was.

The nausea rises, or rather radiates outward. Then comes a quaking convulsion. More mess.

Our commander asks: "Are you OK?"

"Yeah, uh…no, there's…some nausea. The smell maybe…"

Some more quick cleaning. Then: push in the breakers for the radio.

"Loring, this is Watchman. Loring, this is Watchman. Come in. Over."

Breathe and wait, anxious. Choking down another convulsion.

"Watchman, Loring." The voice is distant and clear, the same young duty officer from last time. "Go ahead. Over."

"Loring, we had a NUCFLASH incident on our last Soviet pass. North of the Soviet airfield at Seryshevo. One crewmember Whiskey-India-Alpha with…severe eye injuries. Over."

Confused pause. "Watchman, Loring, I'm sorry. Did you say NUCFLASH? Over."

"Loring, that is correct. It was a nuclear weapon of some sort, detonated...some distance below us while we were on-scope. Over."

"Watchman, you're saying it was a deliberate attack? Over."

Long pause. "That's correct. We had EMP effects on the station. Everything..." (Awful feeling.) "...went out. We are running..." (More stomach badness.) "...reduced systems on battery power. One crewmember is..." It comes. More vomit. Violent disgusting noises.

"Watchman, this...are you getting sick? Over."

"Uhhh...affirmative, Watchman...uhh, excuse me. Loring. We...uhhh...administered Demerol to the station commander, and he became nauseous. And there's been a...ripple effect. Over."

"Watchman, are you sure it's not ARS? Over."

"Say again, Loring."

"ARS. Acute Radiation Sickness. I mean, all I know is...bits and pieces from some book I read. But...if you...uhh, you probably absorbed radiation from the blast. Depending on the dose, you could be getting pretty sick. Over."

"Well that's...fantastic."

"Watchman, I will...uhh, we could patch you through to Cheyenne, but...we're almost at LOS. I'll need to call this in myself. I mean, assuming you'll talk to them via Thule, but...they'll probably want to know sooner. For...decision-making purposes." Infinite heaviness to the words. "Over."

"Copy, Loring." Then: "You may want to call your wife first. Over."

A long pause. "Understood, Watchman. Loring out."

●●●

Five minutes later we are explaining everything again to Thule, the story we'll be repeating for the rest of our lives, however short.

They interrupt us midway through: "Watchman, we're...uh, getting a call on the alert phone. Over."

Anxious break. Floating in space you cannot pace, cannot do much to outrace the nervous energy.

Then: "Watchman, Cheyenne wants us to confirm that you have your Emergency War Order console turned on. Over."

A glance at our opioid-addled blind commander. "Cheyenne...uhh, Thule. We have a crewmember that's blind and...under the influence of narcotics. We're running on batteries, and we're both sick. Not sure how...useful we'll be in a war. Over."

"Uhhh...copy, Watchman. We'll have to...uhh, hold one...we'll patch you through to them directly. Over."

Again the awful wait. Racing towards LOS. It can't come soon enough.

Then, a familiar voice, distant and crackly, but clear enough: "Watchman, this is Cheyenne, speaking on relay. Over."

"Cheyenne, Watchman. Go ahead. Over."

"Watchman, you are hereby ordered to turn on your Emergency War Order console and await instructions. Please acknowledge. Over."

Fist punches fist in frustration. "Uhh, Cheyenne, we...we need to get the fuel cells going, and..."

An edge of anger, barely perceptible. "Watchman, we'll deal with that later. In the meantime you are hereby ordered to turn on your Emergency War Order console and await instructions. Please acknowledge. Over."

Our commander speaks. "Cheyenne, uhhh..." (A weary ill face. Voice somewhat more lucid now.) "...we copy. We'll power up the console." He gives a nod.

Push in the breakers. "Aaand...console is powered up. Over."

"Copy, Watchman. We will have further..." And the radio does, at last, crackle into silence.

"What's our...uhhh...next comms window?" Our commander sounds weary and still ill. But in charge.

"We do have the coverage gap now. It'll be...Siberia, Mongolia, China on the descending node. Thailand or Burma maybe. Indian Ocean, far west of Australia. Then west of South America on the way back up. We probably won't have comms again until CONUS."

"So. Cheyenne Mountain, direct."

"Yeah. If they're trying to have us hit...Moscow or something, it'll still be a few revs. Hours from now. If somebody launches, it could all be over by then anyway."

"We don't know where they've tasked us."

Long pause. "No, we don't. But even so, we're...I mean, we're on batteries here, I don't know if we're even...you obviously can't confirm a launch order. Can you even turn a key?"

A reluctant wait. Then: "I can turn a key."

● ● ●

Around the globe again. Work to turn the environmental control systems back on. Try without luck to restart the fuel cells once more, while our commander makes suggestions blindly between waves of recurring pain. We try to restart the system all at once, and it doesn't work; we try to start it piecemeal, one cooling pump and reactant valve at a time. And: nothing.

"The controllers must be fried," our commander says wearily. "Or the stack got too hot when the pumps went out."

"So, what...batteries?"

"Batteries."

"That'll only keep us going for a few days."

"Yeah."

"The Gemini...they won't have anything on the pad by then."

"No, probably not." A blind grimace. "You've got a ride home, at least."

"If the other X-20 powers up. We had EMP effects, so...who knows?"

"You've got a ride home."

"If they send up a war order this rev, are we gonna…"

"It's…we are…they may be relying on us."

"Well. But still…there's going to be others in…your condition. Beyond the dead, there's gonna be…" The unspoken question: Can you do this to someone else?

"We're…we're a part of this system already."

"You're talking abstractions. This is real now. We are in control of this part of the system. If we don't participate…"

Our commander says nothing. Just floats and thinks. Then: "They might be relying on us."

•••

Again the bright Antarctic. Again the plunge into night. It is late in our workday, almost 2200 hours, a time we'd normally be winding down. But of course there is nothing close to normal about the day.

"How are you feeling?"

"Bit of a headache."

"Do you need another shot?"

"How many more do we have?"

"Two more."

"Let's hold off."

"You're sure?"

"I want a clear head. For whatever's coming."

"OK."

Outside, an incomplete darkness: the moon is out, and the ocean is soft and silver on the ageless Pacific. Everything looks exactly as it must have looked a thousand years ago, when there was no one up here to see it.

But we are not alone. And we are not observers.

At last, the lights of civilization. Lonely distant clusters like campfires on a darkened shore. Mexico, east of Acapulco, the part of the coast that looks southward to nothing.

"We'll be in range of Cheyenne in…probably a minute. We'll have to decide what to say."

"We'll…see what they say first."

"OK."

A few last moments of blessed silence. And then: a klaxon, shrill and real and heartbeat-inducing, accompanied by a swirling tower light. A demon-fevered slot machine announcing a jackpot nobody wants.

The teletype clatters. The teletype is silent.

Our commander: "Was that what I think it was?"

"It was." Float over: a Red Dot 4 message. A summons. "Are we going to do this?"

Distant radio voice: "Watchman, this is Cheyenne. Please set your scramblers. Over."

Our commander: "We should open the safe, at least."

Again the radio. "Watchman, Cheyenne. Please set scramblers. Over."

To our commander: "What's your combination?"

"3-4-6. You should probably set the scramblers, too."

We open his lock—3-4-6—and then our own—2-1-3. Inside, the plastic cases containing the operational instructions. When the safe is opened, the next step is to find and break open the plastic case corresponding to the numeric sequence on the teletype. Inside is a piece of paper. A cookie with a fortune, although this one's predicting a highly specific future to people who won't ever get to read it.

"Watchman, Cheyenne, please come in. Over."

Our commander: "Let's at least respond, shall we?"

At last, the scramblers: "Cheyenne, this is Watchman. Calling secure. Over."

"Watchman, Cheyenne, please acknowledge receipt of Emergency War Order. Over."

Our own voice sounds like a distant dream. "Cheyenne, Watchman. Receipt acknowledged. Over."

The paper simply says:

TARGET LIST: 1

DEPLOYMENT SEQUENCE: 4

CONSOLE CODE: 629973

The bottom of the teletype message says KEY TURN NLT 0800 GMT. Midnight on our workday. Two hours away. There will be time to call down to home. If they're listening.

• • •

Program in the target list and launch sequence. Narrating, for our commander's benefit, the end of the world.

"What does it look like out there?" he asks wearily.

"Peaceful." Arctic darkness over the Taimyr Peninsula, a place we'll never see again. No indications that this is anything but a normal night. We pass over the terminator, and now in the low winter sun the long fjordlike lakes of the Putorana Plateau are visible, slender and icy, nestled in the crooked crevasses of the highlands. Desolate and glorious.

"Do you want to turn the keys now?"

"Why?"

"Get it over with."

"Do you think we're the only ones who got a message?"

"Why would we be the only ones?"

"If this is a...decapitation strike. Or something."

"We can't be the only ones. We were just hit, they wouldn't..."

"What if we are?"

"Then they're really relying on us."

"Let's...call down to Vandenberg first. We have time before the key turn."

"Call the base?"

"Call our families."

The unauthorized communications: never officially acknowledged, never officially sanctioned, never punished.

"You're wanna do that from here?"

"From your X-20. The single sideband."

"Well. You'll get to see if the plane works, at least."

"There is that."

Southward around the earth. Snowy Siberian forests, the cold deserts of central Asia, the high Himalayas, and abruptly, warmth: India, the Ganges plain green and lush before the higher hills to the south. What is there to do? Nothing significant. Inventory the medical locker: what will be left for our commander, once we leave? (18 capsules of Darvon, for when the Demerol runs out.) Use the bathroom over Antarctica. Kill time before...well...

Floating in the X-20 now, the good one. Everything imperceptibly different. After the issues with the station itself, the fuel cell stacks, it seems impossible that it will power up properly. But it does.

Flying backwards over Pacific darkness, the soft moonlit night, the ancient empty ocean that looks the same as it did before civilization, and will probably look the same after. The past receding before us.

At last it is time to call down:

"Kilo-Niner-Yankee-Tango-Yankee, Kilo-Seven-Tango-Romeo -Victor. Do you read, over."

No response.

"Kilo-Niner-Yankee-Tango-Yankee, this is Kilo-Seven-Tango- Romeo-Victor. Please come in, over."

Nothing.

The coast of California crawls past slowly, the electric glory of a million streetlights, a vast mottled pool of coastal light seeping upward into the hills and canyons, and north along the coast, thinning out and then swelling into larger pockets: Oxnard, Ventura, Santa Barbara, Vandenberg.

Did they leave already, when they saw the news? What was on the news—enough to make them leave? "Kilo-Niner- Yankee-Tango-Yankee, this is…"

Somewhere in the distance, a flash. And another. And then: bright meteor streaks.

Eyes closed against the stabbing panic, the swelling horror. But the flashes beneath are bright enough, even through closed eyelids, to know with awful certainty what is happening.

Float back up through the spindle, careful to avoid the windows. Nausea returning.

"It's started."

A grim nod. "Do you want to go ahead and do the key turn?"

If we want to launch, go to page 638.

If not, go to page 640.

(CONTINUED)

"I guess we have to, don't we?" Does it matter, at this point? Maybe not.

We have closed the shade over the living room window. We have helped our commander remove the key from around his neck. We have guided him towards his console.

"Console code: Six-Two-Niner-Niner-Seven-Three."

"I'll take your word for it."

"Key inserted." Guide his hand to the nub of brass.

His echo: "Key inserted."

Float back to the other console. "And countdown to key turn. Three-two-one...and turn."

The spring loaded mechanism resists the gentlest bit, just a tiny bit more than the training device.

"And hold...two...three...four...five." Plus a few extra seconds. Just to make sure.

Nothing has happened. Nothing substantial. But the correct indicator lights are on now.

"And release."

"Nothing happened."

No point troubleshooting the console. If it is supposed to happen, it will happen.

"That's a...helluva convincing training exercise they dreamed up."

"If this was a training exercise…" Grim head shake. If only.

Float off to the bathroom for a much-needed break. And then, about ten minutes after the key turn, comes a sad little shudder, a quick vibration of the station.

Then another.

Then another.

Then another.

Then another.

Then another.

Then another.

Then another.

Then another.

Then another.

We have done our part.

Put on blast goggles and open the shades back up and watch through tinted eyewear as the world ends. Flash after flash after flash.

The lights go out. (Again.) The sounds die down. (Again.)

And now there is nothing to do but await instructions.

Let's go to page 707.

(CONTINUED)

Close the living room shade. Ignore the world outside. Float and wait. Float and wait. Watch the watch hands tick endlessly upwards. Past the time on our war order. It is easy for a few moments to imagine nothing is happening. Everything inside is relatively normal.

But curiosity is too strong.

Blast goggles on. Open the shade.

Far below: flash after flash after flash. How guilty are we in this? The end of the world, happening without our consent or participation. Does it matter that we held back in the end? Will anyone know, or care?

We are a part of this, whether we want to admit it or not. We are part of the system, part of the whole, part of the "we." What the system has done, we have done.

The lights go out, again. The noises fade, again.

Nothing to do but await instructions.

Let's go to page 707.

How did we get here?

Coming out of the last roll reversal at 10,000 feet, the northern end of the Central Valley far below: streambeds accumulating water from the mountains, dark creases in the drab earth leading down to fields and towns. Scanning the roads for signs of life. Hoping and hoping and hoping.

Silence in the helmet. No sense calling down. No sense doing anything but picking the best spot. Coastal mountains to the right, Eureka beyond, but for now just the simple task: bring this final flight to a successful close. If anything constitutes success any more.

This was a mistake, coming down on this side of the mountains. A split-second decision, borne of worry about the rugged terrain: too much caution, perhaps.

Gliding down towards the valley. Beyond the next town there is something that could be a runway. But it seems just a touch too far. Off to the left, the relatively straight and relatively wide pencil-line of asphalt must be Interstate-5. Worth setting down on? That was, after all, the point of steering towards this side of the mountains. But now in the moment, it seems risky. Plus: on the road ahead, a congregated clot: gleaming dots of shiny paint. A traffic jam? Tough to tell.

Ejection it is.

Check the velcro on the pressure suit pocket, the pocket with the picture. No more time to think about it: nothing but the question. The altimeter silently unwinds. From somewhere comes the question, like Chubby Checker MCing a demented round of limbo: How low can you go?

Then again: no point in waiting. Buttocks clenched, back pressed in seat, spine straight. Pull the yellow-and-black rope handle and GO!

A violent blast upwards on a pillar of fire and now the spacecraft is falling away, top hatch fluttering to the side, arcing off in a gentle bank, and there comes two brief seconds of worry about the parachute, but there it is, the risers pulling taut, the sound of the *whoomp* as it catches air, the ejection seat falling away, and above, the most glorious sight, a full canopy, silent in the winter sun.

And now: hanging suspended in the parachute. Pressure-suit-protected from the elements, minus the cool puffs of air through the anti-suff valve. Borne on the wind, drifting west of the interstate. Surveying the alien terrain. Dead grass and distant mountains.

Below and a few miles ahead, the X-20 crashes, a tiny violent puff of dirt.

And now it is...is peaceful the right word? It is empty. On the interstate the clot of cars is visible, a swollen mass spilling off both sides of the road and into the opposite lanes: a massive wreck. No people, there or elsewhere.

Drifting down onto a grassy hillside, a mile or so off the highway. A few bushes and shrubs. Not much.

The ground rises. No way to avoid it. An end to flight.

Watch the trees and grass, trying to gauge the wind. Pull on the risers to land into it. Then comes the rush, and: feetcalvesthighbuttocks and then turning, rolling, legs arcing through the air before coming down again on the other side, a perfect parachute landing fall.

For a few brief seconds it is still clear what to do, the simple immediate tasks trained to Pavlovian perfection: pull at the Koch fittings so the chute doesn't drag, release both risers, grab the parachute and windmill it up in the arms so it's collected and:

There is no one. No one to present it to, no one watching the conclusion of the exercise. (Although perhaps the exercise is not concluded. Next: Survival, Escape, Rescue, Evasion? Survival, at least.)

Slide the visor up. Unlock the helmet. Feel at last the chill of the winter air. Blessed California, not cold cold even this far north.

A lightheaded feeling: the heaviness of everything. Too long in space. Sit for several minutes to rest. Then: an awkward trudge downhill, east towards the interstate, parachute awkwardly under one arm, helmet in other hand, stopping as needed to rest, and wondering:

Where is everyone?

• • •

Still no traffic, and the southbound lanes seem somewhat clear. Cautiously cross them to get a closer look at the first accident on the other side: a station wagon rear-ended by a WV Beetle. What is it about wreckage that's so compelling?

No bodies, thank God. Both cars moved off to the shoulder and abandoned, undriveable. Nothing inside either vehicle that wasn't put there by the manufacturers, save a couple napkins and drinking straw wrappers. In the dirt next to the shoulder, the dim outline of footprints headed the same direction the cars had been going: north.

A look back across the desolate interstate. Dead calm, the other side still empty, a long straight stretch of smooth new asphalt, better than some runways. Still, it would have been a risky landing. Surely it would have been better to come down on the other side of the mountains. Every parachute landing is a gamble, and the rougher the terrain, the worse the risk. But surely it would have been better.

Switch helmet and parachute, to balance out the discomfort. Trudge north. Decide it is perhaps wiser to wear the helmet: warmth against the chill. Put it back on.

Then over a slight rise to: the big one.

It is visible in the distance about a half mile away; it comes into view slowly, a muted metal mosaic, red and green and blue and brown and white, Chevys and Fords and Chryslers and a smattering of Volkswagens, sedans and station wagons and sports cars: cars smashed together, hoods and trunks crumpled and windshields shattered; cars barely touching, upright and scarcely dinged but trapped in the center; two upside-down on the eastern side, another inverted on the west; a few on their sides, wedged in between upright cars by impacts from behind; one fire-blackened spot. There are burnt-out husks of road flares littering the asphalt leading up to the spot, and a couple orange-and-white construction sawhorses placed a few dozen yards downstream, presumably to keep new drivers from adding to the pile. An ugly mass of broken glass and twisted metal, mass-produced Detroit muscle mashed together in rural California, all these cars unique now, at last.

One in the middle looks familiar.

Set down helmet and parachute and scramble onto a crumpled trunk, still careful—absurdly, perhaps—not to snag the pressure suit on a torn piece of metal. Walk reluctantly over roofs and hoods, feeling guilty as the metal dips and dimples underfoot. Eye the shattered windshields, cracks catching the bright sunlight.

No Department of Defense stickers visible. Crane to see the license plate: Nevada.

Behind, out of nowhere: a gunshot *brrrang!*

Jump down instinctively between two cars, less careful about the suit now. Crouch and turn to the source of the sound: a man in jeans and red flannel, rifle raised. "Hands in the air there, comrade!"

"Comrade?"

"Yeah, Ivan. Get 'em where I can see 'em."

Reluctantly raise gloved hands. "Are you…uhh…what seems to be the problem?"

"I want you to get your hands in the air and come out, you Commie bastard. That's what's the problem."

Put hands on the hood of the nearest car to get back up, and: *brrrang!*

"Hup." The rifleman gestures with the rifle like: hands back up.

Back up with the hands. "I can't climb out of here without..." A nod down at the nearest car. "And...uhh..." Turn slightly and dip one arm so he can see the flag patch on the pressure suit. "I'm an American."

The rifle wavers. "An American?"

"Yeah, I'm just...I just came down, and I saw this wreck, and I mean...who did you think I was?"

"One a them." The rifle drops at last; the face melts into contrition. "I'm sorry. I mean, we haven't seen any planes in days. I don't think any of ours are flying. So I figured...maybe they were...scouting things out for an invasion or something."

"I'm...speaking English."

"Well, that don't mean nothing. I mean, you seen those movies. They train them for this stuff. I was gonna ask one of those questions, like who was the Super Bowl MVP, or whatever."

"It's a good thing you didn't. I missed the Super Bowl." Clamber up onto the nearest hood, walk back over, a little more carelessly now.

"I...uhh...you should watch out."

"Well, I don't need the suit anymore, I..."

"No, I mean...some of them cars are radioactive."

"Radioactive?" Step tentatively back over hoods and roofs.

"Yeah. The wreck itself was...well, you're not from around here, are you?"

"I live down south a ways." Lived.

"But not from here in the valley? Not from Beale?"

"Not from the valley, no." Hop back down to *terra firma*. "Not from Beale."

"Yeah. Here in the valley, it's...you get that fog, fills up the whole valley..."

"Yeah, I could...uhh, I could see that."

"So that itself was...I mean, people get in a hurry, visibility drops...you get pileups even in normal situations. But here...the cops on the scene, they realized people was fleeing the fallout zone. Because they'd been stuck."

"Stuck?"

"Jeez, man. Where were you when all this happened? Outer space?"

A smile. Unclassified now, certainly. "Yeah. I was in outer space."

"You didn't have anything to do with all this, did you?"

"Well...it's complicated."

•••

Slow walk north. Rifle on the shoulder of the stranger. Wary, but talking like he needs someone to talk to.

"I mean, for a couple hours, nobody could drive. There was some weird electro-magnetic stuff going on…you'd get started, get on the road, then another one would pop off, all of the sudden your car's turned off, and it's coasting to halt. You could turn it back on, but still. So the day of the war it was hard to get anywhere. But these people…Bay Area, Sacramento, Beale had all been hit, so the next day, anyone east of those places was getting covered in fallout. And they musta realized things would be OK up here, there isn't much in the way of targets up this way. Probably all the way to Portland, just about. So these people…refugees from the fallout zone. Fallout all over their cars, some of 'em. And…well, all this happened."

"Wow." We cross a patch of grass to a frontage road.

"Yeah. I came out on accounta I got a wrecking business. County called me, said we needed to clear the highway. That was when the phones were still workin'. So I came out, took a look. Woulda been a pretty ordinary job. Big, but ordinary. But then I saw that fallout. I said I wasn't gonna do it unless we took care of that. I mean, they were climbing all over cars, tryin' to get people out, and some of these cars, just…dust all over, every crevasse. Well…luckily they already had a fire truck on the scene, out of Red Bluff, and they were just about to leave, but I said, 'Hey, you gotta stay. You gotta hose down the pile!' And they were like, 'The whole pile?' And I was like, 'Yeah, the whole pile.' I mean, it has to be safe enough for me to do my job, right? Which, you figure anyways, best of times it's gonna be a all-day affair. And that's with other wreckers maybe coming down from Redding. But they were busy up there. There was just a lotta wrecks. Foggy night, a lotta people driving late, driving distracted. Lotta people on the road. So it was already gonna be a multi-day thing. And then the topic of payment came up."

Lightheadedness strikes. "Sorry, gotta rest a sec." Stop, hunch down, look up: "Payment?"

"Well, yeah. I mean, I got to thinking, as I was waiting for them to hose things off, how much is money gonna be worth now, anyway? I mean, it's every man for himself now. I gotta look out for me! And I'm gonna clean up this radioactive pile of cars, with no protective equipment, no nothing, and they're gonna...cut a check? I mean, am I supposed to believe the California Department of Public Works is gonna cut a check? Sacramento's gone, man. And the branch office, in Redding, you think they're just gonna come into work the next day like nothing happened?"

"So what happened?"

"Well, there was a lot of refugees, all over on the road. And it was cold. And we'd been arguing, and the head state trooper, this asshole named Mackenzie, he was getting calls on his radio, but even that wasn't working great, the air was all futzed up, and these refugees, they decided they needed to get them somewhere. They commandeered some motel up in town, they were shuttling people up there, and even that wasn't gonna be enough. So Mackenzie calls everyone all around. All of us who were working. And he says, 'Obviously this ain't a normal situation. But we got a few families we need to find housing for. And we're all gonna have to do our part. We all gotta pull together here and be good Christians,' that's what Mackenzie said. And he handed me a family of raggedy-ass niggers."

This obviously seems a bit much. "Excuse me."

"Excuse you, what?"

"That word, it's…offensive."

The stranger spits. "Well, I'm sorry. I didn't mean to offend your…delicate sensibilities. Anyway, they gave me a group of…NEGROES. Just a raggedy little family. Piled in to the back of my tow truck, a bunch of dirty NEGROES. Huddled in the back, some of 'em getting' sick…not even dressed warm enough."

"Are you still…are you still taking care of them?"

"No, they…ahh…they had to move on." An ocean of silence.

We get up. Walk again down the long empty frontage road. Turn right and walk some more. "Well, where are the cops now? Where is everyone else?"

"Cops are down south. We're…I mean, we're trying to establish a perimeter, but you get stuff like this, people coming in, people dying of radiation sickness…I mean, we got farmland, we might be able to make a go of it, but not if we gotta take care of every damn refugee in the state. We gotta defend *our* homes."

"Is that where we're going now? Your home?"

"Unless you got someplace else to be."

"I need to get to Eureka at some point."

"Eureka? On the coast?"

"Yeah."

"Well, that's...a ways away."

"Over the mountains, right?"

"Over the mountains." Snort. "We're back in olden times. 'Over the mountains' means something again. It'll take a week to walk there, at least."

"How long of a drive?"

"Under normal conditions? Three-and-a-half-hour drive. *If* the weather's good."

"Guess I'll have to hitch a ride."

A snort. "Maybe you didn't notice this, but there's not too many people driving nowadays. Gas is good as gold, now."

•••

The walk is long and tedious; a couple more miles along an empty country road—trees and low golden hills, wooden poles and a lonely strand of power lines. We have to stop to rest, multiple times. It is not a natural feeling yet, gravity, walking; all is heavy and uncomfortable.

Then, at last, a white-painted farmhouse, like something out of Steinbeck. Gravel driveway leading back to a separate garage, tow truck parked in front of it, a strand of pines behind. Silent as a tomb, except for the creak of a windmill.

"You don't mind, I'm gonna hose you off," the stranger says.

"Hose?"

"Just make sure you didn't pick up any...fallout or whatever." There is a garden hose on the side of the house, coiled haphazardly like a Don't-Tread-On-Me snake. "My wife thought I was a moron for repairing the windmill a few years back. Said we were fine with an electric well pump. 'Nobody needs windmills anymore,' she said. Well, we haven't had power since the war. Now who's the moron?"

An anemic dribble of water from the hose. The stranger places a thumb over it but it still doesn't show much *oomph*. Each pressure-suited extremity goes under the water in turn, all lingering dust now washed away.

"You know what? We'll probably have you get out of that thing anyway." A nod towards the pressure suit.

"This?"

"How long were you planning on wearing it?"

"I...hadn't really thought that far ahead." Then: "You look like you're shorter than me. Do you have any clothes that'd fit?"

"There's some suitcases out back, in the garage. Think they got clothes in 'em."

The garage is a rickety clapboard thing, dusty and decrepit. Inside are four suitcases, stacked haphazardly, clothes sticking out. Strangely enough, there are in fact clothes that look like they will fit.

Egress from the pressure suit, one last time, keeping the long underwear on. Shiver in the chilly winter air looking down at the pressure suit, this miracle of cutting-edge technology now draped over a wooden workbench next to a dirty shovel. Put on a pair of jeans and underwear and a long-sleeve shirt from the suitcase. A creepy feeling.

Head inside, into the main house, through a clattering screen door and a wooden one badly in need of paint. Inside: clutter and chaos, unopened bills, dirty dishes. Scent of vomit. The stranger hasn't bothered with the lights; he's poured himself a bourbon and sat down in the TV chair, staring at the dead glass as if there's something on it.

A tentative question: "Where is your wife?"

He winces: this is a pain point. "They're…we're…they went away." No indication that any follow-up questions are welcome.

"Is there…uhh…anything to eat?"

"Hot dogs in the fridge. Pan in the cabinet. Help yourself. You're welcome to spend the night. Then in the morning, you can get on to wherever it is you're going."

"All right, then."

"I am gonna need that pressure suit, though."

"Excuse me?"

"Your pressure suit. I'm gonna need it."

"You're…gonna need it?

"You're not usin' it any more, correct?"

"Well, I mean, technically it's…government property."

He chuckles, shakes his head. "Tell you what. You gimme that pressure suit, we just might be able to get you a ride over to Eureka."

• • •

In the evening, pleasant dreams: eating bacon in space with General MacArthur, watching the world scroll by. Wake to: the new awful reality, the unfamiliar heaviness. A dusty farmhouse bedroom in northern California. A world that will never be the same.

It has rained in the night, and there is a chill fog outside. The stranger is not yet awake. Put on the clothes, the same strange clothes from yesterday. Wander downstairs and outside.

Beyond the garage: a pine woods, silent and forbidding. The carpet of needles is moist and supple. It is uncomfortable, walking into this strange place.

Ahead there is an area where the needles have been disturbed. It is a small area, about six feet by six feet, and the disturbance isn't great, but the pine needles are slightly clumped, and there are bits of yellow-brown soil on top.

Clear off a patch of soil, almost without thinking. Despite last night's rain it is still clumped as if someone has dug something recently.

Bend down, not wanting to. Scrape away a couple inches of dirt and there it is: the small black hand of a child.

"They were dying." The stranger's voice. Startling, too close.

Spin to see him standing there in long underwear, bleary-eyed, rifle in hand, not aimed but...menacing. What is there to say, in response? Nothing.

"It was...they had that radiation sickness. They'd driven straight through it. I don't know what all had happened in their car, how they were still on the road, but as soon as I got 'em in the back of the truck, they were throwing up, they were just...making all kinds of mess. It was..." He shudders. "It was hard for me! I couldn't deal with all that, all by myself."

What is there to say? Nothing.

The stranger breathes heavily, arms flexed with tension, rifle...still not exactly aimed, but more menacing. "Look. You show me how to put on the pressure suit, we get you on the road...you don't ever have to see me again."

•••

Back at the big wreck. Under the fog it looks ominous.

The stranger is in the pressure suit, moving clumsily; it is too big, but it fits his purposes. He attaches a metal hook on a cable to the frame of a toppled Buick, makes a motion like: stand back. The winch motor turns and the car falls, and soon it is out of the way.

Another car, a Mustang, has sustained damage; the right front tire's crumpled and bent inward. The stranger finds an attachment point, winches it sideways so it's more or less pointed at the spot made vacant by the toppled Buick. Then he pulls it out.

And now: a red Ford Galaxie, trunk only slightly crumpled, grille pushed in a little from hitting the Mustang, but barely damaged, somehow, amidst all the chaos.

Stare off disconnected as the stranger pulls it free. Once it is on the highway in front of the pile, he returns to his truck, grabs a flat-head screwdriver and a hammer, taps the screwdriver into the ignition, and turns it.

The car comes to life.

The stranger fumbles with the visor of the helmet and flips it up. "You're gonna want to head to 36. That'll get you up over the mountains, all the way to the coast, just about. Really pretty drive. Then you'll pick up the 101, in...Fortuna, I think. Maybe another fifteen miles."

Silent nod.

"Thank you for your service," the stranger says. Extends a hand. "You can keep the screwdriver."

Reluctantly we shake hands.

The car's front seat is uncomfortable. But it is a car. The gas gauge isn't full, but it's full enough.

Put the car in drive. Turn on the radio, curious. Nothing but static. Spin the knob. Still only static.

The feeling comes on, and it's an overwhelming feeling. Brake to a halt, right there on the empty interstate, and put the car in park. Open the door and vomit.

Wipe mouth. Hands on the steering wheel. In a murdered stranger's clothes. Look left across the golden grass, into the fog, beyond which lies the distant mountains.

Three and a half hours.

(CONTINUED)

The sights, the sensations, the trajectory: all are as familiar as an old friend. Weightless body rising against the straps.

Except this time there is no plunge into night at the end of the endless ocean. Instead: Antarctica, clear and bright in the season's light. The vast and empty Ross Ice Shelf, flaking at the edge. Patches of bare snow-swept stone, the flanks of the Transantarctic Mountains, miniscule at this altitude. The awesome lonely emptiness of East Antarctica, high and cold and devoid of life.

We have seen it all now; we have seen the whole world. We can say that, at least.

And then, above the horizon, there it is: the familiar bright speck. A reddish star we're chasing into darkness.

"Watchman, Falcon-2. Comm check. Over." A repeat performance, the same old lines.

Only this time there is no delay, just the familiar voice: "Falcon-2, Watchman, read you loud and clear. How was the ride, over?"

"Not much new, Watchman. May have roasted a pelican on launch, that's about it. Over."

"Sorry, Falcon-2, you said...a pelican? Over?"

"Affirmative, Watchman, he was perched on the nose, and then...fell off, or something. Maybe into the plume. Over."

"Well, we won't tell the nature lovers. Over."

Into night: the empty ocean, moonlit darkness, with silver-feathered clouds hovering over the waters. The Malagasy Republic rotates into view: milky-blue land and civilization, at last, a few scattered outposts on the shore, and one or two lonely blips of isolated light further inland.

Tananarive reads out instructions for the phasing burn. We fire up the transtage. Everything is achingly normal.

On goes the orbit: the Horn of Africa, paler at night than we remember. The Red Sea. Israel, a riot of light after everything before. Turkey, Black Sea, Soviet Union. And this time of year the darkness does not end yet, except with the shimmering green haze of the Northern Lights.

Thule radios up instructions for the approach burn, and soon we're executing it, approaching the station in Pacific daylight. Everything smoother than our memory: no pauses for photography, no—or less—angst about the approach. But the station of course looks different: still there is the slender metal tube, with the spindle and our companion's X-20 on one end. But on the other, beyond the telescope, fat and squat and ugly as a tumor: the orbital bombardment module.

•••

A smooth docking: ease onto the trapeze, and then the familiar metallic groans. Flipping switches, shutting down. And it is time to float up once more into our orbital home.

Familiar sensations: the odd scent of space, our companion pleased to see us. "No need for the grand tour, huh?" he says as we shake hands.

"No, I guess not."

He pushes out of the spindle feet-first and we follow, pulling ourselves through the hatch into the living room. Everything feels slightly smaller, slightly more run-down. Still it is something, being back. Floating free in the interior, watching the vast empty Pacific slide by so far below. It is something, isn't it?

"You gonna get your stuff?"

"In a sec. Just...gotta take it in again."

"Didn't think you were gonna make it back, huh?"

"It did seem doubtful for a minute there."

"We all felt that way at some point. Welcome back."

"It feels different this time."

"You're never the same person the second time you do something."

"It's weird."

"Probably better. They don't have...spy satellites chasing us around."

"You really think they're gonna leave us alone? Now?" A glance at the side of the storage locker: the deputy commander's launch key station has been bolted there since our last visit, with electrical conduit bracketed to the wall and leading towards another console, a few feet more than an armspan away at the lip of the observation module. Familiar objects, new spot.

Our companion shrugs. "Neubeck told me there was a new Zenit right after they brought the module up. It seems like the Russians wanted to rattle their swords a little. Rattle our cage. But the president...well, you know his views on the topic."

"Indeed." Hand to chest: reassurance that under all the garments, the key is in fact still there. A quick prayer that we won't have to use it. Then: open the chest pocket of the pressure suit. A new picture of the family. On the console it goes—as good a place as any. A good reminder of the stakes, if it does ever get to that point; a reminder of what we'll have to defend, or avenge.

•••

Again the next day, the familiar rituals: suiting up, checking every seal and lock, watching the umbilical snake writhe as the pressure gauge drops and we wait to float outside.

Open the hatch and float out. No sounds but breathing. A quick look around, scanning the horizon for an unfamiliar foreign light chasing us over the horizon. But: still nothing.

Our companion's voice in the headset: "Good to be back out there, huh?"

"It is something." Pause to look down at the bleak landscape of northern Quebec, snow-coated and distant under mostly clear skies. Uncountable glacier-carved white-frozen lakes, including one large one like a ring, like a target. "Back home, it felt like it had never happened. Like it was all a distant dream."

"Know what you mean."

"It's like, how much time do you have to spend up here to make the memories stick?"

"Gotta just enjoy it while we're here. Work slow and enjoy it."

"Yeah."

Loring comes on, to guide us through the start of the work. A young anxious capcom, new since last time.

It is all familiar. The task now is to not make any dumb mistakes out of boredom and contempt. But it all goes well enough. Working to get the latest film in the bucket. Stealing glances here and there at the unfamiliar earth, everything upside-down as we fly south. (Mid-Atlantic coast, rivers crooked and irregular, patterned like the veins of a leaf. The Bahamas and their countless blues. Cuba, mottled tan and green. Panama and the jagged little cut between the continents.) Looking up now and again to see if it's really true, if we're doing all this unobserved.

●●●

Soon we are back into the routine. Workdays over the Soviet Union, catching missile sites in daylight as the Russians hustle to deploy more. Near parity now, or so the rumors go.

"Watchman, Thule, calling secure. Over."

"Thule, Watchman. Go ahead. Over."

"Watchman, we have some late additions to your target list. We'd like you to photograph the airfield at Seryshevo on Pass 3. Over."

"Thule, we photographed Seryshevo last week. Any particular reason for the revisit? Over."

"Watchman, it looks like the Mushroom Factory spotted some new interceptor on the runways there. That...uhhh...that prototype they just started showing off at the airshows. Designed to shoot down the B-70. Can't recall the name. Over."

"Thule, that's...what is it? Yankee-Echo-One-Five-Five, maybe? Over."

"That's it, Watchman. It's the one they've been setting records with. Rumor has it they got one up to 100,000 feet. Over."

"Well until we see one outside our window, we won't worry too much about it."

We photograph Seryshevo, a lonely airfield in the Soviet Far East. Everything's cold and new, the winding river nearby now white with ice. It looks like a godawful place to be stationed.

Around the globe, again and again. Pass after pass over the Soviet Union, peering through clouds to pick out our targets. Winter darkness means we've lost the northernmost bits of each pass, and further south almost everything looks different, snow-covered and strange, all the ICBM access roads hard to spot now in the whiteness.

On a pass further west, we see another summer target transformed. A narrow strip of Black Sea coast wedged between open water and snow-capped mountains. Gagra. Memories of the contingency plan: a distant fever dream.

•••

Dinnertime at last. Heating food as Africa slides by below. So much bigger than you see it on the maps: brown and tan deserts of the Sudan giving way to greener lands further south, and the massive lakes of the Rift Valley.

We eat. Salisbury steak, hot in the foil pouches.

"It is amazing how peaceful it looks down there."

"It does look peaceful." Emphasis on *look*.

"You get so used to seeing...borders. Boundaries. Maps in different colors. Asia all red, dots of blue on the periphery. Europe split down the middle. Africa this...checkerboard. Nice to be reminded how...unnatural those divisions really are."

"There are still plenty of natural ones." A smile. "They're called continents."

"Well..."

"The earth used to be one landmass. Everything pieced together like a jigsaw puzzle. But it tore itself apart in slow motion. The Old World, the New World...that was a natural division. The Atlantic gets wider every year."

"But the Pacific gets smaller. We'll all come together again on the other side."

A snort. "Might take a while."

"Except in the Bering Strait. Russia and America, another land bridge. We'll have to get along sooner or later."

A chuckle. "Still might take a while."

•••

Swooping north over Greenland the next day, the radio comes on. "Watchman, this is Thule, calling secure. Over."

"Thule, Watchman. Go ahead. Over."

"Watchman, we've received word of a...probable submarine incident in the eastern Atlantic. The U.S.S. Scorpion has been missing for three days. Navy sonar network picked up what may have been a hull implosion. And a Soviet November-class submarine was spotted traveling on the surface with severe hull damage, heading away from the Scorpion's last-known position. Best guess is there was an underwater collision. Over."

"Thule, sorry to hear it. Are there any...uhh...action items for us at this time? Over."

"Watchman, nothing at this time. We may have some additional targets in the Med if the navy wants intel. Over."

"Copy, Thule. Please keep us posted. Watchman out."

We watch through the living room window as the Northern Lights shimmer far below, like an iridescent alien sea.

•••

Heading south over the Himalayas after a workday pass. As always, an abrupt transition: from the cold deserts of central Asia to the lush plain of the Ganges, with the icy mountains like a fence in between, ragged and impenetrable.

"There's a natural boundary."

"Again with the boundaries."

(A shrug.) "The world's divided. Like it or not. Even when the continents touch, you can't always go from here to there. The Darien Gap, you can't walk from South America to North America. Africa and Asia, not a lot of foot traffic. Not to mention subcontinents. Islands."

We pull out lunch packets. Ham and cheese sandwiches, gelatinized bread.

"The boundaries don't mean what they used to, though. I mean, five hundred years ago, you had no real contact between the Old World and the New. None between…Europe and Australia. Just with…ocean travel, it all became intermingled. The greatest mass migrations in human history."

A snort. "Lot of good it did us. You got…Europeans killing Indians on the Great Plains. Africans sold into slavery in the Americas. Pasty-skinned Brits getting…sunburned in Australia."

"Well that's a…cynical way of looking at it."

A shrug. "You do wonder sometimes if the world would be better off if we'd all stayed put."

"There was migration before that. We all came from Africa. Besides, the way it is today you also get…Negro instructors teaching Germans to fly. Chinese takeout restaurants in Los Angeles."

"When I think of Los Angeles these days, I'm not thinking of…Chinese takeout. I'm thinking of what happened last summer."

"Still. Nobody's isolated anymore. You can go wherever you want, in hours."

"Yeah, but when you get there, you need…guidebooks. Keys to common phrases. You have to wonder whether you're getting ripped off with every transaction."

"Those divisions will fade in time. People sync up over time. Languages that aren't useful die out. People learn the dominant ones. Look at…air traffic control. Everyone has to speak English."

"There already was one language. Right? Before the Tower of Babel, everyone spoke the same. One tongue, for all the peoples of the earth."

"If you take all that literally."

"OK, look at language trees. Any linguist will tell you. Languages all branch out over time."

"And some branches grow back together. Or die off. The places with the most languages are the places with the most islands, the most isolated populations. Indonesia, Papua New Guinea. But even that's ending. With mass culture…radio, television, movies…it'll happen faster. People live together long enough, they end up talking the same. Thinking the same. The earth is small enough now that that it'll happen on a global scale."

"It's small enough now that we can kill each other quicker."
A bitter smile. "People in the same space end up sharing the
same mood. Sometimes that mood is...murderous rage."

Awkward laughter. "Well that's...not exactly comforting!"

An impish smile. "Not *this* space. Not necessarily."

"Better do a little extra cleaning. Just to be on the safe side."

We are alone over Antarctica; we fly back up into night.

This slice of the globe is one of our longer periods of radio
silence: about 4/5ths of a rev. We spend the time as usual:
cleaning, using the bathroom, getting ready for the next pass.
Coming up on Vandenberg, we finally get the news:
"Watchman, the navy is going to formally announce
tomorrow that the Scorpion was lost with all hands. Over."

"Copy, Cheyenne. That's...terrible news. Keep us posted.
Over." It is easy to empathize with submariners after living
up here: life in a tin can, surrounded by a hostile
environment. Isolated and alone.

•••

Another day of recon. The Soviet Union a vast empire of ice
and snow, its northern edges hidden in the globe's winter
shadow. Pictures of lonely airfields, desolate silo sites. Then:
long laps around the planet to see what we're protecting: the
sleeping republic. Dense clusters of city lights, dark stretches
of open country.

"Gotta say...it has been good for us, at least."

"What's been good? For who?"

"Migrations. Boundaries. For Americans."

(Snort.)

"No, really. We've ended up on...probably the best continent for human habitation. Not too hot, not too cold. Wealthy land."

"It is quite a place."

"And the people, too. The fact that people from all over could come together in such a place."

"Except not everyone came voluntarily."

"Well, still. We have an ideal, at least, that different people *can* come together. *E pluribus unum*, and all that."

"We're not 'one' yet. Look at...hell, look at Chicago. Different races, everyone living within a few miles of each other, and they don't talk to each other. You meet a Negro from Chicago, and he sounds like he's from the South."

"That'll change in time."

"I'll believe it when I see it. Hard to be optimistic these days. People self-segregate."

"There are things that bridge the gap. Music...food. Go to any city, you can eat...Chinese, Italian, Mexican. Listen to...jazz, blues, classical. Hell, rock n' roll. Great fusion of cultures. The good ol' melting pot. It's like...metals in an alloy. You can get stronger combinations than you'd get with any one thing individually."

(A head shake.) "It's like…oil and vinegar. Shake it all you want, it'll still separate out in time. God help us if aliens did ever land. We can't even get along with each other."

"Maybe they're avoiding us because we can't get along with each other."

(A skeptical eye.)

"No, really. Keeping an eye on us to see how we handle differences. If we've learned yet."

"Maybe they're plotting an invasion."

(A chuckle.) "Maybe that would bring us together."

"Now *that* is a lot to hope for."

(Long pause.) "It is a worthwhile goal, anyway. For America, at least. The fusion of cultures."

"Except fission is a more energetic reaction."

(A raised eyebrow.)

"No, really. What's it…17.6 Megaelectron-volts for hydrogen fusion versus…what, 200 or so for uranium fission?"

"Fission's a lot more rare. And fusion's a lot more useful." (A nod outside, towards the stars.) "Everything we have came from fusion. Every element on the periodic table, after hydrogen, was made from fusion."

"Except it's not something we can do ourselves. Not in a controlled manner. Not without a lot of…external pressure. I mean…besides an…alien invasion, what force could there possibly be that could bring humanity together?"

"A planetwide disaster."

"Like what?"

"Meteor strike. Supervolcano. Maybe a pandemic."

(A smirk.) "So, nothing positive."

"Christianity."

(Laughter.)

"No, really."

"The victims of the Crusades would like to have a word with you."

"The ideal of Christianity, though. The reality of what Jesus said. That we're all brothers and sisters, all children with one heavenly father."

"Even that. You say 'father,' the women feel left out."

"Well, OK, fine…the Golden Rule. No distinctions there between genders. No distinctions of race or color or creed. Treat people the way you want to be treated."

"Jesus also said, 'I come to bring division. I come to bring the sword.'"

The lights below get fewer and farther between. Smaller populations, huddled together for warmth. Then: "Watchman, Thule, calling secure, over. Not sure if anyone's told you yet, but there is a…standoff of some sort between U.S. and Soviet naval forces in the eastern Med, related to the Scorpion Incident. Over."

"Thule, Watchman, what can you tell us, over?"

"Watchman, apparently the...uhhh Soviet submarine involved was attempting to transit the Dardanelles to return to the Soviet naval base in Odessa. But units of the 7th Fleet are blocking passage of the submarine. The Soviets have mustered their naval forces and are claiming transit rights. Meanwhile we have launched a formal protest and are demanding access to their crew. Latest news is everyone's dead in the water. Over."

"Thule, that sounds like...quite a situation. Any new targets for us? Over."

"Not yet, Watchman. The...uhh...navy has plenty of aerial reconnaissance assets on hand. Vigilantes and such. We may have targets next rev. Over."

"Copy, Thule. Watchman out."

There is nothing new on the next rev. Or after. Nothing but the nagging worry: this is not the end.

•••

In the X-20, flipping switches joylessly. The Single Sideband comms have never been formally acknowledged or punished or approved, one of those turn-a-blind-eye-to-the-telescope situations for our leaders. Still, this feels...risky. And yet necessary.

Time now. "Kilo-Niner-Yankee-Tango-Yankee, this is Kilo-Seven-Tango-Romeo-Victor. Come in, over."

She is there. "Kilo-Seven-Tango-Romeo-Victor, this is Kilo-Niner-Yankee-Tango-Yankee. Good to hear your voice. The news is a little…unsettling this week. Over."

"Kilo-Niner-Yankee, good to hear you too." Pause. Breathe. What can we say? "We've been following it a little. It's easy to see why you're worried. Over."

"Kilo-Seven-Tango, any…instructions for us? Over."

"Kilo-Niner-Yankee, it may be good to be…a little extra prepared this week. Just to be on the safe side. But it'll probably die down soon. Over."

"Kilo-Seven-Tango, say again, over."

"I said it'll die down soon!"

"That's…good to hear. We do have some…other operators at this station that would like to say hello." A pause. Then: "Hi, daddy!" And "Hi!"

"Kilo-Niner-Yankee, it is good to hear you! Your radio discipline is…not what it should be." As much warmth in the tone as possible. "Over."

Mother speaks again. "Yes. Discipline is not what it should be! These little munchkins keep…climbing into bed at night. Ever since you left, even though you're gone, they're…" (Static.) "…me all the way to the edge. Hard to get a good night's sleep." A long pause. "Over."

"Kids, you need to sleep in your own rooms! Over." A glance down: the coastline visible now, crawling past. Two minutes left, at best.

"But we're scared!"

"Kilo-Niner-Yankee, you...have to be scared sometimes! Your mother loves you very much, but she needs to sleep. It's hard to understand when you're a kid, but at night, parents just...want their kids to go to sleep. Over."

The daughter: "Even God?"

"What about God?"

"In the Gospels when the girl died, Jesus said she was asleep. He had to wake her back up. God's our father. Did God want her to go to sleep?"

Anxious glance at the time. "Ahhh...your mother wants you to go to sleep. Listen to your mother. When I'm not here, she's in charge. Over."

Again, mother: "Honey, I don't want to get cut off. It's good to hear from you. Especially this week. You'll let me know if anything changes, right?"

"Kilo-Niner-Yankee...things are OK for now. Stay tuned if you can. I will...ahhh...talk to you soon. Over."

LOS. Power down everything, put the spacecraft back to sleep: that, at least, is easy. Float back to the hammock.

Our commander's in his, wide awake. "You talked to your family?"

"Yeah. Everybody's a little nervous down there."

"Yeah." A pause. "Down there." Another. "What did you tell them?"

"I told them it was gonna be OK."

"OK." He turns towards the bulkhead, the picture of his family. Takes a deep breath. Body still tense, it seems.

This does feel different than before.

•••

Morning for us, early evening for America, we talk once more to Thule.

"Watchman, we just got off the phone with Cheyenne. We believe the Soviets have launched a…manned orbital platform of some sort. Over."

"Thule, uhhh…was that 'manned orbital platform?' Over." Our eyes meet. Anxious expressions on both of our faces.

"Correct, Watchman. It's in a polar orbit. Some planar separation from…" (Static.) "…believe there may be a conjunction later today, but…" (Static.) "…to make sure. Over."

"Thule, that broke up. You said…conjunction later today, over?"

"Watchman, possible conjunction. Over."

We smirk at each other, at the absurdity of it all. "Well, Thule, you'll have to keep us separated. Any news on the submarine standoff, over?"

"Yes, Watchman, the Soviets issued a statement acknowledging an accident. They said it was due to aggressive maneuvering by our captain. And they're claiming they lost a submarine of their own in the western Pacific, just last week. Over."

We trade glances again. A skeptical look that says: well, that's convenient. "Thule, anything else? Over."

"Uhhh, Watchman, apparently there have been...protests outside the White House. Crewmembers' families with signs saying JUSTICE FOR THE NINETY-NINE. And...uhhh...counter-protesters. Peaceniks and what-not. Over."

"All right, Thule, thanks for the heads-up. Over."

"Uhhh, we do have a target list for you! We'll be pushing it up through the teletype shortly. Over."

"Trying to keep it a regular workday, Thule?"

"Hard to think of it as a day down here. We haven't seen the sun since...uhhh, last day of October, I think it was."

"Ouch."

"We do have civil twilight now, at least! Little bit of blue in the sky. I mean, I'm still looking to getting out of here, but there's...light at the end of the tunnel. So to speak. Over."

The teletype starts clattering, rattling our tired souls with the hollow hope: maybe things will go back to normal.

●●●

Photography: far eastern Siberia. A long rev afterwards: Pacific blue, Australian brown, Antarctic white. Still plenty of prep time before the big work, the busy revs over the western Soviet Union.

Then: "Watchman, this is Thule, calling secure…" (Static.) "…at DEFCON-3. Over."

Glances of concern between us. "Thule, Watchman, you said DEFCON-3, over?"

"Watchman, that's correct. Apparently there's been…" (Garbled.) "…clash near the Dardanelles. Related to the standoff. Over."

"Thule, you said a clash? As in actual fighting? Over."

"Watchman, that's correct. Apparently…" (Static.) "…Soviets issued a statement saying they were going to head to the port of Tartus, in Syria, and work for a resolution of the conflict. They…" (More static.) "…to turn away. And then they…tried to make a run for the straits at night. There was a collision between the submarine and one of our destroyers. The submarine sank and…" (Static.) "…ace gunfire between the Soviet and American ships that were trying to pick up the survivors. We're getting reports of casualties. SAC has announced we're at DEFCON-3. The president is scheduled to address the nation tonight. Over."

"Copy, Thule." We look again at each other. Mutual recognition of worry. "Any…uhhh…additions to the target list? Over."

"Watchman, there are some…uhh…new instructions. Apparently Cheyenne would like photographs…" (Static.) "…Kuntsevo district of Moscow. And…" (Static again.) "…some town on the Black Sea coast. Uhh…" (Static once more.) "…Over."

A flood of angst. "Thule, we did not copy the name of the town. Over." Although we know.

(Garbled.)

"Thule, you're still garbled." Panic memories of summer. "Was that...Gagra? Over."

(Static.) "...can get good shots of both...probably obliques of Gagra. Over."

This. This is real.

"Thule, were there other...uhh, instructions related to those targets? Over."

"Say again, Watchman."

"Were there instructions? Specific instructions to treat those pictures differently than any others. Maybe...on-orbit interpretation? Over."

"Watchman, we have received no special instructions. Unless you have, just...send them down in the usual bucket. Over."

"Copy, Thule. Watchman out."

To each other, we speak: "Well that's a relief, at least."

"A relief? Those were the targets from the summer."

"They didn't seem urgent about it. They won't get the pictures for a week. They probably just want to have some intel. See how they look in the winter. Right?"

"Let's hope so."

Those targets are still several revs away. In the meantime we have this pass. We exit the Arctic darkness over the high latitudes of Siberia, already on-scope. Fly down west of the Sea of Okhotsk, headed towards Manchuria. Faces pressed down in the rubber hoods, looking at: nothing. A mass of gray, a blizzard, perhaps. After fruitless minutes, we push up from the scopes.

And then it happens: a flash. Through the large living room window: everything blinding white.

"Jesus Christ, what the hell was that?"

"I dunno, but I am…"

Blinking and rubbing our eyes. Voices spiking with worry. Bright vision ghosts on unsuspecting retinas.

"Was that…"

"That had to be a…"

Unspoken, unnecessary, the fateful word: *nuke*. It doesn't matter if we don't say it. This is real.

"I'm…uhhh, I'm a little…impaired here."

"Uhh…me too."

Trying to paper over anxiety with professional calm. But the questions: Is this the start of the war? And: what if we're stuck up here—sightless? Sounds are fading, too…the normal steady background whir of the gyroscopes, changing in tone as they slowly wind down.

"Did we lose power?"

"We may have lost power."

"That had to be a nuke."

"Well, yeah. This is just like what happened in the summer, right?"

"Right. EMP. Except this was a lot closer."

"It might have been just a warning."

"It was a lot closer."

"Yeah."

"This...this had to be deliberate, right?"

"Well, nobody just *accidentally* sets off a..."

"Right? This was an attack."

"Well."

Some vision fading back in. Blurry shapes.

"There's some...starting to see a little here..."

"Yeah. Is this...flash blindness?"

"You think it's flash blindness?"

"Well, we weren't looking straight at it, right?"

"No."

"It might be flash blindness. They say it's temporary."

"Well, still...this was...they had to be doing this to..."

More blinking. So much unsaid. It does indeed seem that the damage is fading. Sharpness of sight, rising. But also, in every anxious word we exchange, every thought about what just happened, a shared emotion: rage.

• • •

Our first task is to connect the batteries, restore power that way. We are over the ocean, over islands—the Philippines, Indonesia—and the soft bluish glow that comes through the window is enough to read by. Paging through binders and procedures, trying to remember tips that didn't make the checklists, still blinking away spectral shapes.

Reset all the breakers. Panel selector to BATT. The batteries come online without incident: voltmeters and ammeters springing to life. Then: lights. We turn on the gyroscopes and they start spooling back up, but when we push the ECS breakers, everything crashes back into darkness.

"Well that didn't work."

"No, it didn't."

"We need the radios. Let's do that first."

"We do need the radios."

Again: reset all breakers. Verify voltage and amperage. Push the breaker for the lights and they flicker back on. We are just past the empty northwest corner of Australia.

"Radio?"

"Might be too late."

"We need to call this in. It's a long rev to the next station."

"We're past Carnarvon. The fuel cell stack wasn't shut down properly, it might be overheating."

"If there's a chance they're in range, they need to know. The president needs to know that we were attacked."

If we turn on the radio, go to page 683.

If we work on the fuel cells, go to page 684.

(CONTINUED)

"I guess we've gotta try, huh?"

On goes the radio. "Carnarvon, this is Watchman. Come in, over."

No response.

"Carnarvon, this is Watchman. Come in. Over."

Nothing.

"Carnarvon, Watchman. Do you read? Over."

Still nothing. Another minute of nothing. Looking down at the ocean, the Antarctic coast is creeping into view. "We've gotta be well out of range now."

"Yeah."

"Fuel cells it is, then."

"Fuel cells it is."

Let's go to page 684.

(CONTINUED)

The cells don't start up, not right away.

We work the problem patiently, trying different sequences of breakers, powering up coolant loops and pumps, all without result. We start wondering if they're going to come back online, if the controllers were fried by the electromagnetic effects.

But then at last: normal power. The system humming along, output steady, temperatures returning to normal.

Looks of relief. Next: environmental controls. Pumps operating, fans circulating the stale air. Then: gyroscopes. Listening to the slow whine as they spool back up.

Nothing is normal, though. Not really.

"So...next comms is...what?"

Outside, the dark heart of South America. "We might have Antigua, but it's a Class 2 station. Cape Canaveral will be up right after."

"What do we tell them?"

"We tell them we were attacked."

"Are we sure that's what it was? If they'd actually shot it *at* us it would have...destroyed us, right?"

"These things don't work the same outside the atmosphere. No air, no blast wave. It's all...light and radiation."

"Radiation." Such a heavy word.

"We'll talk to Cape Canaveral about the dosimeter numbers. If they think they're bad enough, we might have to abandon the station."

"Abandon it?"

"We could be sick for weeks."

"You think that was their goal? The Soviets?"

(A shrug.) "Maybe."

"So we'll need to go home."

A glance over at the nearest launch key console. "If they don't have orders for us first."

The notepad with the comms windows says it is time. "Cape Canaveral, this is Watchman, calling secure, over."

"Watchman, Cape Canaveral. Go ahead, over."

"Cape Canaveral, we have a NUCFLASH incident to report..."

•••

The normal routines have been suspended. We are winding around the globe, waiting for orders. Stomachs anxious and irritable, either with mild radiation exposure symptoms, or the knowledge of what we'll be asked to do. We are off the console, we have shuttered the living room window. Eyes closed against the world.

But our ears are still open. And coming up over the central United States, the Emergency War Order console comes to life, shrieking and flashing as if demon-possessed The teletype is clattering, and sure enough it is a message. A Red Dot 4.

We look at the printout. FOLDER 6, it says. KEY TURN NLT 0900 GMT. Three hours of innocence, at most. And we were victims first. Surely that counts for something, right?

We look at each other. We look down, whatever down is here. We glance over towards the wallet-sized pictures of our families that are taped near our hammocks.

"Well, we should open the safe."

"Yeah. We should open the safe."

The brass locks, attached to the safe by their shackles, are floating peaceful and horizontal, presenting their number dials towards us. We enter our combinations, those numbers we've kept secret from one another, now in the open at last. 3-4-6 on one, and on the other: 2-1-3.

Inside: the folders are clipped in place to keep them from floating out. Each one holding a hard plastic case, with an instruction sheet inside. A fortune cookie nobody wants to open.

We have pulled out Number 6 when the radio comes on: "Watchman, this is Cheyenne, calling secure. Over."

Reluctantly we answer: "Cheyenne, this is Watchman. Go ahead. Over."

"Watchman, we are at DEFCON-1. Obviously this is..." (Crackle.) "...not a normal workday. We cannot tell you your target, but you should know..." (Hiss.) "...president has decided on a course of action he believes will result in the fewest possible casualties and the best possible postwar outcome. It…" (Static.) "…coming. We cannot avoid it. So we have to win it…"

"Copy, Cheyenne." Stepping on their transmission. Mindless.

"…counting on you to win it…" (Crackle.) "…minutes. Not years or months, weeks or days. Hours and minutes. We're counting on you, Watchman. A lot of us are counting on you. Over."

It is, we realize, the voice of a man under a mountain, a man in a steel bunker mounted on springs that is nonetheless the center of an ugly Venn diagram on some Cyrillic-lettered target map, with God knows how many circles overlapping on that single piece of terrain, and his family somewhere outside, unprotected. How many of those ICBMs can we stop from launching? Can we stop them all? Surely he's wondering.

But what else is there to say? "Copy, Cheyenne."

There is no response. We are at LOS.

Less than three hours of innocence. If we do what we're told.

•••

We crack open Folder 6. A fortune cookie drier and more tasteless than most. One that will come true, if we want it to.

The paper says:

TARGET LIST: 1

DEPLOYMENT SEQUENCE: 1

CONSOLE CODE: 918819

Technically we could turn the keys now; we could turn the keys and get it over with. But we don't. Not yet.

"0900 GMT. That puts us...what, close to Hawaii?"

"Close to Hawaii."

"So we'll overfly Vandenberg on the rev before."

"Yeah. We'll have time to call down."

"Assuming the war starts on our schedule."

"We'll have time to call down."

"Do you think they'll be up?"

"Up?"

"Waiting by the radio. It's...it'll be, what, 11:30 at night for them?"

"They should know to stay up. The president spoke to the country. Right? They said he was going on TV, to address the nation."

"That was before we were attacked. We don't know if he went on. We don't know what he said."

"Maybe he set an ultimatum."

"Maybe he said something else. To buy some time."

"Why would he buy time?"

"So we could do what we're about to do. That key turn time...it has to be a decapitation strike."

"We never got imagery."

"Maybe they don't need it. Maybe they have other intel."

"Such as?"

"Who knows? A crisis like this, people chatter. People have meetings. Maybe they know where Beria's at."

"Maybe. Or maybe we're targeting both targets. And anywhere else he might be."

Silence. Does it matter? Two targets: a small resort town, or an outer district of a major city. Killing: hundreds, or millions. Numbers known by God alone.

Below us the terminator scrolls by slowly as we fly out of darkness high above central Siberia, revealing the intricate frozen beauty of the Putorana Plateau. An icy dawn.

•••

A long silent rev. Taking it all in, thinking. There is not actually much to do. Not much, but everything.

Coming up on California we have split off into our respective X-20s. Not to fly, just to try to talk to our families.

Alone in the cockpit, powering up the radio, flying backwards, watching the moonlit Pacific recede into memory. How many more times will this scene present itself to us? To anyone?

A glance at the watch. It is time. "Kilo-Niner-Yankee-Tango-Yankee, this is Kilo-Seven-Tango-Romeo-Victor. Come in, over."

No answer. Do we want them to answer? Maybe they're on the road already, driving north towards Eureka. Would they have sent a telegram, a personal message? Would they have had time?

"Kilo-Niner-Yankee-Tango-Yankee, this is Kilo-Seven-Tango-Romeo-Victor. Come in, over."

Her voice, innocent and full of love. "Kilo-Seven-Tango, this is Kilo-Niner-Yankee. We were wondering if we were going to hear you tonight. Over."

A flood of conflicting emotions: relief at the contact, admiration for her smooth professionalism and anonymized message, anger that they're living on a target. "Kilo-Niner-Yankee, you need to get the kids in the car and head north, immediately." Pause for effect. "Over."

"Uhhh...Kilo-Seven-Tango, we heard the president's speech. He made it sound like...are you saying something's happening tonight? Over."

"Kilo-Niner-Yankee, I am saying you need to get the kids in the car and head north." Deep breath. "Immediately." Deep breath. "Over."

"Should I...should we tell anyone? Over?"

"We're...we're both calling down." A disorienting glance up, through the open hatch, across the top of the spindle T to our upside-down commander. No way to tell if he's made contact. "The sooner you get on the road, the better. You've got a little time. But you'll need all of it. Over."

"Well, I can't…" (Static.) "…can't just *leave* everyone. Drive past and look at their houses as they're sleeping, *knowing* we're leaving them to…*that*." (Blank space.) "Over."

"Kilo-Niner-Yankee….the sooner you get on the road, the better. If it all happens, we'll…meet you up there. Over."

"Kilo-Seven-Tango, wait, are you…" (Crackle.) "…ing it still might not happen? Over."

Pause. Hand over heart. Key next to chest, weightless but trapped. It is there, it is real. "Kilo-Niner-Yankee, I am saying you need to get the kids in the car. And head north. Immediately." (Pause for emphasis.) "Kilo-Seven-Tango Out."

No need to wait for LOS, or a response. No need for anything but to turn the radio off, and hear the knob's soft final *click*.

•••

Back in the spindle, we confer.

"Did you get ahold of your wife?" our commander asks.

"Yeah, we chatted for a minute."

"What did you tell her?"

"To get in the car and head north."

"I didn't get ahold of mine."

"No?" Angst.

"No."

We gaze out in silence. What else is there to say? The darkness continues, on and on and on. Moonlit mountains of coastal British Columbia, myriad snow-covered islands and inlets, and then: a cloak of clouds. Soon comes the swirling spiky green glow of the Northern Lights. There is still time to not do the thing we have not done.

From the living room, the radio. Float back in, headsets back on, and finally we hear: "Watchman, Eielson, calling secure. Over."

Eielson: Alaska. Not as important as Thule, but an important backstop when we're too far west for Greenland. "Eielson, Watchman. Go ahead. Over."

"Watchman, we…uhh…received a call from Vandenberg saying they missed comms with you just now. Given the current DEFCON status, they wanted us to check in. Over."

"Uhhhh." Guilty glances. "Sorry about that, Eielson. Taking care of some personal business. Over."

"Watchman…" (A tone like: I don't know what to make of that statement.) "…uhhh, be advised there's an object in orbit near you that we're tracking on radar. Based on the plots, we believe there will be a close conjunction over the Soviet Union. Over."

Float back towards the spindle window. Sandwiched between soft gleam of moonlight and the pale reflection of the Northern Lights we can just barely see…something, in orbit. The platform they were talking about. Armed. "Uhh, copy, Eielson."

"Watchman, not sure how much evasive action will matter, but we are recommending a ten-second…" (Static.) "…grade burn with the cold gas thrusters to keep some separation. Over."

"Eielson, do not copy. Posigrade or retrograde? Over."

"Watchman. Ten-second…" (Static.) "…grade burn. Over."

"Eielson, say again. Over."

Eielson crackles off into LOS. The Northern Lights are now a whisper of green; they trail off into nothing.

"Well. Shit. What do you think?"

A smirk. "Flip a coin."

We make the burn and gaze back again at the spindle, at the darkness.

After a few minutes, daylight. Our fellow traveler is fully visible at last, closer than expected. "Well, then," our commander says. "I guess it's time."

His tone leaves no room for the question: Time for what? Again, hand to chest. The key, solid and real. Deep breath: "What if we don't do it?"

"It's…it's a valid order."

"Do you want to do this?"

"Does it matter what we want?"

"If someone gets a launch order off before these warheads land…this could be the end of the world as we know it."

"It could be worse if we don't do anything. We're at DEFCON-1. The president's probably issued other orders."

"We still have a decision to make."

"The decision's been made."

We float back through the hatch into the living room. On the wall, the small photographs of our families. Eyes staring through us: accusing? Strange how the meaning of a photograph changes, once you've seen its future.

"We could be signing their death warrants."

"We could be signing them if we *don't* act."

"We don't know that."

(An exasperated sigh.) "No. We don't know the big picture. But someone does."

A glance back towards the spindle window, towards our adversary. It looks like they're getting closer.

Our commander loosens the collar of his coveralls, reaches inside to pull out his chain and key. Speaks now, emotionless: the voice of formula, the voice of a man playing a role. "We have received a valid launch order. Target List 1, Deployment Sequence 1, Console Code 918819. Do you concur?"

If we concur, go to page 699.

If not, go to page 695.

(CONTINUED)

"I...don't think I can do this. I don't think I can be a part of this." The words feel natural. Reassuring. Surely this is how it's supposed to be. Surely this will all blow over.

"Don't do this."

"I don't think you want to be a part of this, either."

A spike of anger. "Nobody *wants* to be a part of this. We *are* a part of it, already. This is what the American taxpayer is paying us for. To be up here and do this. To keep them safe. The president has issued a war order. It is his decision."

"It's our decision, too."

"This is still going to happen. With or without us. Beria's a...madman. A...syphilitic monster, a rabid dog. If we don't take him out..."

"Nothing's happened yet. We have to give it a chance to blow over. If we turn those keys, there's no chance."

"This is...you're..." Our commander sputters. "This is gonna be the end of your career."

A chuckle. "It's gonna be a short career either way."

For a long moment he is silent.

Float back out to the spindle window. Outside the spot has grown, the enemy spacecraft. Even with the separation maneuver it is not far off, under a mile, in a faster orbit below us; it is apparent now that it is something, a squat metal tube with solar panels. Are they watching us? Are they a threat to us? Do they know that we're no longer a threat, to anyone? The aspect of their craft changes...turning towards us?

We wait for...something. But: nothing.

Their orbital path is crossing ours. They are slightly out-of-plane, and thanks to the evasive maneuver they are faster and lower; they sweep across slowly, from left to right, like a peaceful benediction. And then they pass out of sight.

●●●

"We're going to need to tell them," our commander says at last.

"Yeah. They're probably..." A glance at the clock. "They probably want a confirmation during our comms window with Hickam."

"Yeah, probably."

"Are we gonna stay up here?"

"Well, that depends on what happens, obviously. If it still happens..."

"It might not happen. Nothing's happened yet."

"Except them attacking us. With a nuclear weapon."

"It might not happen."

"It still might.

"Well...maybe we gave them a little extra time."

"The president?"

"Our families."

"If it does happen…" (A long pause. A chuckle.) "If it does happen, Lord knows where we'll be able to land. Might have to…send you down first, so you can report back."

"Would that…even be possible? If it does happen, Thule, Vandenberg, Cheyenne Mountain, all those places will be…"

(A rueful laugh.) "Even if Thule was still standing….even if it was the last place on earth, I wouldn't…" (A head shake.) "No, there's a few of them that might not be targeted, if there is a wider war."

"We could go anywhere."

"We could go anywhere."

"Not sure it'd be worth going to…Tananarive, just to report back."

"Still might stay up here for a little bit after you anyway, if it happens," he says. "Commander's prerogative."

"Why?"

He shrugs, smiles. "Be the last astronaut."

"It might not happen." A gaze out at the peaceful earth. "I hope to God it doesn't happen."

"Well…we'll see."

There is a weird feeling being up here with nothing to do. Out of the loop, just observing.

We call it in to Hickam. Sins of commission, sins of omission: what we have done, and what we have failed to do.

They are not sure what to say.

Still, there is a lightness and a freedom. For the first time in fifteen years, there is nothing to do. We watch the dark empty Pacific, moonlit and midnight blue under softly silvered cotton-puff clouds. We see the Northern Lights again, dancing and dazzling, ghostly and grand. There is a lightness and a freedom...for now.

It doesn't last.

We see the first streak of light punching upwards from the dark of the Barents Sea. Then another. Then another.

We fly south, over icy boreal forests, past Moscow's frozen sprawl. We watch the city crawl backwards towards the horizon, unmolested for a few final moments. Then: a meteor streak, at the edge of our vision. A blinding flash, uncomfortably bright.

All of this is happening, without our consent or participation.

Again the station lights flicker and go out. Again the gyroscopes whir down into silence.

We put on our goggles and watch the end of the world in abstract flashes of green.

Let's go to page 707.

(CONTINUED)

A hard swallow. "We concur. Valid launch order. Console Code Niner-One-Eight-Eight-One-Niner."

We float to our stations. Eyes linked across the gap. Then: each of us looking down at our consoles. Alone with our actions.

"Key inserted."

A deep breath. "Key inserted." This is how it has to be, this is how it was always going to be. The coin has two heads.

"Countdown to key turn. Three-two-one...and turn."

"And turn." As simple as starting a car. Simpler. A smaller key, easier to turn. That's all it takes.

"Hold...two...three...four...five...and release."

Nothing has happened, except that the proper indicator lights are now lit. Nothing has happened at all.

We look each other in the eyes for one painful moment. Look away.

At the spindle window, a nice distraction: the Soviet station is visible now, perhaps a mile off. It is apparent now what it is, shorter and squatter than us, with solar panels at one end, but still: not much different than us. Just another tube of aluminum holding in a bubble of air.

Do they know what we are doing, what we have done? Are they going to attack us? Can they attack us? Do we deserve whatever happens next?

Questions unanswered, unanswerable.

It looks for a moment like they are turning towards us, like they are orienting their station in relation to us.

But nothing happens.

Slowly our paths diverge.

● ● ●

Down across the pristine Soviet Union. Snow-filled forests fading out into flat snowy steppes, marred at the edge of our vision by an erratic icy ribbon, the Volga flowing towards the Caspian. Stalingrad down there, ready to be destroyed again. But maybe, depending on the target list and how it all plays out…maybe, in a sense, liberated…

And yet nothing has happened, beyond the indicators. Nothing has happened. Yet.

Across Iran, the Caspian coast green and beautiful, before giving way to rugged snow-capped mountains. More places we'll never really see, more beautiful places.

"I hope to God they're in the car," our commander says. "I hope to God they're driving."

We are not the same. "My wife wanted to knock on some doors. God bless her, she didn't want to just…leave in the middle of the night."

"What did you tell her?"

A deep breath. Better not to answer directly. "I hope they're all in the car. I hope they're driving."

Southward we fly: the Persian Gulf, the sands of Arabia, bands of lighter tan and darker red. Fragments from an old poem, half-remembered: vast and trunkless legs of stone…the sneer of cold command…the lone and level sands…look upon my works, ye mighty, and despair.

And yet nothing has happened. Beyond the indicators. Why is it taking so long?

"This is a helluva simulation they've cooked up," our commander says.

•••

Bathroom break. Many thoughts. Is there anything to do, any troubleshooting? Is there anything to do but watch, and wait?

Down across the Indian Ocean. The Malagasy Republic. Always on the map it looks like a vast bloated Kentucky turned sideways, although from our altitude it's harder to see it. Should we call Tananarive? Surely no one is targeting Tananarive. Will there be peace there, after this?

Over the empty ocean. Clouds, flecks of ice, icebergs. Sunlit summer Antarctica, the only continent without people, the only one that's never known war. But surely still there is violence, at least around the edges…killer whales eating seals and penguins, cold waters stained by blood…no peace, perhaps, except in the empty interior.

There is nothing to do. Nothing but think, and watch, and wait.

•••

Coming up on Hawaii we call down into the darkness.

"Hickam, Watchman, calling secure. Over."

"Watchman, Hickam. We spoke to Cheyenne a few minutes ago. Our...telemetry is indicating that your console is activated and keys have been turned. Is that correct? Over."

"Hickam, Watchman. That is correct. Nothing has happened yet. Over."

"Watchman...that's...not much consolation. Over."

"Hickam, is there...anything we need to do? Any troubleshooting? Over." Is it moral to troubleshoot in this situation?

"Watchman..." A long pause. A long, long pause. "Our understanding is everything is functioning as expected. Over."

"Thank you, Hickam. On a personal note, this is...not something any of us wanted to happen. Over."

"Watchman, that's...I am...I don't know what to say to that. Over."

"Hickam, I...if you have something to say, feel free to say it. We're all professionals here. Over."

"May God have mercy on your souls."

"Our souls, Hickam."

There is no response.

"He's on an island," our commander points out. "Him and his family. We can go anywhere, when this is over. They can't."

"Where are we going to go, though?"

There is no response.

Northwards we fly, over the moonlit Pacific. Small ugly clouds, gathering together as we approach Alaska. The Northern Lights dance, alien and strange. There is no comfort in the scene. Nothing will be normal again.

Some invisible timer has finished its countdown, some circuit is now complete. There is a shudder as the platform ejects the first warhead. Then another. Then another. Then another. Then another. Thunderbolts from Zeus. Although to think we ourselves have freedom, to think we will not in some way be held accountable for this, is...folly.

For a couple minutes there are no further deployments. Then, another sad sequence of shudders. And then we are spent.

Nothing will be normal again.

•••

Coming down out of darkness over the frozen tundra of the northern Soviet we see familiar sights. Icy rivers snaking across the terrain, branching apart as we follow them backwards towards higher ground. Mottled terrain and cold forests, all snow-blasted and white. General Winter's regular offensive, soon to be followed by a worse warrior. There are clumps of smaller settlements, and then Moscow: sketches of roads, a city etched out of ice. We can see the barest traces of the ring road structure like a skewed spiderweb, like a fractured target.

Then: a meteor streak. We close our eyes before the flash. Close our eyes to what we've done.

On go the goggles.

We wait for the EMP, wait for the station lights to go out again. Somehow it doesn't happen.

There are more flashes further south, off in the distance.

After a few minutes, we take the goggles off. We are over Africa; everything looks normal again. The barren desert giving way to green as the Nile fades out into nothing. Rift Valley lakes, jagged and impossibly long. The drier and more intricate beauty of the south. It all looks exactly as it did yesterday. It all looks exactly as it did.

•••

On the other side of the globe, it is the same. The empty Pacific. We are alone with our guilt.

Alone until Kanton Island.

"Watchman, be advised we are getting reports from Cheyenne of multiple ICBMs inbound. Several stations have gone offline. Over."

A flood of black despair. "Copy, Kanton."

"Watchman, you…you should have another comms window with Hickam this rev, right at the tail end of ours. They may have more info. Over."

"Copy, Kanton."

We call down to Hickam. We get no answer.

The darkness is complete. The darkness is in us. The darkness lasts and lasts and lasts.

Over Europe: more flashes. On go the goggles, again. This time, the EMP is stronger; the station lights go out and the gyroscopes spool down. We leave everything that way, for now. We've done enough. We've done more than enough.

Let's go to page 707.

(CONTINUED)

We do not know our target. But we have a warhead in our payload bay, a single massive warhead, with a preprogrammed target unknown to us. Both Moscow and Gagra are on the other side of the globe, reachable with the current trajectory. Does it matter which one we destroy?

The mission has been prepared in secret. The president is in his airborne command post, awaiting the results of the strike. The payload was prepared in secret. Everything was on a need-to-know basis. And even the launch personnel, it was decided, did not need to know. They are used to secret payloads. They are used to keeping their mouths shut and following orders. Doing their job with blinders on. They are innocent. Or: as innocent as anyone can be, who chooses to participate in such a system.

And now, it is all on us. There is no one else who can stop this.

Approaching now, above (which is below): the coast of Antarctica. Icebergs flaking off the coast and drifting northward to oblivion.

Open the payload bay doors. Arm the panel. Key in the code.

Wait, do you really want to be personally responsible for launching a nuclear weapon? Are you a psychopath? Go back to page 499 and pick something else.

(CONTINUED)

After a few revs the flashes die down. Then finally it is time to remove the goggles.

Everything is disaster in the cold countries of the north. Fires and smoke. Massive plumes billowing and joining one another and riding the prevailing winds high into the atmosphere. Some gaps where one can see patches of snowy emptiness. But far more frequently: blackness, fire, despair.

We turn the station back on, one last time. We stay up and talk, and then fall into periods of silence where the vastness, the incomprehensibility, overwhelms. We succumb to exhaustion and sleep fitfully. We wake and force ourselves to eat, force ourselves to use the bathroom amidst waves of nausea. What is the point? What really is the point, anyway?

On the next day, the smoke has cleared, somewhat.

A smeared series of scars sits where Moscow used to be. A huge mass joined together in the middle, so big a zone of desolation that only at the edges it is clear it is composed of massive overlapping circles, black in the center fading to brown at the outer edges, ragged but still round. Snow surrounds. And hanging above it all, the pall of smoke from millions of dwindling fires, plumes all trailing northeast. Millions of dead souls.

It's almost flat, the scene. Abstract art, an image that seems as unreal as all those nuclear war white papers: maps with fallout patterns drawn in dotted lines, estimated numbers of dead and wounded. Numbers with two commas. But it is real. Not quite flat: a scene with depth and weight. A holocaust on the altar from the priest of Baal's perspective, distant but real. Men, women, children, families. Branches of families. Branches of branches of families.

It is real, and we have made it real. The numbers are not even and abstract; they are unknowable and real. What is there to do but watch in silence? What Hitler failed to do, we have done.

America, too, is destroyed.

Perhaps there are slightly fewer blackened circles, perhaps there are more empty patches. But there is no corner of the country that is safe, no city of any appreciable size that has escaped destruction. Memories of Manhattan: infinite horizons down the wide avenues, limestone canyons golden in the sunlight, pedestrians hailing cabs or stepping off into the crosswalk. Gone. Chicago: another cluster of black circles, new indentations on the shore of Lake Michigan. Gone. Smeared circles strung like black pearls across the Great Plains, destroyed silos strung out along the routes of northern highways. The Green Valley, burnt; our silo crew: God knows. The coast of California blackened and burning, wildfires that will never be extinguished until there is simply no more fuel, from San Francisco clear down to San Diego, including, of course, Los Angeles and Vandenberg. Afternoons on the golf course, or the pier at Santa Monica: no more. Families? God knows.

Stomach tightness, digestive symptoms. Radiation or anxiety? Impossible to tell: no one to interpret the dosimeters. Is there any possibility whatsoever that our families are safe? What is safe on this poisoned planet?

Eureka? Buenos Aires? Tananarive? The New Hebrides? The Sentinel Islands?

At night: glimpses of fires between the moonlit clouds, like glances back in time at the primordial Hadean earth

There are no answers from our earthly stations. Not for some time. The atmosphere is filled with charged particles; our calls down are met by garbled responses that can barely pierce the static. But not everywhere, not everywhere. The American stations, the Australian stations, Lakenheath: speaking to these feels like a useless call into the void. And Thule, especially Thule. Given the time of year and the lack of Northern daylight, we will never know what happened. But we know.

We think of all the people we've known, the ones who might be gone—who are almost certainly gone. Will we ever know for sure? We remember faces, voices: Is a soul more than a memory? Will we ever know for sure?

Eventually we speak to Kanton Island, Tananarive, Ascension. Voices still squelched and distorted by the blanket of ionized air, but audible now. They have been waiting for updates. We tell them what we've seen. They have been awaiting instructions. We tell them we have none.

Again we are passing over Moscow in daylight. A storm has passed through, and coated all the destruction in snow. There are still smoke plumes, but far fewer. Fires extinguished by survivors, or burnt out of their own accord after turning people to ash: God only knows. A cleaner scene by far. A blank slate, an awful thought: wiped clean.

But there is no comfort. There is no way to unsee this.

Where to come down? We think, and talk to our commander.

At the window there is nothing to do but watch, until every passage over the terminator feels like the scrape of a dull razor across a tired face.

● ● ●

At last, sleep. Real sleep, at last.

We sleep but wake to dead reality. What goes up, must come down.

"I guess it's time, then," our commander says.

"We can wait a little while still."

"Does it matter?"

There is no answer.

● ● ●

And now, at last, back to where it all began: the cockpit of the X-20. It powers up without incident. A minor miracle.

When we release from the docking mechanism, there is a sad little shudder. Pause for a quick glance up through the top window at the picture now moving, the interior of the spindle now drifting, now gone forever. A quick prayer: Useless, or no?

We have chosen where to go; we have made our choice, and although we could perhaps delay the transtage burn for a rev or two, or steer the X-20 this way or that once we're through the worst of reentry, our options are far more limited than they were an hour ago, just as those options were far reduced from those of last week, or last month, or last year. Our companion will be up here for a little while longer. The last astronaut.

Glance up at the black sky. Only the brightest stars visible now on the daylit side of the globe, fixed and impassive. Still no sense if anyone is out there, if anyone cares. Just an inner voice—ourselves, or someone else?—that says: Down below. That's where you belong now. Dealing with the consequences.

And it is time to fire the transtage. A brief push transmitted through the back of the ejection seat, and then it is done. And now there is no way to avoid it all. No way but one.

Is this justice? Divine ordinance, a moral lesson, or simply the end of the story? At the end of the world, what is justice for an observer? A participant? What is justice for us? The craft eaten away during reentry by some unseen flaw in the heat shield? A wayward flick of the wrist during the critical phase of reentry—a fast tumble through fiery plasma at twenty-five times the speed of sound? Or a safe trip down, and having to live in the world we've made.

The station falls away. Becomes once again a slender metal baton, and then a bright star in orbit, just above the airglow. Then one last time across the terminator into night. And another glance at the full universe, as the station becomes just a distant red light.

INFINITE BLUES

At last, it blinks out.

And then: waiting for the flames.

Acknowledgments

Reds

Emily Carney was my Deke Slayton for this mission; I talked to her very early in the writing process and bounced some crew ideas off of her, and that was a tremendous help in getting me to decide which MOL astronauts would be worth writing about. She's also been hugely supportive of the Altered Space series. (And she's a very diligent researcher and writer. And she helps run the Space Hipsters Facebook group—possibly the best social media group I've ever been a part of!)

Francis French—a writer of tremendous talent and integrity—was gracious enough to answer an internet inquiry from a random stranger six and a half years ago. He's been a huge source of support, and a friend as well—truly a class act.

Huge thanks to David Hitt for reading and blurbing this. If you're at all interested in the Skylab program—one of our most underappreciated space programs—you need to check out *Homesteading Space*.

In real life, of course, the X-20 and Manned Orbiting Laboratory programs never coexisted, and the Manned Orbiting Laboratory would have been a single-use laboratory, not something orbiting indefinitely. But I wanted to have some fun with this story, damnit.

I owe a huge debt of gratitude to Dan Adamo for his technical consulting work. He took a list of hypothetical ground stations and plotted acquisition times for a spacecraft in a sun-synchronous polar orbit over the course of an average day. This was invaluable in helping me structure the narrative.

Information about the X-20 came in part from *Dyna-Soar: Hypersonic Strategic Weapons System*, edited by Robert Godwin.

I adapted some technical flight dialogue from transcripts of Gemini X.

Biographical information about Henry "Hank" Hartsfield and his political leanings came in part from the excellent memoir *Riding Rockets: The Outrageous Tales of a Space Shuttle Astronaut* by Mike Mullane—one of the best space memoirs ever published, and essential reading for anyone even moderately interested in the shuttle program. I interviewed Col. Mullane by phone on April 14, 2018, which was invaluable in fleshing out my understanding and correcting some misimpressions. By all accounts, he seems like a decent human being—tremendously competent, and an excellent leader—and while I have taken some liberties in the interest of compelling fiction, I hope they aren't outlandishly off-base. If there are substantial differences between my fictionalized alternate-universe version and the real one, or errors in the depiction, they are mine alone.

Information about the workday structure in the Manned Orbiting Laboratory came from "Thirty Days in a MOL: Biomedically Relevant Aspects of a Reconnaissance Mission Inferred From Orbital Parameters" by John B. Charles and Daniel M. Adamo, published in *Quest: The History of Spaceflight Quarterly* 2015 - Volume 22 - Number 2.

Eye in the Sky: The Story of the Corona Spy Satellites, edited by Dwayne A. Day, John M. Logsdon, and Brian Latell, is absolutely essential reading for anyone interested in learning more about American orbital reconnaissance during the Cold War. Many of the themes in the first part of my book were developed from ideas presented by these authors.

The PBS Nova documentary *Astrospies* was also an invaluable documentary for information about the Manned Orbiting Laboratory program and its astronauts.

Information about the Manned Orbiting Laboratory also came from several National Reconnaissance Office documents, including "Preliminary Performance/Design Requirements for the Manned Orbiting Laboratory System," "History of the Manned Orbiting Laboratory Program," "Candidate Experiments for Manned Orbiting Laboratory," and "The Roles of Man in MOL."

The "knock outside" incident was adapted from something that actually happened during one of Hank Hartsfield's shuttle flights, as discussed in his interviews with the NASA Johnson Space Center Oral History Project.

Red Harvest and *The Guns of August* are both pretty great reads, if you get a chance.

Rowland White's *Into the Black* was an excellent space book that helped me with issues related to on-orbit imaging.

The article "Class of '59" in *Air & Space* had invaluable information on the first graduating class of the United States Air Force Academy. I also read through class recollections posted online at usafaclasses.org/1959/

Dark Sun: The Making of the Hydrogen Bomb by Richard Rhodes offered much useful information on hydrogen bomb testing in the Pacific, and on the development of Soviet nuclear weapons.

Readers wishing to learn more on General Curtis LeMay would do well to read *LeMay: The Life and Wars of General Curtis LeMay*, by Warren Kozak, which is an excellent and definitive book on the controversial general.

Information about Lavrentii Beria came from *Beria: Stalin's First Lieutenant* by Amy Knight—essential reading for anyone wanting to know more about this sinister man.

Biographical information about Major Robert Lawrence came from online sources, supplanted by an author interview with his son, Tracey Lawrence, conducted on December 18, 2019. Tracey is a wonderful person and corrected many misinterpretations and imaginings I had about his father, as well as providing much useful biographical information—his father's love of jazz, and his abandoned talents on the piano, his religious tendencies (or lack thereof), and his relationship with his parents. I still did a decent amount of imagining in my depiction of Major Lawrence, and any errors or mischaracterizations are mine alone.

The Thule Broken Arrow incident was inspired in part by the Thule Air Base B-52 crash on January 21, 1968...definitely one of the crazier Wikipedia pages to read.

I worked some lyrics from Silver Jews' highly underappreciated *Tanglewood Numbers* into my writing. Rest in Peace, David Berman.

I interviewed Col. Karol J. "Bo" Bobko briefly at Spacefest on August 9 or 10, 2019, by which point I had already completed much of the manuscript. While the unnamed narrator shares certain biographical information with him, my character is purely a figment of my imagination. Col. Bobko's recollections did help me flesh out some of my impressions about living conditions for the first Air Force Academy class; they also made me realize (belatedly) that the astronauts in question would have moved to Vandenberg at some point.

Whites

Biographical information on General Bernard Schreiver came from *A Fiery Peace in a Cold War: Bernard Schreiver and the Ultimate Weapon* by Neil Sheehan.

The doughnut social after church (and information about the Knights of Columbus) was strongly influenced by the author's fond memories of Saint John Vianney parish in Orlando in the late 80s. Rest in Peace, Charlie Burr.

Some dialogue between Walter Cronkite and Carl Sagan was adapted from the 1966 *CBS Reports* episode "UFO: Friend, Foe, or Fantasy."

Some of Carl Sagan's dialogue was inspired by his thoughts as set down in his excellent book *Cosmos*.

Biographical information on Walter Cronkite (including the Wilhelmshaven raid—which is something I probably would not have believed if it were fiction—and his participation in various national conventions) came from the intriguing and well-researched (if somewhat hagiographic) *Cronkite* by Douglas G. Brinkley. Mr. Cronkite also discussed his thoughts on the importance of open government at his acceptance speech for West Point's Sylvanus Thayer Award, given on September 23, 1997, and attended by the author.

I read Ben Macintyre's *The Spy and the Traitor* to brush up on espionage tradecraft...it's an absolutely riveting book.

Information on Bill Paley, CBS News, the economics of TV and the news in the 1960s, and the general political leanings of various news organizations (and their owners) came from *The Powers That Be* by David Halberstam, a fascinating look at various news media in the pre-internet age.

Pat Frank's *Alas, Babylon* is a pretty fun read, if you're still into Cold War apocalyptic literature after this.

Kennedy's speech was a mashup of his 1960 speech accepting the Democratic nomination, his commencement address at American University on June 10, 1963 (the "Peace Speech") and the "Address at Rice University on the Nation's Space Effort," given on September 12, 1962.

Some of the ideas expounded on by my version of Senator Goldwater were discussed in his book *Conscience of a Conservative*. Other biographical information, including his views on threats as an instrument of warfare, and particularly his thoughts on UFOs (and his request to Curtis LeMay to see any evidence accumulated by the Air Force), came from direct quotes from Senator Goldwater that appeared in the article "AuH$_2$O" in the April 25, 1988 issue of the *New Yorker*.

The album the pet store employee is listening to during the spaceman's second visit is *Forever Changes* by Love—a too-often-forgotten late-60s classic with apocalyptic overtones. It should a part of any serious music collection.

The words that Bob Lawrence quotes from W.E.B. Du Bois come from *The Souls of Black Folk*—essential reading for anyone even moderately interested in race relations in America.

Descriptions of Woodlawn and Englewood in the 40s and 50s came from an author interview with the sculptor Richard Hunt, who went to high school with Major Robert Lawrence.

Conservative tactics used in this narrative's description of the Republican party's nominating process (occupying rooms early, etc.) and other descriptions of Senator Barry Goldwater come from Rick Perlstein's excellent *Before the Storm: Barry Goldwater and the Unmaking of the American Consensus.*

Portions of Senator Goldwater's speech were taken from his 1964 speech accepting the Republican presidential nomination.

Descriptions of the Playboy club in Miami came from various online sources, and from "A Bunny's Tale" by Gloria Steinem, an excellent behind-the-scenes exposé.

I stole the key joke from Townes Van Zandt's excellent *Live at the Old Quarter* album. (Another essential part of any music collection.)

The Kennedy political advertisement described is an adaptation of the famous (or infamous) "Daisy Girl" political ad from Lyndon Johnson's 1964 presidential campaign, created by the Doyle Dane Bernbach advertising agency and Tony Schwartz.

Descriptions of Yuri Andropov and Andrei Grechko came from Wikipedia.

Descriptions and impressions of the Titan missile complex and launch procedures are based on the author's visit to the Titan Missile Museum in Sahuarita, Arizona, and on refresher views of the process posted on YouTube. Thank you to Victor and Lisa for hosting my visit to Tucson, and for the recommendation.

The "positive attitude about nuclear weapons" line came from USAF briefing procedures shown in the BBC documentary *Missileers*, originally broadcast May 25, 2000.

The descriptions of the New York commuter may or may not bear some resemblance to the life of Edward Packard.

Eureka, California was at one point named the safest place in the United States in the event of a nuclear war. The exquisite book *Raven: The Untold Story of the Rev. Jim Jones and His People* by John Jacobs and Tim Reiterman says that Jones and his followers moved there at one point for that very reason. (If you have any appetite for depressing stories after reading this, *Raven* is a phenomenal read about unspeakable evil.)

Descriptions of the USC-UCLA game were inspired in part by the 1968 USC-UCLA game as shown on YouTube.

Information about Richard Nixon came from several sources, particularly the *Politico Magazine* article "How Nixon Turned Football Into a Political Weapon," published October 17, 2017. His statement speculating on the number of casualties he could cause in a nuclear holocaust was adapted from remarks reportedly made by the real-life Nixon to a congressional delegation in the final days of Watergate.

I meant to re-read William Manchester's *American Caesar* for background info on Douglas MacArthur, but ended up reading Arthur Herman's *Douglas MacArthur: American Warrior* instead, and I'm glad I did—it's an excellent read, thoroughly researched, with a lot of new information. One gets the sense that MacArthur was a master media manipulator. And that does seem the danger nowadays—not that we'll lose the freedom of the press, but that the press will continue to surrender its freedom for access, only to be seduced by narcissistic leaders who aren't acting in the public good.

Blues

Titan III launch procedures and dialogue were taken from YouTube videos of launches.

Some launch descriptions and sensations were adapted from recollections from various Gemini astronauts.

Somehow I didn't think to use Google Earth earlier to get a look at things, but it was a huge help in fleshing out the physical descriptions of the earth in this section, and seeing what the approaches to various runways would have looked like to our characters.

Nuclear weapons information came in part from "The Effects of Nuclear Weapons," compiled and edited by Samuel Glasstone and Philip J. Dolan, and "Effects of Nuclear Weapons," a slide show compiled by Alexander Glaser.

Wikipedia continues to be an amazingly useful tool for simple little research tasks, like finding out that Saint Helena didn't have an aircraft runway until the 2000s, or figuring out what direction the runway on Ascension faces. I am amazed that writers were able to survive without it.

Much thanks to the good people of YouTube, especially the ones with enough time and disposable income on their hands to prove that yes, you can actually fire a gun in a vacuum.

If you ever want to—hypothetically, of course—nuke a bunch of cities and get a highly sanitized idea of what might happen afterwards, head on over to Alex Wellerstein's NUKEMAP at https://nuclearsecrecy.com/nukemap/ and have at it. I vaporized Sacramento during the writing of this book. (Sorry, Logan Ryan Smith.)

I have no idea whether any of the historical figures introduced in the book would have said or done anything depicted in this section—hence the vagueness and lack of attribution in the dialogue. But I have no doubt that people, in the aggregate, are capable of such things. Individually, we might be innocent. Collectively, we are guilty.

About the Author

Mr. Brennan earned a B.S. in European History from the United States Military Academy at West Point and an M.S. in Journalism from Columbia University in New York. His writing has appeared in the *Chicago Tribune*, *Newcity*, *The Good Men Project*, and *Innerview Magazine*; he's the founder of Tortoise Books, and was a frequent contributor and co-editor at Back to Print and <u>The Deadline.</u> He resides in Chicago.

Follow him on Twitter: @jerry_brennan

About Tortoise Books

Slow and steady wins in the end, even in publishing. Tortoise Books is dedicated to finding and promoting quality authors who haven't yet found a niche in the marketplace—writers producing memorable and engaging works that will stand the test of time.

Learn more at www.tortoisebooks.com, find us on Facebook, or follow us on Twitter @TortoiseBooks.

www.ingramcontent.com/pod-product-compliance
Lightning Source LLC
Chambersburg PA
CBHW031017030726
47497CB00004B/892